Connie Burns was born and brought up in California. She has degrees in English and Psychology from San Diego State University, as well as a California Teaching Credential. She was recruited by the New South Wales Department of Education to teach in Australia in 1974, and has taught in several high schools in the Sydney area. She has co-written, with Marygai McNamara, four high school English textbooks, including *Literature, A Close Study*, published in 1984. Married with three children, Connie Burns lives in Sydney.

Marygai McNamara grew up in the highlands of New Guinea. She has a degree in English from the University of Sydney and has taught English and History at high schools both in Sydney and London. She has travelled extensively throughout Australia, and especially in the outback. Marygai McNamara has a special interest in women's literature, and has written several plays and short stories. Books published include four English textbooks, written with Connie Burns. She is married, has three daughters, and lives in Carcoar, New South Wales.

IMPRINT

ECLIPSED

Two Centuries of
Australian Women's Fiction

CONNIE BURNS
MARYGAI McNAMARA

COLLINS
PUBLISHERS
AUSTRALIA

To our husbands, Stuart and Tom,
and our six children.

IMPRINT

COLLINS PUBLISHERS AUSTRALIA

First published in 1988 by William Collins Pty Ltd,
55 Clarence Street, Sydney NSW 2000

Copyright © Connie Burns and Marygai McNamara

National Library of Australia
Cataloguing-in-Publication data:

Eclipsed: two centuries of Australian
women's fiction.

ISBN 0 7322 2445 4.

1. Australian fiction—Women authors.
I. Burns, C. J. (Connie Jean). II. McNamara,
M. G. (Marygai Gabrielle).

A823'.008'09287

Typeset in 10/12pt Times Roman by Midland Typesetters, Victoria
Printed by Globe Press, Victoria
Cover illustration: *Lady in Black Dress (Portrait of Mme A. E. K. Cull)*
by James Quinn

Publication assisted by the Australia Council, the Federal Government's
arts funding and advisory body.

ACKNOWLEDGEMENTS

The following pieces have been previously published in the sources mentioned: 'A Glimpse of a Situation', *Clara Morison: A Tale of South Australia During the Gold Fever*, 1854; '*HMS* Anson', *The Broad Arrow, Being Passages from the History of Maida Gwynnham, a Lifer*, 1859; 'How a Woman Kept her Promise', *Pioneers,* 1869; 'My Lodger', *The Australian Journal*, Vol 5, 1869; 'A Blunder', *The Wheel of Life; A Domestic Tale of Life in Australia*, 1880; 'Deposed', *The Woman at Home*, Vol 5, 1895-96; 'The Saratoga Trunk', *A Question of Latitude*, 1912; 'Monsieur Caloche', *A Sydney Sovereign and other Tales*, 1889; 'Gwen's Decision', *Luck of the Leura*, 1907; 'The Chosen Vessel', *Bush Studies*, 1902; 'The Humbling of Sergeant Mahone', *The Ends of the Earth*, 1916; 'A Bush Honeymoon', *A Bush Honeymoon and other Stories*, 1904; 'The New Carpet', *Tales by Australians*; 'A Job for the Parson', *Lone Hand*, 1907; 'The Springs of Human Action', *Old Savage and other Stories*, 1927; 'Their Country', *Sydney or the Bush*, 1948.

The editors and publishers would like to thank the authors and publishers of the following pieces for permission to include them in this collection: 'Conversation in a Pantry' by Henry Handel Richardson, © Margaret Capon, c/o Curtis Brown (Aust) Pty Ltd, Sydney; 'Her Just Necessities' by Mary Grant Bruce, © Mr Jonathan Bruce, c/o Curtis Brown (Aust) Pty Ltd, Sydney; 'Mr Bundock Sat' by Miles Franklin, © Permanent Trustee Co. Ltd; 'Donalblain McCree and the Sin of Anger' by Ethel Anderson, from *Tales of Parramatta and India* by Ethel Anderson, © Bethia Ogden, 1973; 'The Cooboo' by Katherine Susannah Prichard, © Ric Throssell, c/o Curtis Brown (Aust) Pty Ltd, Sydney; 'Young Grief' by Myra Morris, from *The Township*, Angus & Robertson, 1947; 'Habit' by Marjorie Barnard, © Alan Alford, c/o Curtis Brown (Aust) Pty Ltd, Sydney; 'The Urgent Call' by Eleanor Dark, © Michael Dark, c/o Curtis Brown (Aust) Pty Ltd, Sydney; 'You Won't Mind the Ghost?' by Dymphna Cusack, © James McGrath, c/o Curtis Brown (Aust) Pty Ltd, Sydney; 'Sappho' by Christina Stead, from *The Salzburg Tales*, Angus & Robertson, 1966; 'Puzzle for a Later Day' © by Alexandra Hasluck, from *Of Ladies Dead*, Angus & Robertson, 1970; 'Auction Sale in Stanley Street' © Kylie Tennant, c/o Curtis Brown (Aust) Pty Ltd, Sydney; 'The Nurse' © by Nancy Phelan; 'Halcrow Street' © Estate of Margaret Trist; 'Eclipsed' © by Nene Gare, c/o Curtis Brown (Aust) Pty Ltd, Sydney; 'The Snake and Bad Tom' by Olga Masters, from *The Home Girls*, UQP, 1982; 'The Turtle' © by Oodgeroo Noonuccal (Formerly Kath Walker), c/o Jacaranda Wiley Ltd; 'The Shadow' by Gwen Kelly, from *Australian New Writing*, Thomas Nelson (Aust) Ltd, 1973; 'Wednesdays and Fridays' by Elizabeth Jolley, from *Woman in a Lampshade*, Penguin Books Australia, 1983; 'The House to Themselves' by Ruth Park, © Kemalde Pty Ltd, c/o Curtis Brown (Aust) Pty Ltd, Sydney; 'A Northern Belle' by Thea Astley, from *Hunting the Wild Pineapple*, Penguin Books Australia, 1981; 'The Beautiful Climate' © by Elizabeth Harrower; 'Grandfather Tiger' © by Mena Abdullah and Ray Mathew, from *The Time of the Peacock*, Angus & Robertson, 1965; 'The Book of Life' © by Leone Sperling; 'Annie M.' © by Barbara Hanrahan, c/o Curtis Brown (Aust) Pty Ltd, Sydney; 'My Secret Life' © by Glenda Adams, from *The*

Hottest Night of the Century, Angus & Robertson, 1970; 'A Woman with Black Hair' by Beverley Farmer, from *Home Time*, McPhee Gribble/Penguin Books, 1985; 'All Those Bloody Young Catholics' by Helen Garner, from *Postcards from Surfers*, McPhee Gribble/Penguin Books, 1985; 'Mati' © by Gabrielle Lord, c/o Curtis Brown (Aust) Pty Ltd, Sydney; 'The Sex Part' © by Inez Baranay; 'The Space Between' by Kate Grenville, from *Bearded Ladies*, UQP, 1984; 'The Letter' © by Sally Morgan; 'Hospital' © by Ania Walwicz; 'Nothing Happened' by Margaret Coombs, from *Regards to the Czar*, UQP, 1988.

The editors would especially like to thank the staff of the Mitchell Library, New South Wales, the Rare Books Library, c/o Fisher Library, University of Sydney, and the Truscott Library, Mitchell College, Bathurst, for their cooperation.

CONTENTS

INTRODUCTION

This anthology brings to light the creative ability of Australian women writers who have been 'eclipsed' in the traditional study of Australian fiction. Australian women writers have faced many handicaps in trying to write,[1] but the fact remains that Australian women did write. They wrote about human issues and concerns and they explored their experiences as women. Their writing is competent, interesting, entertaining and relevant. Even the early women writers were professional writers whose novels and short stories appeared in abundance in the journals, newspapers, serials and anthologies of the time. In the first half of the twentieth century women wrote almost half of the published novels and it is generally acknowledged that most of the best novelists of that period were women. This writing however had been overshadowed by the beliefs and conventions that have promoted men's writing for the last two hundred years. Women's writing has always been there; it has just been lost from sight. Australians have not had ready access to this eclipsed wealth of Australian women's fiction. This anthology helps to correct this by bringing a sampling of Australian women's fiction back into the light.

One of the many factors which contributed to women's fiction being so inaccessible was that women often found it difficult to get their work published. Catherine Helen Spence's novel, *Handfasted*, written in 1877, and Lesbia Harford's novel, *The Invaluable Mystery*, written in the 1920s, were not published until the 1980s. Other women's problems in getting published have been well documented.[2]

Once finally into print, women writers found it difficult to stay there. One only has to skim the shelves of major libraries and bookshops to discover that women's works are not equally represented. The great women writers: Henry Handel Richardson, Judith Wright and, more recently, Christina Stead, are, of course, well represented. The good, competent woman writer, however, is not as equally accessible as her male counterpart. Rolf Boldrewood's *Robbery Under Arms* (1888) is readily available in any local bookshop while Tasma's *Uncle Piper of Piper's Hill* (1889) can only be found in rare-book libraries. Spence proudly and vividly portrayed aspects of early South Australia in her novel, *Clara Morison* (1854). Although widely acclaimed by the critics at the time of its publication and by others with access to the novel since, both copies held by the South Australian Public Library were lost. No attempt was apparently made to replace the copies. Many other Australian women's works have suffered from similar neglect.

This neglect of Australian women writers is easy to verify. Only eighteen per cent of the work presented in a sample of thirteen anthologies of Australian writing compiled since 1963 was written by female authors.[3] One short-story anthology published in 1981, 'seeking to represent the best in the contemporary Australian short fiction' contained no work by women.[4]

Editors of anthologies are not the only members of the literary establishment to neglect women writers. Women writers were the subject of only nineteen per cent of the essays in eleven books of Australian literary criticism surveyed.[5] Most of that criticism was about Richardson, Wright and Stead, the acknowledged great women writers. The essays on male writers, however, deal with men of varying abilities. Women are often relegated to separate chapters or sub-chapters as if they were a lesser sub-group, not to be included with the mainstream of 'serious' male literature. H.M. Green in *A History of Australian Literature* comments at the beginning of his section on early short-story writers, 'Incidentally, the best of all the short stories was the work of a woman, "Tasma".'[6] Yet he relegates a discussion of her short stories to later in the chapter with the other 'Women Writers'.

References to women writers are often done in a patronising manner. Annie Baxter, a prolific journal writer in early Australia, is dismissed as 'a provocative little devil'[7] by Green.

The male literary establishment and readers in general assumed that women writers were inferior. Women writers such as Henry Handel Richardson and Miles Franklin felt that their writing would be taken more seriously if they were thought of as male authors. Miles Franklin used many pseudonyms and was very careful not to disclose her true identity. Frank Dalby Davison, when discussing women writers in 1933, claimed it was only the woman with the 'masculine mind' who 'really succeeded intellectually'.[8]

Naturally enough women's fiction was often about women and/or domestic life. This was not considered adequate subject matter for serious literature. Caroline Leakey's novel, *The Broad Arrow*, relates the experiences of a female convict transported to Australia for life and was a strong indictment of the transportation system. The social comment and indeed the plot structure is extremely similar to the later novel, *For the Term of His Natural Life* by Marcus Clarke. Leakey's book is about a woman and is now unheard of except by literary historians, while Clarke's book, about a man, has become a part of Australian folklore. Myra Morris and Margaret Trist, who wrote fiction in the 1930s and 1940s about domestic life and the experiences of women ('Young Grief' and 'Halcrow Street') have been forgotten while male writers like Desmond O'Grady and Gavin Casey, whose stories are about mateship and the male experience, are readily available.

The appropriateness of women's subject matter often added another limitation to women's writing. Only certain subject matter was deemed proper for them. When they dealt with improper subject matter such as lust, politics, or feminism, their work was either unpublished or censored and often the women themselves came to feel embarrassed by it. Eleanor Dark regretted having written *Slow Dawning*, a feminist novel which examines how women can live as sexual and intellectual beings. Ada Cambridge's popular fiction was about courtship and marriage, at the time considered proper subject matter for a woman, but this work was later judged insignificant. However, when Cambridge wrote honestly about lust and passion in her poetry in *Unspoken*

Thoughts (1887) the book was suppressed because it was felt her husband's career as a minister of the church would be harmed.

When researching the material for this anthology we discovered a wealth of fiction by Australian women. Obviously no anthology can do justice to this abundance of material. There are many good writers we had to omit. Our most important criterion was that each selection would be enjoyable to read. Since the depth of Australian women's writing needed to be represented, we felt we must include the acknowledged great women writers as well as their lesser known but still significant sisters. The most significant works by many of these women were often novels, however, we have primarily chosen short stories, preferring to include only complete works. Excerpts have been included from the novels of some of the early women writers as it was felt that the worth of these writers' work was not adequately reflected in their short stories. The emphasis of this anthology is on the tradition of women's writing. It is the women writers of the past who have been previously neglected. Where a decision had to be made, we chose the earlier work. Australian women's fiction covers a wide range of subjects, however we tended to select those works more relevant to traditional women's concerns as these were often the very works that had been neglected in the past.

Much of the early women's fiction was about love and marriage, but to dismiss it as just romantic is not acceptable. Many of our early selections demonstrate this. While an unhappy love affair provides the basis for the plot of *The Broad Arrow* by Leakey, the book is about the injustice of the convict system. The selections dealing with courtship and marriage point out the importance of marriage in determining the social and economic position of women in colonial times (Liston's 'How a Woman Kept Her Promise', Cambridge's 'Deposed' and Praed's 'Gwen's Decision'). As well as discussing important issues these stories of love and romance often clearly demonstrate the particular strengths of some of these early writers. Cambridge's 'Deposed' demonstrates her ability to explore character motivation. Praed's 'Gwen's Decision' does not demonstrate her skill evident in her other works in handling the psychological problems of women, but it does provide us with a good example of her wit and humour.

Moral and instructive tales, common in early Australian women's writing, such as those written by Mary Vidal, Ellen Clacy, Maud Jeanne Franc and Mrs A. Blitz, have not been included in our collection. While many of these writers were skilful with character development and/or creating atmosphere, their work was excessively long and would have forced us to omit many selections which would be considered more enjoyable by modern readers.

Some of the selections by early writers particularly demonstrate the skill of these writers with the short-story form. Tasma's 'Monsieur Caloche' is a masterpiece of this genre with its characterisation, use of contrast and its surprising ending. Equally well written are the stories on the loss of innocence and growing up by Richardson and Anderson. Baynton's 'The Chosen Vessel' is a powerful short story that graphically depicts the horrors of bush life, particularly for women. Palmer-Archer's 'The Bush Honeymoon' treats the common theme of women's adjustment to bush life in a far lighter vein, but her skill in this genre is just as obvious.

At the beginning of the twentieth century women started questioning the injustice of their position in society. Bruce in 'Her Just Necessities' humorously looks at women's financial dependence. Devanny's 'The Springs of Human Action' is a powerful exposure of male hypocrisy. In Dark's 'Urgent Call' a dying woman examines her married life and finds it wanting. A woman rejects just such a traditional marriage in Barnard's 'Habit'. Harrower makes a strong critical statement about the repressive nature of man's power over his family in 'The Beautiful Climate'. Gare portrays the classic dilemma of a woman who is torn between meeting the needs of her loved ones and meeting her own needs in 'Eclipsed'.

As early as Elizabeth Macarthur women writers have been aware of problems Aboriginal people have had to face since European settlement. In the 1930s and 1940s Prichard and Drake-Brockman were making strong statements about this issue, but these are white women. Aboriginal women have not written about their own problems until recently. Oodgeroo Noonuccal's 'The Turtle' presents an allegory for the situation of the Aboriginal people, which stresses, in a way no white writer has done, the closeness of the Aboriginal people to their environment. Sally Morgan's 'The Letter' signals the beginnings of a healing process; two Aboriginal women make an effort to claim one of their own, and a part Aboriginal woman takes her first step towards discovering her heritage.

Women writers have shown a consistent concern for other social issues. Cusack's 'You Won't Mind the Ghost?' while being a charmingly humorous tale, is also a plea for sympathy and understanding for the aged. A similar concern for the aged as well as the class problem is shown in Franklin's 'Mr Bundock Sat'. Tennant's 'Auction Sale in Stanley Street' exposes the morbid curiosity of human nature.

Masters and Park look at the incredible vulnerability of children, which has always been a subject for women's fiction. Abdullah in 'Grandfather Tiger' explores this subject as well as the twentieth-century problem of assimilation.

When selecting the modern writers we tried to show the range of styles and subject matter now being approached rather than attempting to include every good modern writer. The modern selections reflect how far women's writing has come since colonial times. There are subjects which were inappropriate, in fact impossible, for earlier women writers, which modern writers attack with vigour. Subjects like rape (Farmer's 'A Woman with Black Hair'), sex (Baranay's 'The Sex Part'), and child molestation (Coombs's 'Nothing Happened') could not have been written even thirty years ago. The subtleties of the problems of sexism are being explored by many modern writers (Astley, Lord, Grenville, Kelly). Old concerns of bureaucracy, racism, old age, migrant assimilation and youth are being treated in a fresh and insightful way. While Dark pioneered the stream of consciousness style in the 1930s, this style has been further developed by modern writers such as Kelly and Hanrahan. Modern women's ability to laugh at themselves is shown by Adams and Jolley. Monologues (Garner) and letters (Jolley) are being used to good effect in the short-story form.

This anthology is made up of writing by women, but literature does not belong to either sex. Australian society as a whole has suffered due to the neglect of women writers. Literature is nurtured by its traditions; one generation is able to explore new styles and ideas developed by a previous generation of writers. When half of that tradition is eclipsed, our potential is reduced. This anthology has tried to make the tradition of Australian women's fiction more accessible. All Australians should benefit from the reappearance of this, the other half of our literary heritage.

> *'Then it was bright again. The stillness left the air and life began again. The eclipse had passed.'*
> *(from Nene Gare's 'Eclipsed')*

1 Suggested readings:

Carole Ferrier, *Gender, Politics and Fiction; Twentieth Century Australian Women's Novels*, University of Queensland Press, St Lucia, 1985, pages 14–19.

Drusilla Modjeska, 'That Still Blue Hour Before the Baby's Cry' in *Exiles at Home*, Sirius Books, Sydney, 1981.

Kate Millett, *Sexual Politics*, Virago, London, 1977.

Elaine Showalter, *A Literature of Their Own: British Women Novelists from Bronte to Lessing*, Virago, London, 1978.

Dale Spender, *Man Made Language*, Routledge and Kegan Paul, London, 1980.

Virginia Woolf, *A Room of One's Own*, Penguin, 1965.

2 Suggested readings:

Joanna Russ, *How to Suppress Women's Writings*, The Women's Press, London, 1984.

Lynne Spender, *Intruders on the Rights of Men; Women's Unpublished Heritage*, Pandora Press, Melbourne, 1983.

3 These are:

Brian James (ed.), *Australian Short Stories, Second Series*, Oxford University Press, London, 1963.

Cecil Hadgraft and Richard Wilson, *A Century of Australian Short Stories*, Heinemann, Melbourne, 1963.

Douglas Stewart (ed.), *Short Stories of Australia; The Lawson Tradition*, Angus and Robertson, Sydney, 1967.

Beatrice Davis (ed.), *Short Stories of Australia; The Moderns*, Angus and Robertson, Sydney, 1967.

Judah Waten and Stephen Murray-Smith (eds), *Classic Australian Short Stories*, Wren Publishing, Melbourne, 1974.

Bill Wannan (ed.), *Bill Wannan Selects Stories of Old Australia*, Macmillan, South Melbourne, 1976.

Harry Heseltine (ed.), *The Penguin Book of Australian Short Stories*, Penguin, Ringwood, 1976.

L. Cantrell (ed.), *Writings of the 1890s; Short Stories, Verse and Essays*, University of Queensland Press, St Lucia, 1977.

Craig Munro (ed.), *The First UQP Story Book*, University of Queensland Press, St Lucia, 1981.

T. Inglis Moore (ed.), *The Australian Book; The Portrait of a Nation by Our Greatest Writers*, Currey O'Neil, South Yarra, 1982.

Kerryn Goldsworthy (ed.), *Australian Short Stories*, J.M. Dent, Melbourne, 1983.

Frank Moorhouse (ed.), *The State of the Art, The Mood of Contemporary Australian Short Stories*, Penguin, Melbourne, 1983.

Leonie Kramer (ed.), *My Country*, Vols 1 & 2, Oxford University Press, South Melbourne, 1985.

4 Craig Munro (ed.), *The First UQP Story Book*, University of Queensland Press, St Lucia, 1981.

5 These are:

A.A. Phillips, *The Australian Tradition, Studies in a Colonial Culture*, Longman Cheshire, Melbourne, 1958.

Grahame Johnston (ed.), *Australian Literary Criticism*, Oxford University Press, London, 1962.

G. Dutton, *The Literature of Australia*, Penguin, Ringwood, 1964.

Clement Semmler (ed.), *Twentieth Century Australian Literary Criticism*, Oxford University Press, London, 1967.

C.B. Christesen (ed.), *On Native Grounds*, Angus and Robertson, Sydney, 1968.

Barry Argyle, *An Introduction to the Australian Novel, 1830–1930*, Clarendon Press, Oxford, 1972.

Chris Wallace-Crabbe (ed.), *Melbourne or the Bush, Essays on Australian Literature and Society*, Angus and Robertson, Sydney, 1974.

A.D. Hope (ed.), *Native Companions, Essays and Comments on Australian Literature (1936–1966)*, Angus and Robertson, Sydney, 1974.

Douglas Stewart, *The Broad Stream, Aspects of Australian Literature*, Angus and Robertson, Sydney, 1975.

L. Cantrell (ed.), *Bards, Bohemians and Bookmen, Essays in Australian Literature*, University of Queensland Press, St Lucia, 1976.

Harry Heseltine (ed.), *The Uncertain Self, Essays in Australian Literature and Criticism*, Oxford University Press, Melbourne, 1986.

6 H.M. Green, *A History of Australian Literature, Volume 1 1789–1923*, Angus and Robertson, Sydney, 1961, page 289.

7 *Ibid.*, page 351.

8 Drusilla Modjeska, *Exiles at Home, Australian Women Writers 1925–1945*, Sirius Books, Sydney, 1981, page 9.

CATHERINE HELEN SPENCE
(1825–1910)

Spence was born in Scotland and migrated to South Australia when she was fourteen. She wrote political and social reform pamphlets, was a newspaper journalist and an internationally known and respected public speaker and lecturer, and was also a founding member of several philanthropic organisations.

Spence thought of herself as a political reformer rather than a literary figure. She led a campaign for more than fifty years for proportional representation, and was Australia's first female political candidate (unsuccessful) in the federal convention of 1897.

Only four of Spence's eight novels were published in her lifetime. She rejected the romantic view of the bush and tried to present life in the colony realistically. Spence's novels often examine the problems of women, particularly the hardships a woman faces in earning a living, even when she has the same ability and perseverance as a man.

Clara Morison; a Tale of South Australia During the Gold Fever (1854) was her first novel and is widely considered one of the best early Australian novels. The main character is sent to Australia by her uncle to make her livelihood as a governess. In the following extract Mr Campbell, an old acquaintance of her uncle, has agreed to try to help her find a position.

A GLIMPSE OF A SITUATION

from *Clara Morison; a Tale of South Australia During the Gold Fever*

Mr Campbell had a very numerous acquaintance, but on inquiry he found that very few of them wanted governesses. Most of them sent their children to school; it was cheaper, and more convenient; some would like a governess, but had not accommodation, for the children had too little room already. Some wanted an elderly person, who had had experience in tuition; but could not think of entrusting their children to a girl of nineteen. But the want of music was the great drawback, for though most of these music-requiring ladies had no piano, they could never think of getting a governess merely to teach reading and writing; they could teach these things quite as well themselves. There was only one lady who would like to see Miss Morison, though even she was afraid she would not suit, and she wished Mr Campbell would desire her to call. It was a nice walk, only four miles and a half out of Adelaide. Mr Campbell gave Clara directions as to her road, which she could not easily mistake, for all the roads go straight north or south, east or west, from Adelaide; and telling her that Mrs Denfield was a high-spirited woman, who did not like contradiction, and though she was very clever she spoilt her children a little, but that she was very amiable notwithstanding, he recommended her to go that very day, that no time might be lost. So Clara took a hurried but kind leave of Miss Waterstone, who promised to write to her whenever there was anything worth writing about, and set off on her nice walk. The sun was over-poweringly hot, and when Clara got out of town, and had to walk between sections fenced with posts and rails, she longed for the green sheltering hedges of her own country. Here and there the corn was left on the field, though it had been reaped weeks ago, and she wondered to see how small and far apart the shocks were. Where the wheat had been reaped by the machine, and the heads

2

merely had been taken off, the long stubble, which is reckoned of no value in Australia, had been either burned or was left standing till favourable weather came. She saw one large field which had accidentally taken fire, and watched the active exertions of all the people about to extinguish it by beating it out with boughs. It had been a very dry winter, and the crops in the plains near Adelaide had been very poor; so that she had no flattering view of the capabilities of South Australian soil. But with all this, there was an appearance of civilisation and comfort in the numerous cottages on the way, each having a small garden, and generally a patch of vines, which were loaded with fruit; and what interested Clara still more, she saw many wells near the cottages, which encouraged her often to ask for a drink of water. She was unused to walking far for so many months, and the road was often so deep in sand, into which her feet sank every step, that she was very thankful when a decent-looking woman asked her to sit down out of the sun and rest a bit. She wiped a chair for the lady to sit on, and went on with her washing. Several children were about her, eating bread and butter with their grapes. They had all dirty faces, but looked healthy enough; their clothes were neither fine nor altogether whole; the furniture was scanty, and altogether Clara did not see that over-powering contrast between the exterior of this dwelling and those of people in the same rank in Scotland which she had been led to expect. But the bread and butter, and the smell of meat baking in the camp oven, and the teapot, which the eldest girl was brightening a little for father's dinner cup of tea, were all very different, and looked as if, whatever crops might be, the labourer ran no risk of being starved.

A little curly-haired boy crept up to her, and asked her her name, where she came from, and where she was going; and Clara, having no motive for concealment, gave him ready answers.

'You're going to Mrs Denfield's; that's where my sister Louisa Jane stops,' said he. 'Mother, this lady is going to Louisa Jane's missis's.'

The mother looked rather curiously at Clara, and said, 'My Louisa Jane is coming home next week, for she can't stand the

3

work nor the rowing she gets there no longer; and them children are enough to tire out the patience of Job himself. I hope, miss, that you ain't a going to be governess there, for the last one had a pretty time of it. The boys and the girls, too, gave her such sauce; and then if she scolded them, their mamma's tongue came cataracting down upon the poor thing; and if Mr Denfield said a word to help Miss Dobson out, I expect he catched it too. Maybe I am too free of my tongue, miss, for Mrs Denfield might be a friends of yours; but I can't forgive her for not letting Louisa Jane come to see me, and forbidding her to take the children out a-walking this way; for she says it is only to have a gossip at her mother's, that will spoil her for a week afterwards. I wonder what missises think servants are made of, if they are not flesh and blood the same as them. Suppose her children had to go to service, I fancy she would like to see them odd times, particular if they lived within a mile. My Louisa Jane did not like Miss Dobson, for she held her head high, and would not speak free-like to the servants in the kitchen; for my maid has a good spirit of her own, and she thinks that as they were all working for wages, there should be an equality. But, as I says to Louisa Jane, mind Miss Dobson wears better clothes than you, and sits at table with your missis, and does no dirty work, so there should be a difference.'

'I had better go now,' said Clara; 'I feel quite rested now. I have not much further to go, I hope?'

'Only a mile and half a section,' said Mrs Watts. 'You'll find it easy; a white house in the middle of a section, with the haystack on the left hand, and the hedge of kangaroo thorn round the garden.'

Clara met the master of the house in the doorway, who was wiping his forehead and calling on Betsy to look sharp with the dinner. He gave a slight bow as he passed the young lady, and hoped she did not feel the weather too hot. But she felt it all the hotter after the temporary shelter, and plodded on more wearily and despondingly than before.

In front of the white house was a very pretty garden, full of

4

a variety of fruit trees and vines; and she saw there two girls and a boy, who were busy picking grapes and devouring them, seeds and stones included. They had no hats or bonnets on, and were very much freckled; they stared for a few seconds at the new comer, who found some difficulty in untying the rope that fastened up the gate, and supplied the place of the lock, which was broken; but they did not offer to assist her, and resumed their pleasant occupation. A sharp-looking girl, whom Clara conjectured to be Louisa Jane, came out.

'My word! Master Henry and Miss Lucy and Eliza,' said she, 'won't your ma be angry to see you out without hats this broiling hot day, and eating them Muscats too. You'll all be ill as sure as I'm here. I'll just run and tell your ma. Come in, there's dears, and get on your hats; you know you'll be sunstruck.'

The two young ladies said that they never wore hats, and that their sun-bonnets were dirty — much too dirty to wear; and scolded Louisa for her laziness in not washing them, and her ill-nature in not giving them their best bonnets when the others were not fit to put on.

Clara had by this time reached the door, at which she knocked. Louisa Jane whispered to the children that most likely this was the new governess coming, at which news they hurried in at the back door, to get into the parlour as soon as she did, and have a good look at her before their mamma made her appearance. So by the time Clara was ushered into the sitting-room the whole of the juvenile Denfields were there ready to inspect her. There was the eldest, Caroline, who seemed to be about fifteen; then James; then the three whom Clara had seen in the garden, and Robert and Emily, first merely looking at her, and then asking her questions.

'What a pretty frock you have on,' said Caroline, 'though you have got it rather dusty with the walk; and your bonnet is very nicely trimmed. Have you been long in the colony, or have you just come out?'

'I only landed last week,' said Clara.

'Then why do you wear your hair in ringlets? they are quite

out of fashion. All new comers wear their hair crimped and stuck out in wavy bands, and it looks so stylish. If you stay here you must wear your hair like that, for ma does not like curls at all. What is your name?'

'Clara Morison,' was the reply.

'It is a nice name, I like it. Our last governess was called Bridget Dobson; wasn't it a horrid ugly vulgar name? but she was a vulgar creature altogether.'

'I do not think it such a vulgar name,' said Clara. 'There was a Mrs Dobson who translated Petrarch beautifully.'

Miss Denfield stared, and continued, 'If you are to be our governess you must give us nice short lessons, and let us play a great deal. I am not too old for play yet, though I am so tall, and I don't mean to give it up till I come out, and I hope that will not be long. There is Miss Robertson came out at fifteen, and I wish you would help me to persuade ma to let me accept the next invitation I get. It would be delightful to dance till daylight. It is never too hot to dance you know, and I would never miss a dancing lesson for the world, but I do hate learning spelling and grammar, and doing horrid sums when it is as hot as this. Ma says she is fit for nothing to-day, and what can you expect of me? Master James, don't break the chairs, swinging upon them like that; and do, Miss Eliza, keep Emily from ma's work-box. She has got everything out of it; and there now, if she has not run the scissors into her hand. Oh Emily, don't cry, it is not very bad. What will ma say?'

But Emily was of opinion that it was very bad indeed, and screamed so that Caroline was forced to take her out of the room to her mamma. Clara saw the other children do a good deal of mischief, and when she mildly hinted that they had better not, they merely stared at her, and went on. Three quarters of an hour elapsed before Mrs Denfield entered, and with considerable dignity requested Clara to resume her seat when she rose to accost her. Mrs Denfield prided herself on two things in particular; first, that she was lady-like, and secondly that she was decided. Her manner was cold, her eye critical, her mouth hard in its expression, and

6

her gait stiff; but still she was, in the opinion of those twenty people who formed her world, such a lady-like superior woman. She was anxious that her children should be as lady-like and firm as she was, but neither precept nor example had hitherto succeeded in producing that result. She had at last adopted the opinion that mothers were not the best instructors of their darlings, but that they needed a subordinate educating machine, such as a governess, to act under their orders, and to cram the minds of children with useful knowledge, without either inspiring any of the respect, or winning any of the affection which was due to the mother, and the mother, alone.

Her cold grey eyes looked Clara over; the result was not satisfactory. As Clara's colour rose at the inspection, she supposed that she had not been accustomed to good society; and as her flexible mouth did not close like a vice, she was of opinion that she wanted firmness. Besides, she was too young, and what some people would think too pretty for a governess, though there was no mind whatever to be found in her face.

'You are, I presume,' said Mrs Denfield, 'the young person in whose favour Mr Campbell spoke to me on Wednesday evening? Miss Morison, I believe, is your name?'

'Yes, ma'am,' said Clara.

'Pray, have you been accustomed to tuition? for I consider that a great point.'

Clara's distressed eyes glanced at the children, who were all eagerly listening, but whether Mrs Denfield thought that they would profit by the colloquy or whether she thought it a good trial of the governess's patience to conduct her cross-examination before her future pupils, she did not take the hint, but looked impatient for an answer.

'I have never been in a situation yet, but I used to teach the little ones at school,' said Clara.

'An apprentice, I suppose,' said Mrs Denfield.

'It was only because I liked it,' said Clara; 'I think there are no such thing as school apprentices in Scotland.'

'Then you are Scotch; yes, I hear you have the accent very

7

strong. Were you at a boarding-school or a day-school, Miss Morison?'

'I have been at both,' said Clara, 'and had instruction at home besides.'

'Are you acquainted with the routine of tuition? Could you give me any idea of how you would go through one day with these young folks of mine?'

'I cannot tell until I know what progress they have made. Probably your boys go to school, and as for the young ladies I must take each separately, as there is such a difference in their ages, and they cannot learn exactly the same lessons,' said Clara.

'I understood from Mr Campbell that you know a little Latin, Miss Morison; and if you could carry on James and Henry for a few months, to prepare them for a good school, I think it would be a good arrangement for all parties. What is the matter, Caroline?'

'Oh, ma,' said Caroline, who just now burst into the room. 'I wish you would come and speak to Louisa, she is so cross with Emily, and was just going to give her a slap, when I said I would run and tell you. And what do you think Sarah is doing, ma? She is scrubbing out your room with the same water she took to wash the passage; all her laziness to save her drawing more water from the well.'

'Servants are the plague of my life,' said Mrs Denfield. 'You will excuse me five minutes, Miss Morrison. Put on your bonnets, my dears, and pick some grapes. I dare say Miss Morison would take a few this hot day if you dip them in cold water for a few minutes to cool them.'

When Mrs Denfield returned it was without her children, to Clara's great delight; she resumed her conversation without delay.

'Caroline, as you may see, is very sharp and observant; nothing escapes her, and as she tells me all that she sees, she prevents these girls from imposing upon me. I feel that under a mother's eye alone can daughters in particular be rightly brought up; and if we should happen to come to terms, Miss Morison, let it be on the distinct understanding that my authority is in no way delegated to you. You teach them such and such lessons, and report to me how well or ill they have been learned, and what their behaviour has been; for my children are of such an affectionate temper that they cannot bear anybody to find fault with them but me. And in the next place, Miss Morison, I wish you to tell me exactly what you can and cannot do. I beg that you will resort to no subterfuges, for children are acute observers, and if you lay claim to any knowledge or skill which you do not possess, you will completely lose their esteem whenever they find it out.'

'I can teach all the branches of an English education,' said Clara, 'and I understand French grammatically. I could give lessons in Latin for the first year or two, and I could instruct the young ladies in plain needlework.'

'No fancy work, knitting, or crochet?' asked Mrs Denfield.

'No, ma'am.'

'No music?'

'No, ma'am; I know only the notes.'

'Don't you draw at all?'

'No, ma'am.'

'Cannot you teach dancing?'

'Oh yes, at least I can dance well; my master always said I was his best pupil.'

'Was he a Frenchman?'

'Yes, ma'am.'

Mrs Denfield hesitated a little, and then said, 'May I ask your age?'

'Nineteen, ma'am.'

'In what vessel did you come out?'

'In the *Magnificent*—in the intermediate.'

'I have met a Mrs Hastie, just come from Scotland; I suppose a fellow passenger of yours. May I inquire from her as to how you conducted yourself on board? Excuse my doing so, for in a colony like this one cannot be too careful.'

'Mrs Hastie knows nothing whatever about me, ma'am,' said Clara. 'We never spoke to the cabin passengers all the voyage. I have no reference except to Mr Campbell; my uncle did not even procure me certificates from the schools and masters I attended, for he thought that Mr and Mrs Campbell's interest would be sufficient to procure me the situation I wanted. Will you try me for a month, and see if I will not suit you?'

'Well,' said Mrs Denfield, 'with so few accomplishments, and no recommendations, I suppose you will be glad of a home. I cannot afford to give you a high salary.'

'I would come for twenty pounds a-year,' said Clara, anxious to bring the matter to some conclusion.

'Twenty pounds a-year! what an absurdly high salary for a nursery governess! If you had known anything of music I might have stretched a point, but I do not consider myself justified in offering you any more than fifteen.'

'That is very little,' said Clara; 'I do not see how a young lady can provide her dress and contingencies on such a small income.'

'I do not care for the young person who occupies the place of governess in my family dressing at all expensively. The plainer the better, provided she is clean and neat. Every governess I have had has assisted me with the family needle-work; and Miss Dobson, to whom I gave fifteen pounds a-year, used to dress two of the younger children every morning. She was no musician, certainly, but she drew nicely; I shall be grieved if Caroline's drawing is to be at an end; and she was very skilful in all kinds of fancy work. I cannot possibly offer you any higher salary, Miss Morison; it is for you to accept or decline it.'

Clara's colour went and came several times during this speech; she knew it would be a most uncomfortable situation, but yet she thought it right to take it; for, according to Mr Campbell's account, this was a fair specimen of colonial ladies, and no other employer might appear before her money was spent, and she was destitute. So she consented to take the salary of fifteen pounds a-year, board and washing (this last in moderation), for instructing Mrs Denfield's seven children.

Mrs Denfield now became tolerably gracious to Clara. She had asked her a great many questions, she had engaged her at a low salary, she had a prospect of her boys learning Latin at no expense;

in fact, she had been decided, and made the governess come into her terms without binding herself in any way. So she was talking rather pleasantly about the colony and the weather, the vineyard and the dairy, and Clara was beginning to think that she would like her a little, when Mr Denfield entered, with the children.

'Ha!' said he, 'a young lady here, and a fair one. Introduce me, Mrs Denfield.'

'This is Miss Morison, about whom Mr Campbell spoke to me.'

'Just so,' said Mr Denfield; 'I am glad to see that it is Miss Morison. I hope you will like Langley, Miss Morison. I am sure, Caroline, and Lucy, and Eliza, you will like this nice lady to teach you your lessons. She does not look at all like Miss Dobson, my dears. Why do you not ask Miss Morison to take off her bonnet and what-do-you-call-it, Priscilla? She must be smothered in them.'

Mrs Denfield was displeased at her husband for admiring the new governess, and at his taking it for granted that she was engaged without its being announced from head-quarters; and still more at his rebuking her for a failure in courtesy. So she changed her mind, and determined that Miss Morison should have another situation to seek for.

'You are always too precipitate, Mr Denfield,' said she. 'I have not settled matters with Miss Morison yet; there are some inquiries to make before a final engagement can be entered into.'

'A final engagement! That sounds very like a marriage,' said Mr Denfield, laughing heartily. 'Never mind, Miss Morison, there are lots of young fellows about here who will be very desirous of entering into a final engagement with you; but in the meantime, we must allow Mrs Denfield to have her way in the first place, and to make your prior engagement as firm and decided as she is herself. Ha! ha!'

'I am sure I shall like you,' said Miss Denfield; 'you look so good-natured.'

'I don't like a woman to teach me,' said Master James; 'I want to go to school like other boys.'

'So you shall, my boy, and Harry too,' said Mr Denfield. 'This young lady cannot take charge of such great unruly fellows as you are; can you, Miss Morison?'

'Miss Morison has promised to do so,' said Mrs Denfield; 'she knows Latin, and says that she can lay the foundation for that language. I hope she can do it well, for it occurs to me that there is some difference between English Latin and Scotch Latin. Is there not, William, my love?'

'Oh! to be sure there is; Scotchmen make all the vowels broad,' rejoined Mr Denfield. I remember a chap, of the name of Macbarnet, coming to our grammar-school from the north, and how terribly he got laughed at among the boys for his way of pronouncing the words.'

'After which fashion do you pronounce the language?' said Mrs Denfield, with such cold severity, that hot as the day was, Clara felt a shiver come over her.

'After the Scotch fashion, ma'am,' said she, flushing under the supercilious sneer of the boy James, who, knowing nothing whatever of the matter, thought it a fine thing to despise ladies' Latin.

'It is of very little consequence, Priscilla,' said Mr Denfield, apologetically; 'Macbarnet was really the best scholar among us, and was never once out in his quantities.'

'I beg your pardon, Mr Denfield,' said the lady, 'but I am disposed to consider it of great consequence; and I am glad I am aware of this point, Miss Morison, for I should have been sorry indeed if you had succeeded in holding it back from me. I will let you know on Monday whether I can engage you, and in case I do, you ought to hold yourself in readiness to accompany the messenger.'

Clara assented, and feeling uncomfortable under Mrs Denfield's eye, she moved to take her leave; having merely tasted the glass of colonial wine that Mrs Denfield had offered her, and leaving both fruit and bread much as she had got them. Mr Denfield went out to open the gate for her, and Caroline followed with a bunch of grapes, which she insisted on her eating by the way; while Mrs Denfield, more displeased than ever, sullenly determined that,

12

whatever might be said on the subject, that girl should never enter her house again, to make mischief, as she was sure to do.

As Clara went home, her heart felt unaccountably lightened. She had observed Mrs Denfield's manner, and was convinced that her answer would be unfavourable; but she was conscious that she had conceded every point, and that she was not to blame for her bad success in her first attempt to get a situation.

So she picked her grapes, and slowly returned to Adelaide, happy in the thought that on this evening, for the first time for months, she could have a little solitude, and even looking forward to a return to Mrs Handy's cordial face with a sort of home feeling. Mrs Denfield's coldness had made her long to return to the boarding-house. The sun was low when she got into town, and in passing Mr Campbell's store, she found it was shut, so that she could not on this evening give him any account of her conversation with his amiable friend.

On reaching home, Clara went straight to her room to obtain a little rest, but was not long left to herself, for in half an hour Mrs Handy tapped at the door, bringing in a cup of tea, with bread and butter; and Clara begged she would sit down to hear about her application to Mrs Denfield, while she took the welcome tea. Mrs Handy was convinced that Mrs Denfield would send for Miss Morison on Monday. She knew very well that Mrs Denfield could afford to give a better salary than fifteen pounds a-year, and concluded by advising Clara to make a stand at first both for more authority and more pay.

Clara said quietly that she did not expect to get this situation, but that even if she did, she was not in circumstances to make any stand. She must come into her employer's terms, or not be engaged at all.

'Well, Miss Morison,' said Mrs Handy, 'I suppose it is all for the best, but things do go contrary with us all sometimes. I am losing all my pleasantest people. There's Mr Haussen has given me notice to-day, and I believe it is just the singing and dancing they make Mr Blinker do in the evenings that sends him off; but I cannot say a word about it, for Mr Oscar and Mr Brown, and some of the others, would leave if I dared to find fault. I don't think you like the noise they make either, and I must say that it would be a great deal more gentlemanly if they would exert themselves to amuse you in a quiet way, than by making game of that poor harmless creature. We have got a new gentleman to-day, who takes half a room till Mr Haussen goes. He is a Jew, a Mr Samuels; but he does not mind about eating pork. He took bacon at dinner to-day, and I was rather sorry to see it, for you know that it is the most expensive article on the table; and I have had Jews who were more particular, and I liked them for boarders very well.'

CAROLINE WOOLMER LEAKEY
('OLINE KEESE')
(1827–1881)

Caroline Leakey was born in Exeter, England. At the age of twenty she came to Hobart to live with her sister. She suffered ill-health and had to return to England five years later. Her first published work, a collection of poems, *Lyra Australis* (1854), deals with sickness and death. Leakey was deeply religious and humanitarian. She became involved with various charities and ran a home for fallen women in Exeter. She wrote for the Religious Tract Society and *Girls' Own Paper*. After her death, her sister wrote her memoir, *Clear Shining Light* (1882).

Her novel, *The Broad Arrow, Being Passages from the History of Maida Gwynnham, a Lifer,* was published under the pseudonym Oliné Keese in 1859. It deals with the problems of the convict system in Australia.

The Broad Arrow is the story of Maida Gwynnham, alias Martha Grylls, who has been wrongly convicted of infanticide and transported to Australia for life. Mr Evelyn and Bridget, free settlers, are in need of a new servant and one of their convict servants has recommended Martha. In this extract they travel out to the convict ship *Anson* to try to obtain her services.

HMS ANSON

from *The Broad Arrow, Being Passages from the History of Maida Gwynnham, a Lifer*

At half past two, Mr Evelyn and Bridget set off for Risdon Ferry, in sight of which the *Anson* lay. From Macquarie Street they reached the ferry at half past three; there a boat awaited parties going on board the ship.

'Now then, miss, hold on, and I'll keep close behind you.'

And Miss D'Urban ascended the companion ladder and stood on the hulk. Her uncle beckoned her to follow him below.

A female standing at a high desk by the open door of the first cabin raised her head and bowed a business-like bow as they advanced. She was evidently the monarch of all she surveyed.

'Is that Mrs Bowden?' whispered Bridget.

The question was overheard and answered by the ruling spirit.

'No, Mrs Bowden is in England. *I* act in her place.' Another, and still more official bow followed. Accompanied by one of the officers, Mr Evelyn and his niece arraigned themselves at Mrs Deputy's bar.

'I want a servant-of-all-work; can you recommend me one, Mrs Deputy?'

'We do not recommend; there are several people eligible, but they will not afford much choice, Mr Evelyn.'

'Except to friends!' drily suggested that gentleman.

Mrs Deputy bowed at once dignity and indignity, and repeated, 'There are several prisoners eligible.' True to the daring contradictions of Tasmanian words and their meanings, 'eligible' is not intended to signify aptness or suitability. A woman eligible for service is rarely fitted for service; the adjective only informs the master or mistress that she is ready to be hired.

'Is one Martha Grylls eligible, Mrs Deputy?'

'Grylls, Grylls, Grylls, let me see?' drawing her finger down the list before her.

The attendant officer chimed in:

'Yes; she becomes so this very day.'

'Thank you, Miss Perkins,' bowed Mrs Deputy, with an air that plainly said, 'I will thank you not to interfere.'

'Grylls, Grylls,' and her finger travelled on.

'You cannot know whom you ask for, if you want her, sir!' whispered the cowed Miss Perkins.

'Thank you, Miss Perkins, perhaps you will leave the arrangement of this matter to me,' again bowed the commandant.

'Martha Grylls is at your service, Mr Evelyn; shall I send for her?'

'I will trouble you, if you please.'

'Would not you prefer my calling several women, sir?' asked the attendant officer.

'I will thank you, Miss Perkins, to call Martha Grylls,' responded Mrs Deputy.

The little officer had no choice but to obey; so bowing obedience, she sidled to the grating which divided the prison from the officers' quarters; and then standing on tiptoe, desired a Miss Snub to send forward 'That Martha Grylls'.

'Ordered forward, Martha Grylls!' shouted a female Stentor; and, uprising from a distant rank, immediately appeared a tall, elegant woman, who, passing Miss Snub with a curtsey, came into Mrs Deputy's awful presence.

She had on the usual brown serge skirt (so short as to show a masculine pair of half-boots), a jacket of brown and yellow gingham, a dark blue cotton kerchief; and a prim white calico cap, whose narrow border was kept in frill by help of a thread run through it, completed her dress. The grotesque coarseness of this attire could not *hide* the inherent grace of the prisoner. Still dignified and beautiful, before her future master stood the wearer of those rough knitted blue stockings and clownish shoes.

Her cap was untied.

'Tie your cap, Martha Grylls,' commanded Miss Perkins.

Martha mechanically obeyed.

'It would better become you, Grylls, to curtsey the same as your

17

mates, than to try to imitate your betters,' continued the little woman, conscious that Martha's obeisance surpassed her genuflecting capabilities.

'The curtsey was meant for *me*, I think, Miss Perkins,' said Mrs Deputy.

In consideration of Martha's presence, the rebuked attendant darted daggers at Mrs Deputy.

Mr Evelyn put a few questions to Martha, all of which she quietly and satisfactorily answered.

'I will hire this Grylls, if you please, Mrs Deputy.'

Preliminaries having been settled, Martha was sent to tie up her bundle, and business being over, Mrs Deputy came down from the tip-top of dignity, and seemed not wholly disinclined for a talk.

'The appearance of the woman decided me at once, Mrs Deputy; to belie *that* countenance, she must be a monster.'

'With a good master she will not belie it, Mr Evelyn. Wise management will do much for her. Her police character is against her, and her crimes you are aware—'

'Yes, yes; but I do not heed the amount of crime: indiscriminate association generally makes it theoretically equal amongst prisoners. It is my opinion that both men and females come out of these probations worse than they went in. Reformations rarely, if ever, commence within prison walls; and reformation the more tardily begins in proportion to the length of durance. We have an extra task to perform on a probationer.'

Mrs Deputy looked much hurt, and exclaimed, '*Here* on the *Anson* surely, Mr Evelyn, you do not call it indiscriminate association: we have distinct classes—bad, better, and best. Surely nothing can be superior to Mrs Bowden's excellent system?'

'Than Mrs Bowden I know no more gifted and prudent Lady-Superintendent; were all officers selected with like discernment, it would be well for the prisoners. Mrs Deputy, may I take my niece through the wards?' asked Mr Evelyn, anxious to avoid a discussion.

The lady only bowed assent; for she was deeply affronted at an attack on a system of which she was representative in place of the highly respected Mrs Bowden: perhaps she was the more deeply wounded, because a conviction of the fallacy of the system already worked in her own mind. It is a natural weakness with many persons to be angry with a scruple they can no longer conscientiously resist. She just deigned to say, 'Miss Perkins, this gentleman wishes to see the *Anson*,' and turned to her desk. The little creature came hopping over with a kind of sidewise movement, not unlike that of an impudent cock-sparrow which can scarcely hop for pertness. Pecking to Mr Evelyn's side, she whispered, 'Though I pity you, sir, I am downright glad to get rid of that woman. The trouble I have had with her!'

This was only meant for Mr Evelyn; nevertheless, it reached the vigilant deputy's ears. 'I am sure *I* shall be glad, Miss Perkins. Often have I been pained by the foolish complaints made against her and poor Lucy Grenlow, when she was here. You know I am obliged to take my officers' part before the convicts; you ought therefore to refrain from bringing such nonsensical cases for me to judge. Had my duties allowed me time to pay particular attention to Martha, I should not have had reason to punish her so much.' As Mrs Deputy was thus properly delivering herself, Miss Perkins stood a deferential listener; she just hopped off in time to hear a mutter that sounded very like—'I have as much trouble with the officers as with the women.'

Bridget clung to her uncle's arm as they passed through rows of prisoners, who were variously employed in working, reading, and learning, it being their school-hour. Each file arose and curtsied as the party passed.

Ever and anon Miss Perkins issued orders to some unfortunate.

'Mary Gull, tie your cap. What, Mary Pike, yours off! The next offence you'll go downstairs.' Mary understood the allusion, and hastily put on her cap.

'Sarah Gubb, you are talking there. Jane Dawson, where's your curtsey? Why don't you rise, Ellen Bracket? Muggins, I shall complain of you.'

'Would you like to walk through the cells, sir?'

They went below. In one cell was a captive, kicking and

stamping violently. Miss Perkins thought fit to soothe her by rapping at the door.

'You don't think that's the way to get out, do you, Stooks?'

''Twas you got me in, you *did*, you beast!'

'If I wasn't very indulgent, Stooks, I should get you double for that,' said the maternal Perkins.

'Is the devil indulgent, I should like to know, you old cant?' cried Stooks.

With a deprecating smile at Bridget, Miss Perkins stopped at Number 10, whence issued an imploring voice:

'Do beg for me; I'm quite subdued, indeed I am, Miss Love. Oh! it's Miss Perkins. I beg pardon, ma'am, I thought 'twas Miss Love,' the prisoner was heard to sigh.

Passing on, they came to stalls where different trades — cobblery, bonnet-making, etc. — were being carried on.

'Do let us go, uncle; it is so dreadful to have these poor creatures made a show of,' whispered Bridget.

'They are accustomed to it,' answered Miss Perkins to the second clause of Bridget's speech.

'As the eels are, eh, Miss Perkins?' asked Mr Evelyn.

'Oh, they keep each other in countenance. We look at them as a lot, not as individuals.'

Here her eyes fell on Martha Grylls, who was waiting, bundle in hand, at the grating.

'Follow us, and don't be talking there, Grylls. I don't wish to lose sight of you.'

'Come along, my woman,' said Mr Evelyn kindly.

'*No*; walk before us, if you please, Grylls. I don't wish to lose sight of you, I repeat.'

Martha obeyed without a word.

All the women tried to give her a nod on the sly; and many anxious eyes followed the party as the grated door closed, and an audible sigh was simultaneously heaved by those whom it imprisoned. Each prisoner envied Martha, and wished it had been her lot to fall to so sweet a looking lady as that bright-eyed girl who smiled on her in passing.

What lay beyond those gates not one could tell. They were as the gates of death—all doubt and mystery beyond. None ever returned to tell of the untried world to which they led.

Strange and vague are the mental picturings the prisoned female forms of the land of her exile, which she knows lies little further than a stone's-throw from her. Some think, on leaving the *Anson*, they are to be turned adrift to all the horrors of an unexplored region; others that they will be driven to market for sale. The cunning and malicious amongst them delight in filling the minds of their less gifted associates with the most terrible apprehensions of the barbarities awaiting them on their departure from their probation. It is with a thrill of cruel suspense that such prisoners first plant their foot on Tasmanian ground.

In this respect the male convicts do not suffer so acutely. Their doubts, hopes, and fears are answered, realised, or crushed almost immediately on arriving at the colony. Their probationary course does not add suspense to sorrow. At once formed into gangs, they learn the worst, and are sent to labour in the roads, or work on public buildings. The torture of suspense is not added to it.

Miss Perkins accompanied Mr Evelyn and his niece to the deck, where she mysteriously beckoned Bridget aside:

'I hope you do not mean to employ Grylls about children.'

She gave a significant wink. 'Of course, though, you don't. You guess why? It is not usual to tell the crime; but really I think it my duty to break rule to you. Do you understand me?'

Bridget looked a negative.

Martha had drawn near enough to hear Miss Perkin's friendly caution. Casting a glance of unutterable contempt on little Perkins, she stepped to Miss D'Urban, and herself solved the significant wink.

'Miss Perkins wishes you to know that I am sent out for murder. She would suggest the impropriety of making me a nurse.'

Bridget turned very pale, and cast an imploring look on the little officer, who, boiling over with injured prerogative, was on the point of reprimanding Martha's audacity, when Mr Evelyn called them to be quick—the boat was waiting.

'Good morning, Miss Perky. We are much favoured by your civilities.'

The officer was hurt at the inharmonious name bestowed upon her, and vented her spite by exclaiming, as Martha was on the first step of the companion ladder:

'I hope you'll behave better *now*, Grylls, or you'll soon learn the difference between factory and here.'

Martha turned abruptly on her. A second more, and she had been on her way back to the cells, instead of on the road to Hobart Town. The crimson cheek, flashing eye, and quivering lip, a second more had met their chastisement; but Bridget's beseeching gesture once more prevailed. Quietly turning from her persecutor, Martha descended the ladder.

'Good-morning, Miss Perky,' waved Mr Evelyn abstractedly, as though his voice mechanically embodied his opinion in a *name* expressive of the little upstart, pecking at him from the deck.

'That horrid woman!' cried Bridget.

A quick nod and frown from Mr Evelyn stopped what further she would have said.

A slight smile overspread the prisoner's face; but it soon faded into a look of anxious sadness. It mattered not to her whether the coast was beautiful or barren; whether the landscape was rendered vital by the upward wreathing of the blue smoke from pleasant homesteads; or whether its desolate grandeur was made more dreary by the long blank masonry of penal life.

She started as from a dream when the boat jerked against the jetty. A ghastly pallor struck her every feature as she stepped ashore. For an instant she covered her face; then, gradually withdrawing her hands, the Maida Gwynnham of olden days discovered herself in the unabated dignity of that upraised head, and in the strength of purpose outshining from the purple depths of those undimmed eyes.

A strength of purpose that even now was to be tried; and if the trial, surprising an unguarded post, be victorious for a season, who shall exult?

She was prepared to confront the hardships of convict existence.

She was prepared for taunts, for jibes, for suspicions, for enemies, and felt that she could face them; but she was not prepared to meet any of these as they were now about to assail her.

ELLEN LISTON
(1838–1885)

Ellen Liston was born in London and came to South Australia with her parents in 1850. She was an accomplished bush woman, and worked as a governess, a teacher and a telegraphist. A staff member of *The Kapunda Herald*, she also contributed stories and verses to *The Adelaide Observer*, and one of her serials won a twenty pound prize from the Melbourne *Leader*. She wrote one unpublished novel, *Jean Kesson*. Her short stories are collected in *Pioneers* (1869).

HOW A WOMAN KEPT
HER PROMISE

'Maggie, you will repent it.'

'Sometimes I am afraid I shall, Harold.'

'Then why don't you break off? It is not because of his position I object; many a highly-educated fellow out here has gone bullock-driving or stock-keeping from the force of circumstances; but this Mark Bedford has had no education, and though his manner and speech are passable for the position he has always been in, yet he is inferior to you in every respect — his tastes won't lie in the bent of yours, and you'll soon be miserable. I say again, why don't you break it off?'

'Because I have promised, Harold.'

'Nonsense; you will be quite justified in breaking your promise, when upon reflection you see it will only bring you unhappiness. Besides, you cannot expect your present friends to associate with him, so he will drag you down to the level of his. Just fancy him in the banker's drawing-room, or here amongst my set.'

Maggie Elliston drew herself up. 'Your last argument has not helped your cause much, Harold; and I will not subject Mark Bedford to the mortification of being looked down upon by my friends. As for him he has none but myself, and I'll take care not to sink below my own level.' The girl turned away, and the conversation, not the first on the same subject, ended.

Was she bound to keep her promise? Would she in time come to repent it? Often and often had Maggie asked herself that question, and sometimes from the depths of her heart she had answered, 'Yes'. But she had promised to be Mark Bedford's wife, and she would keep her word. Unfortunately the opposition of her friends, instead of having the desired effect, only rendered her more determined. Her Scotch blood would not brook being told she must not do this or must do that. She was without father

25

or mother, and thought herself quite as competent as her brothers and sisters to judge of what should or should not be done. It was a matter of wonder to all her friends and sometimes to herself, how Maggie Elliston, who was tolerably good looking, well educated, and generally considered clever, should (when she might have married an Adelaide merchant or tradesman, a Northern stockholder or sheepfarmer) have given herself to Mark Bedford — knockabout hand, as it is called, on one of her friend's stations — a man of but little education, and nothing apparently to recommend him but length and strength of limb, a quiet manner and voice, and a wealth of bright brown hair. He had neither relatives nor friends, for he held himself aloof from the other men, did his work well, and seldom talked. He used of an evening to try and improve himself in writing and spelling, and Maggie having discovered him one night in the kitchen busy over his books, had volunteered her assistance in such a laudable cause, which was gratefully accepted. Some time after his arm was injured in the wool-press, and Maggie's deft fingers used to dress and bandage it for him, because his mistress said the sight of it made her sick. And so Mark fell in love with his fair doctor and teacher, the first, too, who had spoken kind and thoughtful womanly words to him for years. He would have worshipped her afar off, nor dared to tell his love; but she, with her woman's intuition, had found it out, and pitied him first, and then felt something of that tenderer passion which is said to be akin to pity. If she had gone away home then, doubtless it would have died out of the hearts of both. But she stayed on and on, and Mark's love grew deeper and deeper, so that when she was going away and bade him goodbye the evening before, he spoke first of his utter friendlessness when she was absent, and then of his love; and Maggie, pitying him still more, and feeling that she had made him very miserable and was much to blame, also thinking it somewhat of a novelty to be wooed by a man in his social position, consented to be his wife, and repented the next day when she heard him giving utterance to some ungrammatical sentence. But when her friends expressed their disapproval so strongly, she flew off

26

at a tangent, and declared she was not going to be harried into breaking her promise.

Once or twice Mark said to her, 'What will your friends think of this?' and she had replied, 'I don't care what they think.' But she did care a good bit, but more for Mark than herself.

'They will know I am not fit for you, Miss Elliston.'

'They will know nothing of the sort, Mr Bedford.'

'That I haven't a home fit to put you in.'

'We will make a home, Mark.'

Mark sighed, 'I haven't the means.'

'We won't stay in this colony,' said Maggie energetically; 'we will go to New South Wales.'

'And what shall we do there? I go shepherding, with you for hut-keeper?'

'No; we will set up sheep-farming,'

'How can we when I have only saved about forty pounds?' And Mark sadly shook his head.

'But I have a little property in Adelaide left me by my mother, which I shall sell; we shall have to begin in a small way, and work hard.'

'You are not fit for hard work, Maggie; you could not do it.'

'You'll see what I can do, Mark Bedford;' and the grey eyes flashed up.

So Maggie Elliston sold her property, and packed up her goods, and places were taken in a vessel for Sydney. The wedding morning arrived; in the afternoon they were to sail.

Maggie stood before her glass wondering once again if she should repent in the long years before her. 'There is one thing,' she said to herself, 'I am taking this step of my own free act and will, and there are none to blame but myself; so that if in the future I repent never by word or deed must Mark Bedford suspect it.' She had bidden all her friends goodbye.

'I don't ask you to my wedding,' she said, 'because you would only feel uncomfortable; the boys are going (thereby meaning her brothers) just, I think, to see that I am married. There will be no breakfast, no cards, no cake, as Sydney is too far off for a morning call.'

'You will write us of your welfare, Maggie; we shall hear from you,' said her brothers, as they drew her aside on board the vessel.

'You shall hear from me when' — she paused, and her eye caught the figure of Mark — 'when you will be as pleased to welcome Mark as me.'

Moorings were cast off, sails were set, the wharf seemed drifting away; she waved her handkerchief with tears in her eyes, for she loved her brothers dearly. Farther and farther they drift, till she can no longer distinguish them, then she turned and put her hands in Mark's; and it was many a year before Maggie Bedford was heard of again in her old home.

About two years before the time at which I write, and twelve after the Bedfords had left South Australia, there was a family gathering of the Ellistons at the house of Harold. They were also entertaining a stranger within their gates — a gentleman from Sydney who had come round to look at some runs on the Adelaide side, where he talked of settling. He had brought letters of introduction from several Sydney firms to two or three of the family, and was accordingly being entertained with the usual hospitality of the Ellistons. The cloth was removed, and the company were chatting over their dessert. News had come by the English mail of the inauguration of the celebrated author of *Sartor Resartus* as Rector of Edinburgh University; and the conversation turned upon that, then upon education generally, diverged from that to the education of women, and their influence and power in the world.

'I think,' said a lady present, 'that the value of our women's influence must depend upon the quality rather than the quantity of their attainments. Whilst we stuff our girls only with the rudiments of a great deal, and a sound knowledge of very little, polished off with some showy accomplishment, we shall never play a universally practical part in the affairs of life.'

'But, Mrs Rawood,' asked a gentleman, 'would you have a woman leave her home sphere and take a stand in the outside ranks with us men?'

'No; but I would have her take her proper stand in the home. She has enough to do there if she knew but what and how. In many cases she has to go forth as the bread-winner; and in many, where actual necessity does not compel, I think she might help her husband often with advantage.'

'What, help him to work, Mrs Rawood?' exclaimed several Young ladies, 'You wouldn't like to see us do that.'

'Yes; I would like to see you able to take your stand in the position I think God intended you for; as a helpmeet for the men of your families — be they fathers, husbands, brothers, or sons — to train, to raise, to encourage, to elevate, to ennoble, to advise, to assist; and so play your true part in advancement and civilisation. Our sex has always been credited with the power to do a vast deal of good and evil. When we have better knowledge we shall have greater power, more for good and less for evil.'

Mr Marks, the visitor, a tall, quiet-talking gentlemanly man, who had taken his part in all the discussions without any self-assertiveness, but with much good sense and quiet earnestness, now said, 'I strongly support your side of the question, Mrs Rawood, and there occurs to my mind a noble illustration of what a true woman can do; which if you think you would all like to hear I shall be happy to tell.'

All expressed themselves ready to hear, and settled themselves into attentive attitudes, and Mr Marks began.

'I am a sheepfarmer, as you know; well, it is getting on for twelve years ago, I suppose, since I first became acquainted with the lady I am speaking of, whose husband had taken a small run adjoining mine; they were perfect strangers in the neighbourhood, and nobody knew anything about them. They had a tent and a flock of sheep; and the first thing that I heard about them was that the wife shepherded whilst the husband built a hut. The hut was soon finished; then some of my men told me that he had begun fencing in a part of his run, and his wife still tended the sheep. I said to my wife, "We shall not find suitable friends in our new neighbours, as I thought we might; they are only an ordinary working couple." We hadn't many about us, you see, and so had been looking forward to these new arrivals when we learned the run was taken up. A few days after I rode over to have a chat with the man at his fencing. I found him a long-limbed son of Anak, possessed of a thoroughly English nature, of steady indefatigable industry, but evidently of but little education. He was not very talkative, but spoke sensibly as far as the conversation went. I went home past his hut to see if the mistress was at home, and what she was like, but the place was shut up. All around, however, was neat and tidy, and a small piece of ground in front had been fenced in and turned up for a garden. The next thing we heard was that one of our men said the new arrival wore gloves at her work.

'My curiosity was aroused; so the next ride I took was with the view of coming across her, which I did, and was adequately surprised to find a tall, good-looking young woman of some three-and-twenty years, neatly but tastefully dressed in print, with a broad hat of like material, and a pair of doeskin riding-gloves. But she was a lady if she had been dressed in woolpacks; you could have told that by the carriage of her person, by the courteous, easy, well-bred manner in which she addressed you. I had intended to have learnt from her who they were, where they came from, and all about it, but could not ask; for what would have only been friendly familiarity with a less educated woman would, I felt, be inquisitive impertinence to this lady. So I said a few things that the occasion warranted, and then rode away, charmed and wondering. This young lady was evidently very superior to her husband; there seemed a spice of mystery about them which I felt curious to fathom out, but one could not very well get acquainted with people who were never at home, so I thought we must bide our time and see what turned up. Of course authenticated reports came to us from time to time about them and what they did. I think some of my shepherds used purposely to let some of their sheep get into our neighbour's flocks for the sake of going to the house to stay the night, and get their sheep in the morning. And my overseer and stockmen would delay themselves till very late when out after cattle, and so have excuse to beg a night's entertainment. All agreed in expressing great wonderment at the place and its mistress, who, they said, was a perfect genius in all household duties. True she never entertained the men in the little house of two rooms, but made them welcome in the comfortable and cheerful kitchen adjoining. Everybody who has been amongst sheep knows that they should be out of the yard at sunrise and not in till sunset, so that there is but little time for domestic work if the wife is shepherd; but this young lady was up, had put her house straight, breakfast was ready, dispatched, and cleared away, and by the time the sun showed his face fairly both were off to their work, carrying their day's provisions with them; she took needle-work with her, and when not that a book. On Saturdays the husband took the sheep whilst she stayed home to wash and iron, and on Sundays they went together. Lambing-time came on; fencing operations were for the time abandoned, as both were busy with their flocks. Winter set in, and several times I met my fair neighbour dressed in a long garment of waterproof material, with a close-fitting hood of the same, in which she looked perfectly bewitching, and the overseer and several of the men were in danger of breaking the commandment relative to coveting your neighbour's wife. Shearing-time came round. A little while before I had received a note from the husband, asking permission to shear their sheep at my place, as they had no shed nor conveniences, offering to pay a certain sum for the privilege. I readily acquiesced, as a means of making us better acquainted. I had never yet seen husband and wife together, so I wrote and asked her to come and stay with my family whilst the sheep were being shorn and received a polite refusal, saying she should be busily engaged at home during her husband's absence. So I thought my time had not come, and waited accordingly. Of course I cannot tell you day by day what they did, but must speak of the first time I saw them at home, and of the facts that gradually came to my knowledge in after years. I was belated one night returning from a distant township, and thought I would avail myself of their hospitality for the night. It was dark when I got there. I fastened my horse to a tree a little way off, and walked up quietly. I had a mind to see or hear how

31

they spent their evenings. It was summer-time, and the door was open, and I commanded a full view of the interior. The wife was sitting at the table with a book in her hand, alternately reading, explaining, elucidating the different forms of government among nations. Her husband, seated by her, earnestly attentive, asking questions, listening patiently. I reckoned myself well up in the subject she was discussing, but I stood there tired and hungry for an hour at least, intensely interested; then I stole away, got on my horse, and rode up with a great noise. I was cordially welcomed, and soon served with some supper. I looked around me. Certainly my men who had been there had not under-rated the place. The canvas tent had been formed into ceilings for the log hut; the walls were papered and covered with some dark green stuff, against which hung three or four beautiful prints. There was a rough bookshelf, also draped in green, filled with books. The table linen was beautifully fine, the plates and cups were china, the forks were silver. My host was dressed in a gentlemanly light suit, minus a coat; my hostess in a pretty muslin, tastily set off with ribbons. I rubbed my eyes, and thought the old days of enchantment had come back, and that I should wake presently and find myself lost in the darkness of a Sydney forest; but it remained real, and after some hour or so of pleasant and intelligent conversation, maintained on their side mostly by the wife, but so adroitly managed, with appeals and references to her husband, that I remember having at the time an indistinct idea that he was a very clever and sensible man, and his wife only echoed him. We retired for the night, I to lie awake and wonder how all this came about. Next morning before I left I pressed the lady to visit us. She said she would gladly but had no time, her outdoor and indoor occupations kept her fully employed; perhaps she might find time in a year or two. I went off somewhat in a huff.

'What business had a woman like her to marry a man like that for whom she had to work so hard? Soon after I learned, it boots not how, that an hour every evening, and all day on Sundays, and whatever other time could be found, was devoted to the cultivation of her husband's mind, the refinement of his tastes, the instruction of his intellect. However she had come to marry one so inferior to herself, she was determined to stand nobly by him, and raise him up somewhere near her own level; and I noted the success that attended her untiring efforts. Gradually but surely her husband developed, not exactly from an ugly grub to a beautiful butterfly — he will never be quite so brilliant as that — but at least into a very good specimen of moth. You presently know the results of liberal education, and can perhaps better imagine than I can describe the effects of her patient and loving training. He did not lack common-sense and intelligence, only the cultivation and knowledge necessary to apply them, and this his wife supplied him with. One thing I especially admired her for, was that when they were in the presence of others you could never trace aught in her manner or speech to betray her superiority. She always managed, as I have said in the first conversation I had with them, to make you feel that she was indebted to him for most of her ideas. I soon saw why, amidst all the hard work she did, she was so careful of her personal appearance and of the home surroundings. She kept thus ever before him the higher standard of the class to which she belonged, and to which he was to climb. Never did she by the slightest chance take a step back towards his; she felt strongly how much ground she would lose by so doing. I have seen her on horseback tailing cattle day after day for weeks together. I have seen her shepherding in all weathers; helping to draft and brand; harnessing up the horse and fetching a load of wood, or dragging timber for the fences, or busy amongst her household duties; but she never lost caste by it; she was always in everything — by action, manner, speech — a lady. They began with very little, but have been successful; the last four years, especially, have been very prosperous ones. It is a long time now since she left off hard out-of-door work; she only oversees when her husband is absent. They have two children — a boy, about nine, and a girl, six years old. To say that her husband loves her dearly would not express a tithe of his devotion and reverence, for he thoroughly appreciates all she has done and still does for him.

And now, Mrs Rawood, I think you will agree with me that this lady plays her part in life's drama nobly, worthily, and well.'

Mrs Rawood sprang from her chair, exclaiming. 'Tell me her name, Mr Marks, tell me her name, that I may honour her by proclaiming her an example to all my young friends. She is, indeed, a woman after my own heart.'

'Bedford, Margaret Bedford,' was the answer.

'Maggie, our Maggie!' 'Our long-lost-sight-of sister!' 'Our Aunt!' 'Our dear Maggie!' were the exclamations that burst forth; then they were all silent for a little while, thinking of Maggie doing her work bravely afar off, all unaided and alone. Presently, however, Mr Marks was beset on all sides with enquiries relative to Maggie, her husband, and children; and some month or so after, when he had concluded the purchase of a station, and was returning to Sydney to fetch his family, he was loaded with presents and letters for the Bedfords, and brothers and sisters begged him by the friendship that had sprung up between them to lend his assistance in smoothing over the old breach. 'I will do my best,' he said, as he shook hands on the platform at the Adelaide Station; 'but,' he added, with a peculiar smile, 'I don't think Mrs Bedford will *write* to you.' The bell rang, the whistle sounded, the train was off, before they had time to ask him what he meant. Three months passed, but no news of Maggie reached them, though they received a letter from Mr Marks, saying that himself and family would arrive shortly. So, as Harold had asked him to make his house their home during the time they stayed in Adelaide, the Ellistons made ready to receive their guests, who duly arrived one evening, and were announced by the servant. Harold, his wife, and brother, who was also present, came forward with a cordial greeting.

'We are glad to have you amongst us again,' said Elliston, shaking hands warmly with Mr Marks; 'as pleased to see you as —'

'As you are to see me, Harold, I hope,' said the lady, raising her thick veil as she spoke.

'Maggie, it's Maggie's own self!' exclaimed both the brothers, and fond welcomes were exchanged. As soon as the commotion caused by this announcement had subsided a little, Maggie turned to the young people, and said —

'These are my children, your nephew and niece, Harold and Maggie.'

'And this gentleman?' asked her brothers, looking towards Marks.

Their sister's old ringing laugh rang through the place as she answered, 'is my much-loved husband, Mark Bedford. You must pardon him if he has won your regard under an assumed name.'

Ample pardon was granted, and mutual regards satisfied.

'But a pretty story you invented when you first saw Maggie,' said Harold.

'There was no invention in it,' replied Mark. 'I did but assume the character of our next-door neighbour in New South Wales, and repeated what he has often told Maggie and me, only adding a few more home facts with which he was unacquainted.'

Later in the evening, and when alone, Harold said — 'And have you never repented, Maggie?'

'Yes, Harold, many a time during the first three or four years, not because of the physical toil I had to undergo but from the want of mental companionship in my husband. But I never lost sight of the end I aimed at. And I can say,' she added, with a look of pride and affection, 'that for the last five years I have had no thought of Mark but of deep love, respect, and esteem — ay, and pride, too.'

I have not much to add. The Bedfords took possession of their new home. Mark retains the friendship of his wife's family, and has gained that of all in his neighbourhood, so much so, that at a late election for Parliament he was asked to stand.

'No, no,' he replied, with a laugh, 'I am not brilliant butterfly enough for that; but when the day comes that ladies are allowed to sit in Council, I'll head a requisition to Mrs Bedford.'

Nilkerloo, 1869.

'WAIF WANDER'
(c.1840–?)

The identity of the prolific 'Waif Wander' remains a mystery. Almost every issue of *The Australian Journal* from the late 1860s to the 1880s contained one or more of her stories. She is perhaps best known for her series of mystery stories, *The Detective's Album*. She also wrote as 'WW', 'MHF' and 'Mrs Fortune'.

MY LODGER

Why, you know, it was only last summer that I was wearily trudging through Melbourne streets in search of lodgings, and will you credit it that I have to-day arrived at the dignity of keeping lodgers myself! Instead of speaking humbly to crusty old women who scan me from head to foot inspectively, and watch any loose articles, such as a huckaback towel, that may be lying about when I request to see the 'apartment' to let, I have the immense satisfaction of being crusty, and of snapping and turning up my nose at non-eligible inquirers for rooms myself.

Now, I don't care how much inclined you may be to disagreeable fault-finding, you must acknowledge that I have wonderfully improved my condition within the past few months; not that I expect much sympathy from you in any case, oh, no! (although, if you made anything by it, I have no doubt any quantity of that commodity would be humbly at my service), but you are so much in the habit of considering yourself and your judgments as infallible, and of talking of yourself as a reasonable and reasoning creature (fond public!) that you would not venture upon jeopardising your character by denying a fact so obvious.

And although I calculate upon a hearing of my little insignificant interests from you in a general way, in a particular one how idle it would be to attempt interesting you! You walk on Turkey carpets, or at the least Brussels, you do; and you loll upon, oh, so soft and delicious sofas, and in the downiest of easy-chairs; and what do you care about the cost of dingy-looking drugget, or the price of sea-weed mattresses! Faugh! the very idea of the thing makes you ill, doesn't it? but that doesn't trouble me in the least, you know, for it is quite as much pleasure to me to talk of my own petty affairs as it is to you to discuss the most important arrangements connected with your most magnificent *ménage*.

If one has the bump of constructiveness at all well developed, there is nothing more pleasurably exciting than furnishing a house upon nothing. Until you commence to do so with not more than four or five pounds in your purse, and begin to contrive tables and seats out of empty cases, and to convert trunks and boxes into pretty-looking ottomans, you don't know what fun there is in the world. Until you have to scrape pennies together in a way that the careful can only understand, and lay them together to make shillings for the acquisition of some necessary trifle, you have little idea of the comfort to be derived from the most ordinary of necessities; and I have not the least doubt that I have more real pleasure in contemplating at this moment a very pretty rug, bought for the sum of two shillings and sixpence, than you enjoy in looking at the *tout ensemble* of your very magnificent drawing-room, the furnishing of which, I myself am aware, cost you a few cool hundreds.

And when I laid that said rug down in front of a fireplace as white as whitening could make it, and looked from the bright cluster of red roses and white lilies in the centre of it, to my muslin-draped toilet, that you would never suppose to be three empty orange cases, I began to feel the entire satisfaction of having a whole 'furnished room to let'. You might turn up your nose at my clean matted floor, and the efforts I had made to make two chairs look four in my disposal of them in half a dozen different positions; but, thank goodness, I am not likely to have *you* looking for lodgings at my door just at present, although I have seen loftier ideas than yours reduced even lower in my time.

Well, my 'apartment' being in a state of readiness, the next step was to take expeditious measures to lay my claims for patronage before the public, and, of course, considering my means, or rather my want of them, it was necessary for me to do so in as cheap a form as possible. Firstly, then, I wrote several 'cards', stating that furnished apartments might be had at so-and-so, such a street, and these I distributed to the baker and the butcher and the grocer, with the polite request that they would kindly place the same on view in their several windows. Certainly they all promised to be kind enough, and, with one exception, all *were* kind enough, for I made it my business to walk round and see that they had done so; and that disgraceful exception was the butcher, who goes round and rings a bell every day to call out his customers, and I should think the foolish man had since repented his conduct in sackcloth and ashes, for I have not since purchased my pound of 'chuck' steak, or pennyworth of cat's meat from *his* cart.

Now for my own window. I dare say there are many very nice people who feel a little weakness about putting a card in their parlour window, and so advertising the fact that their incomes are not quite so liberal as could be wished, but I do assure you that it was with quite a different feeling I displayed my pasteboard and its unique notice. You see I was so proud of my half a dozen empty cases, and my two chairs, etc., that I was delighted to let everybody know that I really had *furnished* rooms. However, I met with one difficulty at the very outset of preparing my advertisement. I could not decide in what form to make it public.

'Board and residence', eh? in an enclosed card with a delightfully embossed border, and suspended inside the window by a prettily-coloured bit of love ribbon. Very sweet and pretty, no doubt: but there are 'young ladies' where that card is, and gentlemen might be disappointed on seeing my old phiz at the door; and if there is anything in the world aggravating to women 'of a certain age', it must be to read in the male eye that they are considered *passé*, and not worth the trouble of being polite to. No, I couldn't stand that, thank you; and so, what do you say to 'Furnished Apartments to Let'?

Hum! Apartment is a very fine word; could I conscientiously declare that a room, ornamented, or decorated, or whatever you choose to call it, with six empty cases, and two chairs, was a furnished apartment? I don't think I could, I really do not, although I am by no means a straitlaced person (as my lodgers may find when I come to consider my perquisites), and ready enough to stretch a point where my interests are concerned. But beyond a certain amount of cheek I cannot go, and it would be really a bit too far to declare that I was the landlady of a furnished apartment.

'A Furnished Room to Let'. Well, that's sensible-looking, and to the point, and I do like things to seem what they really are, without shirking the matter in the least; but, look here, my card is rather small, and what do you think of the good old-fashioned word 'Lodgings'? I have seen that word in a good many windows in a good many 'old countries', and I rather like the unpretending style of it. You might lodge anywhere — in an exceedingly well-furnished apartment or in a room with a few well-disposed empty cases doing duty for tables, etc.; nay, your lodgings might be 'on the cold ground' for that matter, as the song says, or you might lodge in a gaspipe on Cole's wharf, as does our mythical friend the Peripatetic Philosopher; at any rate, the word describes the thing I have to dispose of accurately, and I have no doubt in the world that disagreeable and evil-disposed persons will be calling me a lodging-house keeper one of these odd days; so, in the name of peace, 'Lodgings' be it.

And 'Lodgings' it was, in the finest old English letters, you can well believe, barring the L. I am sorry to say I failed in that, and that it was difficult, on a cursory inspection, to pronounce that the complete word was not 'Todgings'. Nay, I heard one little wretched *gamin* calling 'Podgings', at the top of his voice, one day, in front of my parlour window; but that was entirely out of spite, seeing that he belonged to the house over the way, where 'Board and Residence' is displayed within the usual embossage, and with the usual bit of ribbon, although truth compels me to declare that the latter is very considerably fly spotted. No, after I had carefully scraped a too long tail off my capital L, and drawn the other tail as near the o as I dared, I think I may with safety declare that the person must be indeed very ignorant who could, for one moment, mistake the word for anything but what it really was, namely, 'Lodgings'.

And so I pinned it up nicely between my muslin blind and the window, and then I went out into the street to see how it showed. Why, it showed beautifully, to be sure, and returned, with a relieved mind, to sit in state and wait for the lodger which it might please heaven to send me. Heaven was, however, pleased to very considerably try my patience, for I waited there at that window days — ay, weeks — before I had the extreme pleasure of talking to my gossips about the sayings and doings of 'my lodger'.

Sometimes one of the passers-by would pause and direct a scrutinising look at my card, and at such times my heart would begin to beat anticipatively; but I soon discovered that those persons were simply interested by the style of my card, and occasionally, I dare say, critically pronouncing on the demerits of my capital L. But of all the disappointments I have to record, that of the old gentleman who was the final occasion (drat him) of the embossed card disappearing from the window of my rival opposite was the very greatest.

I saw this old gentleman appear on the opposite side of the way, and by the keen examining look he was shooting from under his bushy eyebrows, first at one side of the street and then at the other, I was convinced that he was a delightful old fellow in search of 'Lodgings'. How I jumped from my seat, to be sure, and how my heart did really pound at an increased rate when I observed that my card had taken his attention, and that he was making straight across the street in my direction.

He was a rotund, Pickwickian-looking old boy in figure, but he had a sharp and yet half terrified looking expression, not at all suggestive of Dickens's hero; yet I thought him the very acme of old gentlemanliness, as he stood at my garden railing and looked at my old English characters on the card. He looked at it, I say, and thoughtfully shoved up the end of his nose with the knob of his umbrella; and then he hesitatingly turned around toward the street, although his hand was already on the latch of my gate.

I wish that the old — , well, it's no use being uncharitable now that it's all past and gone, but if ever I wished a card at the — , I did the one opposite at that moment, for it caught the old chap's eye, and, like a hawk sighting a fresh quarry, he let go of my latch, and pegged away across the street, to that obnoxious lodging-house keeper over the way.

What could it be? Did my capital L disagree with him, or did the old reprobate catch a glimpse of a chignon and blue ribbon band that *I* saw plainly enough bobbing up and down behind the blind, and watching the old thing's movements with quite as much interest as myself? Goodness knows; but, at any rate, never was a greater disappointment experienced, and had it not been for some hopes that he might return, I am afraid that old gent would not have been followed by many blessings from my side of the way.

Vain were my hopes in this as in many another matter. The old fellow knocked, and was promptly admitted, as you may suppose; and he must have been a person of decided and energetic movements, for five minutes did not elapse ere he reappeared, and was accompanied by the landlady, with so much *empressement*, and so many smiles and nods (with a perspective of the chignon and blue ribbon band), that I concluded the arrangement was made.

It was. In less than an hour the old chap returned in a cab, accompanied by two eminently respectable portmanteaus. He was received by the same smiles and nods, and perspective flitting of a chignon and blue ribbon, and finally the door was closed, leaving me, in the fullest sense of the word, an outsider. Little I thought, when I sighed over the loss of that tasteless individual as an inmate of my apartment, how much he would soon have to do with that very apartment, or how soon the occupancy of mine would make the lodgings of my rival over the way tremble to their very foundations.

Look you, I was in one of my most unamiable moods that afternoon, and can you in your heart wonder at it? When my black cat came purring to remind me that her hour of refection was come and past, I saluted her with such a box on the ear that she made tracks under the sofa, and did not venture to reappear until matters were smoother; and as I desperately began to prepare my usual papers 'for the press' (ahem!) I maliciously made six blots on one page of my MS, just for the purpose of occasioning that compositor a little extra trouble.

'That will pay him out,' I said to myself, 'for the absurd nonsense he puts under my signature at times. There was that last article about the cemetery, for instance; didn't he go and print

42

"brain" for "train" in connection with a "girl of the period", as if such a girl could be supposed to have the slightest *soupçon* of the former.'

Slightly relieved by this piece of retaliation, I resumed my position at the window, just in time to perceive a skippy-looking female pause also at the rival house, just as the chignon and blue ribbon was removing the obnoxious card which had attracted and landed the fish I had hoped to secure as my own prize. The fact of its removal did not, however, affect the female in question, for she skipped to the door, and used the knocker to such purpose that the chignon and blue ribbon were tossed disdainfully as they disappeared from the window. It was a satisfaction to me, as you may well believe, to see that female disappointed over the way; and that her object was lodgings I did not doubt when she turned her back upon my engaged rival, and walked toward my door.

I must describe that lady to you, not exactly as she appeared to me during her approach, for, of a certainty, I was disposed to look upon everything connected with her attractive just at that moment. She was, then, a lady of no few years; perhaps she carried forty of them on her head, but she tried hard to carry them with an air of youth and vitality, which attempt was also evinced in her style of dressing, that was girlish and periodical to a degree.

Perhaps the tight and awfully high heels of the boots she endured, that in some measure necessitated the skipping movement we must term her walk; but I am inclined to believe that it was at least partially assumed, her attire so corresponded with the juvenile activity it simulated. Her skirts were uncommonly short and scant, her ankles as bony as you could wish, and her skinny shoulders well defined, not by nature, but by the tight-fitting waist of a dress of as skinny a make as herself. She carried a parasol in one hand daintily, as if it were a bouquet, and a small leather bag in the other with the tips of her gloved fingers, and by the extreme of the chain, consciously, as if it contained something dirty.

Such was, in appearance, the female who came across the street, and after, with some difficulty, in consequence of the parasol and the bag, opening my gate and stepping in with a little extra skip, performed a 'tat-a-tat ta-ra-ra-ra-ra' upon my door, that would have astonished you. Depend on it, I did not keep the lady waiting, although I am sorry to confess that I did not obey the summons without a considerable increase of the acidity of temper I had been afflicted with since the old gentleman's desertion; so I opened the door with a jerk and inquired her business with as supercilious an air as if I had kept lodgings in London or Melbourne during the whole term of my natural life.

'Have you got an apartment to let?'

'Yes.'

'A furnished apartment?'

'Ye-e-es; what kind of room do you want?'

'Oh! a bedroom — a bedroom for a lady.'

'A single lady?'

'Of course; the room is for myself.'

'Ah! you are unmarried, then?' (How I should like to have added 'still!') 'Well, I am very particular as to whom I take into my house, and expect references.'

'References! I can furnish the best of references, ma'am, if that's necessary,' said the lady, with an angry rattle of the bag chain; 'but in my opinion money is as good a reference as you can have, and I am in the habit of always paying my rent in advance.'

'That, in my case, miss, you would find to be a necessity. Will you step in and see the apartment?'

'Pray, *may* I enquire, is it a front room?'

'It *is* a front room.'

'Ah!' and my lady gave a sigh of the deepest relief, and at the same time a glance which I considered to be strangely directed toward the lodging-house opposite. 'One question more, ma'am, and a most important one — are there any of the male sex about this house?'

'Male sex!' I ejaculated in the utmost astonishment, as the prim lady moved past me into the hall. 'I fail to gather your meaning.'

'I mean have you any gentlemen lodgers or other members of

the sex in the house — in daily communion, I mean?' she explained, with a little simper, and a screwed-up mouth, that I defy you to imitate.

'On, no! I have no gentlemen lodgers; nor are there any males in intimate communion with even the walls of the house, saving and excepting the woodman, to whom you could not have any objection, seeing that he is old and respectable, viz., the father of a large family.'

'I'm glad of that — very glad — for I could not even think of risking my character by residing in the same house as a gentleman. I think young persons cannot be too careful.'

'Certainly not, miss; that is the reason I have such an objection to gentlemen lodgers' (and I thought sadly of the old gent opposite). 'Here is the apartment.'

Yes, there was the apartment, looking so admirable and pretty with its cases decorated, and its two chairs doing duty for four, that I thought it the most mortal of pities it should not become the lodging of a nice, tidy, elderly gentleman. While I was thinking so, my young lady was looking anxiously and carefully from the window, as if the apartment she thought of occupying was on the other side of the street, and she was examining its comforts and capabilities. I thought this rather strange at the time, more particularly when she turned suddenly to me and said,

'I'll take the room, ma'am. What is the rent?'

She was in earnest evidently, as her purse was produced from the bag with the rattling chain as she spoke.

Now I have often had occasion to comment on the impossibility of gratifying the craving desires of humanity, and in this matter I saw myself no exception to the general rule. A few hours before, I should have been only too glad to look forward to the probability of letting my apartment to a single lady of irreproachable character, and a strict determination to take especial care of the same valuable article, and here I was positively half sorry that she showed so decided an intention to locate herself in my establishment. Simply because she was so ready with her money, after I had declared a hundred times over that rent in advance

I would have from king or kaiser! 'Why she has never even looked at the accommodation inside the room!' I mentally ejaculated, 'and there she is, with the open purse in her hand, staring out of the window, as if the most delightful prospect in the world was a brick house with a dingy iron railing in front.'

'And the top of an old gentleman's round bald head, surmounting a little round pair of spectacled eyes, peering over the blind,' I might have added, for just at that moment I observed the new lodger opposite taking a peep at the street; and *my* lodger saw him too, for she drew back and bridled, and looked sheepishly at me, and again devoted herself to the arrangement of terms.

And the terms were arranged, and the old young lady, whose name, by the way, was 'Miss Anna Perkins', went to bring her wardrobe from her former lodgings. And the wardrobe was brought, also in a cab, consisting, outwardly, of one small stereotyped boot-box and four dilapidated bonnet-boxes. Two old parasols followed, in company with a white covered umbrella and a pair of dingy goloshes, and, finally, Miss Perkins, with all her belongings, was 'fixed' among my ornamented empty cases and my two chairs, etc.

And then came my initiation into the comfort of keeping lodgers. Miss Perkins wanted some warm water to perform her ablutions, and I was under the disagreeable necessity of informing her that she might observe the kitchen fire to be out, and that if she wished for warm water, she must kindle it (viz., the fire), and procure the article for herself. Then she requested my assistance in removing the so-called toilet-table from the window to a dim corner of the apartment, as there was 'nothing so pleasant,' she declared, 'as a seat by the window'; 'or so unpleasant,' I mentally added, 'as for an old woman who wishes to be young to see the wrinkles in her face too plainly.'

Early next morning, Miss Anna Perkins was up and out, and all the way to the Eastern Market; and she came home laden with two little red flower-pots; one containing an incipient rose-tree, and the other a very weak myrtle. Added to these were a miniature green watering-pot and a brown-ware teapot of the very smallest dimensions. I was just in the middle of my breakfast preparations when she entered the kitchen and deposited her purchases on the table with a giggle and a skip, and drew the longest breath of relief that her flat chest could afford.

'Oh, I'm so tired! Dear me, you couldn't imagine what a time I've had of it! I don't think I should have really got back at all had it not been for a genteman, who insisted on carrying my watering-pot and flowers.'

'What! one of the male sex?' I exclaimed, in affected astonishment.

'He-he! I couldn't help it. Oh, I do assure you, he perfectly insisted, and followed me so persistently: what could I do, you know? And when he really took my things, almost forcibly, I couldn't struggle in the street, could I, or be rude?'

'Did it not strike you as rudeness on his part at all, Miss Perkins?'

'Well now, there's a great deal in manner, you know, and his was not rude – only anxious to save a lady trouble. And he joked so, I could not, do all I would, help laughing – he-he! He did so enjoy my teapot, and said it was so old-maid-like, that he almost insisted on destroying it, the dear little thing – he-he! But, in spite of all his entreaties, I would not even permit him to carry it for me. It would have looked so, you know.'

I didn't like my lodger – there; and I don't at all mind owning it to you as events turned out. I should fifty times over rather have had a crusty old bachelor to deal with than a vain old woman, that would imagine herself youthful. I don't think there is a more despicable object in the world than this latter, and I never meet with one without the inclination to tell her a bit of my mind on the subject. Perhaps, you will uncharitably gather from this that I have reached such an age myself as to render all attempts at revivification useless; but I haven't, you see, although I am by no means a skipping young lady myself.

My morning avocations performed, I resumed my usual seat at the window of the sitting-room, and, the door of Miss Perkins' apartment being open and opposite mine, I had the pleasure of seeing her arrange her flower-pots in the window, and exhibit her loose muslin-clad arm in using the little green watering-pot for their behoof in the jauntiest and airiest manner conceivable. Indeed, she threw the window so fully up, and fluttered around it so persistently, that I began to fancy she was a little more touched in the upper story than I had even at first concluded, when something or other attracted her gaze to the street.

And just as it was, I saw the old gentleman opposite appear over the blind, or, at least, his round bald head and his round spectacled eyes. He stared—he stared, and his head appeared to grow shiny, as it certainly did grow red, and his eyes rounder than ever; and then he drew suddenly back, as if from some most disagreeable and astonishing discovery. What could it be? I rose up, and looked up the street and down the street, like a true daugher of Eve, but I saw nothing, save Miss Anna Perkins flourishing her watering-pot, and smirking in such a hideous manner, that I felt certain she also had observed the old gentleman with the round eyes and bald head. 'Bah!' I thought, 'she's been making eyes at the poor old man, and terrified him out of his wits. I don't wonder at it, for a husband-hunting old fool is abominable.'

The old gentleman appeared not again; and, after a couple of hours' hanging and lolling around the open window, Miss Perkins dressed herself to kill, and emerged from the front door, performing the *role* of an innocent and lively young damsel to her own admiration. The scrap of ground in front of my residence ought hardly to be dignified by the title of garden, but Miss Perkins made the most of it, as a little area to disport herself in before she passed into the street. She plucked a little scrap of privet and a tiny bit of laurestina, and a morsel of stunted briar, and she placed them daintily together, and smelled them with, oh, such an air! and she finally went out, casting a side-glance at the windows over the way, and patting her lips and caressing her lanky cheek with the small bouquet in a most bewitching manner.

And she sauntered up the street towards the Gardens, with an air of saunter that no person could mistake. 'I am simply going for a stroll' was so evident in her affected dawdle, that I could not help giving vent to my feelings aloud. 'If that old gent over the way does not accept your plain invitation to follow you in a stroll, my most fair Miss Perkins,' I said, 'then your attentions may in future be devoted to some one of the male sex more worthy of, and more likely to reciprocate them. However, I do not doubt that you are stringing, or trying to string, your bow double, and that your "gentleman" of this morning has some slight idea of your stroll in the Gardens.'

'But, bless my heart, is he an old fool after all?' This exclamation was drawn from me by the fact that a moment had scarcely elapsed after Miss Perkins' disappearance from the street, when the old fellow trotted out from his door, and looked keenly in the direction she had taken. And he looked more than keenly — he looked vicious and determined, and like a man who had made up his mind to a certain thing, and would go through with it, even if all sorts of obstacles should be encountered on the way; but for any sake, I beg you to imagine my complete astonishment when the old chap commenced to trot across the street, and finally, opened my gate, with the same pursed-up mouth and frowning brow, as if his determination had at any rate something to do with the sharp rap he presently gave at my door.

I opened it in a sort of daze, and I had no time to wonder. Perhaps an idea that the lodgings opposite did not suit him may have shot across my mind, but if it did, the old man's first words changed it.

'I have something to say to you, ma'am,' he said sturdily, and emphasising his words with a rap of his stick on the ground — 'something about that disgusting lady-lodger of yours; and I want to go inside to your sitting-room, where I won't be liable to be pounced upon by the jade in the middle of it.' And he looked up the street with such a frown and twist of his mouth, while he clutched the cane more firmly in his hand, as if he would not have hesitated to attack Miss Anna Perkins bodily, should she unfortunately make her appearance.

'Gracious me!' thinks I, as I led the way into my sitting-room

49

wonderingly, and saw the old fellow seat himself in my chair, and wipe his face with his voluminous silk handkerchief. 'And now, sir' (aloud) 'will you be good enough to tell me your business?'

'Yes, ma'am, I *will* be good enough—I came here for the purpose of being good enough. Your female lodger is a jade, ma'am, and it is the very greatest satisfaction for me to tell you so.' And the fellow drew in his chin and stamped his foot and his stick, and looked at me as if he considered me in league with Miss Anna Perkins, and one of the same species myself.

'I have no doubt, sir, that you express your opinion, however too candidly I may consider you do it, but pray what have *I* got to do with your opinion of Miss Perkins?'

'Miss Devilskin!' he muttered between his teeth ere he replied. 'Yes, ma'am, you've come to the point, and I expected that you would come to the point. What have *you* got to do with it? Exactly. What will *you* make by it? Just so. Oh, ma'am, *I* know the world—so do you, eh? However, it simplifies matters considerably to have you speak your mind out plainly—not one woman in twenty hundred would have done it; they would have pretended innocence, and immaculate honour, and all sorts of trash. Ma'am, I *hate* women!' Emphasised by another thump of the stick.

'The women are in despair to have gained your bad opinion, doubtless, sir, but I do assure you that I do not personally care one straw whether you hate them or not. Now, sir, will you please tell me what you are driving at, as Miss Perkins may interrupt you before you are prepared?'

'D——Miss Perkins—the jade! That old woman is the bane of my existence, ma'am. She is rendering my existence a perfect hell upon earth! I have the misfortune to be well off, ma'am, and the wretch knows it! If I was a fox, ma'am, and Miss Devilskin was a hound, she could not nose me and follow me out with more persistence; but, by——, I *am* a fox, as far as cunning goes, and that she shall know before long!'

Good heavens! how the stick did go on the floor, and how red the old gentleman got in the face as he flourished his hat about with the other hand! I do declare to you that I began to think of apoplexy and lunacy, and all sorts of disagreeable things, as the excited speaker went on. Suddenly he turned and faced me fully. Turned with a movement, in which stick, and hat, and eyes, and spectacles, and even the very buttons on his coat, seemed to play separate parts of a most extraordinary whole, and asked.

'Now, ma'am, what will you take for Miss Perkins — the — jade?'

'Take for Miss Perkins!'

'Yes, take for Miss Perkins! What's her selling price? Come now, what price, in round straightforward figures, do you put upon that wrinkled, bedizened old fool, Anna Perkins?'

'Ha-ha!' Oh, I couldn't for the life of me help it, the whole thing was so absurd. 'Ha! ha! ha! Oh, sir, I don't think the value I should set upon the dear creature would break any bank; but I do assure you that your meaning is incomprehensible to me. If you wish to buy my lodger, surely you had better apply to herself on the subject.'

'Of course, I haven't explained myself,' he said, looking a little foolish, and moving the end of his stick uneasily on the carpet. 'You know nothing about it — how should you? Bah, I'm an old fool. Look here, ma'am, that jade found me out at a boarding-house in town, where I had been for two years, and where I was very comfortable. She made a dead set at me, I tell you, and in such a barefaced, giggling manner, that I was obliged to bolt for it, to get rid of her. I made a moonlight flitting of it ma'am, and used every precaution. By gad, I even had my letters addressed under cover, so that she might not find me out. Will you believe it, ma'am? I had not been there three days in my new quarters when the wretch took the very room next to mine in the same house, and there she was, grinning at me, and sticking up her bony shoulders before me when I came home to have a peaceable dinner! Man or devil couldn't stand it. Next day, I came here and took a room where there was no other to let, but, by — , the first thing I set my eyes on next morning is that infernal hag making faces at me from your window! I'll buy her out! By Jupiter, I'll buy her out, if it took my last pound out of the bank! I'm not going to be driven about, like a Wandering Jew, in my old days, by a — husband-hunting old curse!'

He couldn't talk any more; he was completely out of breath, and panting with the rage he had worked himself into. And what reply could I make? What could I possibly know of his meaning in buying Miss Perkins out? However, he soon recovered himself, and went on.

'Now do you know what I mean, ma'am?'

'Upon my word, sir, I do *not*.'

'I want you to turn that old Jezebel out! I want to pay for her room! That's what I want, and I don't care if I pay double rent, but out with her!'

'My good sir, if you consider one moment, you will see that it would be utterly impossible for me to be taking money from you for an empty room.'

'Why? I can't see it.'

'You simply offer me a bribe, as I understand it, to get Miss Perkins out of your way. I couldn't accept a bribe, sir.'

'Bribe be — , I only want to pay you for losing your lodger.'

'Yes, pay me for keeping my room empty. Perhaps, the next lady lodger I got might be quite as objectionable as Miss Perkins.'

'Get a gentleman lodger, can't you?'

'I might, sir; but it's only a chance, you know.'

'By Jupiter, I'll take the room and live in it myself, before I'll be beaten!'

'And then Miss Perkins will take the one you at present occupy, and you will be simply out of the frying pan into the fire. Depend upon it, if Miss Perkins discovers your plan, she will just step over into your old room.'

'Will she though?' he said with, I am sorry to say, something very like a jubilant wink (the old scamp!) 'I'll take care of that! The people over there know what side their bread's buttered on. Leave that to me. Now, when does she march?'

'I *must* give her a week's notice, you know.'

'Phew! I'm off to the Dandenong Ranges for eight days, if that's it! At any rate. I'll hide where *she* won't find me.'

'In the Yarra Bend wouldn't be a bad place,' I could not help saying, with a laugh.

'Oh. You're a queer one, you are. There's your money, a fortnight in advance. The change for "extras" — lodging-house extras; oh, *I* know? Good day! I'll be here on the evening of this day week, bag and baggage.' And out he went with a chuckle, banging the door after him, and leaving me sitting with the note in my hand, and feeling funny.

What a scene with Miss Perkins, to be sure! but never mind, I should gain three shillings a-week by the change, not to speak of the chance of setting my own cap at the gentleman lodger. The old silly! Little he guesses what he's doing; never mind, we'll see. With these thoughts, came Miss Anna Perkins, skipping to the gate, and casting such sheep's eyes at the window opposite, as made me laugh loud enough to be heard next door, I dare say.

'Oh, I'm quite fatigued! I'm such a creature! but it's lovely in the Gardens to-day, Mrs —. Oh, dear, how tired I am, to be sure! I must have a cup of tea directly, out of my dear little teapot. He-he! What a nice view you have from this window. Oh, there's Lodgings there too!'

Sure enough the ticket was replaced in the window opposite, and I guessed it was simply a ruse of the cunning old fellow's, and followed it up.

'Yes,' I said, 'there was an old gentleman came there yesterday, but I suppose the rooms do not suit him, for he leaves immediately. I presume that cab is come to remove him.'

Yes. Out came the boxes once more, and out came the old hero himself, and got into the conveyance with an air of triumph, which I should fail to describe. And there stood Miss Perkins, like a transformation, staring at the departure with feelings of disappointment that I could guess.

'By the by, Miss Perkins, I have a rather unpleasant matter to break to you, since I entered into an engagement to let you my apartment yesterday, circumstances have so altered that I find myself under the necessity of giving you a week's notice to leave.

If you prefer leaving at once I shall with pleasure return your advanced rent.'

If I expected any explosion, I was disappointed. The loss of her game affected her too deeply to leave room for any other feeling, so she turned an old withered face without one spark of her recent animation in it, from the window, and said, 'It makes no difference whatever to me; one can always find a room. Is the kettle boiling?'

Well, my ticket with the peculiar L, has disappeared from behind my blind, and I have had an old gent in Miss P's late room, for a week. I have fabricated for myself such a lovely muslin morning-cap (*à la veuve* of course) in which I make the old chap's chocolate in the mornings, that all the widows in the colony would be breaking their hearts for the pattern, could they only see it. Little that old chap guesses what a dangerous house he's got into, for you see, *I'm* not an old maid, and I have that funny old gent's measure to a T already. Already, too, he is beginning to think me the most sensible woman he ever conversed with, and admires excessively my plain outspoken manner, 'so different from most women,' he says; ha, ha! Lord help the old silly!

I mean to tell you something more about my lodgers, for I use the plural, seeing that I am fitting up another apartment to let. I wish I dare give you my address, it would be such a good advertisement, you know; but what would be the use of my writing it, seeing that our Editor would only draw his indefatigable pen right through the middle of it. Ha, there comes my old chap, trotting along, and twirling his stick as if there was not a Miss Anna Perkins in the wide world.

JESSIE LLOYD ('SILVERLEAF')
(1843–1885)

Lloyd was born near Launceston, but lived most of her life on stations in New South Wales. She wrote short stories, essays and poetry for the *Echo* and the *Sydney Mail*, and contributed a regular article titled 'Silverleaf Papers' on bush life for the *Illustrated Sydney News*. Two of her novels were published as serials for the same periodical.

The Wheel of Life: A Domestic Tale of Life in Australia (1880) relates the ironic twists of the life of a woman in colonial Australia. In this extract John Hazelwood has come to ask Agnes's aunt for permission to marry Agnes.

A BLUNDER

from *The Wheel of Life: A Domestic Tale of Life in Australia*

At last he came, and the very sound of his pleasant, genial voice seemed to calm all Agnes's agitation. It seemed to her that it would be impossible for her aunt to refuse anything that he should ask.

During the social meal, which, to our thinking, is the pleasantest of the day, Agnes's pre-occupation caused her to make some mistakes — such as omitting sugar in her aunt's tea, and sweetening John's twice over; otherwise, all passed off well.

After tea Agnes played some of the sweet old-fashioned airs, which are ever new, and then excused herself, on the plea that she would unpack her aunt's boxes that had come from 'Wattle Farm'.

John felt all the awkwardness of his situation, as, no doubt, many others have done before him. He thought, if it had been Agnes's mother or father, the task would have been easier. A thousand ways suggested themselves of leading up to the subject, but none seemed to suit, partly from receiving no assistance from the lady. She had been so wrapped up in self as to have no idea of the love story that had been weaving itself under her eyes, and she had been accustomed to look upon Agnes as such a child, that it had not entered into her head to think that this grave earnest man, of more than thirty years, should think of a mere child such as Agnes, as a woman to be wooed and won.

Time was flying, and still the important subject was not broached. At last John, with startling abruptness, said,

'I am thinking very seriously of getting married. It is time I was settled; I have sufficient means to maintain a wife. What is your opinion?'

'Really, Mr Hazelwood, your question is so unexpected, I scarcely know how to answer you. I think your resolution to marry a wise one, provided the choice is a suitable one.'

'There can be no doubt about that: the lady I love is everything that is gentle and good; and, oh! dear madam,' and here John seized the old lady's hands in the excess of his emotion, 'Can I dare to hope for your consent?'

A flush of surprise and pleasure passed over Mrs Beecroft's already florid countenance, and she said,

'Really, Mr Hazelwood, your question is so very unexpected that I must ask you to give me a little time for consideration. An affair of such moment is not to be decided upon as hastily as the choosing of a dress.'

'How long, my dear madam, do you require? I hope you will consider my feelings in this, and not keep me long in suspense. And then, again, my time is limited.'

'Give me till to-morrow evening; I think I will be able to come to a decision in that time. I feel flattered, highly flattered, by your proposal, for, though still in the prime of life, I know there are so many younger and fairer that you could have chosen.'

John looked rather mystified at this speech, which he thought a singular one. He could not understand what her being in the prime of life had to do with it, and surely Agnes was young enough and fair enough to please anyone. But he merely said,

'Then, I will call again to-morrow evening, and learn my fate, whether I am to be the happiest man in New South Wales, or be doomed to disappointment.'

'She's a queer old woman that; how very affectionate,' he soliloquised, as he walked to his hotel. 'I almost thought she was going to kiss me when she said "goodnight". I expect, after all, she loves Agnes, and she feels affection to the man that has appreciated her worth. I wish, however, she had given me my answer to-night.'

The next morning Agnes was quite surprised to see her aunt look so very good-humoured. John had surely been successful, and she had given her consent.

Whilst they sat at breakfast her aunt remarked,

'Have you ever thought it likely that I should change my condition, and marry again, Agnes?'

57

'Why, no, aunt, I never dreamed of such a thing,' said Agnes, in a tone of astonishment.

'I don't know why you should be so surprised, Agnes; I am not so very old; and, in any case, I have received an offer from a gentleman for whom I feel great esteem.'

Agnes wondered greatly; she knew of no old gentleman who was at all likely to ask her aunt to marry him.

'You know, Agnes,' said Mrs Beecroft, confidentially, 'in the event of my marrying again, you could not expect anything from me; I might have a family of my own. In any case, it would be better for you to take a situation, and be independent.'

'I am sure I am very glad, if it is likely to make you happy, aunt. Who is the gentleman?'

'Well, my dear, I have no doubt you will be surprised. I have not yet decided whether I will accept the proposal. If I do, it will be only on certain conditions. I have no doubt you noticed the gentleman's attentions at Wattle Farm; they were rather marked, but I thought nothing of them. I've been used to attentions; before I married your uncle there were six young gentlemen persecuting me with their love. One of them threatened to blow his brains out, and I have no doubt he would have done so, only he was drowned in a boat accident. I have always thought he was drowned because the state of his feelings would not allow him to make any effort to save himself, although the newspapers said it was because he could not swim.' The old lady became quite sentimental as she spoke of these events of her youth.

'But, aunt, you have not yet told me the gentleman's name, and I am all curiosity.'

'It is Mr John Hazelwood.'

'Oh, aunt, surely you are mistaken. I thought, I thought —'

'And why should I be mistaken?' said Mrs Beecroft, ablaze with anger. 'A likely thing, with all my experience in such matters, that I should be mistaken. He is coming for his final answer to-night, and you will see who is right.'

Agnes could not understand it. Surely John would not play a cruel jest upon her aunt. She must have misunderstood him. In any case, her aunt would not be likely now to give her consent, if she found John meant her niece instead of her. The poor girl was miserable, and dreaded the evening.

Whilst assisting at her aunt's toilet, Agnes never before found her so hard to please; half-a-dozen things were tried on before she found one to suit.

'After tea, Agnes, you can leave the room, and not return. No doubt, Mr Hazelwood is anxious for his answer,' said Aunt Patty.

When John came he looked as happy as Agnes miserable, and he imagined that she had been bearing the brunt of her aunt's temper. And the social meal was over, when Agnes rose to retire, he turned to Mrs Beecroft, after giving the former a reassuring glance.

'And now, my dear madam, for my answer.'

'I have considered your proposal, sir, and have decided that I will accept it only upon one condition—that you remove from the country, and reside in town.'

'Impossible! Quite impossible!' said John, hastily. 'I am not a rich man, and have yet to make my way in the world. My wife would have to reconcile herself to a country life, which, if she loved me, would not be difficult until, should fortune prosper me, I could leave my station to the care of others, and be free to reside elsewhere.'

'Dear John,' said Mrs Beecroft, with a look that curdled his blood, 'when we are married, you will find that I have enough for both.'

Was he asleep and dreaming? Surely he could not have bungled matters so as to lead this horrible old woman, with her infernal temper, and coarse, unwieldy person, to believe he desired *her* for his wife. The thought was maddening. What a dilemma he had got himself into, for he feared to explain matters, lest her wounded vanity should convert the already severe aunt into the niece's unrelenting enemy. He with difficulty recovered his self-possession, and said,

'I could never consent to live upon my wife's means. It would

59

be contrary to all my ideas of manhood. The bush is my home, and there I must abide.'

'Then, Mr Hazelwood, I cannot think your affection is very deep or sincere. Had you been willing to sacrifice your inclinations to mine as regards a residence, I would have risked (what, I have no doubt, my friends would have considered a great act of imprudence) a second marriage, but under the circumstances I must refuse, for I can't, and I won't, live in the bush.'

'Then, madam, as you think the bush is so unsuitable for you, can you recommend me a lady that would suit me as a wife?'

'Oh! I know plenty of suitable ladies. There is Miss Skinner and the two Miss Dobsons, any of whom, I know, would be glad to be married,' said Mrs Beecroft, with some acrimony.

'There is one lady you have not mentioned, who, having been brought up under your care, must be well fitted for the duties of any station. I mean your niece. Will you use your influence with her on my behalf?'

'What, that child. Oh! the idea is absurd, and, besides, I am sure such thoughts as love and marriage have never entered her head; it is not to be thought of,' said Mrs Beecroft, who scarcely liked the facility with which John transferred his affections from her full-blown charms to the child-like niece. But John had now found the use of his tongue, and he so argued and flattered the aunt, that he completely gained her to his side, and she said she would insist upon Agnes accepting him. She wanted to call Agnes down there and then, and tell her to look upon Mr Hazelwood as her future husband, but John urged her not to do so, but let him plead his own cause in his own way, so he took his departure with this understanding.

All the way to his lodgings he kept complimenting himself upon his talents as a diplomatist. He had made a great blunder in almost proposing to the aunt, whilst he meant the niece, but had got out of it without wounding the former or losing the latter, and was jubilant in consequence.

Whilst Aunt Patty went to bed in high good-humour. At the age of fifty, she had had the felicity of refusing a fine young fellow, that any girl would be proud of; and, now he could not get her, he was willing to take her niece, because she was her relative.

To her dying day Mrs Patty Beecroft believed in, and boasted of, this offer, and used to make Miss Skinner green and yellow with envy telling her of it, though the spinster never wholly believed it, and thought there must be a mistake somewhere.

The following day John and Agnes had a great laugh over Aunt Patty's mistake. At the latter's request, Agnes dutifully accepted John as her future husband.

He wanted to get married at once, and take Agnes back with him, but this Aunt Patty would not hear of, and even Agnes thought it would be far nicer to have an interval, bridged over by loving letters, to so suddenly entering into a new life. So it was decided to have the marriage that time twelve months, and John had to hurry home, for a busy time was coming on.

He was not a demonstrative man, and no one, to have seen him part, apparently so calmly, from the fair girl that was all the world to him would have imagined the agony it was to that strong, loving heart to leave her, and with such an uncongenial relative.

> *But men must work, and*
> *Women must weep,*
> *And the sooner it's over*
> *The sooner to sleep.*

And his homeward journey was cheered now by a hope, that was almost a certainty, of one day claiming the girl who had won that true noble heart of his. And each month, as it passed, would bring the time nearer.

ADA CAMBRIDGE
(1844–1926)

Cambridge was born in Norfolk, England, and came to Australia as the wife of a clergyman. Her experiences during this difficult period are recorded in her autobiography, *Thirty Years in Australia* (1903). She began to write for the *Australasian* in order to add to the family income. She published three books of poetry and fourteen novels, most of which first appeared as serials. Her novels deal with love and marriage which are often treated in a satirical manner. Her writing often questions traditional feminine roles and exposes religious bigotry and the 'nouveau riche' of the new colony.

DEPOSED

The little sound that is as common as silence — a familiar step, a murmured word, an open door — one hears it a thousand times with contented indifference, as one hears the singing of the tea-kettle. But one day it falls on the heart as well as on the ear, like the stroke of a swift sword. It seems exactly the same, but one knows at once that it is not the same. In the twentieth part of a second one recognises the voice of a dire calamity. I wonder why?

Tom came into the house by way of the kitchen, and I heard him say to Jane, in quite a quiet tone, 'Where's Mrs Braye?' That was all. I sprang from my chair, wild with terror, dropping my needlework to the floor. For I knew — I knew — I didn't want to be told — that something had happened to Harry. My boy! My boy! I had been scolding him, only an hour ago, for making love to Lily's governess — a minx, whom I had just requested to find another situation — and he had slammed the door almost in my face on leaving me. I had been longing for Tom to come in, that I might tell him all about it, and have a little cry in his arms, and my dignity and authority in the house supported; but now that he was here my tongue was paralysed. And I had no grievance, but an immeasurable remorse.

'Don't be frightened,' said my husband, tremblingly, in a would-be off-hand voice; 'it's nothing very serious — just a bad shaking — I told him that new mare of his wasn't to be trusted, and there was a nasty stone just where she threw him. He's stunned a bit — that's all — no bones broken. I have sent for the doctor. Now look here, Polly —'

He opened his arms across the doorway, but I broke through them, and flew to find my Harry and see what they were doing with him. At the garden gate I met the procession coming in. They carried him carefully on a mattress, and he did not know me. When I leaned over him to listen if he breathed, I saw a little bubble of blood oozing from his mouth; then I knew that he was more than stunned – that it was worse even than broken bones. I left off crying, and became quite calm. I had to.

We were sliding him from the mattress to his bed when Dr Juke arrived, and he made us stop and let him do it; for, though my poor lad seemed unconscious, he panted and grunted in a way that showed we were hurting him – with all our care. The doctor felt and lifted his limbs, and said they were all right, and then undressed him as he lay; I got my large cutting-out scissors, and we hacked his good clothes to pieces – but that didn't matter – until we left him only his shirt and woollen singlet, and even those we cut. And just as we were finishing making him comfortable, as we hoped, he came to and looked at us. My precious boy! His breathing was short and fluttery, and he seemed too full of pain to speak, except in gasps.

'Oh, my side! my side!'

He wailed like a baby – a sound to drive a mother mad.

Dr Juke said, 'Ah, I thought so.' And, having made a little examination, he reported a fracture of the ribs, with some injury to the lung. He whispered something to Tom, and then told me I had better send for a trained nurse, and said it would be as well to get a good surgeon from town also – so as to 'be on the safe side'.

I was willing enough to send for a dozen surgeons – though I had perfect faith in Juke, who was a clever young man, newly out from home, and up to date, an enthusiast in his profession – but I could not bear the thought of a professional nurse. I knew those women – how they take possession of your nearest and dearest, and treat even an own mother as if she were a mere outsider and an utter ignoramus. I protested that I could do all that was necessary – that no one could possibly take the care of him that I should. Was it likely?

'But he will probably want nursing all day and all night for weeks,' said Dr Juke. 'You could not do that unaided. You would break down, and then where would he be?'

'I will telegraph for my daughter Phyllis,' I rejoined. Phyllis was away at the time, visiting.

'Miss Braye is too young and inexperienced,' he objected, with the airs of a grandfather. 'It would not be fair to her. She is better where she is, out of all the trouble. However, there is no need to decide immediately. We'll see the night through first. All we can do for the present is to make him as easy as possible and watch symptoms. The *most* important thing is not to meddle with him.'

This seemed a hard saying, and at first I could not credit it. It was terrible to see nothing done, when he evidently suffered so — more and more as the first shock passed and the dreadful fever rose and rose; but while the lung was letting blood and air into the cavity of the chest, which could not be reached to stop the leak, handling of any sort only aggravated the mischief. The doctor explained this to me when I was impatient, and I had to own that he was probably right. He asked me to see about drinks and nourishment and when I left the room to do so, I had a mind to seize the opportunity for a few frantic tears in private, impelled by the pent-up anguish I could not otherwise relieve.

But outside the door — Harry's door — I came upon Miss Blount. The little fool was crying herself — as if it were any concern of hers! — and looked a perfect sight with her swelled nose and sodden cheeks. Somehow I couldn't stand it — on the top of all the rest. I just took her by the arm, and marched her back to the schoolroom. I hope I was not rough or unkind — I really don't think I was — but to see her you would have thought she was a ridiculous little martyr being led to the stake. I said to her — quite quietly, without making any fuss — 'My dear, while you remain in this house — until the notice I have been compelled by our contract to give you has expired — oblige me by keeping in your proper place and confining your attention to your proper business.'

Just as if I had not spoken — and I am sure she never heard a word — she turned on me at the schoolroom door and clutched at my dress. With both hands she held on to me, so that I actually could not get away from her.

'Oh, tell me, tell me,' she cried, with a lackadaisical whine, as if we were playing melodrama at a cheap theatre, '*what* does the doctor say? Is he, oh, *is* he going to die?'

I replied — cuttingly, I am afraid — that the doctor seemed perfectly well. There was no sign of dying, that I could see, about him.

Then she said, 'Harry!' Impertinent little minx! To my very face! As if she had a right to call my son by his Christian name. I was greatly exasperated; any mother would have been — especially after what had happened.

I answered, '*Mr* Harry is going to die — *thanks to you*, Miss Blount.'

I truly believed that he was, and I honestly thought that it was her doing; because if she had not misconducted herself, and tempted him to do so, I should not have had to scold him, and he would not have gone out in a rage, to ride a young horse recklessly. Still, it has occurred to me since that perhaps I was not quite just to her, poor thing.

Oh, what a night that was! Temperature 103, and a short, agonising cough catching the hurt side, which he was obliged to lie on, because the other lung had to do the work for both. We padded him with the softest pillows in the house, and tried ice, and sedatives, everything we could think of; but we could not soothe the struggling chest, which was the only way to stop the inward bleeding. And he kept up a sort of grinding moan, like a long 'u' in French — worse than shrieks. It was too, too cruel! I wonder my hair did not turn white.

Next day we got the surgeon from town; the day after, the nurse. But I came to an understanding with her before she set foot in Harry's room. I bade her remember that he was my son, and that a mother could not consent to be superseded. She asked if she were allowed to carry out the doctor's orders, and when I said, 'Yes, of course,' she seemed satisfied. She was a good creature. After all, I don't know what we should have done without her. There is a limit to one's strength, and though Phyllis was a great help outside the sick room, we did not think it right —

Dr Juke did not think it right—to let her be much in it.

She came home, in spite of him, as soon as she heard what had happened. She and her brother were devoted to each other. Nevertheless, when I told her of his conduct with Miss Blount, she was quite indignant. She said she would never have believed it of him. At the same time she was firmly convinced, as I was, that Miss Blount had done the love-making and led him on. What a comfort it was to have my dear girl to talk to and confide in! She was not only a lovely young creature—though I say it—but had the sense of an old woman. Lily was quite different. But then Lily was a child—barely seventeen—and she had an absurd infatuation for her governess, such as you often see in a raw schoolgirl. It was a stupid mistake on my part to engage a person of twenty-two to teach her—I saw it now; and I think it a still greater mistake to confer university degrees on such young women. You seem to expect them to be above the imbecilities of ordinary girls, and they are not a bit.

Well, we shut them up together in a separate part of the house, giving them their meals in the schoolroom. We did not want Lily to be losing the education we were paying so much for, and Tom and I just took our food as we could get it. We had no heart to sit down to table. Sometimes he slept for a little and sometimes I, but one or other of us was always on guard; while Phyllis prepared the iced milk and soda, and waited on the nurse and doctor. Certainly the doctor was most devoted; he could not have done more for his patient if he had been his own brother.

I am sure it was the opinion of his medical colleague that Harry could never pull through. He said, in so many words, that the case was as grave as possible, owing chiefly, as I understood, to the accumulation of fluid in the chest, which could not be mechanically dealt with. Nevertheless, the dear boy rallied a little, and then a little more—the fever keeping down in the day-time, and not running quite so high at night—until it really seemed that we might begin to hope. He was such a splendid young fellow, and had such a magnificent constitution. But for that, I am convinced he could not have survived an hour. One afternoon he was sleeping so comfortably that they all insisted on my going out for some fresh air. Tom took me for a walk round the garden, and we planned what we would do for our beloved one when he got well—how we would go for a little travel to amuse and cheer him, to recruit his strength and distract his mind from nonsense.

When I returned, I found that he had awakened from his sleep, calm and refreshed; that he had asked to see his sister Lily, and—that that fool of a nurse had allowed it! Oh, I could have shaken her! As it was, I gave her a talking to that she sulked over for a week. Lily, she said, had only remained with him ten minutes—as if one minute wouldn't have been enough to undo all our work! *Idiot!* And to call herself a trained nurse, too!

As soon as I approached his bed I saw the difference. Not only had he been doing so well, he had been so nice to me, so loving and gentle, as if feeling that all was right between us. Now he was flushed—I knew his temperature had gone up again—and he looked at me as if I were his enemy instead of his mother.

'Is it true,' he said, 'that you have given Miss Blount notice?'

I did not know what to say. Seeing the absolute necessity for keeping him quiet, I tried to put the question aside. But he would have an answer.

'Darling,' I sobbed, 'I am doing it for the best. And you will be the first to acknowledge it when you are yourself again. It is for her sake,' I added, though I'm sure I don't know why I said that.

He continued to look at me as if I were the bedpost, insensible to my tears. And he looked *so* handsome—a fit husband for a queen!

'Mother,' he said, in a stern way, 'if you do a thing so unjust as that I will never forgive you.'

Oh, Harry, Harry! And after all I had done for him—slaving night and day! After all the love and care, the heart's blood, that I had lavished on him for nearly twenty-four years!

'Unjust!' I repeated, cut to the quick. 'My boy, I may have my faults—I daresay I have—nobody is perfect in this world; but my worst enemy cannot lay it to my charge that I have ever committed an injustice.'

He smiled, but it was a hard smile. And the nurse came up, as bold as you please, to tell me I must be silent, as I was exciting him. *I* exciting him! It was then I gave her that talking to.

Well, he had been getting on as satisfactorily as possible up to this point. But now, of course, he went back. His temperature was 104 in the night, and he complained of pains and uneasiness, and turned against his nourishment, light and liquid as it was. When he did get a snatch of sleep, his breathing was as restless as possible. Sometimes it went fast, and sometimes it seemed to stop, and then he would suddenly give a deep snore, and a jump that hurt his side and roused him. After which he would lie still a while, staring at the wall. His eyes were full of fever, and presently he began to talk, and we could not make out what he was saying, except that little hussy's name — Emily. He kept saying 'Emily' — no, 'Emmie' — as if he thought she was in the room. Once I fancied he called me, and when I went to him he put up his poor hands — already so thin and bleached — and I thought he wanted to be forgiven and be friends with his mother again. But, just as I was dropping on my knees beside him to take him into my arms, he said, 'Kiss me, Emmie!' And oh, in such a voice! It made me feel — but I can't describe how it made me feel.

And next day he had a shivering fit, and the day after another, with more fever than ever when they had passed off — a thirst like fire, and pain in breathing, and delirium, and everything that was bad and hopeless. Dr Juke said it meant blood-poisoning, and that he had expected it from the first; but I didn't believe it. For was he not doing beautifully up to the moment when Lily was allowed to see him and upset him with her tales? This time we sent for two doctors from town, and they and Juke were closeted together for an hour after making their examination; and, when they came out at last, they said they were agreed that our boy was in so desperate a state that nothing short of miracle could save him.

I called the girls into my room to break it to them, and we sat on the sofa at the foot of my bed and had our cry together. I was completely broken down. So was poor Lily. She sobbed so

69

violently that I was afraid Harry would hear her. Phyllis was more composed — she always was — and refused to despair as long as life was in him. She professed contempt for the great doctors, and pinned her faith in Juke. Juke had told her that miracles, in his profession, were constantly happening, and that for his part he did not mean to give up the fight until all was over. 'I believe, mother,' said my brave girl, 'that he will succeed after all, in spite of those old fogies. He knows a lot more than they do, and he says there's no calculating the power of youth and a sound constitution in these cases. He says — '

But I was too wretched to listen to her. They were not old fogies to me — those two experienced men — and a young doctor is but a young doctor, however clever; I found it impossible to hope at this juncture. Lily was kneeling by me with her arms round my waist, quite hysterical with grief; and for the moment I felt that she was more in sympathy with me than her sister. I realised my mistake when the child suddenly sprang to her feet — hitting my chin with her head as she did so — and declared she must go to 'poor Miss Blount'.

'Lily,' I cried, as she was flinging out of the room in her impetuous fashion, 'what are strangers at such a time as this?'

'Nothing,' said Lily, in a brazen way (she would never have spoken to her mother in that tone if she had not been encouraged). 'But Miss Blount is not a stranger. She loves Harry, and Harry loves her, and she's broken-hearted, and she's ill, and she's nearly out of her mind, and nobody ever says a kind word to her! Even now that he's dying, and they can't have each other, you treat her as if she were dirt. Poor, poor Emily! Let me go to her! Now that Harry's dying, she's got nobody — not a soul in this house — but me!'

Well, indeed! Who'd be a mother, if she could foresee what would come of it? To have this blow, on the top of all the rest, and at *such* a moment! I felt quite stunned. At first I could only stare at her — I could not speak; then I said, 'Go, go!' and pointed to the door. For I could bear no more.

As soon as she was gone, I turned to my faithful Phyllis, put my head on her shoulder, and sobbed like a baby.

'Oh, Phyllis,' I cried, 'never you get married, my dear! Never you have children, to suffer through them as I suffer!'

She was wiser than I, however. She said she didn't think it was altogether the children's fault.

I admitted it at once. 'You are quite right,' I said, 'and I was wrong. It is not the children's fault. It's the fault of that hateful creature, who has set them both against me. First Harry, then Lily—the very one she was hired to improve and train! Fancy a governess, calling herself a governess, and a BA to boot, corrupting an innocent young girl, a mere child, with all the details of a clandestine love-intrigue! What infamy! What treachery!' I was beside myself when I thought of it. Any mother would have been.

But Phyllis was not a mother, and she was but lukewarm in this matter upon which I felt so strongly. Indeed, I was half inclined to fear that she, too, had become infected by the evil influence amongst us, until I found that it was Dr Juke who had been putting ideas into her head. Dr Juke is undoubtedly very clever, and we were enormously indebted to him; still I have always felt that he was too fond of giving his opinion upon things that were altogether outside his province. It appeared he had been telling Phyllis that it was very bad for Harry to have any trouble on his mind, and that it was absolutely necessary, if we would give him his full chances of recovery, to remove any that we knew of which could be removed.

'After all,' said Phyllis, in a tone that showed how he had talked her over, 'she's a lady-like person enough, and very clever. We must admit that.'

'Clever, indeed!' I retorted. 'To have caught a man like him. And looking all the while as demure and innocent as a nun—as if butter wouldn't melt in her mouth. Oh, Phyllis, it would blight his career for ever!'

'Perhaps not,' she rejoined, tolerantly—for she was too young to know; 'but, even so, I would rather have him blight his career than die.'

'Oh!' I cried. 'And you speak as if *I* wanted him to die.'

Here Tom came in, and when she saw her father she got up to leave us together. I was glad indeed to have him to myself for a few minutes. We, at any rate, understood each other. He has his faults, dear fellow, and I often get impatient with him; but he loves me — he thinks the world of me — he doesn't question my judgment and criticise my conduct, as the children do. I was going to tell him about Lily, and about what Juke had said to Phyllis; but when he took me into his great, strong, kind arms, I was too overcome to utter a word. I could do nothing but weep. Nor could he. We thought how we had toiled and slaved to make our precious boy the man he was — how we had nursed him through his baby illnesses, and pinched ourselves to send him to public school and university, and been so proud of his beauty and his talents and his achievements, and looked forward with such joy to the name he would make in the world; and how we were to lose him after all, just as we were looking for the reward of our love and labours — and in this truly awful way!

Tom said it was quite certain now that he would die. Blood-poisoning had set in; there were swellings in some muscles of his body to prove it — a fatal symptom, as everyone knew. It only needed to spread to an internal organ, and the machine would stop at once.

'And the sooner it's over, the better,' Tom sobbed, 'and the poor chap's sufferings at an end. Ah, Polly, old girl, little we thought of this when he was born, and we were as vain as two peacocks over him! Do you remember the christening dinner, and the speeches, and how he was brought in and handed round to be admired —'

'Oh, don't!' I wailed, in agony. Remember it! Did I not remember it? And a hundred thousand heart-breaking things.

But we had to compose ourselves as best we could, and go back to our dreadful duties; he to see that the doctors had a proper lunch before they left, I to renew my watch in the sick-room — to see the last, as I supposed, of my dying boy.

On my way I came upon Jane, the cook, hurrying along the

passage with a basin of hot broth. Harry was not allowed meat food, so I stopped her to ask what she was doing with it.

'Taking it to Miss Blount,' she replied; and I fancied she did not speak quite so respectfully as usual. 'That poor young lady hardly touches her meals, and it do go to my heart to see her so ill. I thought perhaps a drop of good soup'd tempt her.'

Now I didn't want to get the character — which I am the last person to deserve — of being a hard woman. I am not one of those vulgar creatures that one reads of in novels, who don't know how to treat a governess properly. To me Miss Blount was as much a lady as I was myself, and I had always made a point of considering her in everything. Besides, it was not the time for animosities. All was changed in view of Harry's approaching death. So I took the little tray from Jane, and said to her, 'Go back to your kitchen, and attend to the doctors' lunch. I will take the broth to Miss Blount, and find out what is the matter with her.'

The girl was in her bedroom. When she saw me she jumped up, as scared as if I had been an ogress come to eat her; but when I first opened the door she was kneeling against her bed, as if saying her prayers. Certainly, she did look ill. She had had a very nice complexion — no doubt poor Harry had noticed it — and her eyes were good; but now her skin was like tallow, and her eyes all dark and washed out, and they had a curious empty expression in them that I did not like at all. I put the tray on the drawers and went up to her, and laid my hand on her shoulder. 'My dear,' I said, as kindly as I could speak, 'I have brought you a little nice broth. And you must take it at once, while it is hot, to please me.'

She did not so much as thank me, but just stood and stared in a dazed, fixed way, like a deaf mute. So I did not feel inclined to bother myself further about her, and turned to go. As soon as I did that, however, she spoke to me, calling my name. Even her voice had a sort of lost sound in it, as if she were talking in her sleep.

'Mrs Braye,' she said, 'there's something I have been wanting to say to you.'

'What is it?' I inquired.

'If Mr Harry gets well, I will not marry him—to blight his career. I never would have injured him, and I never will. I would die sooner.'

Well, it seemed rather late to think of that. Still, it showed a nice spirit, and I like the way she spoke of him. She really was a lady, in her way, and—poor thing!—she did look the picture of misery. I am a tender-hearted woman, and I could not but feel a pang of pity for her.

'Ah, my dear,' I said, 'there's no problem of marrying or not marrying now! He's going fast, and nothing matters any more.' Then I kissed her—I kissed her affectionately; and I bade her lie down, and not trouble about Lily's lessons, and told her that whenever there was a change in Harry's condition I would let her know.

The change came a few days later—not suddenly, but creeping inch by inch; and it was not the change we had all anticipated. My splendid boy! Just as he had struggled and triumphed at football and cricket, so his magnificent strength fought with and overcame the poison in his blood before it could deposit itself in vital organs. It was marvellous. The very doctors, accustomed to miracles, could not believe their senses when they counted his pulse, and looked at the little thermometer, and felt the places where the sore lumps had been. For weeks, I may say, we seemed to hold our breath in the maddening suspense, tantalised and intoxicated with a hope we dared not call a certainty; but at last we knew that life had conquered death, and that *this* agony of motherhood, at any rate, was over. Of course he was weaker than a new-born baby—a mere shadow of himself; but he was saved. When they told me, I fell on my knees, just where I stood, and cried in my wild rapture and thankfulness, 'Oh, God! God! What can I do—for all Thy goodness to me!'

They looked at me in an odd way. They all looked at me, even my boy with his hollow eyes. And Tom said, 'Come here, Polly, I want to speak to you,' and took me into our room, and laid his hands on my shoulders. He was six feet in his socks, and weighed fifteen stone, but he trembled like a child.

'Old girl,' he said, 'you'll have to let him have her.'

'Oh,' I replied, 'if he wants the moon, give it to him! I don't care.'

After all, she was a lady, and a BA. He might have done worse. But when I saw the look he turned to her when she ran like a deer to his arms — poor sticks of arms! and how he held her, and crooned over her — oh it was like a dagger in my breast!

Tom came to me, and tried to comfort me. He reminded me that we did the same ourselves when we were young, and that we still had each other.

'You've still got me, Polly, *I* shan't desert you.'

Yes, yes; of course I still had him. But — well, a man can't understand.

LAURA BOGUE LUFFMAN
(1846–1929)

Luffman was born in England and educated in France. She then migrated to Australia where she became involved in the women's movement and was the editor of the *Woman's Voice* magazine. She wrote for South African, American, as well as Australian newspapers, and contributed articles to the Sydney *Daily Telegraph* under the name of 'Una'. Luffman wrote children's fiction, one biography, two adult novels and various short stories.

A Question of Latitude (1912) is about Millicent, a young English girl, and her adjustment to her colonial aunt and uncle, Mr and Mrs Mainwaring, and their family. It records her eventual appreciation of their way of life.

THE SARATOGA TRUNK

from *A Question of Latitude*

Only Mr and Mrs Mainwaring and Lola appeared at the midday meal. Tom lunched in town at a shilling restaurant, and Gerald ate a furtive sandwich in the public gardens. The meal was, if possible, more slatternly than the evening one. Mrs Mainwaring was evidently in a hurry to get it over and prepare for her visitors. Lola, kept at home against her will to answer the door and help with the tea, was steeped in gloom. Millicent, tired, dispirited and out of her element, made no effort to be agreeable. Alone, Uncle John, beaming and hopeful, dispensed the curry with an air that reminded his niece of Charles Lamb's 'Captain Jackson'. Something evidently struck his wife, who glanced across at him questioningly.

('He knows something and he doesn't want to tell Aunt Kitty, and yet he's bursting to let it out,' was Millicent's silent comment. 'I wonder which will win?')

Uncle John went on smiling to himself. Looking up he saw his wife's eyes fixed upon him. He started guiltily.

'My dear,' he began quaveringly. 'I . . . I met Foskett to-day.'

'Oh!'

'And he offered to put me on a good thing — a really safe thing. He behaved most handsomely about it.'

'Oh!'

'So . . . I accepted. I knew it would be better in the end for all of us. And — I really had no time to consult you, my dear.'

'No; I suppose not.'

Mrs Mainwaring rose and began clearing away the things. Her husband watched her furtively.

('He's afraid of her evidently. How horrid for a woman to bully her husband! I *hate* to see a man knock under to a woman!')

Uncle John relieved the tension of the situation by sauntering out on the verandah. Millicent observed that people pushed away their plates and left the table whenever the spirit prompted them to do so. Profiting by this example, she escaped to her own room.

She had just let down her hair, and was standing in her dressing-gown, when she heard curious bumping sounds and a confusion of voices. 'Be careful of the paint.' 'Won't it stand under the arch?' 'Take it into the scullery.' 'Is the door too small?' 'There's nothing for it but the back verandah.'

Looking out, she beheld two stalwart men hauling her Saratoga trunk down the passage, her Aunt Kitty looking on in dismay, and Lola giggling in the background.

'Oh! Cousin Millicent, it's a regular Noah's ark!'

'Noah's ark! Nonsense. It's just an ordinary trunk. I've taken it with me to scores of English country houses,' returned Millicent, with some asperity. ('Dear me, what an uncomfortable country this is! In England the servants would have carried it upstairs and I should have heard nothing about it.') Then she added aloud: 'Why can't I unpack it in my room, and then it can be taken to the box-room?'

But suddenly there flashed into her mind the recollection of the limited space at her command. The contents of that trunk would never go into—one drawer and a tiny wardrobe.

'Well, perhaps it had better be left on the back verandah,' she said resignedly. 'I can go there and take out the things as I want them—just,' she added a little cruelly—'just as we do on board ship.'

And so it came to pass that the trunk, dubbed by the family 'Millicent's Noah's Ark', was dumped down outside the bathroom, where the various members of the family barked their shins against it for many a day.

Millicent with a heightened colour (she hated all this fuss about simple things) unlocked her trunk and extricated therefrom a soft white dress, specially designed for 'afternoon' wear. There were enough frills and trimmings about it to satisfy Lola, who hung over the box in an agony of curiosity.

'Oh, do let me see your things!' she said imploringly.

'Lola, don't worry your cousin. Come and help me to dry up,' cried Mrs Mainwaring. And for once the washing of dishes appeared to Millicent in the light of a beneficent institution.

As she dressed she could hear Aunt Kitty's voice going on and on and on, her uncle putting in a few feeble interjections. She was afraid the lady owned — a temper! Poor uncle! He was evidently having a bad time of it. Well, it was all his fault for not marrying a gentlewoman.

When Mrs Mainwaring made her appearance in the drawing-room, her face bore no trace of ill-humour. Millicent was forced to acknowledge that she looked uncommonly well. She wore a well-made black dress with a deep lace collar and cuffs and a jaunty bow in her hair. As she received her visitors and moved about the little room offering tea and introducing newcomers, her niece marvelled at the transformation. Could this be the woman who, an hour before, had been wrestling with unwashed dishes, pots and pans, arrayed in a tattered bodice? She looked animated, bright, sparkling — although Millicent found little that was scintillating in the conversation, which turned exclusively on local topics. It was difficult for a newcomer to place a word after replying to the stock question: 'How do you like Australia?' The first two visitors dilated on the merits and demerits of their respective 'girls', Aunt Kitty putting in sympathetic adjectives. But the subject soon palled on the English girl, and she was dismayed to find that it formed the staple of the conversation, each fresh arrival imparting thereto some choice item of personal experience.

At last Aunt Kitty created a diversion by starting the subject of music, and, for a time, Marshall Hall's Wagner recitals, Dolores' singing, and the rumour that Melba was coming on a visit to her native land took the place of the iniquities and short-comings of Mary Anne. On this plane, Aunt Kitty was *facile princeps.*

Millicent did not feel attracted towards any of the visitors till a sweet-faced woman dressed in black appeared on the scene. She called Aunt Kitty 'Catherine', and asked at once to be introduced to the English niece.

'You revive very pleasant memories,' she said, holding

Millicent's hand in a lingering pressure and surveying her with a kindly glance. 'I once spent a week with your grandparents at Severn Court — ages ago, when your father and mother were young married people, just come back from their honeymoon.'

'Did you see my mother? Oh! there are so few who remember her now,' Millicent said, with a little tremor in her voice.

Here was a delightful, unexpected link with the old life. Even Uncle John had never seen her mother! She felt her heart warm to this gracious elderly woman.

'Yes, I can see her plainly now: a sweet-looking creature with long golden curls — just the early Victorian kind of beauty. She was very kind to me — so were they all. You see, my husband and your uncle were great friends: they came out together in the same ship. That was why your grandfather invited us to the Court.'

There were other reasons, but these Mrs Talbot forbore to mention.

'I am leaving for the country to-morrow. When I come back you must lunch with me, and we will have a good talk about old times. Sounds as if we were contemporaries, doesn't it?'

All the light seemed to go out of the room when Mrs Talbot returned to her waiting hansom. Millicent felt thankful when the last visitor took her departure.

Aunt Kitty was in high feather. 'Eight more than last time!' she exclaimed triumphantly. 'You were the attraction, Millicent. I began to feel afraid the cake wouldn't hold out! Well, now, I'll go and change my dress and get dinner ready. Only sausages. You won't mind, dear? I can't do much cooking on my "At Home" day.'

Millicent sank down on the sofa and took up a volume of Tennyson: one of Lola's prizes. She felt she needed quiet and rest. Soon the cheerful hiss of frying reached her ears. She shut her book impatiently, and went towards her room.

'Dinner will soon be ready,' Mrs Mainwaring said, popping a red, heated face out of the kitchen. 'Do you want any hot water?'

Under the circumstances Millicent thought it wiser to reply in the negative. She was beginning to eliminate hot water from her scale of the necessaries of life.

JESSIE CATHERINE COUVREUR
('TASMA')
(1848–1897)

'Tasma' was born in London, the daughter of a Dutch merchant. She came to Hobart as a child and was educated there. She wrote for the *Australasian* and the *Australian Journal* and continued to do so after she married and settled in Victoria. Her first marriage was very unhappy and she later used some of her experiences as a basis for her fiction. She divorced her husband and returned to Europe in the 1870s, where she supported herself by doing freelance journalism and lecturing on Australian life and commerce. She remarried, this time to a journalist and member of the Belgian Parliament, and later became the Brussels correspondent for the London *Times*.

Her first novel, *Uncle Piper of Piper's Hill* (1889) was an immediate success. She wrote five more novels and several short stories, and many of these are collected in *A Sydney Sovereign and Other Tales* (1889). 'Tasma' is often cited as the best short story writer before Lawson, and 'Monsieur Caloche' is considered her best work.

MONSIEUR CALOCHE

CHAPTER I

A more un-English, uncolonial appearance had never brightened the prosaic interior of Bogg & Company's big warehouse in Flinders Lane. Monsieur Caloche, waiting in the outer office, under fire of a row of curious eyes, was a wondrous study of 'Frenchiness' to the clerks. His vivacious dark eyes, shining out of his sallow face, scarred and seamed by the marks of smallpox, met their inquisitive gaze with an expression that seemed to plead for leniency. The diabolical disease that had scratched the freshness from his face had apparently twisted some of the youthfulness out of it as well; otherwise it was only a young soul that could have been made so diffident by the consciousness that its habitation was disfigured. Some pains had been taken to obviate the effects of the disfigurement and to bring into prominence the smooth flesh that had been spared. It was not chance that had left exposed a round white throat, guiltless of the masculine Adam's apple, or that had brushed the fine soft hair, ruddily dark in hue like the eyes, away from a vein-streaked temple. A youth of unmanly susceptibilities, perhaps — but inviting sympathy rather than scorn — sitting patiently through the dreary silent three-quarters of an hour, with his back to the wall which separated him from the great head of the firm of Bogg & Co.

The softer-hearted of the clerks commiserated with him. They would have liked to show their goodwill, after their own fashion, by inviting him to have a 'drink', but — the possibility of shouting for a young Frenchman, waiting for an interview with their chief! . . . Anyone knowing Bogg, of Bogg & Co., must have divined the outrageous absurdity of the notion. It was safer to suppose that the foreigner would have refused the politeness. He did not look as though whisky and water were as familiar to him as a tumbler of *eau sucrée*. The clerks had heard that it was customary in France to drink absinthe. Possibly the slender youth in his loose-fitting French paletot reaching to his knees, and sitting easily upon shoulders that would have graced a shawl, had drunk deeply of this fatal spirit. It invested him with something mysterious in the estimation of the juniors, peering for traces of dissipation in his foreign face. But they could find nothing to betray it in the soft eyes, undimmed by the enemy's hand, or the smooth lips set closely over the even row of small French teeth. Monsieur Caloche lacked the happy French confidence which has so often turned a joke at the foot of the guillotine. His lips twitched every time the door of the private office creaked. It was a ground-glass door to the left of him, and as he sat, with his turned-up hat in his hand, patiently waiting, the clerks could see a sort of suppression overspreading his disfigured cheeks whenever the noise was repeated. It appeared that he was diffident about the interview. His credentials were already in the hands of the head of the firm, but no summons had come. His letter of recommendation, sent in fully half an hour back, stated that he was capable of under-taking foreign correspondence; that he was favourably known to the house of business in Paris whose principal had given him his letter of presentation; that he had some slight knowledge of the English language; that he had already given promise of distinguishing himself as an *homme de lettres*. This final clause of the letter was responsible for the length of time Monsieur Caloche was kept waiting. *Homme de lettres!* It was a stigma that Bogg, of Bogg and Co., could not overlook. As a practical man, a self-made man, a man who had opened up new blocks of country and imported pure stock into Victoria — what could be expected of him in the way of holding out a helping hand to a scribbler — a pauper who had spent his days in making rhymes in his foreign jargon? Bogg would have put your needy professionals into irons. He forgave no authors, artists, or actors who were not successful. *Homme de lettres!* Coupled with his poverty it was more unpardonable a title than jail-bird. There was nothing to prove that the latter title would not have fitted Monsieur Caloche as

83

well. He was probably a ruffianly Communist. The French Government could not get hold of all the rebels, and here was one in the outer office of Bogg & Co. coolly waiting for a situation.

Not so coolly, perhaps, as Bogg, in his aggrieved state of mind, was ready to conclude. For the day was a hot-wind day, and Bogg himself, in white waistcoat and dust-coat, sitting in the cool depths of his revolving chair in front of the desk in his private office, was hardly aware of the driving dust and smarting grit emptied by shovelfuls upon the unhappy people without. He perspired, it is true, in deference to the state of his big thermometer, which even here stood above 85° in the corner, but having come straight from Brighton in his private brougham, he could wipe his moist bald head without besmearing his silk handkerchief with street grime. And it was something to be sitting here, in a lofty office, smelling of yellow soap and beeswax, when outside a north wind was tormenting the world with its puffs of hot air and twirling relays of baked rubbish and dirt. It was something to be surrounded by polished mahogany, cool to the touch, and cold iron safes, and maps that conveyed in their rippling lines of snowy undulations far-away suggestions of chill heights and mountain breezes. It was something to have iced water in the decanter at hand, and a little fountain opposite, gurgling a running reminder of babbling brooks dribbling through fern-tree valleys and wattle-studded flats. Contrasting the shaded coolness of the private office with the heat and turmoil without, there was no cause to complain.

Yet Bogg clearly had a grievance, written in the sour lines of his mouth, never too amiably expanded at the best of times, and his small, contracted eyes, full of shrewd suspicion-darting light. He read the letter sent in by Monsieur Caloche with the plentiful assistance of the tip of his broad forefinger, after a way peculiar to his early days, before he had acquired riches, or knighthood, or rotundity.

For Bogg, now Sir Matthew Bogg, of Bogg and Company, was a self-made man, in the sense that money makes the man, and that he had made the money before it could by any possibility make him. Made it by dropping it into his till in those good old times when all Victorian storekeepers were so many Midases, who saw their spirits and flour turn into gold under their handling; made it by pocketing something like three thousand per cent upon every penny invested in divers' blocks of scrubby soil hereafter to be covered by those grand and gloomy bluestone buildings which make of Melbourne a city of mourning; made it by reaching out after it, and holding fast to it, whenever it was within spirit-call or finger-clutch, from his early grog-shanty days, when he detected it in the dry lips of every grimy digger on the flat, to his later station-holding days, when he sniffed it in the drought which brought his neighbours low. Add to which he was lucky — by virtue of a certain inherent faculty he possessed in common with the Vanderbilts, the Stewarts, the Rothschilds of mankind — and far-seeing. He could forestall the news in the *Mark Lane Express*. He was almost clairvoyant in the matter of rises in wool. His luck, his foresight, were only on a par with his industry, and the end of all his slaving and sagacity was to give him at sixty years of age a liver, a paunch, an income bordering on a hundred thousand pounds, and the title of Sir Matthew Bogg.

It was known that Sir Matthew had worked his way to the colonies, acting indiscriminately as pig-sticker and deck-swabber on board the *Sarah Jane*. In his liverless, paunchless, and titleless days he had tossed for coppers with the flat-footed sailors on the forecastle. Now he was bank director, railway director, and a number of other things that formed a graceful flourish after Sir Matthew, but that would have sounded less euphonious in the wake of plain 'Bogg'. Yet 'plain Bogg' Nature had turned him out, and 'plain Bogg' he would always remain while in the earthly possession of his round, overheated face and long, irregular teeth. His hair had abandoned its lawful territory on the top of his head, and planted itself in a vagrant fashion, in small tufts in his ears and nostrils. His eyebrows had run riot over his eyes, but his eyes asserted themselves through all. They were eyes that, without being stronger or larger or bolder than any average pair of eyes to be met with in walking down the street, had such a knack of 'taking your measure' that no one could look at them without discomfiture. In the darkened atmosphere of the Flinders Lane office, Sir Matthew knew how to turn these colourless unwinking orbs to account. To the maliciously inclined among the clerks in the outer office there was nothing more amusing than the crestfallen appearance of the applicants, as they came out by the ground-glass door, compared with the jauntiness of their entrance. Young men who wanted colonial experience, overseers who applied for managerships on his stations, youths fresh from school who had a turn for the bush, had all had specimens of Sir Matthew's mode of dealing with his underlings. But his favourite plan, his special hobby, was to 'drop on to them unawares'.

There is nothing in the world that gives such a zest to life as the possession of a hobby, and the power of indulging it. We may be pretty certain that the active old lady's white horse at Banbury Cross was nothing more than a hobby-horse, as soon as we find out in the sequel that she 'had rings on her fingers and bells on her toes', and that 'she shall have music wherever she goes'. It is the only horse an old lady could be perpetually engaged in riding without coming to grief — the only horse that ever makes us travel through life to the sound of music wherever we go.

From the days when Bogg had the merest shred of humanity to bully, in the shape of a waif from the Chinese camp, the minutes slipped by with a symphony they had never possessed before. As fullness of time brought him an increase of riches and power, he yearned to extend the terror of his sway. It was long before he tasted the full sweetness of making strong men tremble in their boots. Now, at nearly sixty years of age, he knew all the delights of seeing victims, sturdier and poorer than himself, drop their eyelids before his gaze. He was aware that the men in the yard cleared out of his path as he walked through it; that his managers up-country addressed him in tones of husky conciliation; that every eye met his with an air of deprecation, as much as to apologise for the fact of existing in his presence; and in his innermost heart he believed that in the way of mental sensation there could be nothing left to desire. But how convey the impression of rainbow-tints to eyes that have never opened upon aught save universal blackness? Sir Matthew had never seen an eye brighten, a small foot dance, at his approach. A glance of impotent defiance was the only equivalent he knew for a gleam of humid affection. He was accustomed to encounter a shifting gaze. The lowest form of self-interest was the tie which bound his people to him. He paid them as butts, in addition to paying them as servants. Where would have been his daily appetiser in the middle of the day if there had been no yard, full of regulations impossible to obey; no warehouse to echo his harsh words of fault-finding; no servile men, and slouching fast-expanding boys, to scuttle behind the big cases, or come forth as if they were being dragged by hooks, to stand with sheepish expression before him? And when he had talked himself hoarse in town, where would have been the zest of wandering over his stations, of surveying his fat bullocks and woolly merinos, if there had been no accommodating managers to listen reverentially to his loudly-given orders, and take with dejected, apologetic air his continued rating? The savour of life would have departed — not with the bodily comfort and the consequence that riches bring, but with the power they confer of asserting yourself before your fellow-men after any fashion you please. Bogg's fashion was to bully them, and he bullied them accordingly.

But, you see, Monsieur Caloche is still waiting; in the position, as the junior clerks are well aware, of the confiding calf awaiting butchery in a frolicsome mood outside the butcher's shop. Not that I would imply that Monsieur Caloche frolicked, even metaphorically speaking. He sat patiently on with a sort of sad abstracted air; unconsciously pleating and unpleating the brim of his soft Paris hat, with long lissome fingers that might have broidered the finest silk on other than male hands. The flush of colour, the slight trembling of lips, whenever there was a noise from within, were the only signs that betrayed how acutely he was listening for a summons. Despite the indentations that had marred for ever the smoothness of the face, and pitted the forehead and cheeks as if white gravel had been shot into them, the colour that came and went so suddenly was pink as rose-coloured lake. It stained even the smooth white neck and chin, upon which the faintest traces of down were not yet visible to the scrutinising eyes of the juniors.

Outside, the north wind ran riot along the pavement, upsetting all orderly arrangements for the day with dreadful noise and fussiness, battering trimly-dressed people into red-eyed wretches heaped up with dust; wrenching umbrellas from their handles, and blinding their possessors trying to run after them; filling open mouths with grit, making havoc with people's hats and tempers, and proving itself as great a blusterer in its character of a peppery emigrant as in its original *rôle* of the chilly Boreas of antiquity.

Monsieur Caloche had carefully wiped away from his white wristband the dust that it had driven into his sleeve, and now the dust on his boots—palpably large for the mere slips of feet they enclosed—seemed to give him uneasiness; but it would seem that he lacked the hardihood to stoop and flick it away. When, finally, he extended surreptitiously a timid hand, it might have been observed of his uncovered wrist that it was singularly frail and slender. This delicacy of formation was noticeable in every exterior point. His small white ear, setting close to his head, might have been wrapped up over and over again in one of the fleshy lobes that stretched away from Sir Matthew's skull. Decidedly, the two men were of a different order of species. One was a heavy mastiff of lupine tendencies—the other a delicate Italian greyhound, silky, timorous, quivering with sensibility.

And there had been time for the greyhound to shiver long with expectancy before the mastiff prepared to swallow him up.

It was a quarter to twelve by the gloomy-faced clock in the outer office, a quarter to twelve by all the clerks' watches, adjusted every morning to the patriarch clock with unquestioning faith, when Monsieur Caloche had diffidently seated himself on the chair in the vicinity of the ground-glass door. It was half-past twelve by the gloomy-faced clock, half-past twelve by all the little watches that toadied to it, when Sir Matthew's bell rang. It was a bell that must have inherited the spirit of a fire-bell or a doctor's night-bell. It had never been shaken by Sir Matthew's fingers without causing a fluttering in the outer office. No one knew what hair-suspended sword might be about to fall on his head before the messenger returned. Monsieur Caloche heard it ring, sharply and clamorously, and raised his head. The white-faced messenger, returning from his answer to the summons, and speaking with the suspension of breath that usually afflicted him after an interview with Sir Matthew, announced that 'Mister Caloosh' was wanted, and diving into the gloomy recess in the outer office, relapsed into his normal occupation of breathing on his penknife and rubbing it on his sleeve.

Monsieur Caloche meanwhile stood erect, more like the startled greyhound than ever. To the watchful eyes of the clerks, staring their full at his retreating figure, he seemed to glide rather than step through the doorway. The ground-glass door, attached by a spring from the inside, shut swiftly upon him, as if it were catching him in a trap, and so hid him in full from their curious scrutiny. For the rest, they could only surmise. The lamb had given itself up to the butcher's knife. The diminutive greyhound was in the mastiff's grip.

Would the knife descend on the instant? Would the mastiff fall at once upon the trembling foreigner, advancing with sleek uncovered head, and hat held in front by two quivering hands? Sir Matthew's usual glare of reception was more ardent than of custom as Monsieur Caloche approached. If every 'foreign adventurer' supposed he might come and loaf upon Bogg, of Bogg & Company, because he was backed up by a letter from a respectable firm, Sir Matthew would soon let him find out he was mistaken! His glare intensified as the adventurous stripling glided with softest footfall to the very table where he was sitting, and stood exactly opposite to him. None so adventurous, however, but that his lips were white and his bloodless face a pitiful set-off to the cruelly prominent marks that disfigured it. There was a terror in Monsieur Caloche's expression apart from the awe inspired by Sir Matthew's glare which might have disarmed a butcher or even a mastiff. His large, soft eyes seemed to ache with repressed tears. They pleaded for him in a language more convincing than words, 'I am friendless — I am a stranger — I am —' but no matter! They cried out for sympathy and protection, mutely and unconsciously.

But to Sir Matthew's perceptions visible terror had only one interpretation. It remained for him to 'find out' Monsieur Caloche. He would 'drop on to him unawares' one of these days. He patted his hobby on the back, seeing a gratification for it in prospective, and entering shortly upon his customary stock of searching questions, incited his victim to reply cheerfully and promptly by looking him up and down with a frown of suspicion.

'What brought you 'ere?'

'Please?' said Monsieur Caloche, anxiously.

He had studied a vocabulary opening with 'Good-day sir. What can I have the pleasure of doing for you this morning?' The rejoinder to which did not seem to fit in with Sir Matthew's special form of inquiry.

'What brought you 'ere, I say?' reiterated Sir Matthew, in a roar, as if deafness were the only impediment on the part of foreigners in general to a clear comprehension of our language.

'De sheep, Monsieur! *La Reine Dorée*,' replied Monsieur Caloche, in low-toned, guttural, musical French.

'That ain't it,' said Sir Matthew, scornfully. 'What did you come 'ere for? What are you fit for? What can you do?'

Monsieur Caloche raised his plaintive eyes. His sad desolation was welling out of their inmost depths. He had surmounted the first emotion that had driven the blood to his heart at the outset, and the returning colour, softening the seams and scars in his cheeks, gave him a boyish bloom. It deepened as he answered with humility, 'I will do what Monsieur will! I will do my possible!'

'I'll soon see how you shape,' said Sir Matthew, irritated with himself for the apparent difficulty of thoroughly bullying the defenceless stranger. 'I don't want any of your parley-vooing in my office — do you hear! I'll find you work — jolly quick, I can tell you! Can you mind sheep? Can you drive bullocks, eh? Can you put up a post and rail? You ain't worth your salt if you can't use your 'ands!'

He cast such a glance of withering contempt on the tapering white fingers with olive-shaped nails in front of him that Monsieur Caloche instinctively sheltered them in his hat. 'Go and get your traps together! I'll find you a billet, never fear!'

'*Mais, Monsieur —*'

'Go and get your traps together, I say! You can come 'ere again in an hour. I'll find you a job up-country!' His peremptory gesture made any protest on the part of Monsieur Caloche utterly unavailing. There was nothing for him to do but to bow and to back in a bewildered way from the room. If the more sharp-eared of the clerks had not been in opportune contiguity to the ground-glass door during Sir Matthew's closing sentences, Monsieur Caloche would have gone away with the predominant impression that 'Sir Bang' was an *enragé*, who disapproved of salt with mutton and beef, and was clamorous in his demands for 'traps', which Monsieur Caloche, with a gleam of enlightenment in the midst of his heart-sickness and perplexity, was proud to remember meant 'an instrument for ensnaring animals'. It was with a doubt he was too polite to express that he accepted the explanation tendered him by the clerks, and learned that if he 'would strike while the iron is hot' he must come back in an hour's time with his portmanteau packed up. He was a lucky fellow, the juniors told him, to jump into a billet without any bother; they wished to the Lord they were in *his* shoes, and could be drafted off to the Bush at a moment's notice.

Perhaps it seemed to Monsieur Caloche that these congratulations were based on the Satanic philosophy of 'making evil his good'. But they brought with them a flavour of the human sympathy for which he was hungering. He bowed to the clerks all round before leaving, after the manner of a court-page in an opera. The hardiest of the juniors ran to the door after he was gone. Monsieur Caloche was trying to make head against the wind. The warm blast was bespattering his injured face. It seemed to revel in the pastime of filling it with grit. One small hand was spread in front of the eyes — the other was resolutely holding together the front of his long, light paletot, which the rude wind had sportively thrown open. The junior was cheated of his fun. Somehow the sight did not strike him as being quite as funny as it ought to have been.

CHAPTER II

The station hands, in their own language, 'gave Frenchy best'. No difference of nationality could account for some of his eccentricities. As an instance, with the setting in of the darkness he regularly disappeared. It was supposed that he camped up a tree with the birds. The wit of the wool-shed surmised that 'Froggy' slept with his relatives, and it would be found that he had 'croaked' with them one of these odd times. Again, there were shearers ready to swear that he had 'blubbered' on finding some sportive ticks on his neck. He was given odd jobs of wool-sorting to do, and was found to have a mania for washing the grease off his hands whenever there was an instant's respite. Another peculiarity was his aversion to blood. By some strange coincidence, he could never be found whenever there was any slaughtering on hand. The most plausible reason was always advanced for necessitating his presence in some far-distant part of the run. Equally he could never be induced to learn how to box — a favourite Sunday morning and summer evening pastime among the men. It seemed almost to hurt him when damage was done to one of the assembled noses. He would have been put down as a 'cur' if it had not been for his pluck in the saddle, and for his gentle winning ways. His pluck, indeed, seemed all concentrated in his horsemanship. Employed as a boundary-rider, there was nothing he would not mount, and the station hands remarked, as a thing 'that beat them once and for all', that the 'surliest devils' on the place hardly ever played up with him. He employed no arts. His bridle-hand was by no means strong. Yet it remained a matter of fact that the least amenable of horses generally carried him as if they liked to bear his weight. No one being sufficiently learned to advance the hypothesis of magnetism, it was concluded that he carried a charm.

This power of touch extended to human beings. It was almost

worth while spraining a joint or chopping at a finger to be bandaged by Monsieur Caloche's deft fingers. His horror of blood never stood in his way when there was a wound to be doctored. His supple hands, browned and strengthened by his outdoor work, had a tenderness and a delicacy in their way of going to work that made the sufferer feel soothed and half-healed by their contact. It was the same with his manipulation of things. There was a refinement in his disposition of the rough surroundings that made them look different after he had been among them.

And not understood, jeered at, petted, pitied alternately — with no confidant of more sympathetic comprehension than the horse he bestrode — was Monsieur Caloche absolutely miserable? Granting that it were so, there was no one to find it out. His brown eyes had such an habitually wistful expression, he might have been born with it. Very trifles brought a fleeting light into them — a reminiscence, perhaps that while it crowned him with 'sorrow's crown of sorrow', was yet a reflection of some past joy. He took refuge in his ignorance of the language directly he was questioned as to his bygone life. An embarrassed little shrug, half apologetic, but powerfully conclusive, was the only answer the most curious examiner could elicit.

It was perceived that he had a strong objection to looking in the glass, and invariably lowered his eyes on passing the cracked and uncompromising fragment of mirror supported on two nails against the planking that walled the rough, attached kitchen. So decided was this aversion that it was only when Bill, the blacksmith, asked him chaffingly for a lock of his hair that he perceived with confusion how wantonly his silken curls were rioting round his neck and temples. He cut them off on the spot, displaying the transparent skin beneath. Contrasted with the clear tan that had overspread his scarred cheeks and forehead, it was white as freshly-drawn milk.

He was set down on the whole as given to moping; but, taking him all round, the general sentiment was favourable to him. Possibly it was with some pitiful prompting of the sort that the working manager sent him out of the way one still morning, when

Sir Matthew's buggy, creaking under the unwelcome pre-
ponderance of Sir Matthew himself, was discerned on its slow
approach to the homestead. A most peaceful morning for the
initiation of Sir Matthew's blustering presence! The sparse gumleaves hung as motionless on their branches as if they were waiting
to be photographed. Their shadows on the yellowing grass seemed
painted into the soil. The sky was as tranquil as the plain below.
The smoke from the homestead reared itself aloft in a long, thinly-
drawn column of grey. A morning of heat and repose, when even
the sunlight does not frolic and all nature toasts itself, quietly
content. The dogs lay blinking at full length, their tails beating
the earth with lazy, measured thumps. The sheep seemed rooted
to the patches of shade, apathetic as though no one wore flannel
vests or ate mutton-chops. Only the mingled voices of wild birds
and multitudinous insects were upraised in a blended monotony
of subdued sounds. Not a morning to be devoted to toil! Rather,
perchance, to a glimmering perception of a golden age, when
sensation meant bliss more than pain, and to be was to enjoy.

But to the head of the firm of Bogg & Company, taking note
of scattered thistles and straggling wire fencing, warmth and
sunshine signified only dry weather. Dry weather clearly implied
a fault somewhere, for which somebody must be called to account.
Sir Matthew had the memory of a strategist. Underlying all
considerations of shorthorns and merinos was the recollection of
a timid foreign lad to be suspected for his shy, bewildered air —
to be suspected again for his slim white hands — to be doubly
suspected and utterly condemned for his graceful bearing, his
appealing eyes, that even now Sir Matthew could see with their
soft lashes drooping over them as he fronted them in his darkened
office in Flinders Lane. A scapegoat for dry weather, for obtrusive
thistles, for straggling fencing! A waif of foreign scum to be found
out! Bogg had promised himself that he would 'drop on to him
unawares'. Physically, Bogg was carried over the ground by a fast
trotter; spiritually, he was borne along on his hobby, ambling
towards its promised gratification with airy speed.

The working manager, being probably of Bacon's way of

thinking, that 'dissimulation is but a faint kind of policy', did not, in his own words, entirely 'knuckle down' to Sir Matthew. His name was Blunt — he was proud to say it — and he would show you he could make his name good if you 'crossed' him. Yet Blunt could bear a good deal of 'crossing' when it came to the point. Within certain limits, he concluded that the side on which his bread was buttered was worth keeping uppermost, at the cost of some hard words from his employer.

And he kept it carefully uppermost on this especial morning, when the quietude of the balmy atmosphere was broken by Sir Matthew's growls. The head of the firm, capturing his manager at the door of the homestead, had required him to mount into the double-seated buggy with him. Blunt reckoned that these tours of inspection in the companionship of Bogg were more conducive to taking off flesh than a week's hard training. He listened with docility, nevertheless, to plaints and ratings — was it not a fact that his yearly salaries had already made a nest-egg of large proportions? — and might have listened to the end, if an evil chance had not filled him with a sudden foreboding. For, picking his way over the plain, after the manner of Spencer's knight, Monsieur Caloche, on a fleet, newly broken-in two-year-old, was riding towards them. Blunt could feel that Sir Matthew's eyes were sending out sparks of wrath. For the first time in his life he hazarded an uncalled-for opinion.

'He's a good working chap, that, sir!' — indicating by a jerk of the head that the lad now galloping across the turf was the subject of his remark.

'Ah!' said Sir Matthew.

It was all he said, but it was more than enough.

Blunt fidgeted uneasily. What power possessed the boy to make him show off his riding at this juncture? If he could have stopped him, or turned him back, or waved him off! — but his will was impotent.

Monsieur Caloche, well back in the saddle, his brown eyes shining, his disfigured face flushed and glowing, with wide felt-hat drawn closely over his smooth small head, with slender knees close pressed to the horse's flanks, came riding on, jumping small logs, bending with flexible joints under straggling branches, never pausing in his reckless course, until on a sudden he found himself almost in front of the buggy, and, reining up, was confronted in full by the savage gleam of Sir Matthew's eyes. It was with the old scared expression that he pulled off his wideawake and bared his head, black and silky as a young retriever's. Sir Matthew knew how to respond to the boy's greeting. He stood up in the buggy and shook his fist at him; his voice, hoarse from the work he had given it that morning, coming out with rasping intensity.

'What the devil do you mean by riding my 'orses' tails off, eh?'

Monsieur Caloche, in his confusion, straining to catch the full meaning of the question, looked fearfully round at the hind-quarters of the two-year-old, as if some hitherto unknown phenomenon peculiar to Australian horses might in fact have suddenly left them tailless.

But the tail was doing such good service against the flies at the moment of his observations, that, reassured, he turned his wistful gaze upon Sir Matthew.

'Monsieur,' he began apologetically, 'permit that I explain it to you. I did ga-lopp.'

'You can ga-lopp to hell!' said Sir Matthew with furious mimicry. 'I'll teach you to ruin my 'orses' legs!'

Blunt saw him lift his whip and strike Monsieur Caloche on the chest. The boy turned so unnaturally white that the manager looked to see him reel in his saddle. But he only swayed forward and slipped to the ground on his feet. Sir Matthew, sitting down again in the buggy with an uncomfortable sensation of some undue excess it might have been as well to recall, saw his white face for the flesh of an instant's space, saw its desperation, its shame, its trembling lips; then he was aware that the two-year-old stood riderless in front of him, and away in the distance the figure of a lad was speeding through the timber, one hand held against his chest, his hat gone and he unheeding, palpably sobbing and crying in his loneliness and defencelessness as he stumbled blindly on.

* * *

Runaway boys, I fear, call forth very little solicitude in any heart but a mother's. A cat may be nine-lived, but a boy's life is centuple. He seems only to think it worth keeping after the best part of it is gone. Boys run away from schools, from offices, from stations, without exciting more than an ominous prognostication that they will go to the bad. According to Sir Matthew's inference, Monsieur Caloche had 'gone to the bad' long ago — *ergo*, it was well to be rid of him. This being so, what utterly inconsistent crank had laid hold of the head of the great firm of Bogg & Company, and tortured him through a lengthy afternoon and everlasting night, with the vision of two despairing eyes and a scarred white face? Even his hobby cried out against him complainingly. It was not for this that it had borne him prancing along. Not to comfort him night and day with eyes so distressful that he could see nothing else. Would it be always so? Would they shine mournfully out of the dim recesses of his gloomy office in Flinders Lane, as they shone here in the wild bush on all sides of him? — so relentlessly sad that it would have been a relief to see them change into the vindictive eyes of the Furies who gave chase to Orestes. There was clearly only one remedy against such a fate, and that was to change the nature of the expression which haunted him by calling up another in its place. But how and when!

Sir Matthew prowled around the homestead the second morning after Monsieur Caloche's flight, in a manner unaccountable to himself. That he should return 'possessed' to his elaborate warehouse, where he would be alone all day — and his house of magnificent desolation, where he would be alone all night, was fast becoming a matter of impossibility. What sums out of all proportion would he not have forfeited to have seen the white-faced foreign lad, and to be able to pay him out for the discomfort he was causing him — instead of being bothered by the sight of his 'cursed belongings' at every turn! He could not go into the stable without seeing some of his gimcracks; when he went blustering into the kitchen it was to stumble over a pair of miniature boots, and a short curl of hair, in silken rings, fell off the ledge at his very feet. There was only one thing to be done!

Consulting with Blunt, clumsily enough, for nothing short of desperation would have induced Sir Matthew to approach the topic of Monsieur Caloche, he learned that nothing had been seen or heard of the lad since the moment of his running away.

'And 'twasn't in the direction of the township, neither,' added Blunt, gravely. 'I doubt the sun'll have made him stupid, and he'll have camped down some place on the run.'

Blunt's insinuation anent the sun was sheer artifice, for Blunt, in his private heart, did not endorse his own suggestion in the least degree. It was his belief that the lad had struck a shepherd's hut, and was keeping (with a show of commonsense he had not credited him with) out of the way of his savage employer. But it was worth while making use of the artifice to see Sir Matthew's ill-concealed uneasiness. Hardly the same Sir Matthew, in any sense, as the bullying growler who had driven by his side not two days ago. For *this* morning the double-seated buggy was the scene of neither plaints nor abuse. Quietly over the bush track — where last Monsieur Caloche, with hand on his breast, had run sobbing along — the two men drove, their wheels passing over a wideawake hat, lying neglected and dusty in the road. For more than an hour and a half they followed the track, the dusty soil that had been witness to the boy's flight still indicating at intervals traces of a small footprint. The oppressive calm of the atmosphere seemed to have left even the ridges of dust undisturbed. Blunt reflected that it must have been 'rough on a fellow' to run all that way in the burning sun. It perplexed him, moreover, to remember that the shepherd's hut would be now far in their rear. Perhaps it was with a newly-born sense of uneasiness on his own account that he flicked his whip and made the trotter 'go', for no comment could be expected from Sir Matthew, sitting in complete silence by his side.

To Blunt's discerning eyes the last of the footprints seemed to occur right in the middle of the track. On either side was the plain. Ostensibly, Sir Matthew had come that way to look at the sheep. There was, accordingly, every reason for turning to the right and driving towards a belt of timber some hundred yards away, and there were apparently more forcible reasons still for making for a particular tree — a straggling tree, with some pretensions to a meagre shade, the sight of which called forth an ejaculation, not entirely coherent, from Blunt.

Sir Matthew saw the cause of Blunt's ejaculation — a recumbent figure that had probably reached 'the quiet haven of us all' — it lay so still. But whether quiet or no, it would seem that to disturb its peace was a matter of life or death to Sir Matthew Bogg. Yet surely here was satiety of the fullest for his hobby! Had he not 'dropped on to the "foreign adventurer" unawares'? So unawares, in fact, that Monsieur Caloche never heeded his presence, or the presence of his working manager, but lay with a glaze on his half-closed eyes in stiff unconcern at their feet.

The clerks and juniors in the outer office of the great firm of Bogg & Co. would have been at some loss to recognise their chief in the livid man who knelt by the dead lad's side. He wanted to feel his heart, it appeared, but his trembling fingers failed him. Blunt comprehended the gesture. Whatever tenderness Monsieur Caloche had expended in his short lifetime was repaid by the gentleness with which the working manager passed his hand under the boy's rigid neck. It was with a shake of the head that seemed to Sir Matthew like the fiat of his doom that Blunt unbuttoned Monsieur Caloche's vest and discovered the fair, white throat beneath. Unbuttoning still — with tremulous fingers, and a strange apprehension creeping chillily over him — the manager saw the open vest fall loosely asunder, and then —

Yes; then it was proven that Sir Matthew's hobby had gone its extremest length. Though it could hardly have been rapture at its great triumph that filled his eyes with such a strange expression of horror as he stood looking fearfully down on the corpse at his feet. For he had, in point of fact, 'dropped on to it unawares'; but it was no longer Monsieur Caloche he had 'dropped on to', but a girl with breast of marble, bared in its cold whiteness to the open daylight, and to his ardent gaze. Bared, without any protest from the half-closed eyes, unconcerned behind the filmy veil which glazed them. A virgin breast, spotless in hue, save for

99

a narrow purple streak, marking it in a dark line from the collar-bone downwards. Sir Matthew knew, and the working manager knew, and the child they called Monsieur Caloche had known, by whose hand the mark had been imprinted. It seemed to Sir Matthew that a similar mark, red hot like a brand, must now burn on his own forehead for ever. For what if the hungry Australian sun, and emotion, and exhaustion had been the actual cause of the girl's death? He acknowledged, in the bitterness of his heart, that the 'cause of the cause' was his own bloodstained hand.

It must have been poor satisfaction to his hobby, after this, to note that Blunt had found a tiny pocket-book on the person of the corpse, filled with minute foreign handwriting. Of which nothing could be made? For, with one exception, it was filled with French quotations, all of the same tenor — all pointing to the one conclusion — and clearly proving (if it has not been proved already) that a woman who loses her beauty loses her all. The English quotation will be known to some readers of Shakespeare. 'So beauty blemished once for ever's lost!' Affixed to it was the faintly-traced signature of Henriette Caloche.

So here was a sort of insight into the mystery. The 'foreign adventurer' might be exonerated after all. No baser designs need be laid at the door of dead 'Monsieur Caloche' than the design of hiding the loss which had deprived her of all glory in her sex. If, indeed, the loss were a *real* one! For beauty is more than skin-deep, although Monsieur Caloche had not known it. It is of the bone, and the fibre, and the nerves that thrill through the brain. It is of the form and the texture too, as any one would have allowed who scrutinised the body prone in the dust. Even the cruel scars seemed merciful now, and relaxed their hold on the chiselled features, as though 'eloquent, just, and mightie Death' would suffer no hand but his own to dally with his possession.

It is only in Christmas stories, I am afraid, where, in deference to so rollicking a season, everything is bound to come right in the end, that people's natures are revolutionised in a night, and from narrow-minded villains they become open-hearted seraphs of charity. Still, it is on record of the first Henry that from the time of the sinking of the *White Ship* 'he never smiled again'. I cannot say that Sir Matthew was never known to smile, in his old sour way, or that he never growled or scolded, in his old bullying fashion, after the discovery of Monsieur Caloche's body. But he was nonetheless a changed man. The outside world might rightly conjecture that henceforth a slender, mournful-eyed shadow would walk by his side through life. But what can the outside world know of the refinement of mental anguish that may be endured by a mind awakened too late? In Sir Matthew's case — relatively as well as positively. For constant contemplation of a woman's pleading eyes and a dead statuesque form might give rise to imaginings that it would be maddening to dwell upon. What a wealth of caresses those stiff little hands had had it in their power to bestow! What a power of lighting up the solemnest office, and — be sure — the greatest, dreariest house, was latent in those dejected eyes!

Brooding is proverbially bad for the liver. Sir Matthew died of the liver complaint, and his will was cited as an instance of the eccentricity of a wealthy Australian, who, never having been in France, left the bulk of his money to the purpose of constructing and maintaining a magnificent wing to a smallpox hospital in the south of France. It was stipulated that it should be called the 'Henriette' wing, and is, I believe, greatly admired by visitors from all parts of the world.

ROSA CAMPBELL PRAED
(1851–1935)

Praed was born in a slab hut in a remote area of Queensland. In 1872 she married an Englishman and after three lonely years at his station in northern Queensland, the couple moved permanently to England.

Praed published more than forty works of fiction, almost half of which have either Australian settings or associations. Many of her works were psychological novels which dealt with the limitations of marriage. Some of her later novels demonstrate her interest in the occult. Perhaps her best-known works are *Policy and Passion* (1881) and *Mrs Tregaskiss* (1895).

GWEN'S DECISION

It was a typical bush scene, familiar enough of old; but now the girl shuddered at its new aspect of desolation.

A dividing fence of bloodwood slabs, grey and slanting inward from sheer decrepitude; grey-green, long-bladed grass, withered by the fierce December sun; tattered grey-green foliage of gum-trees — oh those everlasting gum-trees! — Long, thin, grey, and spotted stems, crossing each other and extending half-naked branches against a brassy sky which blacked the crest of the range; a rough cart-track meandering down through the trees to the sliprails; and, within the fence, Gwendolen Barnack, her cabin-trunk and bundle of wraps beside her, standing, an image of forlorn wrath.

The train had whizzed away, lost long ago among the thickening gum-forest. There was no shed or stage. By arrangement with the owners of Ballooma cattle-station, passengers were dropped at the sliprails, where, ordinarily, buggy or riding horses awaited them. But there was no horse, no buggy, no apparent means of conveyance awaiting this passenger, just dropped by the train. Gwendolen stamped her foot in impotent rage, but clearly that would not help matters. She determined to wait for half an hour, and then if nothing came — well she did not know what she could do in that case. Ballooma Station was too far for her to walk to it before nightfall. She did not know of any selector's hut in the neighbourhood. But then, she had been away a long time. Probably there would be a selector's homestead somewhere near . . . Oh if she were only back in Italy again! . . . Her thoughts as she waited, went back to the beloved land she had left.

Only two or three months ago she had gazed from her studio window at the dome of St Peter's and the Roman Campagna. She loathed this primitive civilisation, this imprisonment in a barren wilderness bounded by the eternal old gum-trees.

Was nobody coming? She put back her veil and strained her eyes through the grey-green waste — eyes a shade between blue and brown, changing with every passing emotion. One could see now how pretty she was. Slim, straight as the gum-sapling; a little head with gold-brown hair; a determined chin and a kissable but resolute mouth; a complexion that had the exotic brilliancy of a certain type of Australian beauty.

At last! Yes, there was somebody coming at last.

'Yep! Yep!' A crack of whip and rattle of rough wheels. The station buggy appeared, shabbier than ever, and Firebrand and Dozer, the two buggy horses, leaner and worse-groomed than ever of yore. Only the driver sat in the buggy, stooping forward to urge the horses with the bushman's rakish slouch. A good-looking young man, unknown to Gwen, undoubtedly a gentleman, in a new cabbage-tree hat with wide-falling puggaree, clean moleskins, and an alpaca coat carelessly put on over a fresh, blue-checked shirt.

He lifted his hat and leaped from the buggy, standing now before her, tall, muscular, and prepossessing, full of eager apology.

'I'm awfully sorry to have kept you waiting. It's my not having been this road before, and taking it too easy at first to spare the horses. But, as you see, we put the pace on this last mile or two.' The roan and the grey dripped sweat from their heaving flanks. 'It's a good thirteen miles, and they told me twelve,' said the young man. 'Now, Miss Barnack, I expect you're pretty sick at my excuses and are dying to get home. Is this your kit? Do you mind standing at Firebrand's head a minute while I heave up the box?'

He lifted Gwen's trunk as if it had been a valise, and stowed it at the back of the buggy, her bundle of rugs with it.

'That all?'

'Yes, thank you. My heavy luggage is coming later,' Gwen replied, stiffly.

'All right. You get in, then, and we'll be off. Just let me jump on to the box. There! can I help you?'

Gwen disdained the proffered hand and clambered unassisted to the seat beside him.

He gave a few more encouraging 'Yeps' and turned the buggy. Dozer stepped out with brisker courage. Firebrand was a bit of a jibber and required attention. Not till they had covered the first spur did the young man start conversation with his very cross companion.

'Quite comfortable?' he asked.

'Comfortable enough?' she rejoined, tartly. 'I don't find the buggy springs any easier than they used to be.'

'Not likely these bad times. I ought to have greased them.'

'You?'

'Oh, well, I'm doing sort of handy-man this last day or two. Miss Barnack, I don't know how to apologise enough for having made you wait . . . Hold up, Firebrand! No, you don't!' And the whip descended on Firebrand's shoulder and covered Gwen's rather ungracious acceptance of the apology. 'And I haven't given any of the messages and explanations your sister sent,' added the young man.

'I should really like to know,' said Gwen, haughtily resentful, 'why none of my family has come to meet me? I don't think it's kind — or — considerate — in the circumstances' — she could not help her voice faltering — 'to let me be met by a stranger.'

'Yes, I know; it must seem beastly unkind. Only I may say that I don't feel exactly a stranger — in the circumstances.'

He turned on Gwen a pair of blue eyes and a sunburnt, handsome face — almost as good to look at as Gwen's own when Gwen was not in a bad temper. But in the girl's present mood she was unresponsive to his smile.

'I've got to explain why they didn't come,' he went on. 'Mr Barnack meant to, but a butcher rode up this morning on the look-out for a small mob of fat beasts for Christmas. So your uncle went out with all the hands to see what he could muster. That's why I'm here. You see — '

Gwen interrupted with repressed ire. 'I should have thought my sister Marjory, or Aunt Gertrude, who are both fond of driving, might have brought the buggy. Or at least that one of them might have come in it with you.'

'Why, certainly. But I was going to tell you that Miss Marjory had a fall from her horse last week and sprained her ankle pretty badly, so that she's tied up on the sofa at present. And Mrs Barnack—well, the servant—there's only one since the banks began to stop payment—took French leave yesterday, and your aunt couldn't leave the butcher to cook his own dinner, could she?—especially as the sale of those fats is a matter of importance.'

'Yes—yes, I understand now. Poor Marjory! How horrid of me!'

Gwen's impulsive contrition was very fascinating. She looked at the young man with a half-petulant, half-appealing smile. 'It's all the fault of this detestable old bush. I hate it!'

'Oh, I say, Miss Barnack! I can't let you abuse the bush. I'm a right-down bushman myself, and it's a grand place, in spite of its ups and downs. There's excitement in them, too. We're having a turn at the "downs" just now. I went smash like a lot of others, but a stroke of good luck put me on my end again. Me and my mate, you know. And that was a good job for your sister.'

'Why a good job for my sister? And what has your mate got to do with it?'

'You don't know that Miss Marjory and my mate are— There! I've all but put my foot into it. Of course your sister would want to tell you herself.'

'I think that as my sister hasn't troubled to inform me of this important piece of news you needn't feel any scruple about doing so.'

'She hasn't had a chance,' replied the young man. 'It only happened yesterday.'

'It?'

'She and my mate.'

'I suppose you mean that Marjory is engaged to your mate, whoever he may be?'

'That's about it. And he's the best chap ever born in Australia—Frank Haynes, of Tarilpa—yeou know.' The young man had a touch, not too pronounced, of the Australian drawl.

'No, I don't know.'

'Tarilpa is on the Upper Ubi. We were partners there till the Bank came down on us. Then we went prospecting. That was the stroke of luck. We cleared fifteen thousand apiece out of Consolation Reef. Now do you see?'

'Yes . . . I see.'

'We bought Tarilpa on easy terms. Frank and your sister will live on the head station. I've free-selected a pretty twelve thousand acres down the river for a homestead for myself.'

'And you are?'

'I forgot we hadn't been introduced. I'm Alec Grant.'

'Oh, I remember reading about you. You did something heroic, didn't you — saved a party of explorers and discovered Cape York?' Gwen looked interested.

'No, the Dutch did that.' He ignored the rest of the speech. 'Gee up, Dozer! You must sit tight, Miss Barnack. Here's a bit of corduroy.'

The buggy bumped over a stretch of road mended with saplings laid crosswise. After that they struck the home paddock, and the horses stepped freely. Ballooma Mountain came in sight, the sun dipping to its peak. They were skirting the river scrub, whence came whiffs of wild jasmine and the smell of woody earth. A flight of cockatoos shrieked above them; the soft, singing sound in the she-oaks awoke in Gwen wild memories. The bush has a queer glamour which binds even the most unwilling of her children.

The bushman watched it working. She intercepted one of his sideway admiring glances, and it wasn't in Gwen not to respond to admiration. She could not help giving him a smile which invited further conversational overtures.

'Well now,' he said, 'I've supplied you with a good bit of information about myself and my partner, and you haven't told me anything about yourself in return.'

'I should have thought you knew already all the pleasing things they've been saying about me,' she replied ungraciously.

'If I had – which I haven't – it wouldn't follow that they were true,' said he.

'Oh you can take it for granted that they're true,' she replied. 'I'm the prodigal daughter, the rover, the renegade.'

He laughed. 'You have got a fine lot of names together, and I'm sure they don't fit you in the least.'

'Yes, they do. I'll give you a reason for each. I'm the prodigal daughter because two years ago, when Marjory and I were left orphans – you see it's not *exactly* a paraphrase of the parable – I demanded of Uncle Charles, who I suppose in a sort of way stands in a father's place to me, that he should give me the portion of my inheritance, and let me go and study Art – of course with a capital – in Europe.'

'Yes, I see, but he couldn't divide up the station could he? – he being a partner?'

'With a two-third's share – whereas Marjory and I have only one-third between us. I don't blame Uncle Charles for having a two-third's share – he was the eldest and he bought it, and I didn't want him to divide up the station – though it seems that if he'd done it before the bad times came, we might have been better off –'

'I don't see then –' began the young man.

'I'm telling you. There were a few hundreds outside the station which were to be Marjory's and mine some day. I asked for my share of those hundreds – three to be accurate.'

'Which he gave you, and you went off. I know about that. But it wasn't enough was it to study Art on for two years?'

She made a little face. 'No, it wasn't. It was barely enough to starve on. Nobody can accuse me in any way of having wasted my substance in riotous living. I went to the cheapest of cheap *pensions* in Rome, and I went to the cheapest of the art schools. I wish I'd been extravagant and gone to a better one.'

'You'd have got on quicker?'

She made another little face. 'My artistic genius hasn't been able to prove itself – it hasn't had the right opportunity.'

'Two years is a short time to do it in,' said he.

'Especially when you've to count every penny and can't get

beyond a week or two at Tivoli or Albano, in a room shared with another student, during the hot weather,' she retorted. 'I couldn't have done that even, if it hadn't been for the allowance I got out of the station. It wasn't much, but it just paid for my lodging, and what was left of the other money dressed me and did the rest. The beginning of this year, there wasn't any of the other money left. So I wrote and asked Uncle Charles to increase my allowance or to make me an advance, and he wrote back that our bank had smashed like a lot of others out here. He seemed quite surprised that I hadn't read about the crisis, as he called it — but what does one know about Australian banks smashing and droughts killing the cattle, and that sort of thing, in Rome, where one is studying Art?'

'No,' said the young man with an amused little laugh. 'It's a long jump from Rome and art as you say, to drought and dead cattle and Australian banks.'

'Well, Uncle Charles said that it would be all he could do to carry on the station at all, and that Marjory and I couldn't have any regular allowance until times mended — do you think they ever will?'

'Oh yes,' he answered. 'It's always either a boom or a drought with us. We had a few years of boom, and now it's the turn of drought. But this station isn't like the ones out west where a drought means utter ruin — as it did in my case. The creeks down south never quite dry up, and after a bit, you'll see that things will come round all right.'

'And meantime I shall have to vegetate in the bush, and my career will have been baulked,' she said with tragic bitterness.

'I suppose one *could* paint in the bush,' he suggested.

She waved her hand derisively over the forbidding landscape with its everlasting medley of gaunt eucalyptus, arid flat and coarse brown tussocks of unsucculent herbage.

'Paint — *what*?' she asked scornfully. 'Dead logs, stringy-bark gums and blady-grass? There's nothing else, unless you throw in a blackfellow or a kangaroo, or a jew-lizard — which might be interesting to the naturalist, but not from any other point of view.

By the way,' she added, 'we'll pass over the fact that painting is not my particular line of art-study.'

'Oh I didn't know. What was it then.'

'I worked in clay.'

'Sculpting! That's fine. Well I know where I could find you splendid clay in the creek if you wanted to work. And why shouldn't you try an allegorical figure and call it the spirit of the bush?'

'Embodied in a black-gin or a kangaroo — or perhaps the bunyip?' she asked. 'No, I don't feel drawn to that idea.'

'Of course you've got to get into the spirit of the bush before you can feel it,' he said. 'Now to me, there always seems something very grand and wild and weird about the bush. It isn't like anything else in the world.'

'No, it certainly is not,' returned she, loftily satirical. 'You couldn't compare it with Italy for instance.'

He laughed again. 'Not by any stretch of the imagination.'

'I was thinking while I waited for you,' she said, 'of different views I used to love. There was one from a little loggia in the hotel I stayed in at Albano — right over to Rome, with the Alban lake in the foreground, and the Sabine hills in the background, and then the great rolling sea of the Campagna — the aqueducts very far off and the dome of St Peter's standing out — it was pagan and Christian blending. Oh I delighted in Albano. I used to love looking down from the heights into the quiet waters of the blue lake, with the ruins of Domitian's palace on one side, and the old villa with the wonderful garden on the other —'

'Nemi's better,' said he quietly, 'and the walk through that garden with the lake below beats the other one. I wonder if they'll ever fish up those old Roman galleys that are lying at the bottom of Nemi lake.'

'You know Nemi? You've been to Rome?' she exclaimed in surprise.

'Oh a good long while ago. I did my time at Oxford and saw something of Europe as well.'

'Oh!' She appeared to have been silenced by the information.

'You wouldn't have thought it?' he remarked.

'No,' she answered carelessly with more candour than politeness.

'I do like people to be frank,' said he. 'That is a true Australian virtue,' at which she laughed a little discomfitedly. At that moment, Firebrand, the most frisky of the buggy-horses, took fright at the carcase of a dead beast lying near the road, and shied violently, starting off the other horse, so that the two took some clever handling of the reins before they were brought into subjection again.

Gwen could not help remarking the skill of her charioteer, and she felt sorry she had spoken slightingly.

'I wasn't thinking when I answered you just now,' she said apologetically. 'I hope you aren't offended.'

He looked straight at her in a way she liked.

'You might say much nastier things than that, Miss Barnack, and if they were true I'd appreciate you all the more for saying them. Why of course I knew perfectly well this bit of rough bush wood' — and he tapped his broad chest with the knob of his whip — 'never took on 'Varsity polish. I'm a duffer at all that sort of thing — books, society, art. There never was the least use in my trying for a degree.' He administered some gentle correction to the still refractory Firebrand, then said with a certain modest self-complacency; 'But I've got a 'Varsity trophy stuck upon the wall of my humpey, that I'm rather proud of, and I'd like to show it to you some day.'

'What is that?' she asked.

'A pair of sculls — I rowed in the Eight,' he announced gently, and immediately turned the subject from his own achievements. 'You know after all,' he said; 'I don't think there's a great deal in old civilisations — ruined temples and palaces, and broken marble statues, and paintings of saints with halos round their heads — well they are tremendously interesting in their way, of course, but one wouldn't want to live with them always.'

'You didn't apparently!'

'No — I *could* have stopped over there as agent for one of our big meat syndicates that an uncle of mine is director of. I *could* have divided my year between Genoa, Naples and London, and have worked into quite a fine business—think of that! But I decided that nothing would pay me for giving up Australia.'

She stared at him in genuine wonder.

'Well you see,' he said, answering her look, 'I think a free life in the open where a man has to spur up his energy and fight with nature and circumstances for all he's worth, in order to hold his own, is better worth living on the whole. It's splendid to have a hand in the making of a nation don't you think? And there are the political developments in a new country that mean such a lot. Out here we're building up the future, while you artistic folk seem all the time trying at a bad imitation of the past.'

The young lady's lip curled.

'I see we shall never agree in our views of life, so perhaps we'd better not discuss them.'

'You don't see that at all. I'd like awfully to understand yours. Look here, Miss Barnack, you wouldn't believe how sorry I've felt for you, having to give up the studies you'd chosen, all for want of beastly money . . . But I wish you didn't hate Australia so much and want to live out of your own country.'

'Ah, there's where the rover and the renegade come in. Now you see I was quite justified in the names I called myself.'

'You'd have wanted to come back in the end,' he said confidently. 'Nobody can ever get away altogether from what's born in them. But I'm really sorry, all the same, for your disappointment,' he went on, sympathetically. 'Was it absolutely unavoidable?' he added. 'I suppose you couldn't have struggled on over there?'

'Struggled on—How?'

'I don't know exactly but there are ways, I believe, of doing pot-boilers, even in the sculpting line?'

'I suppose so. I never tried them.'

'You'd despise the kind of thing I mean. I was thinking of catchy little terracotta images that one sees in shop windows. I knew a fellow in Melbourne who used to do comic ones. He said it wasn't difficult once you'd got the trick, and he made money by that, when nobody would buy his big things.'

'I'm afraid I didn't get to even that marketable stage of sculpting, and I don't think anyhow that comic terracotta images would have appealed to me. I did start on my artistic career with *some* sort of an ideal,' said Miss Barnack witheringly.

'Lots of people start with tremendous ideals and yet don't seem to make them pay,' he answered. 'Excuse me if I look at art from a practical point of view. I daresay it seems rather brutal to you, but after all, producing marketable wares is the test of capacity as the world goes. Though I don't believe it's a question always of capacity. My idea is that it's the stars. Some people are born to succeed whatever they do, and others to fail, and the worst of it is that none of us know which it is going to be when we start. But I believe Somebody knows . . .' He flicked Firebrand meditatively, then, as she did not speak, he continued.

'Supposing now that it had been seen you were going to fail — perhaps come a cropper over in Italy, and you'd been brought back here to prevent that and because there was something better you didn't foresee waiting for you. That's Fate — I believe in Fate. Miss Barnack, I shouldn't wonder if you were glad some day that you'd been forced to give the other thing up.'

'Glad at having been forced to give up all the beauty of nature and of art that was everywhere around me — all the associations of that wonderful past, which *you* hold so cheap, and I so dear! Glad to give up the life that was congenial to me, the interests that I loved — and to come back to surroundings and occupations and people that I'm not in sympathy with,' she cried. 'I was never fitted to be a backwoods-woman. I've always detested the roughness and crudeness of this place. And it's worse now than it ever was — more poverty-stricken and rougher even than I remember it . . . Good gracious! they've not even had those old dead gum-trees grubbed up yet! This paddock has been a perfect eye-sore for years. Uncle Charles might have made the blacks do that.' She pointed to a patch of 'rung' gum-trees — grey skeletons, which presented the most dismal appearance and were truly, as Gwendolen had said, an eye-sore. They were close to the head-station now, and all the landmarks were familiar to her.

'Blacks are getting pretty scarce along the river, and it doesn't pay to put white men on to grubbing out stumps,' said Alec Grant. 'But I've got an idea, Miss Barnack, those indecent old skeletons shan't outrage your aesthetic sensibilities. I'll plant some native cucumber vines round them — that's the quickest growing thing I know — and before long they'll all be draped in pretty green petticoats . . . Here we are! You won't like me to say "welcome home", but I shall say it for all that.'

Gwen did not answer, and he saw, not without pleasurable amusement, that she was looking about in an excited manner which made him fancy that she was not quite so heartless as she had made herself out to be and that she did feel some natural emotion at her return to her own home and her own kindred. He whipped on the horses and they drove fast along the road bordered by those ghosts of trees, towards a collection of slab, bark-roofed buildings with roomy verandahs connected by creeper-covered gangways. The place looked very untidy — saddles lying about the verandahs; a great heap of rough firewood; bullock-hides pegged to dry on the bark roof of the meat store. Carrion crows circled overhead. From the killing-yard, a little way off, came raucous notes of unclean birds mingling with the bellowings of a mob of cattle. A thick cloud of dust hid the posts and rails of the stockyard.

'They brought in the fats all right,' said Alec Grant.

Mr Barnack, in Crimean shirt and soiled mole-skins, red and perspiring after a day on the run, was Gwen's first new impression of her relatives.

'Hullo! Got up all right. Just in time for Christmas. My word, it's going to be a smoking hot one,' was his greeting. The Barnacks were not a demonstrative family.

Then out came Gertrude Barnack, the young second wife, her sleeves tucked up, her arms floury, her homely face red from the kitchen fire. There was no lack of warmth in her reception of her niece. She kissed Gwen heartily and dragged her along the verandah, chattering all the time, while Alec Grant and the boss unharnessed the buggy-horses. Gwen deduced from this that they could no longer afford the handy man who had acted as groom.

'Oh Gwen, I expect you're hating us,' exclaimed Gertrude Barnack. 'But it was better to have you home while there was money enough to cable you a passage. You can't imagine what terrible times we've been through — almost every bank smashed, and your uncle holding on just by the skin of his teeth. He says he'll do it though. And meantime, we've put down all the extra hands, and sent away some of the servants. We do keep a cook, but the last one went off, so I'm making the scones for your tea and cooking the dinner. We all help, but Alec Grant says that you're a new chum now and should be let down easy and that he'll take half your share of work. Isn't he a good fellow? I expect he's told you all the news. Oh I'm so glad to see you, dear.'

Who could be such an ungrateful wretch as not to respond affectionately to such a greeting? The right sort of squatter's wife was Gertrude Barnack.

'Gwen! Come here, Gwen!' called an eager voice from a lounge in the verandah. 'I can't move, or I'd have gone to meet you.'

All the emotion of Gwen's return concentrated itself in the sisters' embrace.

Marjory was not as pretty as Gwen, but pretty enough, it was clear, to satisfy the young man who had been hanging adoringly over her. Nor was Frank Haynes as handsome as his partner. He had a stronger twang, too, and seemed altogether more 'bushy'. Gwen's antipathy for the native-born Australian male revived.

By and by, Mr Haynes went in search of his 'mate', about whom he had already held forth to Gwen in admiring terms. Indeed, mutual admiration seemed the weakness of the pair. When the sisters were alone, Marjory told the tale of her engagement, which took a considerable time in the telling, and need not be repeated here. It struck Gwen — who among her art-student and literary friends had had opportunities of studying more exalted phases of passion — that Marjory's ideas of love partook of the general crudity of the bush, and that her ecstatic praises of her lover were a trifle commonplace.

'Oh Gwen, isn't he a dear man-thing? And aren't you surprised? Fancy *me*, the plain one, being engaged before *you*! But I'm sure that must be your own fault, darling. Now do tell me, among all the clever romantic people you must have met in Italy — painters and poets and Italian counts and things — *I* should prefer my Frank to any one of them — but, say — wasn't there *one* man for you to fall in love with?'

'Plenty, if I had *wanted* a man to fall in love with, but you see I was in love with my art.'

'Oh, but dearest, you must have found that *very* unsatisfying. I am sure you did, only you won't confess it. And now that you will see for yourself how happy *I* am in being engaged to Frank, and how much better it is to have a nice station of one's own and to make money and be able to take trips to Europe with a husband to look after one than to worry round in art studios by oneself, — why, you'll be quite pleased to stop in the bush and give up all your old ruins and broken gods and rubbish of that sort for the sake of being happy like me in a womanly way.'

'Broken gods!' cried Gwen. 'You may well say that! Give them up for a husband and a station in the bush! Never! never!'

'Oh yes you will,' said Marjory. 'Of course it isn't as if you had made any particular success. Mrs Turnbull — Gertrude's married sister you know, who went to see your work at Rome — I think she must be rather a disagreeable woman — wrote to Gertrude that she didn't see any prospect of your setting the Tiber on fire, let alone the Thames, and that she hoped you weren't likely to be dependent for a livelihood on your earnings as a sculptress. Horrid, wasn't it?'

Gwen burst out hotly. What did Mrs Turnbull know about art? She was a vulgar, ignorant woman who detested her (Gwen) only a little less than Gwen detested her.

'Don't be cross dear. Of course we didn't believe what she said. Still you never did do anything much, did you? And really, art isn't half as good as being married to a man you love and having a nice home like Tarilpa. Now I do want to know what you think of Alec Grant?'

Marjory felt her way clumsily. 'I couldn't help saying to Frank that it was like a sort of fate his being the only one who could conveniently go to meet you at the sliprails . . . Uncle Charles has asked him to stay over the New Year, and we're planning to have a really jolly bush Christmas, in spite of the bad times. I particularly want you to be nice to Alec, Gwen.'

Marjory was not a young woman of tact. After that, for a few days, Gwen was extremely standoffish with Alec Grant. But in primitive conditions, unless you dislike a person very much indeed, it is extremely difficult to be either loftily indifferent or actively disagreeable, and when a girl is thrown all day and every day into companionship with a good-looking, pleasant-mannered man who is not by any means a fool and who is perfectly ready to adore her, it is usually a case either of strong attraction or of definite repulsion, and Gwen's tolerance of Alec Grant's constant attendance upon her did not suggest definite repulsion.

From Gwen's coming back it wanted a fortnight to Christmas. A bush Christmas isn't like an English one. How could it be, with the thermometer 102 degrees Fahrenheit in the shade? Primitive conditions, however, give opportunities for interesting dalliance between man and maid. From these lame Marjory and her lover secured full value, and naturally Grant fell to Gwen. The cook who had taken French leave seemed difficult to replace. Not even a selector's daughter was to be had on a job. So Mrs Barnack made herself responsible in the kitchen, while incompetent, artistic Gwen rashly undertook the housework. The amateur handy-man assisted both. It was impossible to maintain an attitude of dignified aloofness with a young gentleman who helped you to wash up dishes, lay the table, sweep verandahs, and stone raisins for the Christmas cakes.

The crisis came on Christmas Eve. Gwen was in the garden inspecting a gigantic bunch of Black Prince grapes, carefully guarded for the Christmas dessert, and was considering whether she should cut the bunch now or keep it till the morrow, when Alec appeared, proudly balancing, one on each palm, the first two melons of the season.

117

'There! I told you they'd be ready by Christmas Day. I'm going to cool them right away in the tank.'

With that he put them, stalk upwards, in at the round hole of a shallow water-butt, which was half sunk in the ground and was sheltered by the trellis of passionfruit on one side and by grapevines on the other.

'This is the coolest place on the whole station,' he said. 'There isn't water enough to cover these, and I'll fetch them out before the sun gets round here in the morning.'

Gwen decided that she would leave her grapes. The two sat down on the wooden scaffolding that surrounded the tank.

'Miss Barnack, you shouldn't bite a passionfruit. You should suck it the way a snake sucks an egg.'

Gwen shuddered. 'I'm frightened of snakes. Black Billy says there are a lot about.'

Alec took the top off a passionfruit with his knife and handed it to her, watching her with longing admiration as she put her pretty lips to the purple egg. She surprised the look in his eyes and blushed and dropped her own. The young man gave a conscious laugh.

'Kismet! If one is going to be bitten by a snake one will be bitten. If one is going to fall in love with a particular woman she is sure to cross one's path. As I said before, everything is fated. Some people are born under a lucky star, some are not. I'm one of those who aren't meant to be snuffed out—'

'By a snake.'

'Or by a woman. With me what seems bad luck turns to good. I expect it's the same with you.'

'Really!' Gwen was disdainfully incredulous.

'Well, now, if the bank hadn't come down on me and my mate we shouldn't have struck Consolation Reef and got Tarilpa back again. And Frank Haynes wouldn't have come here this Christmas, on the look-out for store cattle, to meet his fate. And I shouldn't have come over after him and met mine.'

'Oh!' Gwen tossed away the passionfruit, avoiding his gaze. Grant proceeded ardently.

'It was Fate that brought the butcher up that day and sent all the men mustering except me; Fate that made Marjory sprain her ankle; Fate that took me in the buggy to the sliprails—to meet *you*. My lucky star smiled on me then.'

Gwen rejoined crushingly: 'All I can say is that if you were born under a lucky star, I'm not so fortunate. It was my evil fate which took me away from all I wanted to do, and dropped me down at Ballooma sliprails.'

'Now I told you I had a feeling that Fate or whatever you like to call it, was saving you from some worse disappointment,' he answered. 'It seems cheeky of me to say so, but that is what I honestly believe, and hope.'

'Ah, you've no faith in me as a sculptress, because I can't see myself attempting an allegorical figure of the spirit of the bush. I know what it is, you've heard Mrs Turnbull's opinion of my work.'

'I've heard nobody's opinion. And I didn't know you were a sculptress until you told me. But I do know that it's the most magnificent and the most difficult thing in the world to make a fine statue. Very few people have done it since the old Greeks.'

'I didn't suppose you knew or cared much about statues—and the old Greeks,' said Gwen.

'Why not? A bushman can read and think as well as ride after cattle—or—'

'Or?' she asked.

'Or fall in love. Gwen, I can't keep it in any longer. The instant I set eyes on you standing there by the sliprails and looking the picture of—'

'Misery and ill-temper,' she put in.

'Well, yes. No matter, I knew that you were the one woman in the world for me, and that my star had led me to her.'

'You are wrong.' The words came as by compulsion.

'No, I am not. Gwen, I love you. I shall never give up trying to win you, and I feel in my heart that sooner or later I *shall* win you. The more you stiffen against me, and try to show me that you hate me, the more I feel it.'

'I don't — hate — you,' she said, slowly.

He laughed trimphantly. 'No, I knew that. And if you were quite indifferent you wouldn't pretend to hate me. Darling, mightn't it be a little bit of the other thing?'

'The other thing?'

'Love, dearest. Will you marry me, Gwen?'

'No, no, I shall never marry an Australian. I'm going back to Italy as soon as they'll let me. Don't ask me any more, Alec.'

And, as if afraid that he would press his suit beyond her powers of resistance, she turned abruptly down the trellis of passion-vines back to the house.

Love and the weather seemed in league that Christmas. A thunderstorm during the night heartened beast, bird, insect, and flower. A delicious, dreamy excitement brooded over the garden. All nature hailed mating man and maid. Involuntarily Gwen and Alec looked across at each other when each opened the other's anonymously-bestowed gift.

Gwen's token to him was a photograph of the Ariadne of the Vatican. He came straight to her and said, in a low voice:

'Ariadne made a false start, you know, but her fate found her notwithstanding.'

Gwen looked down at a queerly-shaped charm that lay in the palm of her hand. Alec's offering to each one of the women was a tiny nugget with a swivel-ring attached — a lucky stone from Consolation Reef. Gwen's bore a curiously perfect resemblance to a heart.

'You shouldn't have given *me* this,' she said.

'It grew so,' he answered, 'and I meant it for a symbol of the other Australian heart that is yours and yours only, whether you choose to wear it here or to throw it away if you decide upon going back to Italy.'

A little later they met again by the grapevine.

'I'm going to fish up my melons,' he said.

'And will you please cut my branch of grapes?'

He cut the stalk with his sharp bushman's knife and laid it in her leaf-lined basket. There were loquats and early figs likewise to be gathered, and the girl and the man lingered over the plucking. A magpie on a bough nearby trilled an acclamation; the butcher-birds hopped inquisitively on to the edge of the tank; a venturesome bower-bird pounced upon a fluff of silk torn by a thorn from Gwen's sash, and by and by carried it off to beautify his bride's chamber. Alec Grant's hand, venturesome also, softly touched the frilleries of Gwen's sleeve.

'I'm going off to Consolation Mine to-morrow,' he said, 'unless you tell me that I may stay.'

Gwen's eyes grew wide and soft as they watched the antics of the bower-bird, but she answered nothing.

'It's Christmas Day,' he pleaded. 'Oh, Gwen, won't you make it the happiest Christmas of my whole life?'

'I — can't — do that,' she said, with the little falter that emboldened his furtively-caressing hand.

It took her hand and raised it to his lips. She shrank, half rebuking, half-accepting, faintly protesting.

'You want me to give up everything I'd set my heart on.'

He touched the nugget-charm which she had let him fasten to a bangle at her wrist.

'Wouldn't an Australian heart do in exchange — a heart that's pure gold — for you — straight from the bush rock — an earnest heart of richer gold and deeper love — if that were possible — still?'

She gathered her resolution. 'No, I can't. Don't urge me, Alec. You must take that as my final answer. And I think you had better go back to your mine and find more gold and give it to someone who'll value it more.'

He dropped her hand at once. 'Very well. To-morrow I shall start, but we won't let this spoil our Christmas. Only I warn you that I shall try again . . . Well, those melons ought to have got fairly iced by the hail-stones last night.'

He pulled up the sleeves of his spotless white coat and shirt, and plunged his arm in at the round hole of the tank. Gwen saw the bower-bird hop away; she thought the sun dazzled her. She heard a stealthy displacement of the water and a faint wash of

121

it against the tank side, then a sudden splash and a grim exclamation,

'By Jove! I'm bitten.'

'Bitten! What—what is it?' she cried.

'A snake!' He drew up his hand from the mouth of the tank; it held the melon by its stalk. On the back of the arm, just above the wrist, was an unmistakable mark—two little blue punctures round which a circle of red was beginning to spread.

Grant looked at the mark, and his face paled and hardened; but he laughed.

'Fate!' he said. 'But I'm not going to be snuffed out—by a snake—or by a woman either.' And he laughed again as he let the melon drop and, pulling out his silk handkerchief, began to bind it round the arm as well as he could with his left hand.

In an instant Gwen was on her knees beside him. 'Oh, let me— quick-quick!'

'All right. Tie it just as tight as ever you can. Now my knife— Don't come too close. I might stain your dress.'

He made a gash in the arm from which the blood spouted and stooped his head to it. But the girl was before him. With a passionate movement she put her lips to the wound and sucked it, the red drops patching her cheeks and her dress, while with one hand she pushed back his face.

For an instant he yielded himself to the overpowering ecstasy of that strange kiss, then almost roughly broke away.

'No, no—Gwen darling—for heaven's sake! You mustn't do that . . . Oh, sweet—you love me. You can't deny it now.'

He had her in his arms. She, too, gave herself up to a moment of ecstasy; only a moment. She seized his arm.

'Come. Are you mad, Alec? Come at once and get brandy— ammonia. Oh, think what it means to me!'

'I don't think of anything but that you love me, and that you are my joy and my life. Dearest, don't be frightened. It will be all right. Perhaps that was only a harmless water snake, after all.'

'Look! Look!' cried Gwen.

Something brown and yellow and shiny wriggled itself up over the edge of the tank, remaining just long enough to verify Alec's words, and disappearing with a flop and a gurgle of the water within. The quick eye of the bushman, and the girl's old-time experience of bathes in the creek, identified the species at a glance. Here in the shallows of the tank an innocuous water snake had found not over-comfortable quarters.

'No poison there,' said Alec. 'We needn't bother about brandy or ammonia. Oh, Gwen, my darling, wasn't I right? Fate sometimes chooses queer instruments to shape her ends. We've got to thank that snake for the happiest Christmas of our lives.'

BARBARA BAYNTON
(1857–1929)

Baynton was born in Scone, New South Wales. She married a grazier when she was eighteen, and when her husband deserted her and their three children, Baynton moved to Sydney and began to write. Her first story appeared in the *Bulletin* in 1896. Baynton remarried twice to wealthy, educated men. She travelled and lived in England and Australia, and was well known as a literary figure and independent eccentric.

Baynton published one collection of short stories, *Bush Studies* (1902) and one novel, *Human Toll* (1907). Her writing stressed the hardship and loneliness of the bush, particularly for women.

THE CHOSEN VESSEL

She laid the stick and her baby on the grass while she untied the rope that tethered the calf. The length of the rope separated them. The cow was near the calf, and both were lying down. Feed along the creek was plentiful, and every day she found a fresh place to tether it, since tether it she must, for if she did not, it would stray with the cow out on the plain. She had plenty of time to go after it, but then there was her baby; and if the cow turned on her out on the plain, and she with her baby, — she had been a town girl and was afraid of the cow, but she did not want the cow to know it. She used to run at first when it bellowed its protest against the penning up of its calf. This satisfied the cow, also the calf, but the woman's husband was angry, and called her — the noun was cur. It was he who forced her to run and meet the advancing cow, brandishing a stick, and uttering threatening words till the enemy turned and ran. 'That's the way!' the man said, laughing at her white face. In many things he was worse than the cow, and she wondered if the same rule would apply to the man, but she was not one to provoke skirmishes even with the cow.

It was early for the calf to go to 'bed' — nearly an hour earlier than usual; but she had felt so restless all day. Partly because it was Monday, and the end of the week that would bring her and the baby the companionship of his father, was so far off. He was a shearer, and had gone to his shed before daylight that morning. Fifteen miles as the crow flies separated them.

There was a track in front of the house, for it had once been a wine shanty, and a few travellers passed along at intervals. She was not afraid of horsemen; but swagmen, going to, or worse coming from, the dismal, drunken little township, a day's journey beyond, terrified her. One had called at the house to-day, and asked for tucker.

That was why she had penned up the calf so early. She feared more from the look of his eyes, and the gleam of his teeth, as he watched her newly awakened baby beat its impatient fists upon her covered breasts, than from the knife that was sheathed in the belt at his waist.

She had given him bread and meat. Her husband she told him was sick. She always said that when she was alone and a swagman came; and she had gone in from the kitchen to the bedroom, and asked questions and replied to them in the best man's voice she could assume. Then he had asked to go into the kitchen to boil his billy, but instead she gave him tea, and he drank it on the wood heap. He had walked round and round the house, and there were cracks in some places, and after the last time he had asked for tobacco. She had none to give him, and he had grinned, because there was a broken clay pipe near the wood heap where he stood, and if there were a man inside, there ought to have been tobacco. Then he asked for money, but women in the bush never have money.

At last he had gone, and she, watching through the cracks, saw him when about a quarter of a mile away, turn and look back at the house. He had stood so for some moments with a pretence of fixing his swag, and then, apparently satisfied, moved to the left towards the creek. The creek made a bow round the house, and when he came to the bend she lost sight of him. Hours after, watching intently for signs of smoke, she saw the man's dog chasing some sheep that had gone to the creek for water, and saw it slink back suddenly, as if it had been called by someone.

More than once she thought of taking her baby and going to her husband. But in the past, when she had dared to speak of the dangers to which her loneliness exposed her, he had taunted and sneered at her. 'Needn't flatter yerself,' he had told her, 'nobody 'ud want ter run away with yew.'

Long before nightfall she placed food on the kitchen table, and beside it laid the big brooch that had been her mother's. It was the only thing of value that she had. And she left the kitchen door wide open.

The doors inside she securely fastened. Beside the bolt in the back one she drove in the steel and scissors; against it she piled the table and the stools. Underneath the lock of the front door she forced the handle of the spade, and the blade between the cracks in the flooring boards. Then the prop-stick, cut into lengths, held the top, as the spade held the middle. The windows were little more than portholes; she had nothing to fear through them.

She ate a few mouthfuls of food and drank a cup of milk. But she lighted no fire, and when night came, no candle, but crept with her baby to bed.

What woke her? The wonder was that she had slept—she had not meant to. But she was young, very young. Perhaps the shrinking of the galvanised roof—hardly though, since that was so usual. Yet something had set her heart beating wildly; but she lay quite still, only she put her arm over her baby. Then she had both round it, and she prayed, 'Little baby, little baby, don't wake!'

The moon's rays shone on the front of the house, and she saw one of the open cracks, quite close to where she lay, darken with a shadow. Then a protesting growl reached her; and she could fancy she heard the man turn hastily. She plainly heard the thud of something striking the dog's ribs, and the long flying strides of the animal as it howled and ran. Still watching, she saw the shadow darken every crack along the wall. She knew by the sounds that the man was trying every standpoint that might help him to see in; but how much he saw she could not tell. She thought of many things she might do to deceive him into the idea that she was not alone. But the sound of her voice would wake baby, and she dreaded that as though it were the only danger that threatened her. So she prayed, 'Little baby, don't wake, don't cry!'

Stealthily the man crept about. She knew he had his boots off, because of the vibration that his feet caused as he walked along the verandah to gauge the width of the little window in her room, and the resistance of the front door.

Then he went to the other end, and the uncertainty of what he was doing became unendurable. She had felt safer, far safer, while he was close, and she could watch and listen. She felt she must watch, but the great fear of wakening her baby again assailed her. She suddenly recalled that one of the slabs on that side of the house had shrunk in length as well as in width, and had once fallen out. It was held in position only by a wedge of wood underneath. What if he should discover that? The uncertainty increased her terror. She prayed as she gently raised herself with her little one in her arms, held tightly to her breast.

She thought of the knife, and shielded the baby's body with her hands and arms. Even the little feet she covered with its white gown, and the baby never murmured—it liked to be held so. Noiselessly she crossed to the other side, and stood where she could see and hear, but not be seen. He was trying every slab, and was very near to that with the wedge under it. Then she saw him find it; and heard the sound of the knife as bit by bit he began to cut away the wooden support.

She waited motionless, with her baby pressed tightly to her, though she knew that in another few minutes this man with the cruel eyes, lascivious mouth, and gleaming knife, would enter. One side of the slab tilted; he had only to cut away the remaining little end, when the slab, unless he held it, would fall outside.

She heard his jerked breathing as it kept time with the cuts of the knife, and the brush of his clothes as he rubbed the wall in his movements, for she was so still and quiet, that she did not even tremble. She knew when he ceased, and wondered why, being so well concealed; for he could not see her, and would not fear if he did, yet she heard him move cautiously away. Perhaps he expected the slab to fall—his motive puzzled her, and she moved even closer, and bent her body the better to listen. Ah! what sound was that? 'Listen! Listen!' she bade her heart—her heart that had kept so still, but now bounded with tumultuous throbs that dulled her ears. Nearer and nearer came the sounds, till the welcome thud of a horse's hoof rang out clearly.

'O God! O God! O God!' she panted, for they were very close before she could make sure. She rushed to the door, and with her baby in her arms tore frantically at its bolts and bars.

Out she darted at last, and running madly along, saw the horseman beyond her in the distance. She called to him in Christ's Name, in her babe's name, still flying like the wind with the speed that deadly peril gives. But the distance grew greater and greater between them, and when she reached the creek her prayers turned to wild shrieks, for there crouched the man she feared, with outstretched arms that caught her as she fell. She knew he was offering terms if she ceased to struggle and cry for help, though louder and louder did she cry for it, but it was only when the man's hand gripped her throat, that the cry of 'Murder' came from her lips. And when she ceased, the startled curlews took up the awful sound, and flew wailing 'Murder! Murder!' over the horseman's head.

'By God!' said the boundary rider, 'it's been a dingo right enough! Eight killed up here, and there's more down in the creek — a ewe and a lamb, I'll bet; and the lamb's alive!' He shut out the sky with his hand, and watched the crows that were circling round and round, nearing the earth one moment, and the next shooting skywards. By that he knew the lamb must be alive; even a dingo will spare a lamb sometimes.

Yes, the lamb was alive, and after the manner of lambs of its kind did not know its mother when the light came. It had sucked the still warm breasts, and laid its little head on her bosom, and slept till the morn. Then, when it looked at the swollen disfigured face, it wept and would have crept away, but for the hand that still clutched its little gown. Sleep was nodding its golden head and swaying its small body, and the crows were close, so close, to the mother's wide-open eyes, when the boundary rider galloped down.

'Jesus Christ!' he said, covering his eyes. He told afterwards how the little child held out its arms to him, and how he was forced to cut its gown that the dead hand held.

It was election time, and as usual the priest had selected a candidate. His choice was so obviously in the interests of the squatter, that Peter Hennessey's reason, for once in his life,

129

had over-ridden superstition, and he had dared promise his vote to another. Yet he was uneasy, and every time he woke in the night (and it was often), he heard the murmur of his mother's voice. It came through the partition, or under the door. If through the partition, he knew she was praying in her bed; but when the sounds came under the door, she was on her knees before the little Altar in the corner that enshrined the statue of the Blessed Virgin and Child.

'Mary, Mother of Christ! Save my son! Save him!' prayed she in the dairy as she strained and set the evening's milking. 'Sweet Mary! for the love of Christ, save him!' The grief in her old face made the morning meal so bitter, that to avoid her he came late to his dinner. It made him so cowardly, that he could not say good-bye to her, and when night fell on the eve of the election day, he rode off secretly.

He had thirty miles to ride to the township to record his vote. He cantered briskly along the great stretch of plain that had nothing but stunted cotton bush to play shadow to the full moon, which glorified a sky of earliest spring. The bruised incense of the flowering clover rose up to him, and the glory of the night appealed vaguely to his imagination, but he was preoccupied with his present act of revolt.

Vividly he saw his mother's agony when she would find him gone. Even at that moment, he felt sure, she was praying.

'Mary! Mother of Christ!' He repeated the invocation, half unconsciously, when suddenly to him, out of the stillness, came Christ's Name—called loudly in despairing accents.

'For Christ's sake! Christ's sake! Christ's sake!' called the voice. Good Catholic that he had been, he crossed himself before he dared to look back. Gliding across a ghostly patch of pipe-clay, he saw a white-robed figure with a babe clasped to her bosom.

All the superstitious awe of his race and religion swayed his brain. The moonlight on the gleaming clay was a 'heavenly light' to him, and he knew the white figure not for flesh and blood, but for the Virgin and Child of his mother's prayers. Then, good Catholic that once more he was, he put spurs to his horse's sides and galloped madly away.

His mother's prayers were answered, for Hennessey was the first to record his vote — for the priest's candidate. Then he sought the priest at home, but found that he was out rallying the voters. Still, under the influence of his blessed vision, Hennessey would not go near the public-houses, but wandered about the outskirts of the town for hours, keeping apart from the towns-people, and fasting as penance. He was subdued and mildly ecstatic, feeling as a repentant chastened child, who awaits only the kiss of peace.

And at last, as he stood in the graveyard crossing himself with reverent awe, he heard in the gathering twilight the roar of many voices crying the name of the victor at the election. It was well with the priest.

Again Hennessey sought him. He was at home, the housekeeper said, and led him into the dimly lighted study. His seat was immediately opposite a large picture, and as the housekeeper turned up the lamp, once more the face of the Madonna and Child looked down on him, but this time silently, peacefully. The half-parted lips of the Virgin were smiling with compassionate tenderness; her eyes seemed to beam with the forgiveness of an earthly mother for her erring but beloved child.

He fell on his knees in adoration. Transfixed, the wondering priest stood, for mingled with the adoration, 'My Lord and my God!' was the exaltation, 'And hast Thou chosen me?'

'What is it, Peter?' said the priest.

'Father,' he answered reverently; and with loosened tongue he poured forth the story of his vision.

'Great God!' shouted the priest, 'and you did not stop to save her! Do you not know? Have you not heard?'

Many miles further down the creek a man kept throwing an old cap into a water-hole. The dog would bring it out and lay it on the opposite side to where the man stood, but would not allow the man to catch him, though it was only to wash the blood of the sheep from his mouth and throat, for the sight of blood made the man tremble. But the dog also was guilty.

MARY GAUNT
(1861–1942)

Gaunt was born in Chiltern, Victoria, and was educated at Ballarat. She was one of the first two women students to enter Melbourne University. When her husband died in 1900, Gaunt moved to London and pursued her writing career. She travelled extensively and her experiences are reflected in her six travel books and seventeen works of fiction, including three volumes of short stories. She wrote three novels set in Africa with J. R. Essex. Her fiction often deals with strong independent women.

THE HUMBLING OF SERGEANT MAHONE

The first winter rains had come with a vengeance. The sun had set and the rain driving before a cutting west wind was coming down in torrents. It had washed the limestone streets of the little seaport town clean; they were slippery and slimy now, almost dangerous to walk upon, and the gas lamps at far distances apart – for gas is dear at Warrnambool – sent out long streaks of light that were reflected on the wet surfaces as in a mirror, and the gutters were running as high as the kerb. All the foot passengers had pulled their collars up above their ears and buttoned their coats close round them. The water streamed from the mackintosh cape of Sergeant Mahone, it trickled off his shiny helmet into his eyes, and his little pointed beard and fierce moustache were limp with wet.

It was a miserable winter's evening, and as he strolled along he whistled to himself a suitable tune, 'A policeman's lot is not a happy one'.

Another man came along the street briskly. He had on only a little short jacket, but he held up his head and put his hands in his pockets as if he defied the elements to hurt him. When he reached the sergeant he swung himself half round on his heels, and pursing up his lips, sent out a sound that was half a defiance and wholly a challenge. Sergeant Mahone stopped dead and the other man looked him full in the face in the gathering darkness and then went on. The light from the lamps streamed out of the big druggist's shop and showed every feature, and the sergeant knew him at once.

'That scamp Bryan O'Daly,' he said. 'Now what devilment is he up to?'

Bryan O'Daly's sins were many. He was known well to the police, but at present he was not wanted on any specific charge, and Sergeant Mahone as he walked on began turning over in his own mind what particular iniquity he might be meditating, for that was a challenge, he was sure enough of that. Burglary? No; burglary was not in Bryan's line. Assault? He had often enough been up for assault, but that was only when he got the drink in him, and was not premeditated. This was evidently premeditated. Bryan wasn't a bad sort if it weren't for that chronic trouble connected with that private still, and, of course — he brought down his hand on his thigh with a sounding smack — of course he was going to run a load of whisky down to the port, and he challenged him to stop him. Sergeant Mahone leaned up against the wall and laughed aloud. And O'Daly thought himself a better man than the whole force of the police ranged against him; and he laughed so loud and so long that the druggist coming to his door to see what fool had the heart to laugh on such a dismal night, remonstrated with him.

'Well, upon my word, sergeant, it's luck that must have come your way. Such a day, too. Pass a little of it on. Nothing to-day has come in at these doors bar five lodge prescriptions and a donkey who wanted a sixpenny bottle of lavender and musk. It won't pay for the gas let alone the rent.'

'Ah, my boy,' said the sergeant, wiping his eyes, 'we've got to look smart these times. It isn't once in a blue moon such a stroke of luck comes to a chap as I've had to-night,' and he vanished in the darkness and the rain in the direction of the police station.

The inspector listened to his story dubiously.

'It was just a piece of cheek on his part possibly.'

'Cheek, was it? He's the cheek of the old gentleman himself, the misbegotten beggar, but he meant it this time, sir. "I'll be runnin' a load of stuff as has never paid duty some time this week or next an' I dare ye to stop me." I'm as sure of it as if he said them very words.'

'Well, well, and it wouldn't tell us much if he did say them.'

The inspector was much inclined to leave Bryan O'Daly alone. He had a high respect for that gentleman's abilities.

'Sure,' said the sergeant earnestly, 'it can come but one way.

His selection's away out Nirrandira way, and the tea-tree scrub's that thick a cow couldn't get through let alone a load of whisky, and they can only cross the river at the bridge at Allansford. To be sure there's Slippery Jim's ford, but it's ten miles up and a devil of a crossing in the winter. If they want to bring the whisky down to Warrnambool, and they do, of course, it'll have to cross the bridge at Allansford. Give me a couple of men, sir, and I'll hold them like winking.'

It was another wet, wintry night when the sergeant and his two men took up their position on the lee side of a big box-thorn hedge on the Allansford road. The bridge was just beneath them, and when every now and again the moon burst through the heavy clouds they caught glimpses of the water running at the bottom of the high banks. Just opposite them was a farmhouse, and the stacks loomed large masses against the wintry sky, and from the chimney every now and then there came a burst of sparks that told of a roaring fire within. It was mighty dull work waiting, and men and horses were fidgeting wearily before even the watch had begun.

'May we light a pipe?' asked one of the troopers.

'Oh yes, it's an open road, and a whiff of tobacco will tell no tales. But mind now, no colloguing with the girls. It's the women spoil these little games.'

'Faith,' said the other man, 'there's only O'Brien's girl to be talking to in this God-forsaken place, and I'm thinking you've the whip hand of us there, sergeant.'

The sergeant smiled in the darkness. He certainly did flatter himself that Maggie O'Brien looked with a favourable eye on his stalwart proportions, and he had every intention, once he had brought off this little affair, to ask her to come and take possession of those comfortable quarters of his in the police camp. But on one thing he was determined—she should have no hand in this business.

It was a dreary night—so long and dreary. Once a belated wood cart passed, once a man riding like mad for the doctor, once a woman crying as if her heart were breaking. There might be tragedy behind all these — very likely there was — but the sergeant kept his men back and they passed. Then there came a long stretch of still, dark, cold, wet night when the minutes dragged like hours, and nothing happened to break the monotony. Long before the dawn broke, cold and grey and reluctant, the people at the farmhouse opposite were astir. The watchers could see the lanterns flitting about the milking yards, and by and by more than one cart passed on its way to the creamery.

Sergeant Mahone rose and stretched himself, and a trooper came trotting casually along the road.

'Here's our relief. Better luck to-morrow, boys.'

The next night was not so wet, but the wind was keen and cold and the sergeant was beginning to weary of his self-imposed task. Still he was not going to confess himself beaten. That stuff must come into Warrnambool, and it must come along this same road. There was no other way.

Nothing came along the road that night. It almost seemed as if all traffic had stopped, and it was very dull and cold. The men moved about uneasily, then hitched their horses to the post and rail fence and lay down under the hedge to get what shelter they could from the cutting wind. A sort of shadow seemed to cross the road a little higher up, and the sergeant started when he felt a hand on his arm. He would have spoken, but the hand quickly travelled to his lips.

'Whisht, don't be givin' me away, sergeant dear. It's yoursilf sure. I thought I seen ye last night. And what are yez waitin' for out in the cowld for the love av God?'

It was Maggie O'Brien, and the sergeant felt his heart glow, and it was no longer a bitter night.

'Whisht, me darling,' he said. 'I can't be telling ye my business. Run in now like a good girl. It's warmth and comfort ye've brought with your sweet self. Go in now.' And bolder than he had ever been, he drew her towards him and would have imprinted a kiss on the lips so close to his own. She yielded a moment, then drew herself quickly away.

'Get away with ye now. Ye're spillin' the tea. I'm just after bringing yez a quart pot of tea, and the scones is just out av the oven. But don't be tellin' a soul now. Me father'd pretty nigh kill me if he caught me.' She started to go back and then paused a moment. 'Yez can give the other poor chaps some, but don't be sayin' 'twas me as brought it,' and she vanished in the darkness and the wild wind covered the sound of her footsteps.

Now a quart pot of hot tea, well sugared and with plenty of cream in it, and another pot full to the brim of light, feathery, well-buttered scones straight from the oven is surely a very innocent love gift, and surely on a cold night a very welcome one. Not the stern inspector himself could have seen guile in such a present, and the sergeant called to the other two and shared it amicably with them.

'Ask no questions now, and be thankful,' said he, and Mounted Constable Campbell gave Mounted Constable O'Neill a poke in the ribs that made him choke over his first drink of tea, but they neither said a word.

Such a long night. Would it never end? The novelty had worn off, and more than once the sergeant had to shake his men into wakefulness. And nothing happened. Once a stray horse lolloped along as if something had startled it, and again a couple of calves strayed up as if looking for a suitable resting place. But nothing else happened, nothing at all. Sergeant Mahone began to think that Bryan O'Daly's crowing was just a piece of bravado to keep him on the alert and wear his life out.

He was very much of this opinion when the dawn broke, and he roused up his now nodding men and took them back to Warrnambool; but evening saw him starting out once more. He must have meant something, thought the sergeant. At any rate he would see the week out.

It was a worse night than ever. A biting wind came from the east that swept right across the road and made the box-thorn hedge that had stood them in such good stead for the last two nights as a breakwind of no use at all. The men groaned and the patient horses hunched themselves up and shivered in the bitter wind. Now if this night, too, were going to be a fruitless vigil their case would be hard indeed. One consolation the sergeant had that the men could not share. He hoped that before the evening had worn away Maggie O'Brien would pay him a visit. She had come about seven o'clock the night before, and not unnaturally as seven o'clock approached he expected her again.

But eight came, nine came; still no Maggie. By half past he had given up hope, and was as cross and grumpy as the men themselves. He drew his cape up over his face and huddled down close to his horse, when suddenly up to his nostrils was wafted the grateful odour he had been expecting all the evening, the smell of warm tea and hot buttered scones, and Maggie was beside him. Where she had come from heaven could only tell, but the sergeant was too pleased to see her to ask any questions.

'Is it yourself, Maggie darling?'

'I couldn't get away before,' she whispered, 'till that bold boy, Terence, was in bed. 'Tis the devil is in him for keepin' his eye on me. But, oh, sergeant darlin', 'tis an awful place yez got. Ye have to be holdin' on to everything for yer life,' as her shawl blew out behind her like a sail.

With one hand the gallant sergeant relieved her of the tea and scones, with the other he held down the shawl round her waist. She did not resist him, and he could see the light in her eyes and feel her warm breath on his cheek.

'Oh, sergeant dear, must ye stay out in the cowld here? It'll be the death of yez, to say nothing of the horses.'

'It doesn't matter about us,' whispered back the amorous sergeant, 'but if anything happens to the horses there'll be the devil to pay.'

''Tis a mercy if they don't take cowld here in the wind,' said she. 'See now, I'll open the gate and ye can put them in the shed in the paddock there. There's room for yez, too, if ye like. But don't tell father for the love av God, and come out before the milkin' in the mornin'.'

The sergeant considered a moment. It was undoubtedly a good offer, and it was made for love of him. He would accept it in the spirit in which it was made.

'God bless ye for a sweet colleen!'

The gate was locked, but the girl, who had grown bolder now and did not seem to mind if the men did see her, took a small key from her pocket and undid the padlock. She pointed to the shed looming up faintly against the dark sky.

'Yez can keep a good look-out along the road from there without bein' in the wind at all at all.'

The sergeant wanted to come back with her but she refused to let him. Her father, she declared, was wandering round, 'restless like wid the wind', and might ask questions.

It was delightfully comfortable in the shed out of reach of the shrieking wind. They all three ate hot scones and drank tea, and the sergeant leaned up against the wall and indulged in dreams of wildest happiness. If he got these smugglers he could have nothing left to wish for. Whether he got them or not he was a very happy man. The shed was close to the road. He would have sheltered there before but that the heavy gate was locked; but this little girl had made everything easy for him, God bless her! And if the night passed slowly it was not passing unpleasantly.

Nothing came along the road, nothing at all. Then about midnight Maggie came again. Her shawl was wrapped tight round her head and she was sobbing bitterly.

'For the love av God, sergeant, come outside wan minit.'

The other men turned their heads discreetly aside. The sergeant was going it strong, they thought; and for a quiet, decent-spoken girl, Maggie O'Brien was making the running.

'Och sergeant, oh sergeant! How'll my tongue be tellin' yez?'

'What is it, Maggie, my girl?' asked the sergeant tenderly, fully making up his mind that her father had found out about the tea and scones, and was making things unpleasant. It was on the tip of his tongue to tell her that she knew she had only to name the day, and the sooner the better, so that he was not much distressed.

'Oh that I should ever tell yez!'

'It's all right, my girl, sure 'tis all right.'

'Oh sure, 'tis all wrong it is. Me father's in the drink, dacint man, and it's murdherin' me mother he is. Come quick for the love av God!'

'Hold on, I'll get Campbell and—'

'Oh, sergeant dear, don't be shamin' me before them, an' me father, too, that's a dacint man when he hasn't the drink in him. It's not yoursilf he'd be mindin' but the other two.' She flung out her hands as if to show she would have none of them.

O'Brien was only a little wizened man. The sergeant thought he could overcome him with one hand if necesssary; so he just shouted back.

'Keep a good look-out, boys, I'll be back in a brace of shakes,' and followed her across the road and into the farmyard.

It was very dark here among the buildings, and he could not have found his way at all but that a warm hand stole into his and guided him. Everything was very still but for the shrieking of the wind among the roofs, and he was going to remark there were no sounds of a scuffle when an exclamation of 'Oh, murdher!' reached his ears, but it did not sound as if the person who cried out were really in fear of her life.

''Tis all right, mavourneen, he isn't hurting her.'

'Come in here,' said the girl, quickly drawing him into a little room with a brick floor and a tiny window high up in the wall. There was a guttering candle standing on one of the shelves, and he could see it was used as a place to keep the milk buckets and milk cans in. Everything was ready to begin work before dawn in the morning. 'Maybe he's quiet now and I wouldn't have ye in if he is. Stay here and I'll slip round and see.'

She gave the hand she held a tender squeeze and was out of the door without waiting for an answer, closing it after her. The sergeant thought he heard the bolt shot and the sound of scampering feet, and a cold sweat broke out over him as he began to think he had been sold. He strode up and put his stalwart shoulder to the door and shook it violently. But it was a stout door and it stood firm. He called, 'Maggie, Maggie O'Brien!' and his tones were by no means lover-like.

'Oh, sergeant dear,' came back the answer in quavering tones, 'sure 'tis that thief av the world, Terence, has played an ill trick on us.'

140

'Open the door, I say, open it.'

'Sure, 'tis Terence has the key. Kape quiet, sergeant dear, or me father'll be hearin' us.' Her voice was broken with sobs now, whether of laughter or tears the unlucky policeman could not tell, but he strongly suspected the former. His love was dying rapidly; still she was on the right side of the door, and it behoved him to see what blarney would do.

'Sure, Maggie dear, 'tis a bolt,' said he. 'Undo it now and I'll give yez the purtiest ring to be had in Warrnambool.'

But she was adamant to his blandishments.

'I'll be findin' Terence,' said she, and he heard her going out into the yard again.

The sergeant turned round, and in spite of his long training and discipline he smashed every tin and bucket he could lay his hands on; he yelled, he shouted, he flung himself against the door, and for all the effect it had upon the household they might have been dead. Then he paused and rested, looking grimly at the destruction he had wrought, and through the open window — that window which was too small for a man to pass through — he heard, borne on the wild wind, the sound he had waited so long to hear, the sound of heavily-laden drays coming down the road.

The language that respectable non-commissioned officer of police made use of on that occasion ought to have raised the roof, but it had absolutely no effect on the door. He listened desperately, there was a challenge, he knew it was Campbell's voice, and — Mahone cursed him solemnly for a born idiot — he only shouted:

'Hold up there, Bryan O'Daly, hold up or I'll make ye.'

'Serves me right,' groaned the poor prisoner, 'for leaving things to a fool-headed recruit. He's not such a fool as to take any notice of that. Ride after him, ride after him,' he yelled at the top of his voice, 'don't let him out of your sight.'

Alas, the wind that brought their voices down to him carried his away. Beside, Maggie O'Brien had very kindly locked the gate again, and they had no means of getting the horses out of the paddocks, as they refused to jump in the dark.

141

But O'Neill made another effort.

'Stop in the King's name,' he shouted, 'or I'll fire,' and the report of two carbines rang out.

'Worse than useless if they didn't shoot one of the horses,' groaned the unlucky sergeant as he heard the horses lashed to a gallop and fleeing down the road to the bridge. Even now a determined man might stop them at the bridge, and he yelled and shouted again, 'O'Brien, O'Brien, I call on you to help in the King's name.'

The constables were getting their horses out of the paddock by the summary method of breaking down the fence. He could hear them at it, but it was too late now. The drays were out of earshot, and he heard, too, a shambling footstep coming along to his door.

The bolt was shot back, and Farmer O'Brien stood before him, a candle in one hand, while with the other he was scratching his head sleepily.

'Faix! is hell broke loose! Och! sergeant!'

'Why didn't you come before?' asked the sergeant, angrily shaking him. 'Haven't I been shouting fit to raise the dead the last hour?'

'Och, faix, who'd be thinkin' 'twas the sergeant of perlice was smashin' my milk cans? Sure the boys does be always stravagin' after Maggie, and I thought she'd locked wan in for the fun av the thing. He'd pay up for certin.'

The sergeant groaned and threw the old man aside. In the gloom he caught sight of other forms and heard some stifled laughter. Then he dashed across the road, got his horse, and clattered down across the bridge.

But it was too late. The whisky was safely brought into Warrnambool and shipped for Melbourne. A nice little keg was also left on the verandah of the police station as a delicate present.

And that was not the end of it either, for Bryan O'Daly sued the police for sticking him up and firing on him when he was peacefully engaged in travelling along the main road with a couple of carts laden with skim milk from the Allansford butter factory.

'Oh yes, to be sure, 'twas late, but wan of the carts had broken down early in the evenin', an' 'tisn't poor folks can be payin' attention to the time when there's work to be done. An' how was the likes av him to know it was the perlice? He thought they was stickin' him up, an' he beat his horses to a gallop, an' 'twas only the Virgin herself saved him when they fired on him.'

And the judge severely reprimanded the police for interfering with an honest farmer and putting him in danger of his life, and he left the court triumphant, and married Maggie O'Brien before the month was out.

And at Warrnambool they always call whisky skim milk.

LAURA PALMER-ARCHER
(1864–1929)

Laura Palmer-Archer was the wife of a station-owner. She contributed short stories to the *Australasian* and the *Australian Town and Country Journal*. Her first published work was a collection of short stories, *Racing in the Never Never* (1899). These stories and others were republished in *A Bush Honeymoon and Other Stories* (1904). Her lively, humorous stories deal with bush life in the 1890s.

A BUSH HONEYMOON

'Oh that a man might know the end of this day's business ere it
comes.' — *Julius Caesar.*

We were married at six in the morning, and now my brand-new
husband and myself are starting to our station home, sixty-five
miles from the little Queensland township. At the back of the
buggy is seated a sleepy-looking old nigger, known as 'Dozy',
whose mission in life is to open gates for Jack, my newly-acquired
spouse.

We are a very brand-new pair indeed. I in the snowiest of white
piqué costumes, white gloves, and white doeskin shoes, and the
daintiest white sailor hat placed atop of my sunny tresses.

I am blue-eyed, fair, and nineteen, but look three years younger.
Jack is seven-and-twenty — quite an old fogey. He looks 'monstrous well', I think, as I steal a glance at him in his serge suit,
spotless linen, and boyish sailor hat. In truth, we are a 'band-boxy'
young couple. My new saddle and bridle are stowed away in the
buggy.

I have noticed Dozy putting in two spades and an axe. Not being
a bush girl, I did not understand why these articles should be
required. A well-filled luncheon basket and strapful of rugs repose
at our feet; but luggage has gone on before, to save weight.

My husband is driving a bridal-like team of four greys, and
we are to have two relays of horses on the journey.

It had been raining in the little township for some days, and
I have heard that some parts of the road are *rough travelling*.

The morning air is balmy, every shrub flings its exquisite
perfume to us, and we pass through groves of wild limes tangled
together by sweet-smelling blossoming vines, and through clusters
of wild orange trees, with their glossy foliage gemmed here and

145

there with tasselled white blossoms. White-and-yellow butterflies flit everywhere.

'Good omens for our happiness, darling!' says Jack, pointing to the butterflies and blossoms.

'Ye-es,' I replied with a gaspy effort; but I am not used to husbands yet; besides, I am a prosaic soul. Jack is sentimental enough for one household. He puts his arm round my waist, and looks unutterable things into my eyes. By all the laws and tenets of new-made brides, I should be nestling to my husband's side, but I am matter-of-fact to a degree; so I put my hat straight — it has suffered during this burst of affection — and then I look up into his face, smile as sweetly as I know how, and squeeze his hand. This answers finely, and Jack smiles like a seraph. I ask the name of his housekeeper, who is to have my home in readiness, and converse about our occupations and tastes. I inform Jack that I adore gardening. He doesn't seem to like these topics, so I squeeze his hand at intervals, keeping a wary eye on Dozy; but true to his name, he is fast asleep, and tumbles out by intuition at the gates he has to open for us.

For twenty miles Jack rhapsodises, and I squeeze his hand in return. It is getting hot and muggy. The smart buggy begins to feel knobby and uncomfortable, and the ruts and gullies shake one horribly. I pull down my gossamer veil, and lift one corner, when occasion demands.

'First change,' says Jack, as we come to a yard where four horses are grazing under the superintendence of a man called Bill.

'Looks dark over there, Bill,' says Jack, pointing to black clouds.

'It does, sir.'

'How's the track farther along, Bill?'

'Heavy and *boggy*; most of the creeks is running. We've had two inches of rain since yer left; the river's pretty high too.'

'The deuce it is!' says Jack. 'Look here, darling; it would be awful to have to go back again, wouldn't it?'

'*Very awful!* Oh, don't let us go back; I'd rather go through any weather than return.'

146

Our fresh horses are now put in, the discarded ones are all following the buggy like dogs. Bill acts as outrider; there are broken boughs lying in all directions, effects of a recent windstorm. Bill removes these obstacles from our road. Dozy is roused up, and pressed into the service. When they come to a fallen tree, the axe is produced and the tree chopped into movable pieces. The sky has become black, with a low rumble of thunder; and then I feel a raindrop on my cheek; then come heavy drops, succeeded by a steady, soaking rain.

'Strikes me we're booked for a storm,' says Jack. He muffles me in rugs and macintosh.

'*Shake it up* now, and let's see what you're made of,' he says, giving the horses a few vigorous cuts.

I fear a thunderstorm, so I cover up my face for some minutes. It is hot and stifling. Now the buggy begins to go *dead slow.*

'We're coming to the worst part of the track,' says Jack. 'This black soil sticks like glue, and we've two miles of it to go through.'

I glance at the wheels. They are *picking up* loamy soil, which sticks like glue. They have a rim six inches wide in ten minutes. The horses pull and strain under the weight.

'Wheels, Dozy,' says Jack. 'Nell darling, hold the horses;' and he and Dozy take spades and set to work to clean the wheels. When they finish, the horses, feeling the relief and a strange hand, start off.

The rain is beating in their faces. I can't drive, but I hang on might and main to the reins and lean back, and mercifully they stop.

Jack and Dozy get up and we start again. Jack resumes his endearments. The lash of his whip tangles in the wheel and draws in the handle. We pull up, and I fancy Jack says 'Damn it!'. . . Oh!

Dozy disentangles the whip, and gives it to Jack, who wipes the lash with his handkerchief, to free it from axle grease, and mops his face unthinkingly a moment after. This leaves a tarry streak across his forehead. I feel a sharp thump between my shoulders, and think it is a joke of Jack's, so say nothing; then comes another blow which brings the tears to my eyes. 'I didn't know you liked practical jokes,' I say.

'What do you mean, Nell?' Jack says, in a hurt voice.

'Didn't you strike my shoulder?'

'No, my darling;' and just then an enormous clod of earth flies over us and strikes the head of our leaders. These clods now fill the bottom of the buggy rapidly.

'Wheels, Dozy,' says Jack.

'No. Let Dozy hold the horses; I'll help with the wheels. I told you I was fond of gardening.' I tear off my rain-sodden gloves and seize a spade, and we clean the wheels. My hat is rakishly askew, and my fringe is hanging in dank rats' tails on my forehead. Poor Jack looks woeful. It is raining heavens hard! The wet has washed the glue out of his sailor hat; it has run down his face and blended with the tarry streak. We are both muddy from head to foot, and my white doeskin shoes — what do they look like?

Then we discover it is lunch time. My husband deposits me on a wet log; my feet are in a pool. I am too tired to care. My hands are blistered from the spade. Alas for us! our luck is out: our luncheon is spoilt by the rain; everything is pulp; oyster patties and chicken sandwiches are doughy masses; the cakes a sort of horrible moist plum-pudding! I try some soaking peaches, and find a flask of whisky, which I present to Jack. The rain trickles down my neck and up my sleeves, and it 'squishes' out of my doeskin gloves and shoes. I am the moistest and most miserable young person alive! I am getting cross. I could cry, but I won't give in. We mount into the buggy again and resume the road. We clean the wheels thrice more. Now we are coming to a gravelly part of the country. There is water lying everywhere. Bill and the spare horses catch us up, and between the noise of the galloping horses and the pour of rain and the wind, he can scarcely be heard speaking; he comes close alongside, and with one hand to the side of his mouth makes himself heard.

'Just seen a *traveller*; all the *creeks is up*, and the river pretty near a *banker* near Mulligan's. Water's comin' down fast. You'll have to go smart to get over with the buggy.'

Jack looks horrified. He lashes the horses afresh; we are now going through sheets of water, the horses splashing it over our heads; we cross our first creek; the water comes into the floor of the buggy, which is unpleasant. In a short time we come to a second creek; it looks very ugly.

'Find us a crossing, Bill,' shouts Jack.

Bill's horse splodges down the steep bank, and Bill's oilskin coat-tails swim on the water. 'Too deep,' he shouts; 'we'll have to go farther up.'

I am now wet up to my poor knees. As we go through, the trace of one of our leaders floats up, and when we emerge at the other side he is kicking furiously. Jack gets in a fury, and shouts at Bill and Dozy to settle the trace. He asks them, 'Don't they *see* the danger?' and 'don't they think the buggy, and what's in it' (poor bedraggled me), 'worth saving and worth looking after?'

The storm rages, and the rain drives in blinding torrents. We are now nearly fifty miles on our road. We come to a boggy place, and the horses go over their fetlocks in mud.

When we get clear, we put on the pace. Jack's idea is to get to the river before too great a quantity of water is coming down, and we race along; the horses go splendidly. We arrive at Mulligan's. Mulligan is an old boundary rider, who lives here with his two daughters. He is the dirtiest old person I have ever seen. He produces 'tay' and '*car'way* bread', as he calls it. I see Jack proceeding to eat and drink. I steal to his side and whisper, 'Did Mulligan make that bread?'

'He did; it's a hobby he has.'

'Sure?' say I.

'Quite.'

'Do you think he was wearing *that* shirt?' I say, pointing a horrified finger at him.

'Most probably.'

'Then I admire your pluck for eating it!'

'I suppose yez knows the river's a banker?' says Mulligan. 'Faith, yez had better go no farther the day; sthay the noight here. I'll make yez very comfortable. The river was ashwim an hour ago.'

I glance round the hut: a goat and her family are under the

table; a hen roosts on the flour bag; the pig is probably under his bed.

'My gerruls will be in soon; 'tis afther the cows they are; but they'll make a few tarts for ye. Now — do stay,' he says coaxingly.

We might have spared our racing, I think bitterly, if the river is so deep already. I look imploringly at Jack, and we take leave of Mulligan. Jack borrows a coil of rope, and we start. As we reach the river, Jack stands up and looks anxiously at the stream. The water is level with the banks. It is a surging, angry, whirling tide. We pull up. Bill and the horses go over first; it is a good swim, their heads are just visible over the water.

'Impossible to get the buggy over,' says Jack. 'I can swim a horse over, but about you — '

'I *can't* swim,' I whimper, 'and I *won't* stay at Mulligan's, and we *must* get home somehow.' I wring my hands. What a diabolical plight we're in!

We get out of the buggy. Jack and Dozy unyoke the horses and tether them to trees. Jack puts my saddle on to one, and mounts another bareback; he ties one end of the rope to a stout tree, and makes a running sling of another piece of rope; he whispers to Dozy, and, driving the saddled horse before him, plunges in. Just as he gets into the deepest part the horse *turns turtle*. Jack disappears. I shriek. Jack strikes out vigorously and gains the far side.

What is to become of me?

Now Jack connects the end of the rope he has taken over with another tree, almost in a straight line.

'Now then, Nell,' shouts Jack from the bank, 'don't be nervous, sweetheart; watch how Dozy works the rope — you're to do exactly the same.'

Dozy seats himself in the rope sling, and works it a yard or two, then comes back.

'No harm, plenty safe, Missee.'

'It *looks* safe,' I say, with scorn. 'Oh, I can't, I *can't*, Jack; I'd rather die,' I wail hysterically and wring my hands.

'You must, you must try it; let me see how brave you are.' I see it has to be done, so Dozy helps me down the bank. I seat myself in the sling and work it a little; I am shaking like a leaf.

'Bravo! bravo!' from Jack. Now I am just in the middle of the river; suddenly the rope sags with my weight. I go deeper. 'Swish, swash.' The water closes over my head – my nose and mouth are filling! my ears sing! I'm drowning! I give muffled shrieks. 'Head up! head up! Hold on Nell; you're safe!' and the rope is rapidly tightened just in time; I was nearly exhausted. I work on and gain the bank. Jack takes me in his arms, pulls me up, and forces whisky down my throat. I throw myself on the ground and cry like a baby. My hair is hanging in a damp mass to my waist; my teeth are chattering.

'Now, Nell, we must ride the rest of the way for our lives,' says Jack, lifting me into the saddle. He doesn't give me time to think; he puts the reins and a switch into my hands; he is riding bareback; and off we go – a sorry pair – through the merciless rain. I cry, and the tears roll down my cheeks; the evening is closing in rapidly; the bats circle round our heads; my mare slips, and shies at everything; my frock has worked up, and is displaying my limbs freely. I am aching all over; the ride is interminable; I turn a deaf ear to Jack's lover-like speeches. I'm really sorry now I ever *saw* him, much less married him. Shall we *ever* reach home?

'Nell, you only look fifteen,' says Jack.

'I *feel* fifteen *hundred*,' I reply crossly.

'Two miles more to home,' says Jack. 'Look, you can see the house, my darling.'

'Th-th-the s-s-sooner we get there the better,' answers his darling waspishly between her chattering teeth.

Thank Heaven! we at last reach the garden gate. Jack lifts me off. 'Run in,' he says; 'Mrs Sullivan will attend to you. I'll just take these horses up to the stables.'

I walk wearily up to the house by the path. Light glows through the ruby curtains. I enter the hall, and seat myself upon a chair to wait for Jack. The dining-room door is open: a table daintily set for two; a mass of delicate pink silk, bestrewn with fairy-like fern fronds, is down the table. An iced bridal cake towers in the centre. I take off my hat and rest my head on the hall table. Would Jack ever come? I am roused by my shoulder being shaken by a motherly dame with a wonderful cap.

'How did yez get in here, anyhow?' she says indignantly. 'Me clean hall, and ye with the dirtiest boots ever I see!'

What a reception for a bride! My voice fails me.

'Me hall in this condition, and me expectin' the masther and new missus anny minnit! Be off with yez to the kitchen,' she says, shooing me with her skirts. 'Till me now, is it wan of Mulligan's gerruls ye are?'

One of Mulligan's girls! This is indeed the last straw! 'I *am* your mistress,' I say, rising to my feet with all the dignity I can muster, and then my head gets strange; and I hear a humming sound, as of a thousand bees; the hall and Mrs Sullivan spin round like a teetotum. The roses in her cap keep bobbing and nodding at me.

'Holy Mother of God! she's fainting, she is!' is all I hear as I collapse limply into the arms of Mrs Sullivan.

ADA HOLMAN
(1869–1949)

Holman was born in Ballarat, Victoria. She wrote for the *Sydney Mail* and the *Sydney Morning Herald* sometimes using the pseudonyms 'Marcus Malcolm', 'Nardoo', or 'Myee'. She published a collection of travel articles, several works of children's fiction, an autobiography, several plays and one political novel, *Sport of the Gods*. Some strong feminist ideas are presented in one of her plays, *The Premier's Wife*.

THE NEW CARPET

Casual callers at Mrs Pierce's weather-board cottage on the edge of her selection were never encouraged to stay too long. Time was too precious a commodity for the widow to waste any of it in chat. Even the local scandals her daughters would have loved to discuss were brushed aside by Mrs Pierce with, 'Well, it's about time to start milking,' or 'Bless me! that jam will be boiling over.'

Bush hospitality was a tradition, of course, but when people worked as she and her sons and daughters did, four cups of tea ought to content anyone, without sitting and sitting as though they had no chairs at home.

Bright young Ellice Walker from the station was a privileged visitor who never taxed hospitality too far. Every member of the family liked to see her tie up her horse at the front gate and drop in for odd moments at any time of day.

'We'll ask Miss Walker about this,' Harriet would say on getting hold of a new recipe for shortcake; 'the quantities look all wrong to me'; or, 'I'd like Ellice Walker's opinion on that short skirt you're wearing, Nell, or what she thinks of Bet cutting her hair off in that silly way.' In fact, Ellice's advice was continually asked, if seldom followed. Sometimes even she volunteered counsel, for she knew Mrs Pierce regarded her as a friend.

The girl knew the family to be far from poverty-stricken, and it vexed her to see them denying themselves every comfort, even necessities, for, she supposed, some problematic 'rainy day'. Although their butter was famous in the district, none ever appeared on their table, every pound being taken into the township for sale. It was the same with the hams, bacon, eggs, vegetables, and honey — all were for the consumption of others, while they themselves lived in beggarly fashion.

This state of things vexed Ellice, and one day when she had

154

been emphatic about its folly Mrs Pierce unburdened herself.

'You see, Miss Walker, I want to get a velvet-pile carpet for the sitting-room. I've been saving up for years, but something else always wanted the money — my husband's operation, Nell's tonsils, and all that; but these last two years I made up my mind to put the egg and butter money aside for it, and I think I'll be able to get it by Christmas. The girls agree we won't have none but a good one, and that means, as you know, a pretty penny.'

Ellice supposed that the absence of a carpet was the reason why 'the sitting-room' was never used. She had accidentally had one or two peeps into this dismal, close apartment, and had been thankful that she was allowed to enjoy the acquaintance of the family amid the plain comfort of the kitchen-dining-room, with its big open fireplace and freedom from all kickshaws, rather than surrounded by horsehair furniture and marvellous crockery vases, not to mention the enlarged photograph of the late Henry Pierce.

The carpet fund was being built up steadily, and Ellice found herself sharing the family excitement. She would hear with distress of a bad week when butter was 'down' and rejoice when eggs went soaring and Harriet's hens rose nobly to the occasion.

It was about a week or two before Christmas that Jimmy, Mrs Pierce's youngest, came breathless to the station, having run the whole of the two miles from the selection.

'Please, Miss Walker, Mother says can you come up first thing tomorrow. We've got the new carpet up from Melbourne and we're going to lay it this afternoon.'

Ellice promised readily, and the next morning, if not quite first thing, at least at a very early hour, rode over to Mrs Pierce's.

'It's a real beauty, Miss Walker,' said the widow, all wrinkling smiles.

With a ceremony that bordered on solemnity she flung open the parlour door and gently pushed Ellice inside. The visitor turned in speechless amazement from the full blankness that met her eyes. She had been prepared for blue roses on a green ground, running up red lattices, but this dull, calico-like article was a distinct shock. Her disappointment, however, was premature. Mrs Pierce was taking slow, important steps across the room, and reaching the corner by the one window, she carefully drew back what Miss Walker learnt was a 'crumb-cloth', and disclosed an even more gorgeous 'velvet-pile' than that conjured up by Ellice's imagination.

'See,' said Mrs Pierce, 'I got a crumb-cloth to preserve it — that was two pounds more, but then the carpet'll last for ever.'

When it was to be supposed that her visitor had sufficiently feasted her eyes on the square foot or so of carpet that had been made visible, its owner deftly drew the covering over it once more, took a packet of tacks and a small hammer from the window-sill, and fastened it tightly over the resplendent vision.

'Why, Mrs Pierce, you're not going to keep the carpet hidden, are you?' remonstrated Ellice.

'Yes, indeed; I'm not going to let a valuable carpet like that be trodden on and wore out and faded by the sun, surely!'

'But isn't the crumb-cloth ever coming off — not when you have visitors say?'

'When I have visitors!' said Mrs Pierce, 'that's just what I got the cloth for. Fancy the state that lovely velvet-pile would be in after a dozen pairs of feet traipsing over it on a Sunday afternoon! That'd be worse than the sun. You don't think, do you, Miss Walker, I'll ever get another carpet? So it isn't likely I can afford to get this wore out, is it?'

Ellice was speechless. She did want to say that Mrs Pierce would have done better to have simply bought a crumb-cloth and allowed the world to imagine a carpet below. Then the money might have been expended on comforts for herself and the children rather than on a luxury no one was to see and would have to take the owner's word for believing to exist.

Such reasoning, it was obvious, would be wasted on Mrs Pierce. To her the pride and joy of possession was that for which she had scorned delights and lived laborious days.

On the lines of Ellice's argument, carpet and sitting-room were equally superfluous, for the family would have thought it ostentatious to use the parlour for their own comfort, while the fear of 'wearing things out' kept them from devoting it to visitors. As a matter of fact, the last occasion on which it had been thrown open was for Henry's funeral service, the occasion on which the shabbiness of the old carpet had so distressed his widow.

Ellice accepted the position as typical and inevitable, and though she never saw the carpet again, continued to hear of its well-being when the sitting-room got its periodical 'doing out' and the sacred floor covering a reverential sweeping.

ETHEL ROBERTSON
('HENRY HANDEL RICHARDSON')
(1870–1946)

'Richardson' was born in Melbourne and was educated at the Presbyterian Ladies' College. Her novel, *The Getting of Wisdom* (1910), is based on her experiences as a boarder there. Her mother took her to Europe to study music, but she abandoned it for writing. *Maurice Guest* (1908), her first novel, is about the problems of a young musician. In 1903 'Richardson' moved to London and isolated herself in order to write, encouraged and attended to by her husband and later her companion-secretary. She returned to Australia only once in 1912 to do research for her trilogy, *The Fortunes of Richard Mahony*, which was based on her father's life. This work is considered a classic in Australian literature.

'Richardson' published one other novel, *The Young Cosima* (1939), three collections of short stories and an unfinished autobiography. She received the Australian Literature Society's Gold Medal in 1929, and was nominated for the Nobel Prize in 1932.

CONVERSATION IN A PANTRY

It was no use, she simply could not sleep. She had tried lying all sorts of ways: with the blanket pulled over her or the blanket off; with her knees doubled up to her chin or stretched so straight that her feet nearly touched the bottom of the bed; on her back with her hands under her neck, or with her face burrowed in the pillow. Nothing helped. Going on in her she could still feel the bumps and lurches of the coach in which she had ridden most of that day. Then the log that had been smouldering in the brick fireplace burnt away in the middle, and collapsed with a crash; and the two ends, rolling together, broke into flames again. These threw shadows which ran about the ceiling, and up and down the white walls, like strange animals.

She was spending the night with Alice, and they had had a fire 'just for luxury', and had sat by it for nearly an hour before going to bed. It would be her last chance of anything like that, Alice said: in schools, you never had fires, and all lights went out to the minute. And their talk had been fearfully interesting. For Alice was in love — she was over seventeen — and had told her about it just as if she was grown up, too; looking into the fire with ever such a funny little smile, and her blue eyes quite small behind her thick, curly lashes.

'Oh, don't you wish we could see into the future, Trix? And what it's going to bring us?'

But though she said yes, she wasn't sure if she did, really; she liked surprises better. Besides, all the last part of the time Alice talked, she had been screwing up her courage to put a question. But she hadn't managed to get it out. And that was one reason why now she couldn't sleep.

With a fresh toss, she sighed gustily. And, where her tumblings and fidgetings had ailed, this sound called her companion back from the downy meadows.

'What's the matter, child? Aren't you asleep yet?'

'No, I simply can't.'

Alice sat up in bed, and shook her hair back from her face. 'You're over-excited. Try a drink of water.'

'I have. I've drunk it all up.'

'Then you must be hungry.'

'Well, yes, I am perhaps . . . a little.'

'Come on then, let's forage.' And throwing back the sheet, the elder girl slid her feet to the floor.

One tall white figure, one short, they opened the door and stepped out on the verandah.

Here it was almost as bright as day; for the moon hung like a round cheese in the sky, and drenched everything with its light. Barefoot they pattered, the joins in the verandah floorboards, which had risen, cutting out their soles. Had they to pass open windows, dark holes in which people lay sleeping, Alice laid a finger on her lips. From one of these came the sound of snores — harsh snores of the chromatic kind, which went up the scale and down, over and over again, without a pause.

Turning a corner, they stepped off the verandah and took a few steps on hard pebbly ground. Inside the pantry, which was a large outhouse, there were sharp contrasts of bluish-white moonlight and black shadows.

Swiftly Alice skimmed the familiar shelves. 'Here's lemon cheese-cakes . . . and jam tarts . . . and gingersnaps . . . and pound cake. But I can't start you on these, or you'd be sick.' And cutting a round off a homemade loaf, she spread it thickly with dairy butter, topped by a layer of quince jelly. 'There, that's more wholesome.'

Oh, had anything ever tasted so delicious? . . . as this slice eaten at dead of night. Perched on an empty, upturned kerosene-tin, the young girl munched and munched, holding her empty hand outspread below, lest the quivering jelly glide over the crust's edge.

Alice took a cheese-cake and sat down on a lidded basket. 'I say, *did* you hear Father? Oh, Trix, wouldn't it be positively too awful if one discovered *afterwards*, one had married a man who snored?'

The muncher made no answer: the indelicacy of the question stunned her: all in the dark as she was, she felt her face flame. And yet . . . was this not perhaps the very chance she had been waiting for? If Alice could say such a thing, out loud, without embarrassment . . . Hastily squeezing down her last titbit — she felt it travel, overlarge, the full length of her gullet — she licked her jellied fingers clean and took the plunge.

'Dallie, there's something I . . . I want to ask you something . . . something I want to know.'

'Fire away!' said Alice, and went on nibbling at the pastry-edging that trimmed her tartlet.

'Yes. But . . . well, I don't quite . . . I mean I . . .'

'Like that, is it? Wait a tick,' and rather more rapidly than she had intended, Alice bolted her luscious circle of lemon-cheese, picked up her basket and planted it beside the tin. 'Now then.'

Shut away in this outhouse, the young girl might have cried her words aloud. But leaning over till she found the shell of her friend's ear, she deposited them safely inside. Alice, who was ticklish, gave an involuntary shudder. But as the sense of the question dawned on her, she sat up very stiff and straight, and echoed perturbed: '*How*? Oh, but Kid, I'm not sure — not at all sure — whether you ought to know. At your age!' said seventeen to thirteen.

'But I must, Dallie.'

'But why, my dear?'

'Because of something Ruth said.'

'Oh, Ruth!' said Alice scornfully. 'Trust Ruth for saying the wrong thing. What was it?'

'Why, that . . . now I was growing up . . . was as good as grown up . . . I must take care, for . . . for fear . . . But, Dallie, how can I? . . if I don't know?' This last question came out with a rush, and with a kind of click in the throat.

'Well, well! I always have felt sorry for you children, with no mother but only Ruth to bring you up — and she for ever prinking before her glass. But you know you'll be perfectly safe at school, Trix. They'll look after you, never fear!'

161

But there was more to come.

It was Ella, it seemed, Ella Morrison, who was two years older than her, who'd begun it. She'd said her mother said now she mustn't let the boys kiss her any more.

'And you have, eh?'

Trixie's nod was so small that it had to be guessed at. Haltingly, word by word, the story came out. It had been at Christmas, at a big party, and they were playing games. And she and some others, all boys, had gone off to hide from the rest, and they'd climbed into the hayloft, Harry MacGillivray among them; and she rather liked Harry, and he liked her, and the other boys knew it and teased them. And then they said he wasn't game to kiss her and dared him to. And she didn't want him to, not a bit . . . or only a teeny weeny bit . . . and anyhow she wasn't going to let him, there before them all. But the other boys grabbed her, and one held her arms and another her legs and another her neck, so that he could. And he did — three times — hard. She'd been as angry as anything; she'd hit them all round. But only angry. Afterwards, though . . . when Ellie told her what her mother had said . . . and now Ruth . . .

But she got no further; for Alice had thrown back her head and was shaking with ill-repressed laughter. 'Oh, you babe . . . you blessed infant, you! Why, child, there was no more harm in that than . . . well, than in this!' And pulling the girl to her she kissed her soundly, some half-dozen times, with scant pause between. An embarrassing embrace, from which Trixie made uneasy haste to free herself; for Alice was plump, and her nightgown thin.

'No, you can make your little mind easy,' continued the elder girl on recovering her breath. 'Larking's all that was and couldn't hurt a fly. *It's what larking leads to*,' said Alice, and her voice sank, till it was hollow with mystery.

'What does it?'

'Ah!' said Alice in the same sepulchral tone. 'You asked me just now how babies came. Well *that's how*, my dear.'

'Yes, but . . .'

162

'Come, you've read your Bible, haven't you? The Garden of Eden, and so on? And male and female created He them?'

'But . . .'

'Well, Trix, in *my* opinion, you ought to be content with that . . . in the meanwhile. Time enough for more when . . . well, when you're married, my dear.' Not for the world would Alice have admitted her own lack of preciser knowledge, or have uncovered to the day her private imaginings of the great unknown.

'But suppose I . . . Not *every* lady gets married, Dallie! And then I'd never know.'

'And wouldn't need to. But I don't think there's much fear of that, Trix! You're not the stuff old maids are made of,' said Alice sturdily, welcoming the side issue.

Affectionately Trixie snuggled up to her friend. This tribute was most consoling. (How awful should nobody want you, you remain unchosen!) All the same she did not yield; a real worm for knowledge gnawed in her. 'Still, I don't quite see . . . truly I don't, Dallie . . . how you *can* "take care", if you don't know how.'

At this outlandish persistence Alice drew a heavy sigh. 'But, child, there's surely something in you . . . at least if there isn't there ought to be . . . that tells you what's skylarking and what isn't? Just you think of undressing. Suppose you began to take your clothes off in front of somebody, somebody who was a stranger to you, wouldn't something in you stop you by saying: it isn't done, it's not *nice*?'

'Gracious, yes!' cried Trixie hotly. 'I should think so indeed!' (Though she could not imagine herself *beginning*.) But here, for some reason, what Alice had said about a husband who snored came back to her, and got tangled up with the later question. 'But, Dallie, you have to . . . do that, take your clothes off . . . haven't you? . . if you . . . sleep in the same bed with somebody,' was what she wanted to say, but the words simply would not come out.

Alice understood. 'But *only* if you're married, Trixie! And then, it's different. Then everything's allowed, my dear. Once you're married, it doesn't matter what you do.'

'Oh, doesn't it?' echoed Trixie feebly, and her cheeks turned so hot that they scorched. For at Alice's words horrid things, things she was ashamed even to think, came rushing into her mind, upsetting everything she had been taught or told since she was a little child. But *she* wouldn't be like that, no, never, no matter how much she was married; there would always be something in *her* that would say 'don't, it's not nice'.

A silence followed, in which she could hear her own heart beating. Then, out of a kind of despair, she asked: 'Oh, *why* are men and women, Dallie? Why have they got to be?'

'Well, now, really!' said Alice, startled and sincerely shocked. 'I hope to goodness you're not going to turn irreligious, and begin criticising what God has done and how He's made us?'

'Of course not! I know everything He does is right,' vowed Trixie, the more hotly because she couldn't down the naughty thought: if He's got all that power, then I don't see why He couldn't have arranged things differently, let them happen without . . . well, without all this bother . . . and so many things you weren't supposed to know . . . and what you were allowed to, so . . . so unpleasant. Yes, it *was* unpleasant, when you thought of undressing . . . and the snores . . . and—and everything.

And then quite suddenly and disconcertingly came a memory of Alice sitting looking into the fire, telling about her sweetheart. She had never known before that Alice was so pretty, with dimples round her mouth, and her eyes all shady. Oh, could it mean that . . . yes, it must: Alice simply didn't *mind*.

Almost as if this thought had passed to her, Alice said: 'Just you wait till you fall in love, Trix, and then it'll be different—as different as chalk from cheese. Then you'll be only too glad, my dear, that we're not all the same—all men or all women. Love's something that goes right through you, child, I couldn't even begin to describe it—and you wouldn't understand it if I did—but once you're in love, you can't think of anything else, and it gives you such a strange feeling here that it almost chokes you!'—and laying one hand over the other on the place where she believed her heart to be, Alice pressed hard. 'Why, only to be in the same room with him makes you happy, and if you know he's feeling the same, and that he likes to look at you and to hold your hand — oh, Trix, it's just Heaven!'

I do believe she'd even like him snoring, thought Trixie in dismay. (But perhaps it was only *old* men who snored.) Confused and depressed, she could not think of anything to reply. Alice did not speak again either, and there was a long silence, in which, though it was too dark to see her, Trixie guessed she would have the same funny little smile round her mouth and the same funny half-shut eyes, from thinking about George. Oh dear! what a muddle everything was.

'But come!' cried Alice, starting up from her dreams. 'To bed and to sleep with you, young woman, or we shall never get you up in time for the morning coach. Help yourself to a couple of cheese-cakes . . . we can eat them as we go.'

Tartlets in hand, back they stole along the moon-blanched verandah; back past the row of dark windows, past the chromatic snores — to Trixie's ears these had now a strange and sinister significance — guided by a moon which, riding at the top of the sky, had shrunk to the size of a pippin.

EDITH JOAN LYTTLETON
('G.B. LANCASTER')
(1874–1945)

'Lancaster' was born in Tasmania but spent part of her childhood in New Zealand. She travelled extensively and lived for some time in Australia, contributing stories to the *Bulletin* and the *Lone Hand*. She published thirteen works of fiction. *Pageant* (1933), a novel which presents the fortunes of a Tasmanian family from 1826 to the twentieth century, won the Australian Literature Society's Gold Medal.

A JOB FOR THE PARSON

'A what?' demanded Jacky.

The Old Woman pulled a kerosene-tin from its home on the shelf running round the shanty wall, puckered her lined forehead at its lightness, and carried it into the kitchen.

'Parson,' she called, over her shoulder. 'A parson. That's what.'

Jacky slowly drew out the nail that buttoned his trousers to his suspenders, and thrust it in again. Then he followed to the kitchen, where the Old Woman was scraping the last stickiness of brown sugar from the kerosene-tin.

'Wot's a parson?' he said, standing on one bare leg, and scraping his calf with the curled toes of the other foot.

'A parson?' The Old Woman glanced up with a streak of colour in her faded cheek. 'He's a chap what buries yer, an' an' gives yer names; but I've forgot what they calls that. An' he splices yer. He spliced Dad an' me—'

'Same one?'

'Dunno. No, I guess not. That was more'n twenty year ago.'

'What are splicin'?'

Delia giggled from the big sheet-iron chimney where she was cramming gum sticks under a cold kettle. She had never seen a parson nor a wedding in all her sixteen years, and she had never read a book. But there are some things which come to a woman by instinct.

'Marries yer, yer chunk,' she explained. 'Makes folk so's they goes away with each other an' takes up free s'lections an' has cows an' kids, an'—'

A big broad bulk blocked the low door; a young man crossed the mud floor with a long step, picked the baby out of the welter of empty tins and wood-ash, and tossed her over his head.

Two piping voices flung the great news at him instantly.

Craig cuddled the baby against his sunburnt neck where she cooed like a homing pigeon, and wheeled on his mother. And there was a red on his face that the sun had not stamped there, and a light in his eyes that never came from Delia's fire.

'What's they kids sayin'?' he asked.

The Old Woman pushed back her scanty hair, and her little thin, alert body was tremulous. For a visitor came to the free selection perhaps once in five years, and a clergyman, never.

'He—he are, Craig. He are comin' ter-morror. Anderson's drovers went past this mornin', an' they told me. I—I was thinkin' as I wouldn't go out ter the grass-threshin' ter-morror. I was thinkin' as I might do a bit o' cleanin' up—seein' as—as a parson spliced Dad an' me.'

Craig looked at her curiously. He had the length and the muscle and the scarcity of flesh that belongs to the worker on a free selection Out-Back, and he had the clumsiness of tongue which such a cramped life must give. But there was a fibre of chivalry in him somewhere, and the quiver in his mother's voice struck it.

'Reckon as a day off won't hurt yer,' he said. 'I kin git a wallop inter it myself arter the ploughin' done. An' you make Delia do her whack o' the muckin' roun'—'

'Craig!' Delia spoke shrilly. 'You jes' dry up!' I bin makin' the butter, an' feedin' the pigs, and mendin' that old hole in the cow-fence—'

'An' lef' the tools out there, o' course. Mother'—Craig's voice was awkward, and his tanned skin was burning—'Mother; did yer know as yer was comin' out ter this here when yer got spliced-up ter Dad?'

Jacky ceased licking the sugar-spoon and stared at so much of Craig's face as the baby's dimpled arms left in sight. Had there ever been, could there ever be any place anywhere but these wide, wide hills of sparse scrub and heavy bush and crab-holes, and this little paling shanty set in the cow-yard with the pig-sties beyond?

The Old Woman rested her thin hands on the table, and she stared down on the thinner wedding ring that the big-jointed knuckles would never lose again.

'I — dunno,' she said.

'But would yer hev comed ef yer had a-knowed? Mother!'

'I — dun —' Then a man's step sounded heavily past the stacked brushwood without, and the Old Woman raised her head.

'You bet I would,' she said, softly, and turning, she cuffed Jacky on the ear with a force that sent the spoon flying.

Craig drew a long breath and carried the baby out to the door, staring through the red of sunset to the sparse tall gums on the farther hills.

'S'posin' I went over an' asked her?' he said to the hills. 'But — how cud I say it? An — she laughin' allers — Lord, kiddie, hold up. *Ah*, ef there was other gels'd guv a chap the wipe o' a kiss like that!'

There was no saddle on the selection, and no neighbour near enough to borrow from. But Craig took the old pack-horse bareback over the crab-holes and up the tracks, and across the muddy bottoms where the hill drainage collects. A little creek tinkled down the hill through shrub and bracken, and an unpainted gate, slung on a wire fence, stood to the right of it. Craig pulled up at the creek-foot, and the blood ran to his forehead. For a girl sat on the gate. A girl with a sunbonnet tipped back, and a shadow of fluffy black hair about her young face. She had a brown hand gripped to the rail either side of her slim body, and she beat her heels on the lower bar, singing softly.

Craig tied the rein to a sapling and came up to the gate. 'Hullo,' he said, flushing.

The girl looked at him without pausing in her song. Then she nodded, slowly.

'What's brought you over the hill?' she asked.

'You,' said Craig with a burst of daring. The girl laughed, beating her heels still.

'I'd a-said it was the hoss. You ain't no good at riddles, Craig.'

The little teeth were white under the curved lip, and the flush of a girl's coquetry was in her face. Craig stared at her, forgetting to answer. Then he said:

'There's a parson comin' ter-morror — from Boulgil.'

The girl put her head on one side.

'A — parson? What's he do?'

'Dunno,' he said. 'Oh, he's a chap what preaches, yer know. In a church — an' — an' wears his shirt outside the rest o' his things.'

The girl threw back her head and laughed again. And, to Craig, the little tinkle of that laughter, sounding out on the still evening air, was the prettiest thing he had known.

'That's all? I seen Dad do that — dippin'-time.'

'He does marryin', too,' he said looking at her steadily.

The girl beat her heels again, and turned her head from him, watching a great grey moth flutter across the strip of widening moonlight by the creek.

'I was thinkin' o' gettin' him ter marry me,' said Craig, desperately. 'Seein' as how there's only a parson by here in 'bout twenty years, yer know.'

'An' the parson's the on'y thing necessary, o' course.'

'What you meanin' — ?'

'Well; there's some thinks a girl part o' the marryin' game. But p'raps you don't. We all has our own 'pinions, o' course.'

Craig pulled his flannel shirt loose at the throat. Neck and tongue seemed suddenly to have swollen.

'I — I was thinkin' as I'd prefer ter have a gel along,' he said, timidly.

'Oh — was you?'

The girl flashed her eyes on him; then flashed them away again. But she did not speak and Craig's skin burnt hotter, until his ears were aflame.

'Ain't yer asked her yet?' she said.

'I — I bin tryin ter. But I ain't got all the words as — '

'Some girls don't take much stock o' words,' said the girl, idly.

Craig stared. Then the man's hot temper in him leapt up and out. He picked her off the gate, and crushed her close in his arms.

'Lordy,' he cried. 'What a durn fool I was! I might a-done this long afore.'

The girl pushed his face away with the flat of her hand.

'Let me go,' she panted; 'let me go!'

'I wun't! Tessie — Tess. There wun't be a parson roun' in twenty year, per'aps, an'—an'—yer *might,* yer know. Tess!'

Delia and Jacky and the baby were going to bed on the kitchen floor when Craig came home, and the Old Woman looked up from the last kerosene-tin boil of dirty clothes in the big chimney.

'Craig,' she said; 'we was thinkin', Dad an' me, as how it 'ud be fine ter git the lot on yer baptised ter-morror. Yer see there ain't a parson come ever' day, an'—'

'Mout as well make him do suthin' fur his tucker,' said Dad, sucking the last breath of black-twist smoke out of his pipe. 'Waste o' him it is as we can't do more. Marshall's over ter She-oak has got five fur christenin'—an' a funeral. An' Macdonnell's he's got a weddin'.'

Craig swung on his heel and went out to the moonlight. That which he had come to tell his family was shut back on his lips again. He looked up at the moon, riding pure and shy among her clouds, and his heart quivered in him. But he had no skill to put the sensation into collected thought. Only he said, as he went to his lean-to behind the humpy:

'If ever I has kids o' my own I wonder ef they'll need the leatherin' these kids are needin'?'

The Old Woman was astir before daybreak, and Craig, coming round the house with the red of dawn in his face, saw a piled heap of refuse outside the door, and narrowly escaped losing an ear as an old broken chopper flew by it. He went down to water the horses with musing in his eyes. Would Tessie one day wear an overall made out of two flour sacks, held round the waist by a bit of string, and a pair of old boots of his with the toes out?

He flung a stone at an impudent magpie strutting on the rim of the creek.

'Not she,' he said. 'She's dainty as a thoroughbred, allers.'

And the magpie halted, cocked an eye at him, then flung back its head, and carolled out such a volume of joyous song that Craig went to his breakfast content. For this was the peal of bells that heralded his wedding morn.

Twice he tried to tell his mother, and twice he gave it up. Then he went into the lean-to, and hauled his best coat out of the kerosene-box under the sacking bed.

'She kin tell 'er,' he said. 'Tess kin tell 'er. Fur the fixin' up'll hev ter be done here, seein' as there's no women-folk over ter her selection.'

It was three hours later, and some of the furniture had been returned to the kitchen, and the rest was stacked under the brushwood, when Jacky shrieked from the rise:

'He's a-comin'. I say, you fellers, he's a-comin'.'

Then sudden shyness seized him, and he dived into the scrub behind the shanty, and lay flat, panting, while the sound of hoofs grew nearer, nearer, and ceased.

The Old Woman was in the door with Dad and the baby. Delia flung a glance round the kitchen. Then she squeezed through the back window; fled to the flour tin, where it stood on the shelf next to the paint; dived a hand in, and smeared neck and wrists with the white.

'Fur gels in the towns hev skin this colour,' she said. 'Reckon as I'll take the conceit outer that Tess Durleton — impident thing!'

The parson was young enough to enjoy even the bumping drive over crab-holes, and ridgy hills and paddocks, where the scrub was half cleared, and the Old Woman's face shone with pride as she led him into the kitchen, where a kerosene-tin of clean water stood in the table-centre.

'Four bapt'sums,' she said, impressively.

The parson looked at Delia and looked away again. And in his eyes was some of the lawless mirth that had been in the magpie's song.

Then Dad made laboured apology.

'Taint much wuth yer comin' all these ways out jes' fur what work I kin give yer,' he said. 'On'y four chil'ern I hev that's livin'. There was another, but it's dead quite a many years. If yer'd come three months since I could a-given yer a first class fun'ral — the Old Woman's dad, yer know. I'm sorry fur him not waitin': but it can't be helped. He's buried some ways out on the corn patch. P'raps yer'd like ter go an' say a prayer roun' there afterwards. I don't mind.'

'T-thanks,' said the parson, hastily.

'Perhaps I — you say you would like your children christened? If this dear little girl —'

172

He held out his arms to the crowing, dancing baby, and the Old Woman cast a quick glance round her flock.

'Git Jacky, Dad,' she said, in firm generalship. 'I seed his leg sticking outer the brush roun' by the pig-sties. An' ef that Craig don't turn up soon—'

'I'm goin' to be Frederica Alberta Lilly,' said Delia. 'I'm sick ter death o' my ole name.'

Dad wheeled in the doorway.

'Mr Parson,' he said. 'Ye're givin' no boy's names ter my gel. I won't hev it. You'll slosh her over wi' Delia or I'll know why. It's bin good ernuff ter cuss her with these sixteen year.'

He shook Jacky by the leg when he caught him.

'None o' yer blamed new-fangled names fur me,' he said. 'I called yer Jack, an' they'll put Jack on yer headstone—ef ever yer hev one, which ain't yer deservin's.'

He bore Jacky, protesting and tearful, back to the house, to see his eldest son lifting his arms to Tess, where she sat still on the bare back of the old pack-horse.

Tess was blushing and sweet as a new dawn, and she ran from Craig sheer into the Old Woman's arms.

'I—he said it was such a chance,' she whispered, hiding her face against the warm heart in the shrivelled little body.

Dad received curt and clumsy explanation from Craig. Then he went to the parson with his shoulders squared.

'Parson,' he said. 'Reckon we're goin' ter guv yer as good a thing as any of 'em all. Here's my son brought his gel along ter be spliced an' she ain't baptised, neither.'

He stood back in pardonable pride, and the young parson looked round the little squalid shanty, halting his eyes on the woman who was wife, and on the other woman, in her arms, who, for love's sake, would dare the same sorrows and the same few joys.

'I am honoured,' he began, with a thread of pity in his voice.

And then Jacky spoke from under the table:

'Yer kin put Bill in my name, too. D'yer hear? Anderson hes a drover called Bill, an' he kin spit further 'n any man I ever seen.'

MARY GRANT BRUCE
(1878–1958)

Bruce was born in Sale, Victoria. Her first writing position was as 'Cinderella', writer of the children's page for the Melbourne *Leader*. She worked as a journalist for various newspapers and magazines both in Australia and in England, and served as editor of both *Woman's World* and *Woman*. She is perhaps best known for *A Little Bush Maid* and the fourteen other children's novels in the Billabong series.

Bruce wrote thirty-seven children's novels (1910 to 1942), a book of Aboriginal legends, and a collection of radio talks. Her works include articles, short stories, and poetry on a wide range of subjects.

HER JUST NECESSITIES

The bride-elect sat in a wilderness of lace and embroidery and raiment of needle-work and inserted ribbons into apertures therein. It was a soulful occupation, and she wore a smile of far-off beatitude. The admiring matron of ten years standing, having duly inspected, armed herself with a weapon similar to the bride's, and settled down to work and the interchange of high ideals. Their talk floated naturally to the halcyon promise of the future — the home in St Kilda, the Brussels carpet in the drawing-room, the household linen (gift of mother of bride), the aluminium saucepans that already made the kitchen glitter even as the last scene of a pantomime. Over the afternoon tea the matron dropped a bomb-like question into the airy structure of romance.

'And what about an allowance for yourself?'

The bride-elect blushed.

'Oh, we never talked about it,' she said. 'I wouldn't like to. Edgar says everything will belong to us equally, and of course it will be all right.'

'I wonder?' said the matron, thoughtfully.

'I don't understand you.' The bride-elect grew pinker. 'With Edgar . . .'

'Edgar is delightful,' said the matron. 'He was a nice boy, and as a man he is all one could wish; and he is absolutely in love with you. But very often the marriages where all thought of business considerations is carefully excluded are the very ones that cause trouble along those lines afterwards.' She sighed. 'Mine was like that.'

'But,' said the bride-elect, round-eyed and uncomfortable, 'I — I thought . . .'

'That John and I are quite an idyllic couple?' finished her visitor, cheerfully. 'Why, so we are, I hope. We're tremendously good chums, even if romance has mellowed down into something more solid, if not so thrilling. But I'm not likely to forget some of my experiences in my first years of married life—those that arose through money matters.'

'But how can they signify?' asked the bride-elect, 'when everything is common property . . .'

'Ah, that's an old idea,' said the matron. 'Of course, it's literally true, in theory. It's in practice that it works out so irregularly. John assured me that all he had was mine, and—at the altar— presented me publicly with his assets. It was a different matter when we came down to business. A man is brought up to be the lord of creation, and, in hard fact, he has generally no intention whatever of handing over all his worldly goods.'

'But one doesn't want him to.'

'No, one doesn't. But have you ever thought, Dorothy, of what it will be to ask Edgar for every penny you want? I don't mean household expenses, but your own little personal needs—tram fares, afternoon tea money, an occasional cab: the sort of thing you can't manage without cash?'

'No,' said Dorothy, blushing yet more fervently. 'I thought— after one was married—that sort of thing would not be difficult. One takes it for granted.'

'Don't imagine that you can,' said the matron, putting down her cup firmly. 'That's the way I entered my married life. I had been brought up with very vague notions on financial matters. Father gave me an allowance, a little more than was necessary for my actual expenses; the margin was a variable quantity, depending on my own management. If I needed more—well, one made levies on whichever parent appeared the more malleable. There was nothing to hurt one's pride. Father had appeared to me all my life as a more or less ample cornucopia, from whom supplies came as a matter of course. Unless I knew that a bad season had made things "tight", I had no compunction about asking for pocket money—it never was much. I didn't know anything about housekeeping bills; personal expenditure was all I had to think of. My allowance was definitely my own, and I was hardly even thankful for it. But the feeling of independence it gave me was more than any mere monetary consideration. I found that out after it stopped – on my marriage.'

'But you weren't very poor, were you?' Dorothy asked.

'Why, no, John explained to me beforehand – it was out on the river in the moonlight, and he was more or less coherent – how our finances would be. I knew that house rent would not be a pressing problem, and that, since he could afford to give me a maid, there would be no need for me "to sully my fingers with house work". To pursue details further seemed not only mundane, but a waste of time. After the honeymoon was over I found myself with a neat home, an ample supply of clothes, assured credit at the shops, and no money in my purse. John was just as dear as ever. But we hadn't met on a business basis at all; he was my lover still; but all the same, he was an outsider man, and it seemed to me simply incredible that I should ask him for money. You can't quite put it into words,' said the matron, looking out of the window. 'Only a woman would really understand. Put it this way. You take it for granted that Edgar should pay for afternoon tea when you meet him in town. But you can imagine asking him to give you the money for your boots being soled?'

'Why – Mary?' said the little bride-elect.

'I found that being married made it no easier to ask John for my cobbling money. It seemed to me impossible that I could go to a man who had not known me until a year back, and get silver for my personal expenses. Possibly I was a fool, seeing that he was my husband but there are many women that are fools in the same way. Especially at first, the dearer relationship seems a thing quite apart from the hard facts of keeping house together, and I was desperately shy of John. I don't think for an instant that he realised it. You see, the average man is curiously slow to understand that his wife hesitates to ask him for money. Comic papers – they are run by men – assure him otherwise; they draw moving pictures of his wife searching his pockets while he sleeps, and demanding, at the point of the bayonet, when he wakes, anything she has failed to find. And there is not one man in ten who is not, unconsciously or consciously, on the defensive about money.'

'I suppose,' said Dorothy, 'that if he hasn't much he feels he must be economical.'

'Quite so. But I was as many other women — most women are — just as economically inclined as my husband. I knew quite well that we could not waste money, and I had every respect for John's efforts to save. We did not arrange a definite housekeeping allowance. John paid the bills, and I went to him for money for odd expenses. From the first I went half apologetically. Not that he ever grumbled, but the feeling was always there that I was asking for a grant, not taking what was mine as an equal, according to our before-marriage theory — and yours. I would tell him what I wanted the money for, and he would hand it over; his strongest attempt at a protest being "If you're sure you want it, dear." I never asked him without being very sure indeed.'

The little bride-elect ran ribbons steadfastly, thoughtful eyes bent downwards.

'John never understood,' her friend went on. 'He pooh-poohed all idea of a personal allowance, and he cannot see now why, after eight years of married life, I made such a definite stand for it that I got it. He could see no humiliation for me in the necessity of coming to him for every penny. It was the natural thing, he said. But it was not the natural thing for a woman who has known anything like independence; it is a galling restriction and a totally needless one. I tried to make him comprehend by reversing the situation — picturing him obliged to come to me for money for tobacco, odd drinks, games of billiards, even the evening paper he buys coming home — and he thought I was mad. Well, if I am, it is a kind of madness that every married woman would understand. I do not spend a penny more now than before; in fact, I save, for I can count on a definite sum, and I put it in the Savings Bank to draw on; and already I have a little nest egg there. At no time did I wish to spend on foolish things. My money goes on the house, the children, or John himself. Why, before I had my allowance I couldn't even give the dear soul a birthday present without his knowing all about it!'

'I don't quite see the justice of it,' Dorothy said. 'If the wife does her part in the home, surely she should be entitled to independent control of a little of the family resources. Mother says that I shall have to do my part in helping to save what Edgar earns.'

'You will probably work just as hard as he works,' said the matron. 'Since the first year or two my hours have been infinitely longer than John's — and the woman gives up far more than the man. She earns all she gets. Just arrange with Edgar to pay your dress allowance into the bank monthly; whatever he feels that he can afford. It won't make you a spendthrift: you will learn what you can save out of it, and retain that feeling of independence that is dear to every woman, no matter how much she cares for her man. I can never make out why some men desire their wives to be implicitly dependent on them. After all, it's a partnership, not an autocracy!'

The matron put on her gloves with care, and said goodbye affectionately. In the street she paused, thinking aloud. 'But I wonder will Edgar love me?' she mused.

MILES FRANKLIN
('BRENT OF BIN BIN')
(1879–1954)

Franklin was born and brought up in the Monaro region of New South Wales, the fifth generation of a pioneering family. Her first book, *My Brilliant Career* (1901), caused such a furore in her home district that Franklin moved to Sydney in 1904. There she worked as a freelance writer and became involved in feminist and literary circles. Later she moved to America where she edited a feminist magazine. Franklin went to Europe during the First World War and remained there until her return to Australia in 1933.

Franklin used many pseudonyms, the most frequent being 'Brent of Bin Bin'. She published twelve novels, one in collaboration with Dymphna Cusack, *Pioneers on Parade* (1939). *All That Swagger* (1936), considered her best work, deals with four generations of a pioneering family and demonstrates a love and understanding for her country. She also published a book of literary criticism, an autobiography, and a biography of Joseph Furphy written with Kate Baker. Franklin wrote over twenty unpublished novels and plays. She left her estate to establish an annual literary award for an Australian novel.

MR BUNDOCK SAT

An elderly gentleman named Bundock, wearing baggy mended trousers was sitting on a coil of rope and perspiring in the humid tropical atmosphere. The one reception room in the Third Class was a passage furnished with a piano and park seats behind a grille. Through this the people of the promenade deck could peer as at gorillas in a zoo. This place had been filthy at the port of embarkation; now it was packed with coolies bound for wherever coolies are shipped after a term in the guaniferous mines of Oceania. Actuated by mercy and a spirit of fair play, Mr Bundock and others had surrendered the apartment following their inspection of the hold without daylight or ventilation allotted to the Asiatics, who, nevertheless, were paying the same rates as other passengers. The steward who truculently pointed this out did not divulge that he demanded from each coolie ten shillings or a pound. Civil and uncomplaining, they were to him less troublesome and more profitable travellers than poor white men.

The white men breathed curses against the Company as they stepped over the seasick or tubercular forms of the orientals to gain the only access to the deck. Three flights aloft from the cabins, a few square feet among derricks, lifeboats and other gear were delimited by peremptory warnings to THIRD CLASS PASSENGERS. An awning was spread only in the immediate neighbourhood of the Line, and for days when heat or wind was not unbearable, rains swept the deck like a hose.

Mrs Lawlor, the widow, had Mr Bundock's private deck chair, her daughter, the belle, his private cabin stool. Earlier, when he had been about to claim his chair, a cabin passenger warned him that it was Mrs Lawlor's, and continued to sprawl in it until she appeared. With the manner of a superior to a transgressing inferior, the assistant-purser then seized the cabin stool almost from under its owner and handed it to the belle. She was belle of the whole ship, and naturally pleasing, but the assistant-purser was dependent upon his uniform for distinction. He fawned upon the First Class, was civil to the Second and snubbed the Third, with the exception of the widow and the personable flapper with the extravagant clothes. Both mother and daughter reserved their charms for the assistant-purser. Neither had any urge to court a shabby old man who was travelling Third.

Mr Bundock considered the assistant-purser as bumptious a nonentity, in an albino slinking way, as he had ever met, but the belle always bade good-morning politely. He found the widow a weariness of the flesh, he not being a servant of the flesh, and she of the flea-brained order who continually explained that she was travelling Third merely for experience.

Mr Bundock was travelling Third because he was strapped for cash but had to be in London before a certain date. The bottom had dropped out of the wool-growers' utopia, developed by the war in Europe, so that for several seasons west of the Darling Mr Bundock had been burning good merino staples because to do so was cheaper than sending wool to market. He was sustained in the discomfort of the lopsided coil of rope by his sense of humour.

'There is such a thing as being too good, Mr Bundock, and you are a fool,' observed his cabin companion, a battered old walrus disfigured by *gutta rosacea*, who himself hankered to rest in one of Mr Bundock's seats.

He knew the South Seas as well as Mr Bundock knew his sheep and horse runs, and his perpetual thesis was that there was no real affection in the whole wide world. Mr Bundock did not refute this, his thoughts being tinged with bile induced by an unrelieved diet of meat and boiled puddings, and the results of nausea. The TSS *Manawatu* was a roller, and the Pacific, in that season, a bounding main.

Mr Bundock had no doubt of his foolishness and poverty. His depression deepened as he totted up his disabilities. Like the widow, it was his first time he had travelled Third. He was going down the financial scale—and at his age. Yes, his *age*. He had too much age for anything but an antique. He was no cavalier. He had a full beard. Shaving was not worth the effort when a man was sixty, though the wife nagged about his resemblance to an old wolf or bison.

He was reserving his good suits for the United States and London, and a joker horse-playfully had torn up some of his shipboard wardrobe. Mr Bundock felt that it would be of no consequence if he died on the coiled rope in full view of the leaping porpoises. An able seaman brusquely requisitioned the rope. There was no compulsion to be polite to Third Class passengers on this line; for the time, it had a monopoly, and its officers set the fashion in insolence.

Mr Bundock found that another pair of trousers had been ruined by tar. The only seat available was the deck so he leaned on the taffrail and reviewed his career aboard. There were few passengers to whom he had not extended some help or courtesy. Why, for a change, could not someone else be the giver, he the receiver? Some were gifted in making others pay, but Mr Bundock lacked such power and was also deficient in pretentiousness.

Life appeared as drab as Egypt's sands when bereft of the sun. There lacked peace—in Mr Bundock's case there also lacked place—for meditation. In the practically empty First and but half-filled Second Saloons the comfortable apartments were not used for repose. The passengers invaded the limited Third Class space and perched or stood about for a sight of the belle, and frankly admitted that there was such a 'punk' crowd forward that boredom penetrated to the spine.

The First and Second Saloon passengers were free to take the few spots open to Third Classers, but no reciprocity was involved. Yesterday, the belle, with assurance gained by attentions from the pursers and engineers, had taken a seat on the promenade deck, and was shooed away by the chief steward who pled that he was forced to take notice of complaints. People who were paying more for their passages than others did not like to have those others sharing the luxuries.

'Serves the brutes jolly well right!' remarked the assistant-purser of some more males, who also had been ordered to their Third Class lair when taking a breather on an unpeopled top deck roofed from torrents of rain. In the case of the belle, his findings were against the complainant, a glaringly fifth-rate woman with bleached hair and bare legs. Some very young flaps adorned the stockingless cult, but in this case it confirmed middle-age by exposing varicose veins. The varicosed one had hoped to banish the belle. The disconcerting result was that she banished also that lily lad the assistant-purser. The varicosed one, having complained of a Third Class person, could not join in the trek aft in search of livelier society.

The assistant-purser was championing the belle, the special conditions of sea discipline enabling him to extend his protection with confidence. The widow descended for an afternoon nap; the belle took her place in Mr Bundock's chair, and that blighter, the assistant-purser, drat him! as usual sat beside her on Mr Bundock's stool and entertained her with petty disclosures about the financial straits or personal weaknesses of the passengers. Mr Bundock — risking a third pair of trews on a capstan — was unmanned by the inevitableness of increasing age and weariness. The young were so cruel. They would tread the old underfoot if they dared.

Along the deck at that moment trod a maiden, arch-belle of the ship, at three, First Class in every particular. The assistant-purser clucked at her and called her by name to air his status. The adult belle leaned forward, making herself more lovely by exclaiming, 'You darling little pet! Come to me!'

The infant, who spent her days in a sea of adulation, imperiously dismissed the assistant-purser and ran from the belle. The belle pursued her, but without response.

'She doesn't like any of us,' said a good-natured young man, 'and she'll always be able to pick and choose.'

So dainty, so bewitching, she electrified the idle onlookers. An extraordinary figure, with waxed moustache to proclaim masculinity; a stiff white suit, field glasses and camera as evidence of travel; who for ever walked up and down, up and down in loudly creaking yellow boots, who was never seen speaking to anyone, whom no one addressed, assumed human aspect as he watched the child. Mr Bundock's nausea abated.

The little maid went towards him. She held out her tiny hand clasping a melting sweet. She proffered it with increasing urgency in a clear piping voice, 'For you, nice man. Put it in your mouf.'

'Don't let her worry you,' called a musical voice from the companion way. A remarkable resemblance showed whence came the infant's beauty.

'Children never worry me,' said Mr Bundock.

'I loves you. Do you love him too, Mummy?' demanded the small siren.

'Won't you take my chair?' invited Mr Bundock, seizing the opportunity to slide it away from the assistant-purser while the belle was on the other side of the hatch.

'Thank you,' said the beautiful young matron, accepting.

'Excuse me, my stool,' continued Mr Bundock, dispossessing the usurper.

'Don't let her tire you,' said the lady. 'She is too imperious in her adorations and prejudices.'

'Take me for a wide,' commanded the arch-belle holding up her arms.

Mr Bundock hoisted the wee beauty to his shoulder and strode the deck triumphant.

ETHEL ANDERSON
(1883–1958)

Ethel Anderson was born in England to Australian parents. She was educated at Picton, New South Wales, and later in Sydney. She married a British officer and spent ten years in India with him, then returned to Sydney in 1926. Anderson wrote for magazines in India, England and America. She wrote two volumes of poetry, three collections of short stories, and two collections of essays. Her satirical stories, often about triumphant women, are filled with wit and irony.

DONALBLAIN McCREE AND THE SIN OF ANGER

It was some few months after Aminta's wedding that Donalblain McCree, five yesterday, woke up in his room in Mallow's Marsh Vicarage. He was not, even yet, used to waking up and finding that miracle, the earth, precisely where he had left it when, on the preceding night, most reluctantly, he had closed his eyes.

For this reason he had pulled his cot alongside the window, the better to survey his inheritance, his chin on the sill.

He liked to make certain nothing was missing.

The sun? Ah, there it was! With a sunrise in full swing.

It was an elaborate effort which entailed much flinging about of amber and gold, a particularly happy effect having been achieved by piling cumulus shapes right to the zenith of the sky, then topping these with three cirrus clouds of a bright coral pink which floated like gondolas in a sea coloured a pale pistachio nut green.

Even Donalblain recognised this as a successful experiment. He turned his chin up the easier to observe it and the sun, caprice itself, hereupon sent out a ray that dropped down through steep stairways of cloud to touch the eager face as if to caress it, as if to say (misquoting Baudelaire), 'This child pleases me'; while the warm sunshine vibrated like far-off chiming bells to articulate in dancing motes the promise of the sun: 'Child, you shall live under the influence of my kiss. You shall be beautiful in my way. You shall love all that I love, the earth, the trees, the sands, all sights, all sounds, all life, rivers, hills, valleys. You shall love through my influence places you have never visited, the memory of scents you have never known shall stir your heart to ecstasy, and my light shall bleach your blond hair and bronze your white neck, and dye your blue eyes to an eternal blue that will never fade.'

Yes, on that radiant spring morning the sun (in his own tongue) said something like this — something of this he said — as Donalblain leaned far out of the window to make sure that the whole of the empyrean was there. Yes, it was. But were such scudding clouds really necessary? Oh, surely not another wet day?

Was the swallow's nest still under the eaves?

Yes, it was.

There was the butcher-bird impaling a lizard on a thorn.

There were the ring-doves who always had the air of falling off a branch before settling on it, pegged, a row of eight on the orchard wall — an erection of grey stones innocent of cement.

Donalblain heard little 'Guinea-a-Week' twittering unseen, but piercingly near, and his chirping soul responded.

The child liked everything in the world except Hasty Pudding, but he found the horses too hoofy, the cattle too horny, the dogs too bouncy and barky for perfect companionship; it was the birds he loved. He had even steeled himself to listen without fear to the curlews calling 'kerloo, kerloo' as they swept in flocks over the roof on windy nights, or danced on moonlight nights in the boggy paddocks; bald, with patches soaked through with the white gold reflection of water; thatched, with shivery grasses and tussocks of Kumbungi, and extending, chequered by grey three-rail fences right from Mallow's Marsh Vicarage to the Razorbacks.

It is hardly to be credited that the sound made by two eyes opening could be heard all over the Vicarage, yet, directly Donalblain peeped himself awake, every woman in the house was aware of it. His mother, meandering like a long 'M' in the middle of a double bed, and, since her husband's death, sleeping with the sheet over her face, would lift a corner of it, smile, and replace it. His sister Juliet in the next room to his would throw her pretty legs over the side of her truckle-bed and feel for her slippers. His grandmama, majestic in a four-poster fringed and curtained in maroon, who, like most old ladies, never slept, would pause in her calculations, her difficult sum in mental arithmetic — 'If four new milch cows would bring so many more pounds of butter to be sold in Parramatta market, how long would it take to save the money necessary to send Donalblain to Trinity College, Cambridge, where his grandfather had been before him?' His grandmama was determined he should go there!

The Vicar's wife was convinced that though St Paul might possibly be an inspiration to saints and martyrs, who need not, of course, be people of much social standing, only the classics, only Horace, could create a gentleman. Mrs McCree had no use for 'Nature's gentlemen'. Indeed, she was really desolate that there had not been, that there never could have been, an Epistle from Horace to St Paul.

On this particular spring morning, all these family manifestations having happened as usual, the three maids who were engaged in turning out the drawing-room were also immediately aware that Master Donalblain was awake. Cook Teresa, smiling, handed her millet broom to Min, the new housemaid, and hurried to the dairy to pour out from the bubbling bucket the glass of new milk, warm, which Juliet, who had found her slippers, was to carry upstairs to her brother. In the interval Tib, the housemaid-emeritus, getting up from her knees, in which posture she had been 'lifting the nap' — where there was any — from the Turkey Carpet (already twice swept) with a besom no bigger than a shaving brush, poked a head enveloped in a duster out of a side-window to engage Donalblain in that light badinage for which she had a talent; her undoing. Cook Teresa would allow no such pleasantries as those Tib had engaged in with the new boy, Dan O'Leary; this Tib felt to be unreasonable in a woman who addressed Donalblain as 'Young Tinker', 'Young Turk', or even 'You Limb' (of Satan, being understood).

On the day after his grandson's fifth birthday Mr McCree, who had long noticed that the women spoilt Donalblain, also woke the moment the child stirred, to feel an impression, which had for some time been teasing the back of his mind, harden into a resolution; it was in obedience to this impulse that the old man bent his trembling steps uncertainly to the kitchen, just after eleven o'clock.

At this hour, much like a seagull scrap-fishing in the wake of a tea-clipper, Donalblain was to be found hovering in Cook Teresa's rear. Yes! There he was! Already he had not done too badly! He had accepted with red, moist, pursed-up lips a mouthful of cream, robbed a basin of rich gleanings of yellow batter, cajoled a generous munching of lemon-peel, and, yes, been given, ever so kindly, a whole delicious cumquat in syrup!

There was sunlight in the kitchen.

The room was gay with the rustle of work in progress.

Three maids all in Delft-blue cotton, worn summer and winter alike (for who could feel the cold when active?), and demure in starched white caps and aprons, in which they took pride, were red of face and arm, for the immense stove, roaring up the flues, was in the act of roasting a sucking-pig.

Like salmon in a Scottish fishing-lodge, or bloaters in a Yarmouth cottage, sucking-pig was no dish *de luxe* at Mallow's Marsh Vicarage. There were always so many male pigs, porkers that must not be kept, and, being a glut in the market, could not be sold, born in the six sties in which, this season, six shameless sows had each produced a litter of thirteen piglets—all of the wrong sex, that it was indeed an economic necessity that they should be eaten.

Mrs McCree was well aware that Mrs Noah and Mrs Job must have known a great deal about life that has not come down to us; she was in their class; but—*seventy-eight young hogs*! Oh, even Mrs Noah, even Mrs Job, would have considered this too much! Just the last straw!

In the face of this misfortune the Vicar's wife, quite losing her nerve, had talked with such severity to the man who kept her pigs that he, usually so meek, had rebelled, and, scratching a straw-coloured mop of hair, kept repeating querulously 'Phut, Mum, phut had Oi to do with ut? How could Oi help ut?'

Today the grateful smell of cooking pork grew every moment more perfect in bouquet, the sizzling of the crackling, the bubbling of beans in a pot grew every minute more full of promise, as, sitting at the freshly scrubbed and sanded table, Lulu, the between-maid, cut white kitchen-paper into picot-edged flounces, meant to hide the nakedness of the dresser shelves and the high mantelpiece above the stove. Her big curved scissors with the vandyked blades snapped and clapped as the spirals of paper lace increased and the roll of paper diminished. Min, sitting beside Lulu, being instructed by Cook Teresa in the more finicky art of fashioning frills for cruets, cutlets and hambones, plied her small scissors on an accompanying *pizzicato*.

Both maids would have been cooler in the housemaid's pantry, but, no! they preferred the hot kitchen with its constant coming and going of male visitors.

On Mr McCree's entrance all four menservants had sheepishly withdrawn from the open doorway; Cook Teresa was in the habit of giving them all a sup at eleven — nothing much — nothing that would startle the household bills; a pewter tankard of small ale, or penny ale, perhaps, or a glass of sparkling cider — both home-brewed.

In this feminine air of comfort, plenty and security, Mr McCree recognised the enemy of his sex. In this cloying, this enervating atmosphere, this 'monstrous regiment of women' the Vicar saw his grandson's undoing; he would become 'soft'. His manly character would be ruined.

Since the poor child had now no father, his grandfather was determined to warn him, to point out to him the dangers lurking in the society of females, and he took him by the hand and led him out through the orchard to the fallen pear-tree, their usual trysting-place, Donalblain's ducklings following.

Every woman looked out of a window to watch them. Eight faces appearing at the toy-like, white-curtained casements in the old-fashioned Vicarage walls, which were like those of a doll's house, painted to look like red-brick or a cardboard building in a harlequinade, registered the same fear, the same knowledge: 'He is going to set the child against us.' Intuitively the women realised this — rightly.

Sitting on the lichened trunk of the fallen pear-tree, which had a living branch or two because the tree had not completely pulled its roots out of the soil when it fell, and some remained to nourish

191

it, Mr McCree nipped his grandson between his knees, and firmly held his restless hands, to keep them from fiddling with the ducklings, and he looked intently at the child with his kind, wise eyes, which were yet as blue as those which looked blandly back at him.

'Donalblain, you are five years old,' Mr McCree began in his quavering, hesitant voice; he had been made speechless by a stroke a year back, and was only just regaining his power of clear articulation. 'I am your grandfather, eighty-four years old. Soon you will be alone, with no father, no brother, and only three women to look after you.'

'It is too sad,' Donalblain said, tears filling his eyes.

'No, it is not a bit sad,' Mr McCree said, testily, 'it is merely inconvenient. Well, now, listen well! If a man has land or a house he can leave his land or his house to his sons, or his grandsons. But I have no land, and no house.'

'Can't I have this land? And this house?' Donalblain asked, looking round him with a wondering air.

'No. These belong to the Church. They are not mine. When I die they will go to the new Vicar of Mallow's Marsh. Well, now, if a man has tools he can leave them to his children, or his grandchildren. But I have no tools to give you. The only tools I had with which to earn a living have been an old book, and a quill pen and a halting tongue. And it cost my father a lot of money to teach me to read the old book, and write with the scratchy quill, and speak with the halting tongue.'

'Mr Noakes, the gardener, has got a pick, a shovel, a pruning hook, a scythe and a wheelbarrow,' Donalblain volunteered, as he looked across the neat, gently swaying branches of the trees planted in narrow arcades in the orchard, to where the four men were digging a drain.

'Yes, so he has. And he can teach his sons to use them, but I can't teach you to use my tools because I am too old and you are too young. However, there is one thing I can tell you, and that is this. You are too big a boy to hang round the house with the women all day long.'

Donalblain was only half-attending. Working one hand free from his grandfather's weak grasp, he swooped on the duckling which was sipping at his boots, and turned it upside-down. A scientist, satisfied with a deduction, he dropped the boat-shaped morsel of yellow fluff and, slipping his hand into his grandfather's again, prompted, dutifully, 'Yes, Grandpapa?'

But his thoughts were with his ducklings. Would they soon lay eggs?

The sun, now quite a fiery affair, was negotiating the bend between the Church tower and the henhouse, and it threw a few diffident shadows across the blossoming fruit trees; across the pears, each bearing a hint of fruit in the last remaining fuzz of vanished petals; the cherries with their dancing and triumphing clusters in full blaze, the red threads left in the peach-branches each shielding a swelling bead that intended to be one of the immense Yellow Mondays for which the Vicarage was famous.

'I have no land, I have no house, I have no tools, I have no money, but I have my integrity,' Mr McCree said, and as he watched his grandson's rosy face which blossomed no less radiantly than the blossoming trees, the old man thought, 'How can I explain the meaning of "integrity" to so immature an intelligence?'

'Mr Noakes says I am to avoid women as I would the Devil,' said Donalblain.

Hearing this, Mr McCree felt a slight lessening of the burden on his conscience; his burden, it appeared, was to be shared; his grandson was, apparently, to be accepted into the garnered wealth of the experience of the world of men; he was to be Everyman's son. Every bit of wisdom each man had gathered for himself he would, in all kindness, be ready to hand on to those who followed him. Of course, so it had always been; so it would always be.

The old man smiled, the sweet smile of age, of one helpless yet unaware of his helplessness, and his whole face brightened with that same look of doting fondness which he had so reprobated in the women of his household.

'Yes,' the boy continued, 'Mr Noakes says, if you meet a girl and a death-adder, kill the girl and cuddle the adder. He says it's safer.'

Sitting in his threadbare black cassock on the grey bole of the fallen tree, Mr McCree, who had served his God devotedly for over sixty years, felt that none of his own experiences had brought him any knowledge so salty. He considered, half astonished, the implications of such an attitude. He was, himself, warning his grandson against the deleterious effects of a woman's love; of a woman's affections. But, need one go so far?

'Little dears,' he murmured to himself, forgetting Donalblain, and sipping as a bee sips at the memory of some flowering hours. And there was his wife, of course, what a good woman she had been — Still —

'You must beware of women.'

'Yes, Grandpapa.'

'You must never allow a woman to get the whip hand of you. They are weak creatures.' Delving again into the depths of his memories, he added, 'Sometimes you must protect them from themselves.'

'Yes, Grandpapa.' Donalblain was mystified, but he was a polite child.

'You must look after your poor grandmama, your mother, and your sister, and make enough money to keep them.'

The Vicar of Mallow's Marsh looked at the small church in which thirty years of his life had been spent, mostly on his knees, where, in all happiness, he had learnt the beauty of holiness and the delight of serving his God. But his had not been a profitable life as regards material things, no, not at all! And when he had passed to his rest, and joined the Communion of Saints (as he was assured he would, meeting, he hoped, several other men from Trinity), the ninety pounds a year with which his labours had been rewarded would cease to support his family — and then? What would happen to them? He had saved nothing.

Sighing, he collected further scraps of experience to dole out, hopefully, to his grandson.

'You must have faith.'

'Yes, Grandpapa.'

'You must be a man.'

'Yes. May I begin now?' Donalblain looked eagerly up. 'May I have a catapult? May I shoot at the birds, and keep them from eating the seed?' He had often asked this before, but he saw that his grandfather was in a yielding mood. 'I would not hurt the birds! Only frighten them. That boggart Mr Noakes put up is no use at all.'

There is nothing that so becomes an orchard as ecclesiastical black, however faded it may be, and Mr McCree's cassock, swishing across the green springing orchard grasses was a telling contrast to that amazing medley of cumulus clouds, the exulting cherry trees.

His rosy face, bright with the animation of coming manhood, hopping along to avoid the persistent, nibbling beaks of his ducklings, Donalblain McCree, in his blue smock, chattered away to the old man in the easy confidence of an equal. 'I see your point,' he said, 'Sir' — this was his first claim to the status of an adult. 'I will stand on my own feet (as you tell me) and hang by my own tail (as Mr Noakes advises). I will be careful about women, too, Grandpapa!

'*More wheat*

More to eat!'

the child chanted, in sheer joy of being alive, as they joined the four men, working at the drain. 'That's a poem,' he cried out to them gaily.

Everyone there, Mr Noakes, Boy Bob, Man Jonathan, and Dan O'Leary, the new hand, all agreed that it was a good poem, and putting their picks and shovels and mattocks aside, they combined in the manufacture of a catapult, contrived from the fork of a cherry-tree, a piece of garter elastic and the thumb of an old glove. Everyone there tried the sling out and gave Donalblain good advice, and each man had his own theory about the art of flinging a stone.

Standing beside Mr McCree, who looked on, smiling, Dan O'Leary, the new man, said in a humble, ingratiating voice,

'Indeed, Surr, it's a privilege for us poor folks to spake to the Quality. It does us poor folks good, Surr, just to see the faces of the High Folks.'

He gave a sort of scrape with one foot, and his bold, handsome face took on an expression of gentle humility.

'Why did you wink at Mr Noakes, Dan?' Donalblain, who stood on the far side of the boy, asked, interested.

'Wink, is ut? It was a tear, Master Donalblain. I've had a sad life an' all, and it's new to me to be stepping alongside the gentry, that it is!' And he slid a fierce, angry look sideways at the child.

The other men kept wooden faces and no more was said.

Donalblain, then, with his new catapult, went off to the wheat-field, to drive the birds from the newly-sown seed. He was proud and happy. He could see all the other men at work, and he, too, was at work, and he, too, was becoming a man, and, what was more, his grandfather had promised him a fourpenny-piece, a Joey, as a reward for his labours.

So he sent stones as high as he could, standing under the larks that hovered, pouring out their full hearts, near a heaven that was entirely blue from one horizon to the other. Resplendent, two Wampoo Pigeons, birds of passage, bound for the scrub, rested a moment on the arms of the scarecrow, the boggart, that had been there so long that inkweed was growing out of his hat. A family of 'grey jumpers', called 'The Twelve Apostles', next came hopping over the ground, and when Donalblain, taking careful aim, flung a pebble their way (but not too near) they flew to the branches of a tree on the edge of the wheat-field, ascending from branch to branch in a series of leaps, all the time calling out indignantly and harshly at the disturber of their meal. These birds gave Donalblain lots of fun, and he would break off work sometimes to tell his ducklings how silly they were. And he would refresh his love for his ducklings by rubbing their soft yellow down against his cheeks.

'Do not think, darling, that little scissors-grinder does any harm, because he eats only spiders, my pet,' Donalblain told his eldest duckling, and he did not shoot at these birds when they came chasing their tails over the ploughed clods of earth. But when a whole flock of lorikeets came sailing and swooping in their scalloped flights to assail the cherry-trees, the child had moments of great activity; he thought of nothing else, rushing to the borders of the wheat patch for pebbles, making his ammunition of the smallest he could find, so that they could not hurt even the tiniest bird, and slinging stones wildly about.

'Jerrygang! Jerrygang!' he shouted in the exuberance of his joy, and he rolled about in the grass, and the sun shone, and the faintest of zephyrs disturbed the tranquillity of the older blossoms, and wafted their discarded petals about like snow in the warm, soft air that smelt more of honey than of anything else. The Vicarage wall-flowers were out in the Vicarage garden, and their scent came puffing over the field in fragrant gusts of heavier air.

Far off the Razorback hills were a deeper blue than the sky. Nothing stirred in all the waving miles beyond the Churchyard, for the larks had all left the earth, preferring heaven, and the cattle, since it was noon, were out of sight, preferring the consolation of the river and the lower ground, where the cool water ran thinly over the flattened rushes. The men had gone to their noonday meal. There was not a soul about and the sunlight purred like a cat.

It was then that Donalblain noticed Dan O'Leary standing on the far side of the field, watching him. There was something threatening about his still figure, in its three-flounced cape coat and tall hat, and he looked very big. In that flat country even lambs looked like Leviathans. In that beautiful hour the child felt some misgiving in his heart. He hoped that Dan would go away. He pretended that he was looking for stones close to the orchard wall, and that he did not see him.

Donalblain had hoped all along that a big bird, a bird so large that he would not hurt it if he hit it, would come along, and now his wish was fulfilled, for a wild tribe of currawongs, whistling and wailing and behaving in their usual noisy abandon, came rioting down from the hills. They walked and strutted about, picking up sticks and looking coy, and setting their black heads

197

on one side, in their indecorous courtship. 'Let us build nests' was what they were saying to one another, and the cachinnations of the older birds at some shy first-nester were amusing to hear.

Donalblain forgot Dan O'Leary.

He had a handful of stones in the pockets of his Nankin breeches — new yesterday — (and with straps that went under his jemimas, his elastic-sided boots — new, too), and he was fitting a stone into his sling when he saw that Dan, unseen, had come round the orchard wall and was standing not two feet behind him.

'Oh, Hello, Dan,' he said, to disguise his trepidation.

'Hello, young master,' Dan said, amiably. 'You are learning very fast to use your catapult, aren't you? But you don't seem to hit much, I notices.'

'I don't aim to hit the birds, only to frighten them away.'

'You don't seem to have frightened them currawongs.'

'I've only just begun to frighten them. I scared away the Twelve Apostles, and the lorikeets.'

'They never stay long. They were going in any case.'

Dan was a very handsome lad with curly black hair and dark brown eyes that were apparently black, for their pupils had no light in them; they looked flat, and had no depth in them, and reflected nothing back; and his nose was tip-tilted, and his ears pointed, and his arms, Donalblain noticed, were so long that his fingers, as he stood there holding his bundle, reached his knees. Though he smiled with his big, curled, hungry mouth, there was a wind of fear that seemed to blow about him; he was a figure alien to the calm and peace of that happy hour.

Donalblain felt nervous. He fitted the stone which had fallen out of its place back into his sling, and let fly, to miss a sitting currawong not ten feet away.

Dan laughed heartily with a show of good-fellowship.

'Come, young master! I'll teach you how to hit a bird!' he said, and stretching out a large, hairy hand, he took the catapult, and, stooping, picked up a stone, and said to Donalblain, 'You watch me hit that currawong! I'm a dead-sure shot, I am!' He drew the elastic well back, twanged off his missile, and the eldest duckling, quite in a different direction to the big piebald bird at which he was aiming, fell dead, and its head hanging almost off its neck.

Dan clicked his tongue.

'Dear me, now! Isn't that misfortunit? To hurt your duckling! That was the last thing I wanted for to do!' Dan said, watching the child's face fade from red to white.

He would have run over to the bird but Dan put his foot on the child's foot, and said, smiling, 'Wait a bit, little master! I must aim better next time!'

'You are hurting my foot, Dan,' Donalblain said, trying to pull it from under the big, heavy boot.

'Am I, indade? Oh, no, master, I wouldn't for the world hurt the likes of you, indade an' I wouldn't! Why should I?' He pressed his boot harder down on the small resisting foot under his heel. 'It's mistaken entirely you are!'

'Just you watch me,' Dan continued, fitting another stone into the catapult. 'I'll hit that currawong over there – beyond the scarecrow! It's a long shot, that – just you wait.'

The second duckling flopped about, with the soft embryo of a wing trailing on the wheat blades.

'Tut an' tut! Sure an' isn't that the Divvle an' all? Where my cunning gone to, ava? I'm ashamed of meself – to shoot that wide!'

Dan stooped, to look directly into Donalblain's smarting eyes.

'I'd best put the poor thing out of its misery, now.'

Dan knocked the third duckling out with his next stone.

Then the fourth, the fifth, the sixth.

'I hope I am not discommoding you with my foot, Master Donalblain?' he asked in a gentle, polite tone. 'It's the difficulty I find in aiming straight, that's what it is, that makes me lean so heavy on your toes; shall I lift me foot?'

'Yes, please, Dan,' Donalblain said, setting his lips.

Dan lifted his boot and then stamped it hard down on the child's small foot.

He made an exclamation of annoyance.

'Now, aren't I the fool of a man? I thought I was stamping on that snail there, Master Donalblain. I don't know what's come

199

over me this noon, that I don't first kill all your ducklings when I aims at them blasted currawongs, and then I hurts your foot — stampin' on it — like that!' He ground his heel on the child's instep.

'Does that hurt, little Master?'

'Yes, Dan.'

'With its new boots an' all!' Dan murmured softly into Donalblain's ear. 'Would the other foot be feeling it less?'

He brought his foot down.

Donalblain stood, his lips set, looking at his ducklings.

The one with the broken wing still struggled, bleeding, to get out of the trough of earth into which it had fallen.

'Don't you think it would be kinder to put that duckling out of its pain?'

'Yes, Dan.'

'Come over here, then, just stamp on it with your boot, that will give it comfort, like. You'd like to be kind, wouldn't you, young Master?'

'I don't want to hurt my duckling.'

'Oh, it's being cruel to be kind, that's what it is, just like me! I'm teaching you something, that's what I'm doing, but I'm just a clumsy oaf, just a poor man, Master Donalblain, and I don't rightly seem to have the gift of it, like my betters. They can thrash my back with a cat-o'-nine tails, and do me good, see? Because they're the Quality, and can't go wrong. But I'm no hand at it.'

Dan walked across and stamped on the duckling.

It was said, in medieval times, that a man in the paroxysms of an overpowering rage had white eyes.

When, for instance, King Arthur ran 'wood-mad', Mallory tells us he had white eyes, and Langland gives 'Ira', anger, white eyes.

What was so dreadful to see in Donalblain, a child transported with rage, was just that same alarming manifestation. When he saw Dan stamp on the wounded duckling, in his fury his eyes became white; the pupils turned inwards, as it seemed, and slewed round out of sight like a Medium's eyes in a trance. His vibrating feet stamped up and down on the grass, in a swift staccato tattoo, a rapid churning! Up and down! Up and down! Donalblain's legs moved so quickly that they were difficult to see, like flails on a windmill, or like a man trying to keep his place on a treadmill. They whirred up and down. And he thought not at all of his bruised feet which were next day to show black and blue.

The child's hands beat wildly in front of him, sawing the air in a demented fashion, threshing it, hitting out with all his might when, running over, he got close enough to batter Dan O'Leary's knees—he could reach no higher. And the tears fell in immense bright drops, a clear, incredible torrent, pouring down his now flushed, now scarlet face, round which his yellow hair stood out almost on end, and a sort of high keening noise, a most curious whinnying sound came whistling out of his wide-open mouth, moist and dripping with saliva.

It was a noise so piercing that it seemed impossible that he could be making so strange, so clamorous a shrieking; an animal braying, a primitive echo from the first abortive transports of man.

Dan O'Leary was amused and gratified.

At that moment he almost liked Donalblain.

He stuck the catapult back in the little boy's breeches pocket and started tickling him.

At this last outrage the inverted eyes came back into focus.

Donalblain turned and ran back over the ploughed field, over the once-hopeful arena of his first initiation into the service of his fellows, racing back through the shadowy orchard, where so lately he had stood, a happy child between his grandfather's knees; he ran pelting back, still screaming at the top of his voice, past the laundry, the kitchen door, along the narrow strawberry-beds, screaming, screaming in that high ass-like bray of sheer terror.

Every woman's face again appeared at the Vicarage windows.

Eight alarmed, compassionate women, leaving those points of vantage, rushed out to meet the child, and even his mother, throwing aside her novel, jumping up from her rocking-chair, after one wild look from her bedroom window, rushed downstairs so quickly, her white spotted wrapper streaming out behind her in the wind of her swift passage, that she was the first to reach

201

him, and Donalblain flung himself into her open arms, that maternal refuge, and cried till he slept.

Like that first Dove sent out from the ark, Donalblain had come home. Of the death of his ducklings, of the knowledge of evil, of cruelty, which he had gained in that moment of his initial experience of the world outside the nursery, he spoke never a word. He answered no questions. Instinctively he conformed to the masculine code.

There is nothing so mysterious as the way that the seeds of the future germinate in the character of a child.

It is a miracle like that of a bud, which has, folded in it, the uncurled petals of the rose.

It is time's triumph, like the fashioning of the cone, the brass cone, which is to be the trumpet, silent until breath animates it, till breath blows the fanfare for which, from the first casting of the instrument, preparations had been made.

On that spring day the child Donalblain's destiny was made manifest; it was made coherent on that spring day when, on waking, he approved of the sunlight, when his teeming heart was united with the singing bird's, when he and little 'Guinea-a-Week' sang their psalm together; when he was happy among the women of his grandfather's household, when (with the eyes of a scientist) he studied his duckling, and with the eyes of a dutiful child he looked up at his grandfather to learn, without speech, the meaning of the word 'integrity'.

On that spring noonday when, without rancour and being for the first time conscious of a sense of duty to others, of the pleasure of service, of a male desire to protect the weak, when he drove the birds from the patch of wheat; his family's bread; and then, seeing the death of his birds, felt in his young, untried heart the anger of the Saviour unable to save, of the pitiful soul unable to exercise the virtue of pity, or to save the helpless, the suffering, or to master (with his puny strength) the evildoer; in that moment, when Donalblain realised that he was helpless in the presence of cruelty, or wickedness, his fierce emotion operated like a dye, like woad, like murex, to colour his whole nature. Like a piece of cloth, dipped in a vat, to come out purple, he was metamorphosed, by that moment of his childhood, his youth, his manhood, his age.

Yes, Donalblain's character was stabilised by all that he suffered then. His experience on that bright noonday made him the child, the youth, the man he was always to be; the crisis of that encounter, the agony of that defeat, which taught him he was not omnipotent, that he was powerless in the presence of sin (it is a lesson all must learn), stood like a peak in the accumulated sensations of his whole life.

Like a child he cried himself to sleep. Like a child he accepted the comfort of his mother's embrace, but deep in his heart he had learnt all he was ever to know of man's capacity for grief beyond the reach of consolation.

He had exhausted himself in this knowledge.

That night the moon, caprice itself, looked down on Donalblain, sleeping by the uncurtained window, sleeping with his cot drawn as close as he could get to the wide-open window, and the moon said (misquoting Baudelaire), 'This child pleases me.'

And the moonbeams dropped down through gigantic stairways of parting cloud, and streamed, unimpeded, through the panes of glass, the doubled panes of the pushed-up window, high above his head, and touched his face as if to bless it, as if to caress it, to print on it the splendour of the human knowledge of good and evil, of sorrow, or joy, and this radiant light became articulate with the moon's promise:

'You shall live under the influence of my kiss. You shall be beautiful in my manner. You shall love all that I love, water, clouds, silence, darkness and the illimitable sea.'

And from that day and that night, the sun was Donalblain's brother, and the moon was his sister, and in his long, useful and distinguished life, though love informed him, he cared to make no nearer relationships.

But Tib, the housemaid-emeritus, the girl of sixteen, knew nothing of such depths when, after the moon rose, she slipped out from her attic to join Dan, who was waiting for her behind

203

the orchard wall in his three-tiered driving coat and rakish hat; clothes which Mr Noakes had called 'a nob's togs', and had asked him how he came by them?

Tib had her neat carpet bag, bright with roses as big as cabbages, which had enclosed in it the wardrobe which the Duke of Wellington himself had chosen for female emigrants; a mixed bag of eight calico garments (in the selection of which the Duke had betrayed a singular innocence) and two pocket-handkerchiefs, and one Huckaback towel, she wore a dress of grey linsey-woolsey, and a coal-scuttle bonnet, into which, with great daring, she had stuck a rose.

The child had a month's wages—the twelfth part of two pounds—tied in a corner of her handkerchief, and she was not afraid of anything that might happen to her.

Though man's inhumanity to man may make angels weep, Nature shows a singular and impartial beneficence, bestowing on king and tinker alike the best earth has to offer; Dan, walking in that soft moonlight night through the orchard with Tib, the simulacra of last year's apples, the dust of last autumn's toad's-meat crumbling and dispersing under his footprints, was triumphant.

While the lovers trudged the long miles into Parramatta his voice murmured untiringly, as he told Tib all he had suffered and all he meant to achieve.

And they delighted in each other, the strong, handsome young man in the pride of his manhood, and the innocent girl in the beauty of her budding womanhood; and they had no fear of each other, or of the future.

And peering out through the white muslin curtains of her bedroom window Donalblain's mother, the young widow, watched them go, and her tears fell faster than Widow Dido's, indeed they did.

KATHERINE SUSANNAH PRICHARD
(1883–1969)

Prichard was born in Fiji, the daughter of a journalist, and grew up in Melbourne and Tasmania. She worked as a governess, a teacher, a freelance journalist, and was social editor of the women's page of the Melbourne *Herald*. She founded support groups for women and several writers' organisations. Her awareness of the inequalities in society led her to become a Marxist, and in 1919, a founding member of the Australian Communist Party.

Prichard wrote eleven novels, three collections of short stories, one book for children, a travel book, two books of verse, two plays and some political pamphlets. Her novel *Working Bullocks* (1926) stresses the importance of the working man and his closeness to nature and his environment. *Coonardoo* (1929) was one of the first Australian novels to explore the Aboriginal experience with understanding and to examine the possibility of love between an Aboriginal woman and a white man. Prichard's play, *Brumby Innes* (1940) was not performed until 1972 due to its explicit treatment of racism and sexual relationships.

THE COOBOO

They had been mustering all day on the wide plains of Murndoo station. Over the red earth, black with ironstone pebbles, through mulga and curari bush, across the ridges which make a blue wall along the horizon. And the rosy, garish light of sunset was on plains, hills, moving cattle, men and horses.

Through red dust the bullocks mooched, restless and scary still, a wild mob from the hills. John Gray, in the rear with Arra, the boy who was his shadow; Wongana, on the right with his gin, Rose; Frank, the half-caste, on the left with Minni.

A steer breaking from the mob before Rose, she wheeled and went after him. Faint and wailing, a cry followed her, as though her horse had stepped on and crushed some small creature. But the steer was getting away. Arra went after him, stretched along his horse's neck, rounded the beast and rode him back to the mob, sulky and blethering. The mob swayed; it had broken three times that day, but was settling to the road.

John Gray called: 'Yienda (you) damn fool, Rosey, Finish!'

The gin, on her slight, rough-haired horse, pulled up scowling.

'Tell Meetchie, Thirty Mile, to-morrow,' John Gray said. 'Miah, new moon.'

Rose slewed her horse away from the mob of men and cattle. That wailing, thin and hard as hair-string, moved with her.

'Minni!'

John Gray jerked his head towards Rose. Minni's bare heels struck her horse's belly; with a turn of the wrist she swung her horse off from the mob, turned, leaned forward, rising in her stirrups, and came up with Rose.

Thin, dark figures on their wiry station-bred horses, the gins rode into the haze of sunset towards the hills. The dull, dirty blue of the trousers wrapped round their legs was torn; their short, fairish hair tousled by the wind. But the glitter and tumult of Rose's eyes. Minni looked away from them.

At a little distance, when men and cattle were a moving cloud of red dust, Rose's anger gushed after them.

'Koo!'

Fierce as the cry of a hawk flew her last note of derision and defiance.

A far-away rattle of laughter drifted back across country. Alone they would have been afraid, as darkness coming up behind, was hovering near them, secreting itself among the low, writhen trees, and bushes; afraid of the evil spirits who wander over the plains and stony ridges when the light of day is withdrawn. But together they were not so afraid. Twenty miles away, over there, below that dent in the hills where Nyedee Creek made a sandy bed for itself among white-bodied gums, was Murndoo homestead and the uloo of their people.

There was no track; and in the first darkness, which would be thick as wool after the glow of sunset faded, only their instinct would keep them moving in the direction of the homestead and their own low, round huts of bagging, rusty tin and dead boughs.

Both were Wongana's women: Rose, tall, gaunt and masterful; Minni, younger, fat and jolly. Rose had been a good stockman in her day: one of the best. Minni did not ride or track nearly as well as Rose.

And yet, as they rode along, Minni pattered complacently of how well she had worked that day; of how she had flashed, this way and that, heading-off breakaways, dashing after them, turning them back to the mob so smartly that John had said: 'Good man, Minni!' There was the white bullock — he had rushed near the yards. Had Rose seen the chestnut mare stumble in a crab-hole and send Arra flying? But Minni had chased the white bullock, chased him for a couple of miles, and brought him back to the yards. No doubt there would be nammery for her and a new gina-gina when the men came in from the muster.

She pulled a pipe from her belt, shook the ashes out, and with reins looped over one arm stuffed the bowl with tobacco from a tin tied to her belt. Stooping down, she struck a match on her stirrup-iron, guarded the flame to the pipe between her short, white teeth, and smoked contentedly.

The scowl on Rose's face deepened, darkened. That thin, fretted wailing came from her breast. She unslung from her neck the rag rope by which the baby had been held against her body, and gave him a sagging breast to suck. Holding him with one arm, she rode slowly, her horse picking his way over the rough, stony earth.

It had been a hard day. The gins were mustering with the men at sunrise. Camped at Nyedee well the night before, in order to get a good start, they had been riding through the timbered ridges all the morning, rounding up wild cows, calves and young bullocks, and driving them down to the yards at Nyedee, where John Gray cut out the fats, left old Jimmy and a couple of boys to brand calves and turn the cows and calves back to the ridge again while he took on the mob for trucking at Meekatharra. The bullocks were as wild as birds: needed watching all day. And all the time that small, whimpering bundle against her breast had hampered Rose's movements.

There was nothing the gins liked better than a muster, riding after cattle. And they could ride, were quicker in their movements, more alert than the men; sharper at picking up tracks. They did not go mustering very often nowadays when there was work to do at the homestead. Since John Gray had married, and there was a woman on Murndoo, she found plenty of washing, scrubbing and sweeping for the gins to do; would not spare them often to go after cattle. But John was short-handed. He had said he must have Rose and Minni to muster Nyedee. And all day her baby's crying had irritated Rose. The cooboo had wailed and wailed as she rode with him tied to her body.

The cooboo was responsible for the wrong things she had done all day. Stupid things. Rose was furious. The men had yelled at her. Wongana, her man, blackguarding her before everybody, had called her 'a hen who did not know where she laid her eggs'. And John Gray, with his: 'Yienda damn fool, Rosey. Finish!' had sent her home like a naughty child.

Now, here was Minni jabbering of the tobacco she would get and the new gina-gina. How pleased Wongana would be with her! And the cooboo, wailing, wailing. He wailed as he chewed Rose's empty breast, squirming against her; wailed and gnawed.

She cried out with hurt and impatience. Rage, irritated to madness, rushed through her; rushed like waters coming down the dry creek-beds after heavy rain. Rose wrenched the cooboo from her breast and flung him from her to the ground. There was a crack as of twigs breaking.

Minni glanced aside. 'Wiah!' she gasped with widening eyes. But Rose rode on, gazing ahead over the rosy, garish plains and wall of the hills, darkening from blue to purple and indigo.

When the women came into the station kitchen, earth, hills and trees were dark; the sky heavy with stars. Minni gave John's wife his message: that he would be home in about a fortnight.

Meetchie, as the blacks called Mrs John Gray, could not make out why the gins were so stiff and quiet: why Rose stalked, scowling and sulky-fellow, sombre eyes just glancing, and away again. Meetchie wanted to ask about the muster; what sort of condition the bullocks had on; how many were on the road; if many calves had been branded at Nyedee. But she knew them too well to ask questions when they looked like that.

Only when she had given them bread and a tin of jam, cut off hunks of corned beef for them, filled their billies with strong black tea, put sugar in their empty tins, and they were going off to the uloo, she was surprised to see Rose without her baby.

'Why, Rose,' she exclaimed, 'where's the cooboo?'

Rose stalked off into the night. Minni glanced back with scared eyes, and followed Rose.

In the dawn, when a cry, remote and anguished flew through the clear air, Meetchie wondered who was dead in the camp by the creek. She remembered Rose: how she had looked the night before. And the cooboo—where was he?

Then she knew that it was Rose wailing for her cooboo in the dawn: Rose cutting herself with stones until her body bled: Rose screaming in a fury of unavailing grief.

MYRA MORRIS
(1893–1966)

Morris was born in Boort, Victoria. She wrote articles for magazines and newspapers, verse, short stories, one children's novel and two adult novels. A collection of her short stories, *The Township* (1947), demonstrates her skill in writing about women in domestic situations.

YOUNG GRIEF

Marie Louise ambled along the edge of the earthern tennis-court, her stubby school shoes kicking up the water in the puddles.

She was cold with a coldness that seemed to come less from the wind that swept round the convent corners than from the hard core of misery inside her. Her little claw-like hands were tinged with purple. Her face had a bleached look. It was an odd, unchildish face with a high, knobby forehead and a chin that was pointed when you might have expected it to be square. With her combination of dark skin and startlingly blue eyes she had vaguely the face of a Siamese cat.

Sister Perpetua, who always made jokes, had said that about the Siamese cat. And now Sister Perpetua was dead, and her sharp, sweet voice, her impatient laughter, would no more be heard in the schoolroom or the long vine-walk where the nuns took their recreation.

The bell from the red-brick church was tolling as if the effort of tolling hurt it somewhere. Marie Louise listened with her head on one side, waiting for the little crack that came in the middle. Cling-clang . . . cling-clang . . . Slower than the metronome that beat with a maddening evenness in the cold parlour while you practised your Czerny exercises. Much, much slower than that . .

Cling-clang! Sister Perpetua was gone. She hadn't been ill very long. Only three days since she had suddenly staggered in from the garden veering over a little like a tall ship in a gale. It was her *heart*, the girls had often said, whispering together. Sister Perpetua's heart . . . Look at her red lips! Red as a poppy. Strange and beautiful in that austere white face . . . Dear Sister Perpetua standing under the stair-hall window with her hands folded away in her long sleeves . . . Sister Perpetua looking down her high-bridged nose with a little secret smile . . .

211

Reverend Mother had told the girls at study hour. They had put away their books and jammed down their desk-lids without a sound. Then they had cried, and it seemed as if everyone had been crying for days . . . red eyes . . . voices chanting from the chapel . . . silences and the furtive sound of doors opening and shutting . . .

Marie Louise drew a deep, shuddering breath. Sister Perpetua's 'favourite', the girls called her. 'I'll never be happy again,' she whispered. 'Never.' She broke off a little blackened stick from an orange-bough and scratched on the damp earth of the tennis-court. 'I'll never be happ —' she printed and stopped as suddenly as she had begun.

Cling-clang! Cling-clang! Oh, that bell! They were going to the funeral that afternoon, all the girls. They would walk two by two, and wear black gloves and stockings, and black ribbons in their hair . . . The girls were in the chapel now. Because Marie Louise's mother had a different sort of religion that did not countenance flowers and candles and incense, Marie Louise did not go into the chapel ever, but stayed in the schoolroom under the eye of tottery old Sister Carmel, or kicked her heels alone in the garden.

Marie Louise spent a great deal of her time in the garden. It was a sad-seeming garden now. The paths after the rain were washed a pale silvery-lilac, and the air flowed over them soft and lilac too. The orange-trees round the tennis-court looked hard and stiff, as though they had been cut out of painted tin, and the shallow creamy cups of the scented syringa had their wet, yellow insides stuck together.

Marie Louise ducked her head and smelt the richness of the damp syringa-cups, and her two long plaits swinging out tapped at her thin shoulders. They were lovely plaits, thick and golden, the colour of sun-splashed hay. Marie Louise loved to feel her plaits knocking against her shoulders. But better still, she liked to feel her hair floating in a silken cloud round her tingling neck. She was vain about her hair. Terribly vain. 'The sin of vanity,' Sister Perpetua had called it. 'But I love my hair, Sister Perpetua.' 'Then you should cut it off to the glory of God.'

'Ah, Sister Perpetua!' Marie Louise cried, rubbing her cold little hands together. All the girls — the little ones, and you were still 'little' at twelve — were doing something for the memory of Sister Perpetua. Tessa Stuart, fat as butter, who guzzled chocolates in bed, was going to eschew the sin of gluttony . . . Eileen Murphy, swift as an arrow on the tennis-court, had left her racket ungreased, because she wasn't going to play again. Too often she had played tennis while leaving Sister Perpetua's little tasks undone.

'And I,' thought Marie Louise with a sudden sharp anguish of spirit, 'I shall cut off my hair to the glory of God and the memory of darling Sister Perpetua.'

Yes, she would cut off her lovely, lovely hair. She would show it to the girls. 'Look what I did!' . . . But not now . . . Not till after the funeral, when she would run upstairs to the streaky mirror at the end of the little dormitory . . . The thought of the scissors going through her plaits, the sound they would make, made her screw up her eyes and tremble. Blindly she walked towards the school, knowing that the bell had stopped ringing, though she still heard it inside her head.

They went two by two down the long country road, between paddocks that were thick with winter-whitened grass. The hearse in front rolled along very slowly, but the girls had to walk fast to keep up. Splash, splash through the puddles, through the cart-wheel tracks that were filled with pinkish water. Marie Louise was panting as she cried. Close to her, Tessa plodded awkwardly. There was a bulge in her blazer pocket that was hard when she lurched against Marie Louise.

At the cemetery a wind was blowing, and the white tombstones in the grass looked like the play-things of giants' children that had been left where they played. The wind made a moaning sound in the she-oaks, and wrapped the wet ribbons of grass round the legs of the mourners, who stood back from the grave.

Marie Louise, touched with terror, stood staring at the red, crumpled face of old Father Slattery and the little wavering group

213

of people who, the girls had whispered, were Sister Perpetua's relations.

'It's terrible,' she thought. 'Nothing will be the same any more . . . It was silly to worry over a little hole in my tooth or whether my algebra sums would come right . . . I don't mind any more about mummy not coming up from town to take me out. I don't *want* to go out.'

Father Slattery's voice had stopped. People were moving away towards the cemetery gate. Misery, misery . . . Marie Louise rubbed her harsh black gloves together with a scraping sound, and whimpered. Tessa was tugging at her sleeve.

'Marie Louise, we're to drive back in Mr Dennett's car,' Phyllis said. 'Only the big girls will be walking. Bags I sit next to you.'

A little gleam of interest shot into Marie Louise's sapphire eyes. Oh, goody, goody! That gorgeous car of rich Mr Dennett's that was like a shop window with its glass and silvery stuff! She had often watched it glide past as she hung over the convent balcony. Who would have supposed —

In the car she sat forward a little, squashed and squeezed between a multiplicity of black, writhing arms and legs, but pleased to be sitting on a red upholstered seat that had springs like an old buffalo-lawn. Next to her Tessa was pulling a crumpled bag of sweets from her pocket.

'Have one, Marie Louise?'

'I couldn't.' Marie Louise, thinking of Sister Perpetua and the long grass in the cemetery, pursed her lips.

'Eileen? Gracie?' The bag made a timid round and came back unscathed.

'I couldn't either.' With a little sigh Tessa thrust the bag in her pocket. 'They're chocolate bon-bons,' she said regretfully. 'Those with different-flavoured middles. Blackcurrant and raspberry —'

Marie Louise, conscious of outrage, quelled her with a look, and watched the moving needle of Mr Dennett's speedometer past Mr Dennett's shoulder . . . forty . . . fifty . . . past fifty. Nearly sixty . . . Marie Louise knew a moment's ecstasy. *She* loved high speed, though mummy, who was an actress on the stage, nearly fainted when they were past forty. Oh, it was lovely, lovely to be going nearly sixty in Mr Dennett's glass and silver car!

She got out stiffly at the convent, her ecstasy dying in the cold, grey silence of the garden, where the nuns were walking smoothly like ships sliding over water. Remembrance rushed at her. 'I've got to cut off my hair. I've got to cut off my hair to the memory of Sister Perpetua, because I'm vain of my hair and it's a sin. I love my hair . . . I love it . . . I'll get my little snubby-nosed scissors out of the work-box that mummy gave me! One cut — two cuts — and it will be all over — before I get into bed.'

But Sister Joseph, her eyes sewn in red silk, was mounting weary guard in the dormitory. Marie Louise let the cold scissors slide back into her blazer pocket.

'I'll do it in the morning,' she told herself with a feeling of relief. 'Early — long before the others are up.'

But she didn't wake. Tessa's chirping voice roused her. Tessa was fully dressed, and she had a smear of chocolate round her mouth.

'Marie Louise, Marie Louise, get up, get up! The bell's gone ages ago and Sister Joseph's as mad as a hornet.'

Marie Louise sat up, her small brown face thickened with sleep. What terrible thing had happened? Oh gosh! She had slept in! A bad mark if she was late down and another if she was untidy. Must be quick. A rush into the bathroom, a sprinkle of water under the tap. Then into her blazer over her crumpled blouse. There was something hard in the pocket. Marie Louise remembered as she tied the ribbons on the ends of her plaits. Oh, the scissors, the scissors! She was going to cut off her lovely hair! Oh, Sister Perpetua, Sister Perpetua, there's absolutely no time now . . .

She was down the stairs and into the cold refectory only a little late, with her stockings wrinkled and her tie askew. The girls were talking and laughing and the sun was shining on the big grey-enamel teapot at the end of the table. Breakfast was good to eat, but —

'Go upstairs directly you have finished, and dress yourself properly,' Sister Joseph told her sternly.

She was on the landing when Tessa caught her up.

'Oh, Marie Louise, your mother's come early. She's come to take you out. She's in the parlour. You're wanted at once.'

In the parlour, mummy, with buckles on her shoes, was sitting under the picture of St Sebastian stuck with arrows. She was laughing.

'Well, my pet?' Marie Louise's mother had a caress in her voice that had charmed thousands. The charm was there now. 'Coming out with me for all day? Is it too cold for ice-creams? Shall it be the "Arcadia"?'

'Oh, mummy!' Marie Louise's blue eyes glittered and danced in her brown face. 'They have those ones with brown on the top and pink underneath . . . And mummy, you'd have died! We came home yesterday in Mr Dennett's car at nearly sixty. Sixty! It was lovely. Mummy, have you been—'

'Yes, I went to see your precious dancing-master.' Mummy smiled and passed her hand over the smooth golden top of Marie Louise's head. 'He's going to let you be the fairy queen in that ballet they're doing. Because of your hair, he said. It *must* be long—like yours.'

'Oh, mummy, I'm so happy!'

Marie Louise jigged with joy, pulled herself up at the door, and stood decorously aside with her eyes downcast. Gosh! She'd nearly disgraced herself. Barged into Reverend Mother . . .

'Make yourself presentable, child. You're a disgrace!'

'Yes, Reverend Mother.'

Marie Lousie danced away. On the stairs she met Eileen, who was swinging her racket and whistling as she padded down in her sneakers.

'Oh, Eileen, I'm going out for the day! Whoosh! And I'm going to be a fairy queen in the dancing-class ballet! All my hair spread out like this!'

A crazy pirouette and her pleated skirt was whirling. Something fell out of her pocket. The scissors! Marie Louise stooped down and picked them up. 'Gosh! I must put these back where they belong.'

JEAN DEVANNY
(1894–1962)

Jean Devanny was born in Ferntown, New Zealand, into a working class mining family. She developed strong feelings about the rights of the working class and was active in the New Zealand labour movement. Devanny moved to Australia in 1929 where she became a prominent agitator, writer and orator for the Communist Party. In addition to pursuing her career as a novelist, she took various other jobs to help support her husband and three children. In the last years of her life she retired from political activities to concentrate on her writing.

Devanny wrote nineteen works of fiction, some of which are set in New Zealand, and three non-fiction books about Queensland. Her first novel, *The Butcher's Shop* (1926) was banned in Australia and other countries due to its feminist and socialist attitudes. Her works, such as *Sugar Heaven* (1936), examine the union movement as well as women's rights to sexual and economic autonomy. Four of her novels have remained unpublished.

THE SPRINGS OF HUMAN ACTION

The Socialist was in one of his intolerant, intolerable moods. Usually he was a likeable sort of chap; companionable, even tempered and immensely interesting. But there were times when his ever-ready, whimsical satires were summarily discarded for a brutal disclosure of the facts of life as he saw them; when his dry, pleasant manner fell from him like a disguise to expose the hard reality compounded of desires and aspirations dammed by his understanding.

In these moods he was distinctly obnoxious to his companions. Of course the most of them liked to be called 'socialistic', for a little magic air of intellect and superiority clung to that condition in their environment, the West Coast mines of New Zealand. But there were limits, they considered, to the socialist philosophy. All very well to convert the world from a place where the idle capitalists had all the good things to a place where the workers had them, and the bosses were put to work; it was natural for a man to sympathise with that sort of 'science', but when it came to, say, a question of a man's home, or his marriage, well, then it was time to discuss limitations. This rot the Socialist was talking now. — It angered some of the miners who were seated with him around the big open fire in the hut. Others were uneasy; the four card-players at the card table behind cast peculiar side-glances at him from time to time.

'Isn't it possible for you to follow a thing out to its logical conclusion?' he demanded hectoringly. 'You can't limit science! You can't annihilate a fact by denying it or refusing to recognise it! For Christ's sake face the facts of life and accept them! And if you've got the guts deal with them!'

'What do you mean by that? Deal with them! How deal with them?' asked an elderly man with the drawn throat and emaciated face of the 'dusted' quartz miner. He coughed, then added: 'You said that under capitalism our wives were just our property, like our tools; that the socialist philosophy establishes that. Suppose we accept your word for it. How could we deal with it? How do you?'

'Well, you can deal with it in two ways. You can arrogate to yourself every freedom your economic position allows and restrict your wife in the same proportion. The law will allow you to do that. That action would be quite logical and right and moral according to present-day ethics. Or you can do as I do — apply the morals of the future regime to your own individual case to-day. Refuse to make a woman your chattel by tying her to you legally; regard her as a human being like yourself with all the rights and privileges of a human. And that doesn't mean only those rights and privileges which you demand for yourself. You might be the sort of man that asks very little of life; she might be the sort of woman that wants a lot, that needs a lot from life. She might need other men, for instance —'

A chorus interrupted him here, some voices jeering, some sarcastic, some plain angry. They all knew his marriage was not legalised, of course. That did not matter, though they would rather he did not speak openly of it — savoured of disrespect to the woman — but the last item, 'she might want other men' —

But the Socialist dominated them.

'That's right! Bellow like calves when your own property instinct is scratched! It is all right to deprive the capitalist of his privilege but don't put a hand on your own. Oh, no! Hypocrites! Ignoramuses!'

They listened now, frostily.

'How many of you men here, the married ones,' he looked round the twenty-odd men, 'are unfaithful? You all are. I am myself. But one mustn't even mention unfaithfulness in connection with your wives. Property instinct! The capitalist will sacrifice his sons in war to protect his property; you workers will commit murder to protect your property interests in your wives.' He stopped moodily. 'People that make trouble over love matters ought to be shot.'

The men near him exchanged shifty glances. Then one of the card-players, a big dark fellow, took up the conversation while he swiftly dealt the cards.

'So you don't object to it in your wife Jimmy?' he asked. There was a queer note in his voice. In the quiet that fell on the room with the asking of that question, the Socialist caught that queer note. He whirled with astonishing quickness, caught the other's eyes suspiciously and answered significantly:

'I will not object if my wife ever is.'

The other's look dissolved in a bland smile.

'Just so!' he said quietly, and turned away.

A breath of relief seemed to settle on the atmosphere of the hut. The Socialist was sensitive to it and frowned. But he added:

'I'd be a nice sort of cur if I did. So would you.' He knew enough of the other's 'frivolities'.

Just then the door opened to admit a young man of handsome, boyish appearance, a particular friend of the Socialist's. At once the same card-player greeted him with:

'Hallo, Bill! Jimmy here has just told us that he won't object if his wife goes wrong.'

A heavy flush suffused the face of the newcomer. He stopped uncertainly and glanced from one to the other.

'Wha-at?' he quavered.

The Socialist felt an unaccountable venom rise up in his throat, a compound of many emotions. He was puzzled, for one thing; he felt he was being 'ragged', and he could not see why; but he was mostly the victim of a peculiar, unpleasant new sensation for which he had no name. He looked around, searching for a clue. The old quartz miner avoided his eye and leaned over to cough. So he turned to the man at the table and sneered:

'You seem to find my opinions very amusing to-night. You know, there's not much to choose between the men and the women in this little burg, Phillips.'

The other sprang up, sending the cards flying.

'And what the hell do you mean by that?' he spat out.

But the newcomer interposed. He stepped between the two and

clapped a hand on the Socialist's shoulder.

'Aw, cut it out. What sort of talk is this, anyhow? You ought to be ashamed! The night's only beginning. Come and have a game at my hut, Jimmy.'

There was a general move; things had got too lively. The whole incident had been extraordinary and the older men were a trifle serious. Eventually only two single men were left sitting alone by the fire.

'Funny, you know,' one remarked to the other. 'Sex is a queer thing—the way it takes men.'

'The way it takes husbands, you mean,' the other corrected.

The Socialist refused the proposed game of cards, however, saying he would get along home. He went off alone along the gritty coke path that traversed the crooked street and as he walked he tried to shake off his queer perturbation by getting an understanding of it. Why had he made that remark to Phillips? It had popped into his head and out of his mouth before he had got its meaning. Its meaning was unmistakable, he saw now. God! What a thing for him to say! It really meant that Phillips had been getting at his, the Socialist's, wife, and he had understood and retaliated by showing up the other woman. 'There was not much to choose between the women and the men.' True enough, so far as Phillips' wife was concerned, but as for his own—The Socialist felt himself an unmitigated blackguard. How could he explain to those chaps? Nohow. It couldn't be done. He had stigmatised his own wife, and she about the only young wife in the place that a man could trust. And so pretty, too, so popular. He loved to pop in at the dances sometimes, just to see the way the fellows sought her as a partner. (He did not dance. He preferred to philosophise.)

Again, why had he said it? Something had been called for, he thought even now, by the peculiar note in Phillips' voice, but anything but that! Taking up the man in a way that he could never have meant. For Phillips was not a bad sort. A good woman was a good woman to him; nothing could have been further from his mind than an insinuation against the Socialist's wife. He had an

221

animus against the Socialist's ideas, that was all, and was probably 'shi-acking' him to judge of the sincerity of his views. Well, he would show them, if ever the opportunity arose. Just let that dear little girl claim the privilege he usurped for himself and he'd show them! It would be hard of course, but he'd do it. Well, the incident was finished. No use dwelling on it.

Yet the flavour of it clung around him as though he had not understood; had not sifted it sufficiently. He had a passion for analysis.

He passed by a house from which a great deal of noisy merriment proceeded. He stopped and listened and, recognising various voices raised in laughter and snatchy song, smiled and turned back. It was early yet, not nine o'clock, and he knew Margie would not be home till twelve. This was one of her dance nights. She had gone off to a little settlement three miles away, to a weekly affair. The unpleasant episode in the hut had upset his routine. Other dance nights he chatted and played cards in the big hut with his cobbers till eleven at least.

He knocked at the front door of the house determined to be gay, but the itch of the incident persisted, in spite of himself, a rowel to his temper.

The crowd at the house were mostly 'homies'. Usually the Socialist enjoyed their strange speech, their vulgar ways of making merry, but to-night the unmusical dialects of Lancashire and Cornwall disgusted him. He had even lost his taste for their beer — and it was proverbial that the 'homies' ' beer was as good as New Zealand's, anyhow. They were lavish 'shouters', more spendthrift than the New Zealanders in this direction, a little overcome by the big wages of the new country which to the native miner were small, hardly sufficient for his higher standard of living. They pressed the Socialist to sing in their routine manner.

All would fill their mugs or cups or glasses with beer. Then one of the women would sing out jovially: 'Now so-and-so will sing for us. Won't he?' All would take up a chorus:

'Of course he will! Of course he will!' in a regular chant. They would all drink. Then the woman would call:

'Didn't he say he would? Didn't he?' The chorus:

'Of course he did! Of course he did!' Another drink. The woman:

'He said he would?' The chorus:

'And — he — will!' In a great voice and with a mighty clapping of hands.

The person called on never failed to respond unless he was a 'no-sport', in which case he would be left out of the next re-union. The Socialist responded. He got to his feet and sang 'Barney Google' with great success. He was the cleverest fellow in the place and found it easy to introduce local personalities into his song, to the great edification of his audience. The women screamed with laughter and all pounded on the table.

But the Socialist could not stomach it for long. Even in the midst of his song, Phillips': 'so you don't object to it in your wife' and the queer note in his voice recurred to him, and once when it happened — A gush of fiery fluid seemed to shoot from his heart to his brain, to whiz around in his head, deafening him so that he lost the sound of his own voice; blinding him. He got away in half an hour.

Back in the night air he doggedly resolved that he would have this thing out with himself. Something was wrong with him apart from the ass he had made of himself and Phillips' 'shi-acking'. What?

The Socialist's pet formula was 'be honest. Don't try to evade disagreeable facts.' He was proud and fond of his honesty which others did not like. Well, he would not shuffle here. This new experience must be analysed and pigeon-holed against future necessity. Just for a second the Socialist felt a wish to be like those other chaps, wrapped around with the safe old usages of custom. Life was simple to them. They followed the blind trail of their emotions; felt no urge to set up precedents; no call to adapt their daily life to science. But he suppressed the wish as the plaint of a coward. They were common men whom aspiration had never even brushed with the tip of its wings. He was the Prophet, the blazer of new trails; a unit of the vanguards leading the hosts of Progress.

The Socialist felt himself rise on the wings of his faith in himself; in his stark acceptance of whatever conditions, whatever trials of the flesh and spirit his exalted position as leader might impose. In the impulse of his quickening spirit he freely and exultantly caught up the truth of the episode that had passed and dealt with it. Dealt with it on the heights of his momentary spiritual flight, forgetting that his feet still heavily trod the earth. It was his way, the unconscious sophistry of the Visionary who cleaves to his ideal with the fervour that even reason finds invincible.

He had been jealous. That queer note in Phillips' voice; his friend's flush and embarrassment, the general feeling in the hut, had awakened suspicion in him, suspicion of his wife, of his Margie, who had never once, in all the ten years of their life together, betrayed so much as a hint of unfaithfulness, or even of discontent. And that suspicion had engendered jealousy. He would have taken his oath that jealousy was an emotion impossible to him. Had he not thought out the matter of sex relations in all its ramifications? He and Margie together had discussed every phase of sex and agreed that jealousy was impossible where understanding existed. He filled with love and pride in his Margie at the thought of her wise words on the subject. Well, he had that night discovered that there were more springs to human action than he had thought.

He wanted to forget that gush of fiery fluid to his brain. Jealousy had taken him unawares. He had not recognised the emotion at its inception. Strange how the male in him had reacted to Phillips without apprehension by his brain. But now that he understood, now that he recognised his vulnerability, never again! Recognition meant control; meant that he could apply his understanding, his socialist philosophy, to the matter and so inhibit jealousy. He could reason it away the same as any other complex the cause of which was understood.

He must recognise that Margie might sometimes want other men, just as he had wanted other women. Of course it was hardly likely, scarcely possible, seeing that she was getting on in life now, and had been faithful for ten years.

For all the talk he and Margie had had on this subject of sex, he saw now that they had merely played with the thing. He had glibly enunciated heroic principles and lines of action and she had seconded them. But he at least, had not recognised till now the real possibility of being called upon to vindicate those principles. Funny that, he thought, in view of his own unfaithfulness.

Well; he did realise it now and perhaps it was just as well. He wanted to stand on solid ground. If this incident had not awakened him he might have come slapdash up against the real thing some day and done something rash, made a fool of himself, done something in opposition to his principles that would have damned him for ever in his own sight and that of his kind.

His spiritual wings were beating their way to earth again when he ran into a lady friend; a special lady friend who greeted him gaily and detained him with small talk. The Socialist was feeling rather at a loose end now, so was nothing loth to linger. It was Saturday night; no work to rise early for on the morrow, and Margie was not home. His emotions had been titillated, too, by his upset, so before very long he was pleased at the encounter. The woman, rather pretty, with the volatile attraction of the promiscuous among her sex, had many times before given practical evidence of her preference for the Socialist. They soon sauntered away into the dark.

But the exigencies of domestic life hurried the woman home; so it was still early, not ten o'clock, in fact, when the man approached his own front door. His thoughts were lingering on the little sexual interlude, pleasantly, for the Socialist liked his comforts, the thread of his own satisfactory domestic relations winding among them. A lucky beggar, certainly, to have landed a woman like Margie. All the same he could have — have done more — for his principles — have given a better lead, perhaps, if he had been called on personally to vindicate his philosophy. His honesty recognised that. Oh, well, it might come yet. If Margie ever said she wanted another man he would fade out of the picture with a 'good luck, old girl', if it broke his heart. It would, too, just about.

225

It struck him here (really, the night was one of revelations for the Socialist) that he had not given Margie the chance to decide whether she would care to 'fade out'. He flushed in the darkness, and stayed his steps a little to consider this. Why had not he? Certainly he had not deliberately decided to hide his unfaithfulness from her. No, it was custom, the damnable habit in the man, making of it a thing of no importance, calling for no particular attention, and yet — If Margie did it, he would expect her to come to him at once, before she actually committed herself, indeed, to save him from the baseness of 'cuckolddom', to allow him the exhibition of heroic magnanimity in effacing himself, in handing her over. If Margie did it it would mean the entire readjustment of their lives — to him — a cataclysmic force; an eruption that could do no less than bury the whole delightful companionship of their ten years together beneath its lava.

The Socialist winced. He could not escape that other habit — honesty, nor his passion for analysis. He saw that now for the first time he was really honest about his sex relations with Margie. He saw that all his clatter of principles, which in themselves were solid, had been hypocrisy. Only ten minutes before he had sauntered off into the dark with another woman, had quaffed at the cup of sex delights with her and without even bothering to justify himself — A mere nothing, a pleasant little incident not worth causing Margie a moment's trouble. But if she — Was he so much different from those other chaps after all? He broke out into a sweat. Perhaps here was the reason for that queer note, the strange attitudes of the fellows. They realised his hypocrisy and despised him. They made no pretensions of unordinary sex principles, even if they were socialists: the old double standard was good enough for them. Yes, he had been different but not enviably so. He had boasted of virtues they knew he did not possess; he had thundered forth principles they knew he did not act up to. He had been dishonest. He had practised their way of life while hypocritically pretending another. They all knew that Margie was faithful to him while he was unfaithful to her.

The Socialist saw himself as very small goods indeed. But he bucked up in no time. For it was finished now, that hypocrisy. He only needed to understand to act. It seemed that theories and philosophy were not enough in themselves. One had to have the practical experience of life in order to deal with it. But the practical experience was useless without the philosophy. Right action necessitated understanding – of causes. The reason why ordinary people were always botching their sex relations was because they were ignorant of the fact that the morals and sex life of the period were resultants of its economic life. Those people were unable to apply reason. But he and Margie were different. He would tell her as soon as she came home and if she finished with him would take his medicine.

But the Socialist did not really think it would be so serious as that. After all, women did not feel these things as men did. Male supremacy down through the ages had bred in woman a tolerance of the mate's faithlessness that that same supremacy had inhibited in man. He and his kind stood for sex equality in man and woman and knew it would be a feature of the future regime, but the very philosophy upon which their ideals were based taught them appreciation of the actual existing relations. Margie would probably cry and forgive him. And he would cut out the other women.

It was the rotten life they were compelled by conditions to live. No refinements, no amusements other than dancing which he hated (a good job Margie like dancing, it kept her occupied). And the women of the times were forced to seek some sort of excitement outside the squalor of their horrible tin shacks. (He and Margie occupied a fairly decent little house.)

Then in the contradictory way of thoughts he decided that there was really no reason why he should have lapsed in the matter of marital fidelity, for Margie was a passionate woman; always ready, usually seeking, in fact. He had sometimes thought that perhaps a little, just a tiny fraction less sexuality would have improved her. What was it that woman had told him that night. Oh, that one man was no good to a passionate woman. And he, probably with Margie latent in his mind, had told her laughingly to speak for herself. But Margie, bless her, was in love with him. Perhaps that constituted the difference in the two women. He hoped she continued so.

He had come to a stop a few yards in front of his home to finish his soliloquy in the night air. Now he made to go on but his steps were arrested again by a gleam of light which shot athwart the night from a side window of one of the back rooms, Margie's bedroom. (They occupied separate rooms.) Someone in there had suddenly struck a light. The Socialist was surprised. Margie must be home and it only ten o'clock! What had happened? She could not have just entered either, for he had plain view of the road leading to the back door. Why had the light only just flashed on? He hurried to the little front porch and fumbled for the knob of the door, his shoes clattering on the board floor. As he pushed the door back he heard a sort of scuffling from the back, from Margie's bedroom. He stood still and called out:

'Is that you, Marge?' but already his extreme sensitiveness had caught an inkling of peculiarity, of untowardness, and the half-second of dead quiet that followed his call stirred a clamour in his mind of a thousand questioning incoherent voices. Before he knew it he was at her door, turning the knob. It was locked. But he heard the key turn and it opened on the instant, disclosing Margie—Margie clad in nothing but a clinging woollen body garment. Her back was to the dull kerosene light.

The Socialist did not know what to say. He felt flustered as though he had done something wrong. He wanted to ask why she had locked her door, an unprecedented thing as far as he knew, but instead tried to smile and stammered:

'Hallo, Marge! What's wrong? It's only ten o'clock.'

'I—I got a headache at the dance and came home,' she answered, and the quavery note of her first word or two struck a chill to the heart of the Socialist. Then she added briskly: 'But you are early, too. I was just getting into bed. Didn't expect you till your usual time.'

'I'll get you a cup of tea if you've a headache,' the man said slowly, jingling some coins in his pockets and staring at her. She

228

came close and threw her arms around his neck.

'Do, there's a dear, Jimmy. The fire will only need a poke. I banked it well.'

He did not stoop at once to her lips as he usually did but let his eyes wander up and down her pretty arms, over her neck. Then he kissed her mouth slowly. He did not enjoy that kiss. It seemed stale, somehow. He thought that perhaps he had spent himself on the other woman. He continued to stare into her face. She patted his cheek with a rough little hand and asked:

'What are you staring at me like that for, you old owl? Haven't been drinking, have you? I can smell beer.'

He pushed her away suddenly, none too gently.

'I can smell something too, and it isn't beer,' he said grimly.

'Well, you can't smell anything on me but powder,' she answered sharply, a trifle defiantly.

He knew she had deliberately misunderstood him.

What was the matter? The Socialist felt that the whole world had turned over that night. Something was the matter with Margie! She knew that he thought so too, and was 'stalling' him. She faced him with real defiance now. He felt a queer prickling all over his body but mostly at the roots of his hair. His tongue ran over and over his lips. Something seemed to be piling up on him; something grotesque, laughable but hideous. He felt that there was a way of escape from it, too, but could not marshal his faculties sufficiently to take that way. He saw fright spring up in her eyes and did not know it was born of the fearsome aspect he himself was assuming.

She looked so lovely, standing there almost nude, so gloriously intimate. Her bustered golden curls were tumbling everywhere, almost into the eyes which were fearfully holding to his.

But the Socialist suddenly felt as though her nakedness were sinister, bad. He wanted to cover it up. It seemed that other eyes were looking at her, too; men's eyes, lewd eyes, chasing all over her coral body that had to be only his.

'Where's your nightdress?' he ripped out. A slow pallor spread over her face, down over her neck. She glanced around helplessly, then plucked up and with a show of bravado answered:

'It's none of your business where my nightdress is. What's the matter with you, anyhow? You're mad! Get out into your own room! You must be drunk.'

'Put on your nightdress!' he ordered harshly, feeling himself mad, right enough, in some strange way, but unable to help himself. There was something he had to admit to himself and he would do it better if he could not see her body. He trembled with awful emotion and stepped across the room to pick up her nightdress, which he could see lying in a heap on the floor beneath the open window. But she stepped in front of him, saying hurriedly:

'No, not that one. That one is dirty. That is why I didn't put it on. I'll get a clean one.'

There seemed to be significance in everything she said or did, to him. A clean nightdress, even, was suspicious. She was so urgent about it. Why be urgent about a nightdress? He looked at the one on the floor carefully. There was not much of it; a yard or two of lawn, yet it looked bulky, somehow, humped up. There *was* something urgent about it! He looked down into the woman's face, struggling with himself, though he could not get what the struggle was against.

'Jimmy!' she whispered. 'What is it, Jimmy?'

He threw her aside, bent down and grasped that little heap of lawn and there, lying awkwardly as though they had been dropped in haste, was a pair of man's boots.

The Socialist cackled. No other word could describe his strange cachinnation. And now he could see that her bed behind the door was badly rumpled. He groaned, unawares. Her fear was lost in an access of sympathy. She put her arms round his body below the shoulders and pressed her head into his neck, sobbing:

'Don't take it hard, Jimmy! It doesn't matter! It's only an incident. You should understand, Jimmy. It doesn't matter at all. I love you the same. Darling!'

He shook himself and loosened her hold; coughed again and again to expand his throat against the iron band that had closed around it. His head was clearing now. He was marshalling his faculties and making for that way of escape. Reason, understanding— The male in him had blotted them out but now that he was himself again—

Why in hell hadn't she covered herself up?

The cloud of hateful unreason descended upon him again. His gaze tore up and down her loveliness as if to brand her in every part with the fire of his jealousy. He saw her with the other man's eyes of lust; saw her— Jesus Christ! Could his life go on with that picture in his soul? Up from his heart to his brain came that gust of fire to beat in his temples and smear his eyes with red. His hands came up too and out, the fingers curved like talons.

She stifled a scream, dodged him and ran from the room, bringing him to himself with a jerk. What had he meant to do? To strangle her? Margie? By God! He grew limp with sickening, pallid fear. 'Margie! Margie!' he cried and sought her hurriedly. She had locked herself in another room but came out at once, wrapping an old coat of his around her as she came. The Socialist gathered her to him and begged her forgiveness.

'By God, Margie! By God! What it is to be a man! But you should have told me before you did it. Why didn't you? We always agreed that you would tell me if you liked another man better than me. I'd have let you go.' She dropped her eyes from his.

'I don't like him better than you. I don't like him at all, really.'

This turned him cold. He looked away from her and tried to get what that admission meant. It was not hard to get. It means that she was just another—Mrs Phillips, another like his lady friend of that night. 'One man is no good to a passionate woman.' The Socialist's soul filled with an anguish unspeakable, the anguish of broken trust in something he had reverenced. He thought of his boasted understanding, of his boasted cynicism. He knew himself now for a little child. His Margie, so good, so kind, so sweet and loving! He knew so much about women. Too much not to recognise now that Margie was an 'old hand' at this game. He grew furiously angry, in a sane manner, at the way he had been 'tricked'. Phillips' queer note; all the rest of it. He let her go suddenly, saying coldly:

'I'll get you that cup of tea.' She followed him out into the kitchen and sat down by the table, wondering visibly, gauging his temper. He poked the fire viciously through the bars. He hated himself and her; hated everyone and everything for the hash the incidents of that night had made of his preconceived notions. His fetishes had failed him; his reason and understanding. An escape? A warden-ship? He understood right enough. He wished he didn't. He knew, now that he was himself again, that this thing did not make Margie bad any more than his own adultery had made him bad. He could even admit that probably her sweetness, her graciousness, was born of the very sexuality that had demanded 'more than one man'. He could admit, even then, in his honesty, but Oh, the hell of bitterness the admission opened up for him! His very understanding caged him, his reason. Inhibited him from easing his hurt by punishing her, by leaving her, by believing in her 'badness', as those other common fellows would do. His principles, which he had imagined would be his safeguard, his protection, were proving instead a rack. He and his kind believed in the absolute sex equality of man and woman, believed in freedom of action for the individual. Well, Margie had only emulated his own example. He was caged. But here he remembered that she did not know of his adultery. This perked him up a lot; promised him some legitimate satisfaction. He would tell her of his own adultery. That would hurt her as hers had hurt him. Childishly he gloated over his power to hurt her as she had hurt him. He filled the little copper kettle at the sink, put it on the fire and then sat upon the table near her. He leaned towards her with a harsh laugh.

'Well, Margie,' he began, but before he could get any further the relish of his intended announcement dropped away. He was chilled and his intention crushed out of him by the sudden realisation that it would give him no satisfaction at all to tell her. No satisfaction at all! How was that! Oh, the Socialist knew, right enough, what it was. The very next instant he had recalled the fiat of society that the man's adultery mattered nothing because it signified nothing, but the woman's was the crime of crimes because it made for ambiguity of descent in a 'property' world. He understood that the inherited instincts of the ages were transcending the power of his reason and knowledge. It did not matter one whit if Margie knew of his own adultery, not from the point of view of his sufferings over hers. There was no ease for him, no surcease anywhere. He remained leaning towards her with his mouth open, gathering up and reflecting in his eyes the terror born of this complete realisation.

The woman could not understand his expression. She looked puzzled and piteously sympathetic.

'Oh, Jimmy, how can you take it like this? It isn't reasonable. Think of your own women, Jimmy. Have I ever fussed over your women?'

It seemed æons to the Socialist before he took that in properly. At last he asked queerly:

'So you knew — of my women? You knew?'

'Why, yes, Jimmy. I've always known. I knew the first time, I believe.' She reached out a hand and stroked his head. 'I knew. We have been very happy together, Jimmy — I understood.'

'Well, well,' said the Socialist. He got off the table, went to the dresser and brought two cups to the table; then went back and got two saucers. She had understood, ay? He understood now, too, by God, but it affected him differently. However, she was right; her attitude was the only one if they were to continue living together. He must conquer himself. What was she saying? — 'Make too much of this silly sex act. It doesn't mean anything, really. It is the smallest thing in life. It takes up only a moment or two out of millions of moments. The things that matter are comradeship, congeniality, friendship and kindness. You have told me this a hundred times, Jimmy. But we shall have to separate if you are going back on all your own philosophy.'

The Socialist mechanically put the cups in the saucers, then took out a handkerchief and wiped his brow.

'You are quite right, Margie,' he said. 'Quite right.'

She rose and went to him, drew down his head and kissed him. He returned her kiss, feeling better now, a little. Then the kettle boiled over and she turned to the stove. The Socialist thought: 'She must be right. I must apply reason. If reason can't triumph over emotion, mind over matter, there is no hope for the world. No hope! What was it he had said! Oh, no hope for the world In a second their meaning seemed transmuted into opposite significance. No hope — no hope!

Margie had bent down to the hearth to dust it. She was so tidy and methodical. The Socialist looked at her and thought dully, to the accompaniment of that 'no hope', 'I'll make the tea.' Margie knocked the poker from the fender to the floor at his feet. It clattered and the Socialist stooped and lifted it out of her way. No hope! What was it he had said! Oh, no hope for the world if Science — SCIENCE!!! He clutched at his throat with one hand. Something was happening to him. He felt it and struggled — some hideous thing was creeping into his brain; like hot wine, exciting him; like myriads of maggots, torturing him. His eyes turned inwards and saw pictures in his brain, pictures of men's eyes, lewd eyes, lust-inflamed eyes; of hands clutching at naked women. No, not women; just woman, and that woman was Margie, his Margie! Science!!! The Socialist laughed maniacally, to himself. He thought his laughter pealed out like cracked bells and echoed round the world, it was so loud, but really he made no sound. But he did not want to laugh. Laughter would not stop the gnawing maggots in his brain; the hot wine sizzling; the men from pawing at his naked Margie. There was something else he had to have! What was it, ay? Let him be quiet, just one second, and it would come to him. It was very close, he knew. Right beside him; at his feet; in his hand. Ah! He knew! He had it!

No hope if science failed, ay? Well, he — had hope — had surcease from his torment. The hideous pictures were blotted out; the soft, pulpy maggots withdrew from his brain; the wine flowed like silk, like ribbons of floss, which had somehow entangled themselves in the golden curls of her hair.

She got up off her knees, his Margie, and half turned to speak a word. He saw the softness of her smile, saw the gentle gleam of her wide intelligent eyes. She looked so placid, now, the

Socialist thought. It was rather a pity there was no other way. But life— Ah! she knew he was going to do it! He wished she hadn't turned around. Her horror, her terror, her wild cry of his name! No matter! No matter! No more men would paw her!

Her skull shattered so easily, though the poker seemed so light.

MARJORIE BARNARD
(1897–1987)

Barnard was born in Sydney. She graduated with distinction from the University of Sydney. Her collection of short stories, *The Persimmon Tree and Other Stories* (1934), is made up of carefully structured stories of inward, mostly female experiences. Barnard also wrote history books, literary criticism and children's stories. She was made an Officer of the Order of Australia for her services to literature in 1980.

Barnard collaborated with Flora Eldershaw on historical studies, literary criticism and five novels, including *A House Is Built* (1929). Their last novel, *Tomorrow and Tomorrow* (1947) was heavily censored when first published because of its apocalyptic view of Australia's future. It was finally published in its uncensored form and won the Patrick White Award in 1983.

HABIT

Miss Jessie Biden was singing in a high plangent voice as she made the beds. It was a form of self-expression she allowed herself only when there were no guests in the house, and she mingled the hymns and sentimental songs of her girlhood with a fine impartiality. She made the beds with precision, drawing the much-washed marcella quilts, with spiky fringes, up over the pillows so that the black-iron bedsteads had an air of humility and self-respect. The sheets, though not fine, smelt amiably of grass, and the blankets were honest, if a little hard with much laundering. With the mosquito nets hanging from a hoop, which in its turn was suspended from a cup hook screwed into the wooden ceiling, the beds looked like virtuous but homely brides.

Jessie stopped singing for a minute as she pulled the green holland blind to the exact middle of the window, and surveyed the room to see if all were in order. She had very strict notions about the exact degree of circumspection to which paying guests were entitled. Yesterday everything washable in the rooms had been washed, the floor, the woodwork, the heavy florid china on the rather frail, varnished wooden washstands. The rooms smelled of soap, linoleum polish and wood. The lace curtains were stiff with starch. Indeed, there was more starch than curtain, and without it they would have been draggled and pitiful wisps.

As every door in the house was open and it was a light wooden shell of a place, old as Australian houses go, and dried by many summers, Jessie could quite comfortably talk to Catherine, who was cooking in the kitchen, from wherever she happened to be working. But presently, the rooms finished, she came to stand in the kitchen doorway with a list of the guests they were expecting for Easter, in her hand.

The kitchen was a pleasant room looking on to the old orchard,

237

a row of persimmon trees heavy with pointed fruit turning golden in the early autumn, squat, round, guava bushes, their plump, red-coroneted fruit hidden in their glossy dark leaves, several plum and peach trees, one old wide-spreading apple tree and a breakwind of loquats and quinces. Beyond again was the bush, blue-green, shimmering a little in the morning sunshine.

Catherine Biden, too, was pleasant, and in keeping with the warm autumn landscape. Her red-gold hair, fine, heavy and straight, made a big bun on her plump white neck, her milky skin was impervious to the sun and her arms, on which her blue print sleeves were rolled up, were really beautiful. In the parlance of the neighbours, neither of the sisters would see forty again, which somehow sounded duller and more depressing than to say that Catherine was forty-two and Jessie forty-six.

'I'm putting the Adamses in the best room,' Jessie was saying, 'because they don't mind sharing a bed. And Miss Dickens and her friend in the room with the chest of drawers. Mrs Holles says she must have a room to herself, so it will have to be the little one. The Thompsons and Miss George'll sleep on the verandah and dress together in the other room. The old lady and her niece next to the dining room. That leaves only the verandah room this side, for Mr Campbell.'

'It's quite all right while the weather is cool,' said Catherine, in her placid way, rolling dough.

Jessie looked at her list with disfavour. 'We know everyone but Mr Campbell. It's rather awkward having just one man and so many women.'

'Perhaps he'll like it,' Catherine suggested.

'I don't think so. His name's Angus. He's probably a man's man.'

'Oh, if he's as Scotch as all that he won't mind. He'll fish all the time.'

'Well, all I hope is he doesn't take fright and leave us with an empty room.' The Easter season was so short, they couldn't afford an empty room.

'I hope,' said Catherine, 'we don't get a name for having only women. We do get more teachers every year and fewer men, don't we?'

'Yes, we do. I think we'd better word the advertisement differently.'

She sighed. Jessie, growing stout, with high cheek bones and a red skin, was the romantic one. She had always taken more kindly to this boarding house business than Catherine, because of its infinite possibilities — new people, new chances of excitement and romance. Although perhaps she no longer thought of romance, the habit of expecting something to happen remained with her.

Their father had married late. This house beside the lagoon had come to him with his wife and he had spent his long retirement in it, ministered to by his daughters. When he and his pension had died together, he had not, somehow, been able to leave them anything but the house, the small orchard and the lovely raggedy slope of wild garden running down to the water. Jessie, in a mood of tragic daring, advertised accommodation for holiday guests, carefully copying other advertisements she found in the paper. This expedient would, they hoped, tide them over. That was twelve years ago. A makeshift had become a permanency. In time, with the instrumentality of the local carpenter, they had added a couple of rooms and put up some almost paper-thin partitions. It looked as if they had developed the thing as far as they could.

They both still looked on their home as something different from their guest house. It was vested in that company of lares and penates now in bondage to mammon, but some day to be released. 'Our good things,' the sisters called them, the original furniture of the house, the bits and pieces that their mother had cherished. The big brass bed that had been their parents' was still in the best bedroom, though the cedar chest of drawers with pearl buttons sunk in its knobs and the marble topped washstand had gone to raise the tone of other rooms. The dining room was very much as it had always been. The sideboard with the mirrors and carved doors took up the best part of one wall, and set out on it was the old lady's brightly polished but now unused silver coffee service. The harmonium, with its faded puce silk, filled an inconvenient amount of room by the window. The old people's enlarged portraits, an ancient, elaborate work table with dozens of little compartments, and other intimate treasures not meant for paying guests, but impossible to move out of their way, gave the room a genteel but overcrowded appearance. In the dining room in the off season it was almost as if nothing had ever happened.

In twelve years Jessie's hopefulness had worn a little thin and Catherine's gentle placid nature had become streaked with discontent, as marble is veined with black. Sometimes she asked herself where it was all leading, what would happen to them by and by and if this was all life had in store? She began in a slow blind way to feel cheated, and to realise how meaningless was the pattern of the years with their alternations of rush and stagnation, of too much work and too little money. Of their darker pre-occupations the sisters did not speak to one another. In self defence they looked back rather than forward.

The guests began to arrive at lunchtime. Angus Campbell was the last to come, by the late train, long after dark. Catherine went up to the bus stop with a lantern to meet him. He saw her for the first time with the light thrown upward on her broad fair face, and he thought how kind and simple and good she looked. His tired heart lifted, and he felt reassured.

Undressing in the small stuffy room they shared, next to the kitchen, Jessie asked her sister, 'Do you think he'll fit in all right?'

'I think so,' Catherine answered. 'He seems a nice, quiet man.'

'Young?' asked Jessie with the last flicker of interest in her tired body.

'About our age.'

'Oh well . . .'

They kissed one another goodnight as they had every night since they were children, and lay down side by side to sleep.

The shell of a house was packed with sleeping people, all known and all strangers.

Angus Campbell evidently did not find his position of solitary man very trying, for on Easter Monday he asked, rather diffidently, if he might stay another week. He was taking his annual holidays. When the other guests departed, he remained. One week grew into two, then he had to return to Sydney.

He was a tall, gaunt, slightly stooped man with a weather-beaten complexion—the kind of Scots complexion that manages to look weather-beaten even in a city office—and a pair of clear, understanding, friendly, hazel eyes. His manner was very quiet and at first he seemed rather a negligible and uninteresting man. But presently you discovered in him a steadfast quality that was very likeable. You missed him when he went away.

When he was alone with the sisters, life settled inevitably into a more intimate rhythm. They ate their meals together on a rickety table on the verandah, where they could look over the garden to the lagoon. He would not let the sisters chop wood or do the heavy outdoor work that they were accustomed to, and he even came into the kitchen and helped Jessie wash up while Catherine put away. He did it so simply and naturally that it seemed right and natural to them.

One day he began digging in the garden, and, from taking up the potatoes they wanted, went on to other things. 'You oughtn't to be doing this,' Jessie said. 'It's your holiday.'

'You don't know how I enjoy it,' he answered, and his eyes, travelling over the upturned loamy earth to the blazing persimmon trees and the bush beyond, had in them a look of love and longing. She knew that he spoke the truth.

He went out fishing and brought back strings of fish for their supper with pride and gusto, and then had to watch Catherine cook them. There seemed to be something special about Catherine cooking the fish he caught.

He helped Catherine pick fruit for jam and she was aware that for all he was thin and stooped he was much stronger than she, and it gave her a curious, pleased feeling. Jessie, alone in the house, could hear their voices in the orchard, a little rarefied and idealised, in the still warm air.

Angus Campbell told them about himself. He was a clerk in a

secure job and for years he had looked after his invalid mother, coming home from the office to sit with her, getting up in the night to tend her, his money going in doctor's bills. She had often been querulous and exacting. 'The pain and the tedium were so hard for her to bear, and there was so little I could do for her. Of course I remember her very different. No one could have had a better mother. She was very ambitious for me, and made great sacrifices when I was a boy, so that I should have a good education and get on. But I never did — not very far.' It was evident that he thought he owed her something for that disappointment. Two months ago she had died and he missed her bitterly. 'She had become my child,' he said. He felt, too, the cruelty of her life that had been hard and unsatisfied, and had ended in pain. Now there was no hope of ever retrieving it.

One day it rained, great gusts of thick fine rain that blotted out the lagoon, and Angus, kept in, took his book on to the verandah. Passing to and fro doing the work, Catherine saw that he was not reading, but looking out into the rain. Then he went and stood by the verandah rail for a long time. She came and stood beside him.

He said, 'If you listen you can just hear the rain on the grass and among the leaves — and smell the earth. It's good, isn't it? The trees are more beautiful looming through the mist — the shape of them.' Marvelling, she saw that he was half in love with the beauty that she had lived with all her life.

A magpie flew through the rain, calling. He laid his hand on her shoulder and she was a little shaken by that warm and friendly touch. The eyes he turned on her still held the reflection of a mystery she had not seen.

'He is very good,' said Jessie to her sister when they were alone that night.

'And kind,' said Catherine. 'The kindest man I've ever known.'

Neither of them thought how few men they'd known.

Jessie raised herself on her elbow to look at Catherine as she slept in the faint moonlight, and thought how comely she was, sweet and wholesome.

When Angus had, at last, to go, he said he would be back for the weekend. They kissed him. He was to arrive on the Friday by the late train again, and Catherine prepared supper for him before the fire, for it was getting cold now. She took the silver coffee pot, the sacred silver coffee pot that had been their mother's, and put it to warm above the kitchen stove. She cast a half defiant glance at Jessie as she did so, but Jessie went and took the silver sugar bowl too, and the cream jug, filled them, and set them on the table.

Angus asked Catherine to go out in the boat with him or to go walking, and then he paid Jessie some little attention. But they both knew. One Sunday, perhaps it was the fourth weekend he had come, the autumn was now far advanced, he and Catherine went for a long walk and he asked her to marry him. He took her in his arms and kissed her. She felt very strange, for she had never been kissed before, not by a man who was in love with her. They walked home hand in hand as if they were still very young, and when Catherine saw Jessie waving to them from the verandah she stood still and the unaccountable tears began to flow down her cheeks.

They said, everybody said, that there was no reason why they should wait, meaning they had better hurry up. The wedding was fixed for three months ahead.

It was a curious three months for Catherine. When Angus came for the weekend they would not let him pay his board, and that made a little awkwardness. Even calling him Angus seemed a trifle strange. He did not come every weekend now. Once he said, 'It seems wrong to take you away from all this beauty and freedom and shut you up in a little suburban house among a lot of other little houses just the same. Do you think you'll fret, my darling?'

Catherine had never thought very much about the beauties of nature. So she just shook her head where it rested against his shoulder. Still, her heart sank a little when she saw his house with its small windows, dark stuff hangings and many souvenirs of the late Mrs Campbell. It seemed as if sickness and death had not yet been exorcised from it.

243

Catherine and Jessie sewed the trousseau. 'We must be sensible,' they said to one another, and bought good stout cambric and flannelettes, though each secretly hankered after the pretty and the foolish. Catherine could not quite forget that she was going to be a middle-aged bride, and that that was just a little ridiculous. Neighbours, meaning to be kind, teased her about her wedding and were coy, sly and romantic in a heavy way, so that she felt abashed.

A subtle difference had taken place in the relationship of the sisters. Jessie felt a new tenderness for Catherine. She was the younger sister who was going to be married. Jessie's heart burned with love and protectiveness. She longed, she didn't know why, to protect Catherine, to do things for her. 'Leave that to me,' she would say when she saw Catherine go to clean the stove or perform some other dirty job.'You must take care of your hands now.'

But Catherine always insisted on doing the roughest work. 'He's not marrying me for my beauty,' she laughed.

Catherine too thought more of her sister and of how good and unselfish she was, and her little peculiarities that once rather irritated her, now almost brought the tears to her eyes. One night she broached what was always on her mind.

'What will you do when I've gone?' she asked in a low voice.

'I'll get Ivy Thomas to help me in the busy times,' Jessie answered in a matter-of-fact voice, 'and in between, I'll manage.'

'But it will be lonely,' said Catherine weakly.

Jessie cast a reproachful glance at her. 'I'll manage,' she said.

Catherine was no longer discontented and weighed down with a sense of futility. Another emotion had taken its place, something very like homesickness.

As she did her jobs about the place she thought now, 'It is for the last time,' and there was a little pain about her heart. She looked at her world with new eyes. Angus's eyes perhaps. Going down to the fowlyard in the early morning with the bucket of steaming bran and pollard mash, she would look at the misty trees and the water like blue silk under the milk-pale sky; at the burning autumn colours of the persimmon trees, and the delicate frosty grass, and her heart would tremble with its loveliness.

One evening, coming in with the last basket of plums — ripe damsons with a thick blue bloom upon them — she stopped to rest, her back to the stormy sunset, and she saw thin, blue smoke like tulle winding among the quiet trees where a neighbour was burning leaves. She thought that she would remember this all her life. Picking nasturtiums under the old apple tree she laid her cheek for a moment against the rough silvery bark, and closed her eyes. 'My beloved old friend,' she thought but without words, 'I am leaving you for a man I scarcely know.'

It would seem as if the exaltation of being loved, of that one ripe and golden Sunday when she thought she could love too, had become detached from its object and centred now about her home. She even became aware of a rhythm in her daily work. Objects were dear because her hands were accustomed to them from childhood. And now life had to be imagined without them.

'Wherever I am, I shall have to grow old,' she thought, 'and it would be better to grow old here where everything is kind and open, than in a strange place.' It was as if the bogey she had feared, meaningless old age, had revealed itself a friend at the last moment, too late.

Jessie lit the porcelain lamp with the green shade and set it in the middle of the table among the litter of the sewing. She stood adjusting the wick, her face in shadow, and said:

'We'll have to have a serious talk about the silver and things, Cathy. We'd better settle it to-night before we get too busy.'

'What about them?' Catherine asked, biting off a thread.

'You must have your share. We'll have to divide them between us.' Jessie's voice was quite steady and her tone matter-of-fact.

'Oh, no,' cried Catherine, with a sharp note of passion in her voice. 'I don't want to take anything away.'

'They are as much yours as mine.'

'They belong here.'

'They belong to both of us, and I'm not going to have you go away empty handed.'

'But, Jessie, I'll come back often. The house wouldn't seem the same without mother's things. Don't talk as if I were going away for ever.'

'Of course you'll come back, but it won't be the same. You'll have a house of your own.'

'It won't be the same,' echoed Catherine very low.

'I specially want you to have mother's rings. I've always wanted you to wear them. You've got such pretty hands and now you won't have to work so hard . . . and the pendant. Father gave that to mother for a wedding present so as you're the one getting married it is only fit you should wear it on your wedding day too. I'll have the cameos. I'm sort of used to them. And the cat's eye brooch that I always thought we ought to have given Cousin Ella when mother died.' Jessie drew a rather difficult breath.

'You're robbing yourself,' said Catherine, 'giving me all the best. You're the eldest daughter.'

'That has nothing to do with it. We must think of what is suitable. I think you ought to have the silver coffee things. They've seemed specially yours since that night — you remember — when Angus came. Perhaps they helped . . .'

Catherine made a funny little noise.

'I don't want the silver coffee set.'

'Yes, you do. They're heaps too fine for guests. They're good. What fair puzzles me is the work table. You ought to have it because after all I suppose I'll be keeping all the big furniture, but this room wouldn't be the same without it.'

'No,' cried Catherine. 'Oh, Jessie, no. Not the work table. I couldn't bear it.' And she put her head down among the white madapolam and began to cry, a wild, desperate weeping.

'Cathy, darling, what is it? Hush, Petie, hush. We'll do everything just as you want.'

'I won't strip our home. I won't.'

'No, darling, no, but you'll want some of your own friendly things with you.'

Jessie was crying a little too, but not wildly. 'You're overwrought and tired. I've let you do too much.' Her heart was painfully full of tenderness for her sister.

Catherine's sobs grew less at last, and she said in a little gasping, exhausted voice. 'I can't do it.'

'I won't make you. It can stay here in its old place and you can see it when you come on a visit.'

'I mean I can't get married and go away. It's harder than anything is worth.'

Jessie was aghast. They argued long and confusedly. Once Catherine said: 'I wish it had been you, Jessie.'

Jessie drew away. 'You don't think that I . . .'

'No, dear, only on general grounds. You'd have made such a good wife and,' with a painful little smile, 'you were always the romantic one.'

'Not now,' said Jessie staunchly.

'I'll write to Angus now, to-night,' Catherine declared.

She wanted to be rid of this intolerable burden at once, although Jessie begged her to sleep on it. Neither of them had considered Angus, nor did they now. She got out the bottle of ink, and the pen with the cherry wood handle, which they shared, and began the letter. She was stiff and inarticulate on paper, and couldn't hope to make him understand. It was a miserable, hopeless task but she had to go through with it.

While she bent over the letter, Jessie went out into the kitchen and relit the fire. She took the silver coffee pot, the sugar basin and the cream jug, and set them out on the tray with the best worked traycloth. From the cake tin she selected the fairest of the little cakes that had been made for the afternoon tea of guests arriving tomorrow. Stinting nothing, she prepared their supper. When she heard Catherine sealing the letter, thumping the flap down with her fist to make the cheap gum stick, she carried in the tray.

Although she felt sick with crying, Catherine drank her coffee and ate a cake. The sisters smiled at one another with shaking lips and stiff reddened eyelids.

'He won't come again now,' said Jessie regretfully, but each added in her heart, 'He was a stranger, after all.'

ELEANOR DARK
(1901–1985)

Dark was born and educated in Sydney. In the early twenties she wrote some poetry and short stories for magazines. She wrote ten novels, and in many of these, such as *Prelude to Christopher* (1934) and *Return to Coolami* (1936), she has used a stream of consciousness technique. Dark is perhaps best known for her trilogy, *The Timeless Land,* which accurately traces the development of white settlement in Australia from 1788 to 1814. Her work reflects a love for Australia, and an understanding of the plight of the Aborigine and the destructive effects of Western civilisation. She has received many literary awards, and was made an Officer of the Order of Australia in 1977.

THE URGENT CALL

She had sometimes thought it strange that they had not become, after all these years, so used to the shrill summons of the telephone bell at night as to sleep through it, undisturbed. But no, when she considered it she knew herself—even the inner and unconscious self which might be supposed to stand sentinel during sleep—too much the slave of that telephone to ignore it, to forget it, even for a moment, day or night.

And now, waking with the start, the instant acceleration of her heartbeats, the vague sense of crisis that it always caused—feeling her husband stir, grunt, sit up and fumble at the foot of his bed for his dressing-gown, she thought with a weary resentfulness how merciless a tyranny it had been. In the early days when her energy and youth had rebelled at the restriction of her liberty, she felt bitter about it sometimes. But lately—what matter, after all? She was tired of such society and such diversions as Carawatha had to offer—had been tired of them for years. When one was old, slavery to a telephone became faintly ridiculous. And she was old. Yesterday, her sixtieth birthday had made her old. At fifty-nine one is still clinging to the last outpost of middle-age, but at sixty, one is old. One can let go, and admit—

Philip had found his slippers and was half-way to the door. It would ring again before he reached it. She saw him for a moment silhouetted in the doorway as he switched on the hall light, and it occurred to her for the first time as being strange and rather dreadful that she should know so accurately how he looked at that moment, bulky and dark, his head turned towards the telephone, his arm outstretched to the switch, his shadow lying along the floor and then climbing grotesquely at right-angles for a couple of feet up the wall.

And then moving. Moving in front of him out of sight, to leave her listening for the click of the lifted receiver and the sound of his bored voice.

But to-night as he spoke her momentarily caught attention wandered. A case — urgent, of course. She thought with the cynicism that comes to people who know both sides of a situation at first hand, that every case was urgent — to the patient. And to the doctor? One in — how many? Fifty? A hundred? She herself, periodically twisted on her bed with pain, understood the 'urgency' that sent stammering husbands and sons to peal at the night-bell and face, chafing, the doctor's calm questions and deliberate preparations. And from the other — the inside of the surgery door, she knew, too, how entirely without urgency her own case was. Thought, looking away from the lighted hall into the grateful dimness of the room, what a matter of routine and habit even this suffering of hers had become. At this very moment the pain, dulled by the hypodermic, nagged away at her and she scarcely heeded it. Urgent! She surprised herself by giving a tiny laugh which, anxiously, self-consciously, she turned into a cough. But he wouldn't have heard. He was talking himself, and listening, concentrating on the mangled directions which someone was giving him. She heard his bored voice sagging, sentence by sentence, into a veritable abyss of contempt.

'God, what a fool!' said his tone. *'God, what a blasted fool!'*

The receiver went back on to the hook quietly, evenly. No irritation of his mind, however acute, translated itself into meaningless physical gestures. He came back into the bedroom, and she shut her eyes quickly to escape the sudden glare of the electric light as he switched it on. And when she opened them again he was, most strangely, not reaching for his clothes where they lay on the chair by the bed, but standing still, with his head turned as though his attention had been suddenly caught, and staring at her. She asked indifferently, from habit, 'Accident?'

'No. Confinement.'

He turned away and began dressing in his methodical, unhurried fashion. She (while one part of her brain began to puzzle — worrying like a dog at a bone over that strange, intercepted look of his) drifted off again into the meandering thoughts which her own question had interrupted.

What happened to you, she wondered, when you came to the stage of admitting nakedly to yourself that you no longer cared for your life? Not, actually, that you wanted to be rid of it, but that you had acquired a kind of negative outlook — neither hoping nor dreading, neither liking nor disliking — for love and hate, of course, had long since faded into that, like a vividly-dyed scarf bleached into neutral tones.

He said, shrugging himself into his coat, 'Feeling any better?'

Ah, that was it. The part of her brain that had been puzzling relaxed into a faint amusement. He had noticed, suddenly, how ill she looked. She answered. 'Yes, the pain is a good deal easier now,' and shut her eyes again.

Marriage. How extraordinary a relationship! As if two people, by telling their thoughts, by flinging their beliefs and opinions at each other, by welding, desperately, their bodies together, and by spending long years of days and nights side by side, imagined they could evade or conquer the dreadful solitude of every human soul! Here they were, she and Philip, after thirty-five years together — strangers. And yet, how intimately, how unmercifully they knew each other — up to a point, and no further. Intimate strangers —

Urgent! She started awake, roused from the drowsiness that had been drifting over her by the click of the front door as Philip closed it behind him. The word was in her mind, clanging like a loud bell — like a fire-alarm — Urgent! Urgent! Urgent! Actually the suggestion of the word was having its effect on her. She was very broadly awake, slightly excited, eager, apprehensive, anxious, exhilarated.

What about? She asked herself the question, scornful, but a little breathless. Had she not just been thinking of the still monotony of her physical life and the passive drifting that had come to be her mental existence? What possible urgency, then, for her?

She had thought afterwards that it was only the mist lying softly over everything, and the dark pines appearing up through it as she had seen them do in Scotland, that had made her first homecoming endurable.

Sydney, grey and glistening wetly under the drizzling sky had had a rather reassuring look. The easy-going air of its narrow streets (which suddenly jerked away at an angle, as though they had forgotten something and were off at once to fetch it) was not to be withstood). Those hours had been her first with Philip, too, after four years of separation; no wonder, perhaps, that there had been a reassurance, a glamour, oddly as they went under the gloomy sky. He had taken her almost straight from the boat to the church. She had scarcely begun to feel her physical balance restored before she was thrown into the strange mental confusion of finding herself Philip's wife.

The next morning, however, had found the new country already less glamorous, and an hour in the train that bore them west brought her to the verge of panic. He was pointing out places to her, and her tired brain rang with names, that had no meaning. She remembered that she had said, forcing a laugh, 'But to me it looks as if we were coming to the same station over and over again!'

For there was no kindly reassurance in this landscape. It did not break out into little woods like laughs, nor collect itself into neat fields, gathering their fences demurely about them; it had no hedges, no lanes, no little criss-crossing byways — only one long, naked, relentless-looking road that fled on beside the train with a singleness of purpose that was intimidating. Only mile after mile of dark green, sombre trees, and dull green sombre undergrowth. Only a few houses, and those, too, rather dreadful in their solitude and the starkness of their shape and colouring.

It was dusk when they came at last to Carawatha — half past five, and a winter evening. Cold — colder, she thought, shivering into her overcoat, than England — and damp and bleak. But as she saw the place spread out below, falling away from the high ridge along which the railroad picked its way, some vague sense of sudden familiarity warmed her. It did not look so bad, after all; lonely, yes, and rather dreadfully huge, but there was Scotland in it, somehow — in the bite of the air, in the vagueness of the mountain country with its alien trees half-veiled in mist.

The street, now wide and concreted, bordered by flourishing shops, alive with cars and people, had been more like a track in those days. Philip had held her arm and guided her past ruts and slippery places. No lights except the gleam of a window here and there broke the grey evening, swiftly gathering into night. She remembered a thrill of nervousness as she walked down the hill beside him. Surely nowhere in the world grew trees as grim as these that fringed the road and dripped on to her shoulders. One had been used to thinking conventionally of yews and cypresses as the gloomy trees — but surely the dark profusion of their foliage seemed almost smug beside the gaunt white nakedness of these gums. The bark hung from them in strips and tatters; she thought that they looked like starving prisoners, defiant in their rags.

At the bottom of the road, in the dark shadows, Philip had stopped suddenly, dropped his suitcase, and taken her in his arms. Only snatches of what he had said came back to her now. 'So lonely —' 'Like Heaven to have you here —' '. . . to make you happy —' But she knew that they had clung to each other, and all the glamour had rushed back on her like a fire, all her strength and optimism flared up anew. She kissed him, tears on her mist-wetted cheeks.

They had walked after that with their arms about each other, ridiculously, in a wild, reckless mood of joy and union. Only one thing remained clearly in her mind of that night. The strangeness of it, the very intensity of her emotions seemed to have blurred it in her mind to something that was less a memory than a sensation — until she came, in her methodical march of recollection, to the moment when she had put her hand on the gate.

He had turned, stopped, put down the suitcase, still in a silence they had felt neither wish nor power to break. Her right hand, released from his warm clasp, went out to touch the dim, white-painted gate before her. Its hardness, coldness, wetness, ripped through her mood of beatitude like a jagged knife through silk.

253

The eyes she lifted, peering beyond to the shadowy house, were startled, vaguely apprehensive.

Now, turning a little on her pillow, shrugging a little mentally, she told herself that there must be *something* in being in love. Some power of receptiveness, some acuteness of understanding, some mysterious sixth sense that made you, for a little while, at least, strangely one with your beloved. For in that brief second her hardly-formed misgiving had communicated itself to him. He said nothing, but she knew that he had felt it. She said nothing, but he knew that she knew. Naked and dismayed their souls confronted each other.

The house, shut up for three days, greeted them with a smell of dampness and linoleum. He struck a match and lit the gas. Her smile was ready. Snatched from her consciousness and spread briskly, efficiently over her face, it met his anxious eyes, challenged them, and won. Pulling off her hat she found words. 'It's good to be home — such a long time travelling — '

She was caught into his arms, and the merciful obliterating force of their passion and past loneliness lifted the night away on the wings of its illusion. They slept, and woke to a world of brilliant sunshine.

From the doorway she had watched him drive off in the little trap that took him to his more distant patients, and still, even after he was out of sight, stood there with her finger to her cheek staring absently at the curve of the road, and wondering —

There was a change in him. Four years did make a difference, of course, but not such a fundamental difference as she dimly felt had been wrought in Philip. He had been a light-hearted lad, and he was now a serious-minded man — well, that was not unnatural — if it had been only that. She could not have told where he had betrayed it, but a change was there. Was it cynicism? She was not clever — the subtler shades of analysis had always escaped her. Even now, at sixty, she told herself, grimly, it was only the 'patter' that she knew — only the jargon of psychology that she had picked up from the years with Philip. So she had stood there on the verandah, and arrived, finally, at no better conclusion than that he was 'different, somehow — '

Her virtue had always been that she was 'practical'. It was a virtue which, casually attributed to her once or twice in her childhood, had become her beacon light. She had striven towards it. She had added, with the lust of a collector, ever more and more accomplishments to her list. Not frivolities, but useful things. She could sew, of course, and knit, and crochet. She had learned with an almost religious fervour, to cook superlatively. She could saw a bit of wood and drive a nail. She was an 'organiser'—a leader and driver in all things that require energy and a certain eager belligerence. Already she was on the alert to catch these unknown Australians out in—in—in what? In anything! Just to convince herself, perhaps, of a superiority which, alone in an alien country, had seemed very necessary to her self-respect.

Superiority! She moved suddenly on the bed, a movement which, caused by a sharp stab of mental uneasiness, brought a gasp of physical pain to her lips. Why in the name of Heaven should she be thinking so terribly to-night? Never before had she known so intimately that queer, hostile, lonely girl who had been herself nearly forty years ago. What did that girl matter now? Why should she lie here in the semi-darkness adding to her bodily torment the misery of remembering days long past—happily long, long past! Superiority! That word stuck and rankled. She realised that for the first time in her life she was doubting it. Clutching at it she began to peer about the dim room; she needed no light to tell her of the soft depth of the carpet, the rich texture of the curtains, the exquisite embroidery on the bedspread now folded with mathematical neatness on the couch near her feet. The street lamps, filtering through lace curtains, touched the silver on her dressing-table to points of brightness, and threw one soft bar of light across the rose-coloured eiderdown, and two diamonds that glimmered on her thin, white hand.

Fleeing still from thoughts less welcome she began to roam in imagination through her beautiful house; at her feet the rare wood of the floors shone softly like satin beyond velvety carpets; her bathroom glittered; (with a nervous twitch of annoyance she thought of what Mrs Osborne had said of it—not to her, of

255

course, but these things always found their way back. '*A perfect menace of nickel and porcelain! It positively snaps at you: "Be dirty if you DARE!"* ' A silly woman, Mrs Obsorne. One of those women who run down anything better than what they have themselves.)

But her moment of housewifely pride had passed, leaving her feeling curiously defenceless again. For that, after all, had been her consuming passion. For this house and all its luxurious comfort she had worked and Phil had worked for nearly forty years. She began actually to tremble at the new and awful knowledge that had come to her — the realisation that all her life had gone by in the pursuit of something so utterly unsatisfying as a lovely house. Things passed in a flash while one was striving. One missed them. She remembered vaguely a picture of the *Pilgrim's Progress* — something about a man with a muck-rake — who missed a crown while he was grubbing in the dirt. What then, was the crown? Wearily she wondered if it was children. After all, one could not help being childless. She remembered the helpless rush of anger and jealousy that had filled her in the early days when Mrs Osborne had said briskly, just after her first baby was born: 'We're going to have one more when this one is about three, and that's all.'

And, surely enough, along had come the small daughter just after the son had celebrated his third birthday. There were women who could plan and control and limit — and there were those who went empty-armed all their days. Well, they survived. They turned their energies to something else. She tried for a moment to remember the name Phil's psychology books gave to that, and then decided cynically that the name mattered little to *her* — she had been *doing* it all her life. But had she? To-night she was not so sure. To-night she had to admit that for her, at least, children were the crown — and had she found any substitute even dimly satisfactory? Ah, it was all very well to talk of muck-raking! Things happened so slowly — one hope merged into another, a desire for this became, imperceptibly a desire for something entirely different. When, at what stage of her life in this town had that early ambition to push her husband and her husband's practice merged into — into — ?

Grimly she lay still, forcing her thoughts onward. Into a mere lust for personal possessions; an overmastering need to know her own husband more successful than the other doctors, her own house more beautiful and more beautifully directed than any in the town, her own clothes more expensive, her own car more sumptuous —

Well, she had all these things. Yes, so far she could still say she had them all; but what was coming? The defeatedness of old age clutched at her suddenly — that was something one could not fight. Philip was nearly seventy, and Osborne a mere forty-seven or forty-eight. She herself, for all her straight figure and handsome head of silvery hair, was sixty, and Osborne's wife about thirty-nine. Well, their turn would come! Young Hartigan was barely thirty, and his wife a mere flapper. They would push the Osbornes out someday. She felt a stab of regret that she would not be there to see it, and a sharper stab as she realised that probably there would be no question of pushing. In her new clear-sightedness there was no blinking the fullness, if not the happiness of their lives. There would be no pushing of such people. They ran their own existence. And she knew bitterly that from the beginning — from that first morning when she had stood at the door of their little cottage to wave goodbye to Philip, she had been driven, driven, driven —

Now when it was all over, she cared nothing for what people said; but in those days public opinion had been, unadmitted even to herself, her driving force. It *had* to be, she thought angrily, when your bread and butter, your future, the future of the children you hoped you were going to have, depended utterly on the verdict of this same public. The humiliation of it! Their malice, their heedlessness, above all their ignorance, had been a perpetual thorn in Philip's flesh — and he could not, or would not dissimulate. The burden, then, had fallen on her; to smile where he had frowned, to chat when he had snapped, to heal the raw patches of irritation and hostility which he had made.

Thoughts came to her now whose strangeness she was quite unable to express. From that last point in her musings an idea expanded and blossomed, giving her mysteriously the answer to a problem which, cheek in hand, she had pondered so many years ago. That change in Philip—that 'something different' was a conflict between two almost paradoxical emotions which grew increasingly side by side. Respect, passionate admiration for mankind—and an intellectual contempt equally passionate, for the average man. He had called them once—during the war, it was, 'sublime asses', and she, packing socks and pyjamas for the Red Cross, had been slightly shocked. One did not call 'our boys' asses, even with 'sublime' in front of it. Anyhow, she had thought irritably, coaxing a sheet of brown paper from its wrinkles, there was no sense in it; asses were not sublime—they were just—well, asses.

Now that she came to think of it most doctors seemed to have that feeling. Even Osborne, imperturbability itself, hid it, she felt sure, behind his everlasting one-sided grin. But Philip didn't hide it. She herself had felt that speculative eye on her. His very habit of retiring suddenly from any argument with her—his way of giving her the last word as one might give a child a toy—were enough to make her feel that she was a mental outsider.

She had cried once, knowing it untrue:

'You know I'm right! You don't care to argue with me!'

And he, thin and grim and polite, had answered:

'Argument calls for a certain amount of logic on both sides. You haven't an ounce of it in your whole composition. You're just a Martha.'

Well, perhaps it was true; she didn't claim to be brilliant. But logic or none, it was *she* who had pushed the practice, she who had earned, in the truest sense of the word, this ease and luxury, this pleasant position of importance in a rapidly growing town.

And she hadn't always been a Martha. Even now, old and sick as she was, she could remember the early days and the heart-stirring sweetness of them; she could remember when there had been love between herself and Phil—love that was a real bond, love of the spirit — not anything like the queer emotion that she sometimes sensed uneasily in the Osbornes — sharp, bitter, restless — a thing, she felt sure, less of the spirit than of the body and the brain.

And yet it seemed to last. Was that, perhaps, the real test of love — not its ideals, its aspirations, its expression, but simply its staying-power? Defeatedly she put her arm under the bedclothes, drew the sheet up closely round her shoulders, shivered a little.

How she had worked! A wild rebellious nausea rushed over her as she thought of it — a frantic hatred of floor-polish and sandsoap, and dusters and brooms and grease and saucepans. Martha! It was easy to jeer. The house had to be kept clean. She couldn't help it if she was particular. She was made like that. A tap unpolished, a spotted window-pane, a dusty cupboard-top — what could one do but clean them? There they were — a ceaseless mental irritation silently accusing her until she dealt with them.

What had she not sacrificed to that house — forced Phil to sacrifice? Her youth, her temper, her health — she had flung them all on that fire of fierce acquisitiveness which had begun so innocently as a small warm flame of wifely enthusiasm! Now that it all seemed so remote, so unimportant, she was lost in a blank wonder at herself. Fiercely, almost thankfully, in her passion for economy, she had adopted the Australian woman's attitude of relentless domesticity. In the early days she had kept no servant at all. Even now, so irrevocably was she in the grip of her habit, she kept only one — and her hands twitched irritably on the rose-coloured eiderdown at the very thought of Gladys, dancing up there at the Casino with her young man, the whole of her week's wages on her back, and too sleepy to-morrow morning to dust the surgery properly —

And there had been that absurd lawsuit —

It had hurt her at the time with a torture that was almost physical. For years afterwards she had literally flinched at the remembrance of it. She, weary and irritable from domestic toil and the unrelenting tyranny of the telephone to be told that her house was not clean! To have it shouted from the housetops — to

259

have her cupboards and floors, her windows and shelves, discussed in every cottage, even, actually starred in the miserable little local paper. Of course it had been only spite on the part of old Miss Barlow. She had seemed to imagine that because a doctor rented her house she was entitled to free medical attention. Well, she wasn't. And if Phil was too weak to tell her so, of course his wife had to do it. Her temper, never far below the surface, had bubbled up, overflowed, rushed down on the tight-faced little spinister like lava from a volcano.

'You call a doctor out in the middle of the night and expect not to pay him for it! He has his living to make — and let me tell you it's to your advantage he should make it, for you'd get no other tenants for such a miserable, ramshackle, inconvenient bit of a place — there's that bathroom, it's the worry of my life! And the way the rain comes through into the kitchen — !'

And the tight-faced spinster, gripping her umbrella in both hands like a club, had rapped it excitedly on the stone doorstep and cried out shrilly:

'There's nothing wrong with the place if it were only kept *clean*!'

When the old woman, fiercely muttering, had gone, she had walked down her little hall over the polished linoleum feeling stunned. Almost, for a moment, she had doubted herself! The accusation was so grotesque that it was impressive. She peered about for dust, and would have abased herself in shame for one grain of it. There was none. She knew there was none. Had she not gone round herself with her slightly damped duster, polishing the rungs of the chairs, the carved intricacies of the sideboard till they shone?

And yet, of sheer spite, the old woman had brought her lawsuit. It had failed, of course; but it had been. It had dragged her domestic reputation into the question, and never (so she realised to-night) had she succeeded in escaping from that question-mark. Everyone else had long-since forgotten it. Only she herself had always felt it there, pricking like a microscopic thorn, goading her on — on —

Martha!

'Oh, God!' she thought passionately. 'To have my life again!'

As if shocked into activity by so extraordinary a desire, pain leapt at her again out of its forgotten lair. She was suddenly nothing but a mass of pain, clutching at the bedclothes, clutching at her breast, gasping for breath. She was afraid now; death was coming close to her just as she had realised the preciousness of the life she had so madly squandered. She listened feverishly to a passing car — but it was not Phil's — it was going on, up the hill. The first delirium of agony passed slowly, and she lay exhausted, her thin body twitching under the rose-coloured quilt. Dully, mechanically following deep-worn grooves of thought, her brain took up its burden again.

Someone was ill — very ill — in pain. Philip must be summoned. It was urgent.

The word clanged relentlessly. Urgent, urgent. She must get to the telephone and ring up Philip. But she did not want — oh, how desperately and painfully she did not want to go to the telephone. She hated it; it was her gaoler, her accuser, her tyrant. It was the symbol of her long, weary, aimless life. And even as she thought she was dragging herself out of bed. Messages for Philip must be delivered. If it had not been such a long way — so many miles of thick carpet and satiny floor — if she were younger, of course, it would not be so hard to get to the telephone — but the case was urgent, and she must hurry.

And then, again, one's eyesight was not good. She had thought that she was quite close to it, and yet when she stretched out her hand to the receiver she touched only the air. Now she had it, and its hard, cold rim was against her ear. She spoke clearly into the unhearing wires:

'You must ask the doctor to go at once — it is very urgent —'

She felt a deep relief as she lay there. She had got the message to Philip, and now she needn't worry any more. But even thick carpets were curiously hard to lie on — and cold. The telephone on the wall above her looked enormous — it filled the world. She had left the receiver dangling. She must get up and put it on the hook again, or the calls would not come through —

A little flame of rebellion shot up.

Oh — let it be. Let it be.

She turned away her head.

261

HENRIETTA DRAKE-BROCKMAN
(1901–1968)

Drake-Brockman was born in Perth and educated in Scotland, Western Australia, and New South Wales. She studied English and French literature at university.

Drake-Brockman wrote short stories about the outback, using knowledge gained from her extensive travels there. Her fiction often shows sympathy for the Aborigines and for the loneliness of women in the bush.

She published five novels, several plays, and a collection of short stories; and edited several popular anthologies.

THEIR COUNTRY

From the camp—tent and flies pitched back to the road, facing the mountains—they could see the summit of Toolbrunup and the long lines of the Sleeping Beauty.

Toolbrunup rolled from their tongues as easily as for generations it had rolled from the tongues of their people; but they no longer knew its meaning. The Sleeping Beauty—there was no native name for her, though they had learnt to trace her, a white man's Beauty, lying face to the sky, hair sweeping back in a Garboesque torrent of rocks immovably there for centuries before the earth knew Garbo.

But the camp knew Garbo. One night they had gone to the pictures in the hall, back in a town on the railway-line. They'd been parked right in front; there had been a bit of fuss about letting them in at all. But Charlie had just cut-out on a small shearing job, and his money was dam' well as good as anybody else's, he told the ticket-man. That's how it happened young Ada saw Garbo and pointed out in a high excited giggly voice the way her hair grew off her forehead like the Sleeping Beauty's hair, back at the mountains.

That was the only bit of interest in the silly film. The second half of the programme turned out better, fellers on horses and girls who could live in tents and cook a damper. When Mickey Mouse turned up, well, that was a real chuck-in—they all got pains laughing. They still got pains laughing, whenever Ada took off Mickey Mouse.

She was a bright one, Ada, and no mistake. Old man Paddy, who still mumbled blackfeller talk through his purple lips into his grey beard, got properly wild when Les Mick started hanging round Ada, round about the time she turned eleven. Les Mick wasn't the proper man for Ada, said old man Paddy, Les was *windong* for Ada.

Ada's mum laughed. Hadn't they got over that blackfeller stuff a long time back? Hadn't she and all the girls married anybody they happened to fancy, same as other Australian girls? Ada's fat old mum could talk — she'd had a job, she had, with some of the settlers, when she was a kid. Properly brought up, she was. And she'd got Ada before she got a husband, too. Ada was a proper bright one and no mistake. Wasn't Ada's white dad all sorts of a big man in his town now? Ada could do what she liked.

There was quite a crowd in the camp. Charlie had splashed all his cash buying the horse and cart to fetch them out there to the ranges, where Les Mick had picked up this job of mustering stragglers in the thick mountain scrub. Charlie had his woman Winifred and their tribe of kids. Then there was Les himself, who was Winifred's brother, and old man Paddy, who was Charlie's uncle. Les Mick had fetched along his friend Harry Clark. Besides Ada and Ada's mum, there was Jo, Ada's mum's husband, who was lame, and all their kids, and four dogs — two kangaroo bitches and a couple of any-sorts. Actually the two kangaroo bitches and old man Paddy were the only full-breds in the camp. But Ada was the only one of the whole bunch, except for a couple of toddlers, who showed white much in the skin.

Ada's mum soon had their bit of a tent shipshape — blankets and chaff-bags made into bunks, the gramophone set up on a box, a fox-trot going. Jo lit a fire and put the billies on to boil. Charlie's Winifred slung their fly from the back of the cart, for the old man to sit under with his pipe. Charlie took the dogs to see if he could start up a roo. Les Mick and Harry Clark went out to scout round and see what hunting for stragglers in the heavy scrub was going to be like. Les tried to get Ada to go out with them, too, but she wouldn't. The old man might have saved his worry, Ada didn't like Les any more now she was fifteen than she had before!

Everyone reckoned Ada was dippy and should have had a boy a long time ago. But Ada thought of Garbo and kept her dippy thoughts to herself. She was a happy kid. She loved her fat mum and the toddlers and above everything she loved being out there

264

close to the mountains. She would never leave the mountains!

She could have got a job back in town as a servant, any day. But she didn't want just to wash dishes and clothes and buy lollies and face-powder and have boys, any more than she wanted to hitch up with Les Mick and cart round a tribe of kids like her mum, and live in a tent. Ada didn't quite know what she did want. But she always felt happy out near the mountains. She could act Mickey Mouse there, and make the camp die laughing; she could sing songs learnt off the gramophone and make up dances to her songs.

She poured water out of their big petrol-tin tank into a tin basin and had a wash. She did her hair in front of her mum's cracked mirror and tied a pink ribbon round her head. Then she went and stood over by the road and looked out for Charlie. If he'd got a roo, or even a brush, it'd be real good, they'd grill the steaks over the coals after the sun went down. The sun lay low and gold in the west already. Behind the camp, in the east, against a ribbon-pink sky, dark-blue—like she'd seen the sea once, when she was a little kid. Ada sang under her breath.

At last she spotted Charlie. He wasn't coming round by the road at all, but through the scrub, bent almost double under the weight of a big boomer. Watching Charlie, Ada missed seeing Ron McGovern ride down the road and draw rein, abruptly, caught by what he saw.

What Ron saw was a slender smiling excited youngster, with a pink ribbon tied in her hair, clean-cut against the dark scrub, haloed by the rosy sky. He saw her first, and the picture she made stamped itself so deeply over other pictures of girls he'd got in his mind that he felt she might have been the first girl he had ever seen.

Then he saw Charlie come staggering up, saw the cart and the fire and the tents. One bit of him saw those, noted their meaning, while the rest of him watched Ada. She moved, she laughed out loud and ran to help Charlie, and the fact of her breeding ran away before the grace of her, almost before Ron McGovern knew he had realised it.

He reached the camp-site just as Charlie chucked his burden on the ground.

'Good night,' he said.

Charlie looked up, blown, his chest heaving under his blue shirt, the sweat standing out on his fine black skin.

'G'day,' he gave back pleasantly, and kicked aside the dogs from the carcass. Ada went to chase them. But first she glanced up at the fellow on the horse.

She saw instantly that he was young and white. His red hair and two bright blue eyes made his forehead, where he'd pushed his hat back, show up like a white bandage across the tan of his face. He looked straight at her, though he was talking to Charlie. Something in his look made her stop dead. Before she could pull her eyes away, she knew why she'd never got keen on boys. Or married Les Mick.

'That's hard work, dammit,' Charlie grunted, kicking the carcass. 'Three mile I've lugged that dam' thing. But we gotter have meat.'

'Yous live out here?' asked the white man.

'Um. For now. We come out mustering stragglers. Town's no good t' us. Won't let the kids t' school like they used when I was a boy — moan if we go t' the pictures, give y' a job now and then if y' lucky and expect a feller t' live on rations. Flour and sugar and a pincher tea! Gorblimey, and I c'n do a job er work with any man! Like t' save the cash and get a block out here and run sheep, I would. This country round here, it's our country, old man Paddy there says. I reckon it could run sheep, a few enough f'r us. What you reckon?'

'Hope so. Just taken up a block further out meself.'

Charlie grinned. 'Want any fencing, boss, or scrubbing down?'

McGovern took a packet of cigarettes out of his pocket. 'No boss about me, yet. I got t' do me own hard yakka or go under. Have one?'

Charlie's arm came up for a fag. 'Thanks.'

'D'you mind if I feed here tonight? I got me tucker with me.'

Charlie said easily, 'Good-oh. If you lent us a hand with that roo, we'll be no time.'

Often in the next few weeks McGovern left his humpy to share a meal at Charlie's camp. Charlie, Les Mick and the rest of them, set up a sort of base camp for the women and kids, for old man Paddy and lame Jo, in one of the gullies, while the younger men went ranging. More than one day, McGovern lent a hand to Charlie, and once or twice Charlie, Les Mick and Harry Clark went over to McGovern's to work on the place. Les didn't cotton to McGovern, though. Old reason, old story. Only that to Ron McGovern and Ada it seemed new and different.

At first, Ron had a bit of a fight with himself. Ada said nothing, but her eyes and her smiling lips and the songs she sang out on the gully-slopes soon told young McGovern the rightness of it.

The day came when Ron thought it damned silly she wasn't with him all day and all night, across with him in his humpy, helping him build up his place. So he asked Charlie about it.

Charlie said: 'She's a quarter-caste, Ada is. Ward of the Government. The Department says who'll she marry. And if y' don't marry her, they'll quod you f'r anything else. That is, if they find out.'

'Are you married t' Winifred?' Ron demanded.

Charlie laughed, 'We ain't so white as Ada, so they ain't so fussy. She's my woman, I stick to her. That's all.'

'Well, I reckon Ada's my woman. I'd stick to her.'

For a long moment Charlie said nothing. Then his eyes turned on Ron's and held them straight. 'Would you?'

Ron said yes, he would.

Charlie fell silent again. 'Well then, Ron,' he said slowly. 'I reckon you'd better not ask anything. The Department, they want her t'marry Les Mick. Les's been asking f'r years. Only Ada won't. She's not easy, Ada.'

So Ron didn't ask anybody except Ada. And she just took her pink ribbon and her two dresses and her toffee-tin full of little treasures, and went over to Ron's humpy. Her mum didn't mind. Ada was that happy, now she'd got a house of her own and a bed! Ron was going to build a bathroom even, when he got on enough to buy tanks and a bath. Ada didn't even worry when one day Les Mick cleared into town along with Harry Clark. Charlie did, a bit. He kept it under his hat though; he reckoned Les was one of themselves and wouldn't hurt Ada.

Ron was out fencing and Ada on her own, when the police turned up.

He wasn't a bad sort, the constable, and he could see by how well Ada kept the humpy how happy she must be; though as soon as she set eyes on him she stiffened up like a chilled carcass. The constable couldn't get anything out of Ada, her frightened eyes kept twisting to the door.

Ron came home singing at the top of his lungs, hat shoved back on his red head so the white stood out on his forehead. When he saw the police car, he stopped dead, frozen up like Ada. The constable wasn't so easy with him.

'Don't you know it's a criminal offence to cohabit with one of these here half-castes? She's a ward of the state, Ada is. We're going to take her back into town with us right now. You can explain after.'

Ada ran to Ron, she clung to him, she didn't call out. The sound of her soft begging voice was worse than any singing out. 'No, no—don't let them, Ron, don't let them take me away!'

'She's my woman,' said Ron stoutly. 'I'm ready to marry her.'

'Oh, are you? Well then, why ain't you done it? You come along and tell that to the heads.'

Ron's hand on Ada's hair moved very gently, up and down, as if she'd been a little kid. He said slowly, stammering a bit: 'I ain't because—because I got a wife already.'

Of course on paper, on the file in the office marked: 'ADA SMITH, Quarter-Caste' etc. etc., it appeared moral enough. It was reasonable to suppose that a certain young man called Ronald McGovern, who had left a white wife in the lurch, would not, divorced, make a good husband for Ada Smith, quarter-caste. It was only reasonable to suppose he would leave her in the lurch too, sooner or later. Obviously, McGovern was no sort of a husband for Ada; she was one of the Department's best girls. Moreover, he had broken the law for a start by taking her off to live with him like that, without a by-your-leave. Obviously, he could be no good. Whereas this Les Mick who wanted her was one of her own people, a good worker, and very much in love with her. Had been for years. Surprisingly faithful, in fact. On paper, a very pretty, suitable little romance.

While this inquiry into the case of Ada Smith went on, Ada stayed at a Government Settlement. She grew thin and yellow. She would not open her mouth to speak to anybody.

Ron did his damnedest. Only when he realised resistance was hopeless did he decide to clear out. Ada, they said, hadn't even asked for him, didn't appear interested at all. So after another fight with himself, Ron decided he'd better not even see her again to say goodbye—it might upset her. He wrote a stiff little letter, telling her he was clearing out, that she'd best marry Les Mick and forget all about him.

Ada was obstinate. She refused to marry Les. She could not read her letter properly, but she blotted it with tears. She kept it in a little bag made out of a handkerchief and hung round her neck by her pink hair-ribbon.

As she refused to marry Les, the Department put her in a job as a servant in the city. After a month she ran away. The police found her again, out at the mountains, back in camp with her mum and Jo, Charlie and the rest. There was no hiding, then, what was up with her. So they let her be. Ada could go into the district hospital when her time came. The police explained the matter clearly to her mother, the girl seemed so sullen; as if she did not care or understand what they said. Her mother understood, though. So that was all right.

Late one night, Charlie drove Ada into hospital in the cart. The matron laughed, and said Ada was lucky to get there in time— the baby nearly raced her! He was such a pet, creamy instead of tomato-red. All the nurses ran in to see him. They wanted to make his little mother smile and feel happy. They could not discover why she was not happy, why she grew so restless if they took the baby away to let her sleep. She did not sleep at all, if they took him away. So they had to break rules and let him be, in bed with her; and then she would sleep sound enough, with him tucked in close to her side, his hand clinging on to a pink ribbon round her neck that she wouldn't be parted from, either.

On the fourth morning, the night-sister, starting on washing rounds before she went off duty, found Ada's bed empty. It had happened before; these half-caste women often cleared out! Once one got up inside twenty-four hours so as not to miss seeing a buck-jumping show twenty miles away in another town.

Ada was all in when she reached the camp near the mountains. But by the time the police looked her up again she had got over her gruelling. The baby was doing well enough. No need for worry. The police told her she could have a tin of milk added to the camp ration allowance, one tin a week, now she had a baby. Then they went back into town.

Little Mac — that's what Ada called her baby — grew up in the camp, sturdy, red like his father, and soon playing happily with the other kids and his mother, who recovered her smiles at his antics. Mac turned out to be a strong kid, no sore eyes or running ears, like most of them, on their flour and sugar and one tin of milk. But he was too white to be left with his mother for long.

When he turned six, the police came out, took him away from the camp, and put him in a Home. He had to be given his chance. He had to be educated.

Ada was older and had a bit of sense. She had known for a long time they would take Mac away from her some day. She didn't fight when the police came, or cry or kick up a fuss at all. She just said goodbye to her mum and Jo, to Charlie and the rest, and went along up to the city with little Mac.

She asked for the Department to get her a job as a servant again. If they let her have a job near the city, Ada said, she could go and see little Mac on her days off.

It was hard to leave him in the Home. He clung to her; he cried his dad's blue eyes all red and sore-looking. But there were other kids in the Home, white kids without parents, and the women in charge were kind. Mac would soon be one of them, the women said, they'd look after him well, Ada needn't fret.

Ada ran her dark eyes over the women as once Charlie had run his eyes over Ron McGovern. She reckoned they were speaking the truth. The Government said she couldn't look properly after little Mac, they said she couldn't give him all he should get. But these women could. He'd grow up here into a white feller like his dad. And she'd have her job and buy him presents with the money she earned.

Ada did well in the new job the Department got her. 'Good-natured, clean and efficient', her mistress reported, 'and reliable'. She told her friends Ada was miles better with children than any of the white girls she had employed.

Sometimes Ada did think it funny she should be left to mind white kids while their mother played cards, when the Government said she wasn't capable of minding little Mac! But she tried to feel happy and think about the education Mac was getting. The only catch was, the women at the Home hadn't seemed keen on letting her go to visit him as much as she'd planned. They said if she went too often she'd only upset Mac.

She saved up for a whole month. She was so excited when the day came she could hardly walk up the dusty path to the Home.

Mac must have been told she would come. He was standing clutching the gate, peering through the bars, waiting.

She had presents, lollies and a train and a toy dog, things like she'd seen in store windows in the south and wanted when she was a kiddie herself. At first Mac wouldn't even look at the toys, though. He flung himself at her. When she stooped he nearly dragged her down, clambering into her lap. 'Mum, Mum, Mum! —' he couldn't find anything else to say and his arms hugging fit to choke round her neck were the best thing she'd ever felt.

Afterwards he looked at the toys and laughed and laughed with pleasure till his dad's eyes almost vanished with laughing. He looked fat and happy enough, Ada decided, though he wouldn't let go of her hand, not even to play with his new toys. She was glad he liked them, she'd had to argue to be allowed so much of her wages to spend on toys. The Department said what she was to spend.

At tea-time little Mac dragged her off to show to his cobbers. Most of the kids hadn't got any mums at all. But *he* had!

Ada felt very happy when she went back to her place. Mac sniffed a bit, she'd sniffed a bit herself; but she was coming soon again, she'd promised, and she would fetch more nice toys. Ada even sang under her breath as she used to down by the mountains, before they took Ron from her. She undressed quietly and got into bed. She was sorry that she could only see a brick wall and drain pipes out the window, she'd like to have seen trees and the night sky. But little Mac was growing up along with nice white kids, into a white feller like his dad before him, and she'd got to not mind the brick walls till Mac was big enough to make a place like his dad had, where she could work and help him.

Ada missed a week, then went out to the Home again, all laden up. This time Mac wasn't waiting. She supposed they'd thought perhaps she wouldn't come, hadn't told him so he wouldn't get disappointed. She went out through the Home into the play-yard at the back. Mac stood in the far corner with a crowd of youngsters. He didn't seem to see her, so she called out.

He looked across. But he didn't move.

'Mac,' Ada called. 'Mac, it's mum!'

He seemed to wriggle behind the other kids. She thought he must be shy and went across.

'Mac, dear, it's mum — see what I've fetched this time,' she coaxed, hesitating.

His blue eyes looked fiercely up. She couldn't make it out. She knelt down. The children stood watching, stone-still. Ada put out her arms to Mac. He screamed. He hit her face.

Stone-still, the children stood for a second. Then they burst into screams and shrieks of laughter and ran off, screaming with excitement.

'Go away,' screamed little Mac, hitting Ada's face, beating her. 'Go away! You're not my mum. I won't have you for my mum. Go away. You're black!'

DYMPHNA CUSACK
(1902–1981)

Dymphna Cusack was born at Wyalong, New South Wales. She was educated at the University of Sydney, and worked as a teacher until she had to retire due to chronic illness.

Cusack wrote twelve novels, The first, *Yungfrau* (1936) was a strongly feminist book. She collaborated with Miles Franklin to write *Pioneers on Parade* (1939), and with Florence James to write *Come in Spinner*, which won the 1948 *Sydney Daily Telegraph* competition. Cusack wrote three travel books, two children's books, and eight plays. Her work has been translated into many languages and has been published in thirty-four countries.

She was awarded the Elizabeth II Coronation Medal in 1953, and was made a Member of the Order of Australia in 1981 for her contribution to Australian literature.

Cusack's work tackles social problems like racism, fascism and alcoholism. Her work also explores the issues of war and nuclear weapons.

YOU WON'T MIND THE GHOST ?

'Of course, Miss Robinson,' I said, almost too heartily, for I was anxious to get away, 'I shall bring them back with me to-night.'

Miss Robinson whispered apologetically. I discovered that her voice rarely rose above a whisper.

'No trouble at all,' I repeated, 'I'll pick them up before the chemist closes. But I may be rather late. I'm catching the picture-bus from Manly.'

She smiled—a half-deprecatory, half-apologetic smile that revealed chipped, ill-fitting false teeth. Although I had been her neighbour for three years, till now I had had no more than brief glimpses of her, flitting like a shadow round the little tree-shrouded house, and I looked at her curiously, for she was a legend in the district.

'I wouldn't trouble you at all only that Ophir looks so sick, and when he gets one of these attacks, only those powders of Mr Carlin's do him any good. And since I hurt my leg, I find it so difficult to get on the bus—'

I sympathised with her injured leg, but she waved away all reference to it as 'nothing serious' compared with Ophir's disorder—induced, I privately considered, by too much high living. There wasn't a handsomer, plumper, or lazier cat in the district than her great golden Tom, and she took my sympathy and admiration with the smile of a mother hearing praise of a loved child.

'I shall wait at the gate for you and save you the trouble of walking up—'

'You mustn't do that—the bus may be here any time between twelve and half past. It depends on what time the pictures come out. Besides, it's so cold these nights. I'll bring the packet up to the house and leave it on the verandah if you're asleep.'

274

'Oh, I shan't be asleep. That is my busy time, and I want to give Ophir a powder as soon as they come.'

I wondered what there was to keep a middle-aged woman living alone, so busy at night. Scarcely housework — the place was too small for that. Certainly not the garden — (my neighbour on the other side conducts a nightly crusade against snails!) — but here a jungle rioted unchecked to the verandah — a tangled mass of thin saplings and an aromatic underbrush that acted as a rampart against a curious world.

Gossip said that Miss Robinson had gone a little 'queer' from long nursing of an invalid father, a retired clergyman of the hell-fire-and-damnation school, who, when he could no longer dictate to a parish, turned the full fire of his evangelical zeal on his daughter. She had let the place go 'to rack and ruin' since his death. She never went out and the tradesmen left their goods in a box at the gate — 'not enough to keep a canary alive' was the consensus of their opinion, broadcast to anyone prepared to discuss the foibles of a neighbour.

'I'll whistle as I come up the path,' I said, 'then you won't be nervous.'

'I'll be looking out for you. Be careful not to slip on the stones.'

'I have a torch, so I'll be quite all right.'

'It is kind of you. I really wouldn't trouble you only that my leg — You're sure you won't mind the ghost?'

I had been answering her vague comments absently, mentally calculating the time I had to get down the hill for the bus. Now my mind came back like a dog checked on a chain. I blinked as I focused on my neighbour with new interest. Her sparse grey hair flew round her head like a ripe dandelion, and her skin looped in folds of pinkish flesh, terribly marred by a wine birth-mark that stretched from temple to jaw. Out of this unlined mask, under its nimbus of hair, her eyes smiled, limpid and very young. Now she was smiling at me apologetically again. I gaped, turned a mental somersault, concluded I had heard wrongly — assured her I didn't mind whatever there was to mind, then somersaulted again when she said, wistfully, 'It's a very nice ghost.'

I heard my bus toot as it came round the bend and privately waved it goodbye. It isn't every day one is hauled by the scruff of one's spiritual neck out of the placid contemplation of a winter morning-mist still trailing in the hollows, dew bright on the grass and spiders swinging intricate webs against the sun. Not every morning that a gaunt, raw-boned woman hobbles to her gate, and breaks the silence of years by asking you in the first five minutes of conversation whether you mind the ghost!

'No,' I said dazedly, 'I don't mind ghosts at all.'

'Oh, but this isn't an *ordinary* ghost.'

Now, I am the product of a materialistic age and my experience of even ordinary ghosts is nil. But I agreed with Miss Robinson's opinion of her ghost, just as one agrees with a mother's estimate — however mistaken — of her child's potential genius. The warmth of my response, and possibly the need to talk to someone after years of solitude broken only by Ophir's uninspiring companionship, released a spate of confidence.

'You see,' she said, resting one big red hand on the gate and leaning over as though she feared that the bush might hear her whisper, 'you see, I don't usually talk about my visitor. But now that you've so kindly offered to bring Ophir's powders, I feel that it is only courteous to tell you that I entertain him every night after twelve.'

'How nice!' I murmured.

'You being a writer, I thought — well, I thought you would understand and not take the conventional point of view. People do talk so.'

I agreed that people did talk so. Then I saw that the knuckles of her misshapen hands were white as they gripped the top of the gate support, and realised that I was — by purest chance — receiving a confidence so sacred that the solitary heart was shaken to utter it.

'You'll understand, then, won't you, if you should come a little early and meet him on the path?'

I nodded dumbly, essaying a smile that went a bit shaky at the corners. At my apparently matter-of-fact acceptance of her explanation, she sighed with relief, and leant closer.

'You'll recognise him easily. He's so handsome and has a dark pointed beard — such pleasant company! But he always wears a dressing gown! So unconventional, you know. He's travelled, too.'

A fleeting picture of George Lambert's self-portrait flipped in and out of my mind. Forever after, Miss Robinson's nightly visitant was for me an exotic silk-clad figure striding the dark like an earth-bound Flying Dutchman. Pointed beards, I remembered, would have been the acme of masculine glamour in her vanished youth.

'You're sure you won't mind?' she asked again, peering at me with translucent, short-sighted eyes, as blue as winter seas.

'Quite sure,' I replied as I gathered up my bundles and prepared to make a flying dash for the bus that was tooting in the distance. 'Quite sure.'

But at quarter past one that night — the bus had broken down as usual — I wasn't so sure. My torch had failed and I hesitated with my hand on the latch of the gate. There was no moon and the stars crackled with coloured fire in the frosty air. Shadows darker than grape-bloom shrouded the scrub-lined narrow path.

Suddenly out of the darkness there floated down the hill a tinkle of laughter — so light and fresh — so exquisitely joyous that it set the hair prickling on my scalp. A mopoke was calling dismally in the bush, and I stood rooted to the ground, assuring myself that it was no laughter I heard, but the call of some night-bird.

A single light shone through the trees, and for one foolish minute my heart creaked as rustily as the gate under my hand. I opened it cautiously, and closed it behind me. The clack as it settled on its hinges completely unnerved me.

'Take a pull of yourself, girl,' I said, hearing the sand grate under my shoes on the rocky path.

I regretted that I had not let Miss Robinson come to the gate to collect the powders for her wretched, overfed cat. Now there stretched between me and the light, a hundred yards of winding track, close packed with matted scrub.

'Get along, Mary! You'll catch another cold!' But there was a chill running in my veins that was not entirely physical.

The path was almost a tunnel in places, so overgrown had it become. Each darker shadow was a silk-clad figure waiting in the dark. Each lighter patch a pallid face gleaming with its own faint light. I remembered my promise to whistle. I pursed my lips; then that ripple of laughter — unbearably happy, drifted down to me, and my rigid lips could emit no sound.

When at last I stepped into the shaft of light from an uncurtained window, sweat was running down my forehead. I mounted the steps to the verandah, stepping lightly for some reason not clear even to myself.

I need not have worried. Through the open window I could see my neighbour 'entertaining'. There was a wood-fire in the grate and the smell of burning gumleaves came to me, pungent and comforting. In a stiff-backed chair, Miss Robinson sat, presiding over a spindly table set with her 'best' china — I knew it was her 'best' for it was the kind, fluted and inadequate, that had stood inhospitably unused on a little table in my grandmother's drawing-room for as long as I could remember. She was modestly collared to the neck in a frilled blue dressing gown — vintage 1910 — this 'unconventional' garb selected, no doubt, in deference to her visitor's informal attire. Her childish eyes gleamed with excitement in the lamplight, and a single rose drooped rakishly over one ear. On a cushion by her side, Ophir lay, his golden eyes fixed unfalteringly on the empty armchair on the other side of the table.

With a coy simper, she leaned forward to place a slice of cake on her 'guest's' plate — little finger upraised in the fashion that the district regarded as the height of gentility. She was smiling that sweet, deprecatory smile I have so often seen women smile when complimented on their cooking. There was a light tinkle of laughter as she leant back in her chair and played coquettishly with the rose in her hair. Yes, I swear that raw-boned, gaunt Miss Robinson played coquettishly with the rose in her hair — to an audience in an empty chair! Then she looked anxiously to the window, a quick frown darkening her face. She was listening for my whistle I thought, but the expression of her face was not one of pleasant expectation. With an appealing gesture — great hands fumbling clumsily with a wisp of lace handkerchief, she explained that only the direst necessity would have forced her to risk an interruption.

'You won't mind Miss Stone, will you?' she pleaded anxiously in a penetrating whisper. Then after a pause in which I could almost hear her being reassured in the very words I had used that morning, she added, with a sigh of relief —

'She's not an ordinary girl, you know. She writes.'

I knew myself an intruder. I took a last look at Miss Robinson's radiant face in its halo of flying hair — the red rose dangling grotesquely against the redder birthmark. I looked once more at Ophir — his golden eyes mirroring the fire as they gazed unfalteringly upon the empy chair. Then I put the box of powders upon the doorstep, where she could not fail to find them, and crept down the path.

Behind me, a ripple of laughter assured me — had I wanted assurance — that the handsome bearded ghost in his silken dressing gown was proving as 'good company' as ever.

CHRISTINA STEAD
(1902–1983)

Stead was born in Rockdale, New South Wales. She trained and worked as a teacher. In 1928 she left Australia, not to return until 1974, and lived for extended periods in Europe, England and the United States. Stead, who always considered herself an Australian, was nominated for an Australian literature award in 1967, but was ruled ineligible due to her extended residence overseas. She won the Patrick White Award in 1974.

Stead wrote eleven novels of which *The Man Who Loved Children* (1940) is perhaps her best known. *The Salzburg Tales* (1934) demonstrates her brilliance as a writer of short stories in both her range of subject matter and her versatility of style. Many of her uncollected stories were published posthumously in *Ocean of Story* (1985).

SAPPHO

The sea froths, the coroneted swans cover the cliff with their feathers, a groan bursts from the belly of the sea, black as blood. Sappho has sung to the sea-king's daughter, who steals the keys of jasper and opens the prison gates for her to pass out. The waters divide, and Sappho, with shut eyes, her white amorous body asleep, and still and pale as a sandy beach under the last embraces of regretful seas, passes upward, drawn by the desires of the hosts of heavenly virgins. With the sound of the surge, the swans burst from the cliff, leaving it sable, and, closing round Sappho, bear upward in their flight, a sweep of long wings into heaven. The misty beam of the moonlit night strikes on the swan's plume as it shoulders away the dark, and glistens on the dark eyeball: left and right, the line re-forms as they rise and fall along the dewy uplands of air. Ever they climb precipitously up the steep of night, spirally as a Babylonian tower. The sinuous waves have long ago been calmed beneath them, and sleep like frost: the forests and lakes are dark, like the secret locks of young women. They pass out of the cone of night, and they see the earth struck by sunlight, smiling as it imperceptibly rolls over the twilight strand into the surf of dawn.

The swans pass through the groaning meteors and the yelping winds and tempests of the upper air: their wings, wearing, drop feathers and down, which, a month after, come to earth, as the snow that falls in white climes. They cross the red, blue, green yellow and white rivers which shine in the rainbow, they cross without danger the blue burning plains and the rivers of corrosive gold which show when the pavilions of air are rent by thunder: they hear the growling of the bears, escape the hoofs of the charioteer who treads the tails of comets to dust, and make signs to all the impudent Zodiac. As they pass by the Maiden, Sappho stirs in her sleep, and her nostrils, hitherto obstructed by the bad cold she caught two days ago falling into the Mediterranean, expand. The first flush of blood gushes into her cheek as they pass swift as light through the palaces of Perihelion and Aphelion, cleaving the bowing and murmuring company of astral mandarins, with coloured topknots according to their magnitudes.

But now the solar system is past, and they are in the pathless waste. Only the instinct of the coroneted swans, who are fed on dragon-flies every morning at the heavenly gate, can guide her over the steppes of the Middle Distance. It is past: the heavenly light begins, as the dawn with us, only with all those known delights heightened in their transcendental way to delights inconceivable: this I say, who relate it, for I cannot conceive what they may be. Now the hosts of virgins and all the saints of the calendar, even the full tale of saints of these latter days, sing faintly as sings the morning star to the lover who has watched all night in the shrubbery: the noise grows louder, as surf to tempest-tossed ears: it sings about them as sings the drenching summer rain: and Sappho wakes.

'Where are we, O dearest Swan?' says she to the nearest crowned head, resting so lightly on its long stalk of pleasing form.

'We approach the gates of pearl,'-said the Swan, singing now, as do the heaven-born swans.

'Who is there to receive us?'

'The Virgin, the Lords of Heaven, Buddha, Confucius, the hosts of martyrs and saints, Venus, Diana and other celebrities, the Muses with elegantly-poised feet, the Graces in their naked chastity, all, all you knew on earth and under sea.'

'What will I wear? I am naked!'

'The future director of the Moscow Art Theatre, yet unborn, will study your type and tell you!'

'Whom shall I have to love me?'

'The Lord, the saints—'

'Hm! Hm!'

'—the nymphs and oreads—'

'Pallid souls!'

'—Ariadne, Andromeda, Cassiopeia—'

'Too sentimental!'

'—Lilith, Dalila, Potiphar's wife, Cleopatra, Thaïs, Ninon, Catherine the Great, Ste Thérèse—'

'Too religious!'

'—all the daughters of Eve!'

'But Eve?'

'On Wednesdays and Sundays,' said the Swan, 'she visits Heaven to see her numerous descendants, but at other times she stays on earth, refusing to give up her little notions.'

'Is today Wednesday?'

'Alas, there is a wretched innovation here, the Gregorian Calendar,' said the Swan, 'I never know what day it is now.'

'Give me a mirror,' said Sappho.

'There are no mirrors in heaven, for no one can make reflections there,' said the Swan, shaking his head.

Sappho pouted, but she reached for an asphodel floating past in the air, and twined this in her hair, shaking from it as she did so seaweeds and pearls put there secretly by the sea-king's daughter. 'Lend me a pen,' said Sappho, and the Swan made haste to do so. Sappho began frowning and counting on her fingers: 'This sapphic metre is the very dickens,' she said. Presently she said to the Swan, 'Do you know a rhyme for Leda?'

'Certainly not,' said the Swan coldly: 'and I hope you were not taken in by that very tall story of Leda's, none of us swans was. But it was generally believed by a population ignorant of biology, and we have been much annoyed by those forward water-nymphs ever since.'

'Don't take on so,' said Sappho: 'but I admit a girl is lucky who lives in antiquity, a taradiddle is as good as coin of the realm.'

'There you have it,' said the Swan indignantly. 'Take Semele: she had a happy conceit: she bothered no one.'

They now arrived at the gates of pearl on the crystal shore. St Peter pulled aside a little shutter and looked out through a grille, a razor in his hand and his face covered with suds. 'You are very early,' he observed amiably, 'but do come in. I took you for a gentleman who has been too much with us lately. He contributed to the rebuilding of the Delphic oracle, and has always treated the cloth honourably; and then, that loafer Mercury slept late and permitted him to be caught short on the stock exchange. Most unfortunate; and he positively insists that we cover his losses!'

'Very reasonable,' said the Swan, ruffling his feathers. 'There is a good deal too much *dolce far niente* in this place: look at yourself, not shaved at this time of day!'

'I've a good mind to grow a beard,' said St Peter ruefully. 'Beatitudes are so frequent now that I have no time to dress for dinner: and here, as you know, we still feel manna maketh man.'

They entered. Tents of silk covered endless lawns, harps twanged of themselves in the air, so that the blessed should not have to work, for it was an honourable society living entirely on its capital of faith and good works. The Lord, an old-timer, conscious of his rustic origins, sat and listened valiantly to the Earl of Chesterfield, Brillat-Savarin and Vedius Pollio, but he could not keep his eye from glazing, nor his foot from idly waggling.

An angel bore down on Sappho, and politely but firmly took from her fist her pen.

'I can't write here?' said Sappho, surprised, knowing that the holy are addicted to the Word.

'No,' said the angel, 'it is a very old regulation, first imposed by the Lord (God bless him!), who is a writer himself, as you have probably guessed from the number of his writings, both attested and apocryphal, scattered about the earth. The day after Heaven opened, two journalists came here and immediately started rival journals: the interpretations they gave of the Gospels and their disputes under the heads of theophany, theogony and theopathy were so ridiculous and bitter, that the Lord himself was assailed by religious doubt: but he was wisely advised, and since then there has been no literature in heaven.'

'This is very painful to hear,' said Sappho.

'You will get used to it,' said the angel putting the pen back in the Swan's wing. 'Besides, you will soon be perfect, therefore your interpretation of celestial phenomena will be the same as everyone's, so you will have nothing to say.'

'And I will be perfect!'

'Naturally!'

'I won't feel any more hunger, toothache, suffocation, ambition, love, the wind, the sun or the sea?'

'Your questions are typically sentimental,' said the angel shrugging his wing.

'But, goodness me, I want to see Eve and love her!'

'This is Thursday,' said the angel. 'By Sunday you will be too perfect to love her.'

'Where is she, O, where is she?' cried Sappho, much agitated.

'How do I know?' said the angel. 'She earns her living by snake-charming: she is at present, hm, let's see, in Lesbos. Yes, look through the terrestrial telescope over there on the rampart, and you'll see her in Lesbos.'

'In Lesbos!' cried Sappho. 'A malediction! And I in heaven! But I must see her for whose charms the whole world was eternally damned by a jealous god.'

Sappho leapt to the platinum wall of heaven, and plunging her glance through the variegated universe, she found the earth's surface. There, as in a silver mirror, she saw a beautiful and holy face, fair as Psyche's, passionate as Medea's, terrible as the Medusa's, calm as Hera's, in which the forces of love and self-love, as of life and death, perpetually made war.

'What divinity! What frailty!' said Sappho. The beautiful face seemed to her to cloud. 'Something annoys her, some regret her brow, some gnat her bosom, some worm her heel,' said Sappho: 'I must go! At that sight a storm of passions so bitter and burning has risen in my breast, that I cannot stay any longer from her side.' And spreading her arms like the albatross as he takes off, she leaped towards the far sea's polished mirror, into which, in error, she had been gazing.

'There she goes,' said St Peter with self-possession, putting away his razor. 'So much the better. The housing problem is really getting acute here.' He fed to the swans their dragon-flies. 'Besides,' he said to the chief Swan, 'she would have had no luck with Eve: Eve and Adam are a most devoted couple, they say.'

DAME ALEXANDRA HASLUCK
(1908–   )

Hasluck was born in Perth. She graduated from the University of Western Australia and worked as a teacher. She has written historical and biographical studies including a memoir of her mother and a biography of Georgiana Molloy, and has edited the letters of Lady Audrey Tennyson and Lady Broome. She has also published her autobiography, *Portrait in a Mirror* (1981). Her only work of fiction is a collection of short stories, *Of Ladies Dead* (1970). In 1970 the University of Western Australia granted her an honorary Doctorate of Literature, and she was made a Dame of the Order of Australia in 1978.

PUZZLE FOR A LATER DAY

Lady X was on her deathbed. She knew it and it did not worry her at all. She was eighty-eight years old, and she had had a good life.

'I never know why the thought of death worries people so much,' she used to say when she was only eighty. 'After all, it has to happen, and when one is very tired I am sure it will come as a relief.'

But now she could not say this to people, for circumstances had tragically altered, so she kept it to herself. People did not like being reminded of death in the third year of the war.

At eighty-eight, she still retained something of the beauty of her youth — the setting of the eyes and their lovely blue, the fine delicate nose, and the air of fragility and rareness, which, once deceptive, was now real. Suddenly all energy had left her and she had taken to her bed. Her daughters, of whom she had two, did not know whether to be alarmed or irritated by this, for they could see no reason for it. She was not sick. However, they installed a nurse in the comfortable apartment in Chelsea, and they dutifully came to see her almost every day.

Sometimes she wished they wouldn't: they were such very dull girls — or women, as she supposed she ought to think of them. In her hours of reflection she used to wonder how she ever came to have Ursula, thin, dyspeptic and devoted to good works; and Audrey, stocky, blunt almost to rudeness, and at the moment, in the Women's Auxiliary Armed Services.

'They take after Alaric, of course,' she muttered. 'Poor dear Alaric, so proper and so scandalised if one did not do the right thing.' And she laughed a little.

It was Lady X's custom, to fill in the long hours of waiting for what must come, to choose episodes that had taken place in her

287

life, and think herself back into them, seeing again the people concerned and the strange exotic backgrounds, for much of her life had been spent as the wife of a colonial Governor in outposts of the British Empire.

On this day of days, as it was to be, she propped herself up in bed to look out of the window that looked down the street towards Sloane Square. While the light lasted she could see the red buses moving, and the busy crowds intent on their little lives, now under continual threat. When the light faded, the nurse would come in and draw the blackout curtains.

Perhaps because of the gathering darkness, she chose from her memories the brightest place she could think of, the land of almost perpetual sunshine — Australia. The funniest thing had happened there. She chuckled as she remembered. Oh, it was many a year since she had thought of this. Whatever could have reminded her of it?

'I know. It was Audrey's bloomers, those awful khaki Army issue underclothes she showed me today. I laughed at them and she was cross, and crosser still when I said I'd rather wear none. "Mother!" she said. "How can you? You must have worn far more peculiar and longer pants in your day!" '

'Yes, but they weren't uninteresting.'

Lady X laughed at the thought of her daughter's face, and laughed again at the thought of what her daughter didn't know. The sound of her laughter brought the nurse bustling in. 'Gaga, poor old thing, laughing at nothing,' she thought as she moved about, tidying up, straightening the bedclothes and tucking them tightly in.

Lady X gave as strong a kick as she was capable of, to untighten them, and suffered her pillows to be plumped up.

'Please do not draw the curtains yet,' she said firmly. 'I like to see the world go by. I will ring when I want you.'

Thank heaven the air of authority still remained with her: the ghastly female — no, not ghastly, just impersonal and efficient — withdrew. As she went, Lady X began to chuckle again.

Alaric had been twenty years older than she when she had

married him. He had had a distinguished military career, and when he was offered a colonial governorship, he was pleased to accept. She had quite liked the idea too, and they spent five quite pleasant years in Trinidad, where both the children were born. Then they moved on to one of the colonies of Australia, a very different environment, and one that took a little adjusting to. Perhaps she had adjusted a little better than had Alaric.

'Poor dear, he just couldn't approve of some of the Australians he was forced to meet. I remember how he would come into my boudoir sometimes, as red as a turkeycock, and positively bursting at some piece of social awkwardness he had encountered. I used to say to him, "But Alaric dear, does it really matter?" '

'Of course it matters,' he'd splutter. 'Not only do they speak as though they were my equal, but they have the impertinence to offer comment. I won't stand for it, you know! I won't stand for it. And their women are no better. I am uneasy with them all the time, in case they do the wrong thing.'

'What sort of wrong thing?' she would wonder. But he couldn't say. It was just a thing that 'wasn't done'.

'And finally, the thing that "wasn't done" was done by me,' she thought to herself, and again it caused that uprising of laughter. As it had at the time, she remembered. She had always had a peculiar sense of humour. Alaric had been wont to explain to her that she really had no sense of humour at all, no women had; but he granted her she had at least a sense of the ridiculous.

'But what is the difference, my dear?' she used to ask. And then he would reply loftily that if she didn't know it only went to prove the point. To this there was no rejoinder, at least not aloud, for she was a tactful woman. She merely thought, as she thought now, that to laugh was one of humankind's great protections, and there were many kinds of laughter.

'And many kinds of reasons for it,' she told herself. The grey veils of night were falling one by one over the view down the London street, and the people she could see hurrying home were not laughing and had little reason to, with the grey days of war growing dimmer and dimmer. She was glad, so glad, that she would not have to last through as many such days as they would, poor things. And she sent her mind back determinedly to the sunny country, the land of Australia.

It had been in the same month as this when the thing had happened — November; but there the foggy November of London was the wondrous beginning of summer — blue skies, a true azure, the air balmy and languorous. It was the time for garden parties, before the weather got too hot, the sun too burning. And for some particular Important Person, she just did not recall whom for they were no longer important, Government House had turned on a garden party in the late afternoon. The gardens were looking gorgeous, blazing with colour, threatening to dim the colours of the gowns that would be worn. With this in mind she had devised for herself, and managed to convey it to her dressmaker and her milliner, a turnout of the softest grey chiffon, cool and becoming, the long skirt draped to her slim figure, the straw hat upturned at the back and piled with pink roses.

The gown was not the easiest thing to get into, her rather elderly maid peering and groaning about the lines of hooks and eyes. That hat, too, had to sit just so, and what with these things and the long tight white kid gloves needing buttoning, and the buttonhook missing just at that moment — she was running a little late. Sir Alaric was a stickler for punctuality and usually she did not give him a moment's anxiety, but this time the day was warm, the rice powder clung in patches to her face, the maid was not as dextrous as usual. In short, she felt flung together, but there was no time to worry about that — she had to get downstairs.

When she did descend the splendid staircase, looking, she hoped, serene and *soignée*, it was not to find Sir Alaric awaiting her. The hall was empty save for a young aide-de-camp, visibly agitated, who rushed towards her, spoiling the effect she had hoped she would make.

'Oh, Lady X,' he gasped, 'His Excellency said, I mean, he asked me to say, that he had gone on ahead to the State entrance and would await you there. He asked me to say that people were already arriving and . . .'

'I know,' she had said smilingly. 'He said, "And they would expect us to be there"?'

'Well, yes,' he said, gazing at her as though he were not hearing the question at all. 'Yes, that is — er,' he drew breath and gasped again. 'How lovely you look,' he said, but his voice was so thickened that she could hardly understand. He was new at Government House and very recently from England, very young and impressionable.

'How sweet, how divine,' she had thought. 'I do believe he quite worships me.' And he had certainly given some of the symptoms in the week or so that he had been with them. She had encountered them before, so she knew.

'Thank you. You *are* kind. I needed that for reassurance. One never quite knows if one's dressmaker has really brought off the effect. I know I'm late, but not very, surely? Let us hurry down the corridor to the State entrance.'

And off they went, she grasping the side of her skirts for easier transit, he, breathing rather noisily, striding beside her.

The corridor was long, connecting the main dwelling with the State reception rooms. It was hung with dismal photographs of preceding Governors and their apparently grim-faced spouses. As she hurried past, she accorded them a look and her usual kindly thought that the photographer had not done justice to them.

And then! And then! She halted at the very end of the corridor, perforce, since her feet were stopped.

'Good Heavens! *Damnation!*' she thought. 'Whatever has happened? Oh Lord, it *would* have to happen now!'

She knew from the feeling that the drawstring of her drawers had broken and they had fallen down.

Whatever to do? And no time, no time!

This was a crisis for which her breeding had given her poise but no advice. She had to use common sense, of which Sir Alaric had often told her women had absolutely none. She had not believed him then, she did not believe him now.

'Captain Norris,' she had said crisply. 'I need help. I am, as you might say, hamstrung. In other words, please get rid of these.'

291

And she stepped out of her drawers, picked them up, and handed them to him.

Captain Norris was twenty-three, intelligent, young and fair-faced. He had been struck with the loveliness of Lady X from his first arrival. She was now in an awful spot. What should he do? Whatever *could* he do? Nothing in his Army training had quite fitted him for this, except to deal smartly with the impossible.

He snatched up the fine lawn lace-trimmed unmentionables from her, raced into the nearest cloakroom, which happened to be the gentlemen's, flung the fragile pretty things up behind the high top shelf of gentlemen's hats, and thought, 'That will keep for a while.'

Then he had another thought: perhaps he'd better cover them up. And he seized one hat after another from the shelves and flung them up to the top shelf. Most of them were derbys and bowlers, cloaked by gentlemen who did not wear a topper. A military cap followed them. He was a little mystified that they did not form a pile but seemed to disappear. Then he noticed that there was a slight recess behind the shelves down which hats and drawers had apparently fallen. All to the good, the drawers would be completely hidden. He gave no thought to the five or six angry gentlemen who would be demanding missing headgear at the end of the afternoon; nor could he imagine that it would be seventy years or more before those hats were discovered in the course of the cloakroom's belated remodelling. No, he thought he'd really fixed it up, and went back to Lady X. She was standing cool and tranquil, unmoved and apparently unembarrassed, which was far from what he felt himself.

'Oh Lord,' he thought. 'I wonder if it's all right. How can she go on? There is no time, no time at all. His Ex. will be ropeable. She is due to meet the guests.' And his heart was wrung, even while it for some reason beat faster.

Lady X was almost as exercised as he, but she at least had more experience of handling situations. She knew she had only to stand there beside her husband, smiling, bowing, asking the expected question, making the expected observation, giving the expected congratulations; and no one would know that she was actually thinking: 'No drawers!'

It was not unpleasant, she felt behind the expected remarks, to feel oneself without drawers. It was cool, untrammelled, nice. One became aware that one had legs. But she could also feel, in fact almost scent, the apprehension of young Captain Norris behind her. Oh bother the boy, did he have to make her have a sense of guilt?

Time passed. Her tiny kid shoes grew tighter. The receiving line could relapse, and the Governor and his wife could mingle among the guests. The soft air poured down, the breezes wooed the plumes of the ladies' hats; gentlemen removed their toppers and became more complimentary as the afternoon changed to early evening, the champagne flowed, and the cool air soothed. She went from one group to another, the Aide behind her, young Captain Norris. At length they arrived at a place in the garden where there was a small terrace behind hedges.

'Aren't we in the wrong place?' she had asked. But again the strong breathing, the sense of his nearness.

'No! No. Not for a moment,' he begged. 'Just for a moment. You can spare that much. I must tell you . . .' his voice had faded off, and he had come closer. He was very tall; it made her feel fragile and tiny, she who was good average height and (as the gossip columns described her) well-built. She liked the feeling.

'But, my dear Captain Norris, we have to think of the guests,' she had reminded him. 'I have not made the rounds by any means yet.'

'Oh, *confound* the guests!' he had said, and she had tried to exhibit shocked horror, but she had not been so horrified when he had suddenly taken her in his arms and without permission kissed her strongly and with a passion she had not felt for some years.

She had sighed, 'Oh dear, oh dear, I don't know what to do. This is quite wrong . . .' And he had pressed his lips to hers again and silenced her. And she had kept feeling, 'No drawers! I should not be doing this!'

And then—it seemed hardly a second that they had been so secluded—Sir Alaric had suddenly appeared at the end of the terrace, suave in his grey frock-coat, his Aide behind him. They had fallen apart and studied the flowers.

'I've been the rounds,' Sir Alaric had announced in his usual waffling, pleasant way. 'Have you? I wouldn't mind if we left soon. Captain Norris, has my wife talked to almost everyone?'

Captain Norris, very erect, very correct, replied that she had.

'Oh well, my dear, shall we retire?' the Governor had said, and they did. And nothing was solved, if anything had to be. After all, he had only been a little effusive, the Captain.

Awful idea: knowing as he did, that she had no drawers, since he had had to dispose of them—had he thought to take advantage of her?

The thought of Captain Norris taking advantage of her in Government House gardens during the night of a garden party made her chuckle again.

The nurse came in again, and said reprovingly, 'It is almost dark now, your ladyship. Shall I draw the blackout curtains? Anything may happen.'

'Oh yes, draw them now. Anything might happen,' she agreed, and really that had been the situation, such had been her mood at the time. That warm evening long ago had passed. They had retired from the gardens. The usual conventional dinner had followed, with his glances directed at her till she had had to make herself appear frothy and social and trivial, while feeling the sharp sense in her inmost heart: 'This is the last time for me. I shall never feel this again. He thinks it is love but it is not. It's something else quite nice. I don't think it would ever have got to this point if my drawers had not descended. It gave him the chance to speak, to act. Oh Lord, what shall I do? He is too nice to dismiss but the situation is impossible. He cannot stay here.'

But she had not had to make the decision. The next few days

were full of appointments and social occasions, and then they went to the country for the weekend, taking one of the other Aides. When they returned, she learnt that Captain Norris, owing to illness in his family had unfortunately had to take ship for England. There had been no goodbyes, so sudden had been his departure, according to her husband, and she had not questioned it.

She just regretted the tall young man, and wondered where he had hidden her drawers, for she had not heard anything about them since she had handed them to him. What on earth could he have done with them? They were her favourite pair, handmade by Madame Ferrault, trimmed with ruffles of the finest Valenciennes lace that took her maid ages to press, with narrow blue ribbon threaded through the insertion between every three rows. A masterpiece, and lost.

Several years later, Lady X and her husband had returned to England, their term over and the sunny land behind them in their memories. Memories, however, were not important, for the Empire was engaged in a war with the Boers in South Africa. Various regiments had departed from England and from the colonies. In England, she was expected to be interested in the troops from Australia. And she had been. She had visited the hospitals for returned troops quite religiously—if that was the right term. And one day, on her rounds, she had arrived at a bed. The occupant was comatose; the nurse had informed her of his serious condition; and as she looked at him she had recognised the fair head on the pillow, the lean look of youth, the look that she remembered. Captain Norris, the one that she recalled with the keenness of the last of her youth. Captain Norris, Australia, the end of a period. Dear Captain Norris.

The fair head on the pillow could not look at her, it hardly breathed. She took the cold hand, something she had never done before! She looked at the full young lips. These she had known. She bent and kissed them, gently and sweetly, remembering only the sunny days, the strange and ridiculous situation in which she and this young man had found themselves at the end of the earth. And Captain Norris died with her kiss on his lips. Both of them of no importance, both of them part of a period, and sharing a memory of the sunny land.

She thought now of the situation that had caused all this; the breaking of the tape in her drawers. Funny wasn't it, that such a small thing could cause a feat of memory over fifty years?

Captain Norris had died during the South African campaign. Alaric her husband had died soon after they had returned to England after their next posting. Only she was left. And she still did not know what had become of her drawers—a question she might have asked Captain Norris, had he been conscious when she saw him in hospital.

Would they be found by future ages? Or had some house-maid long since retrieved them, thinking the worst of her mistress (for they bore her name-tape) while taking them for herself?

The night, the long everlasting night, descended on Lady X, and she slept with a smile on her lips that baffled her worthy daughters. What had she got to smile about?

A trivial memory to die on, but at the end, as good as any other.

KYLIE TENNANT
(1912–1988)

Tennant was born in Manly, New South Wales, and studied at the University of Sydney. She had many jobs, including chicken farmer, book reviewer, journalist, publicity officer, barmaid and editor. She travelled the roads with the unemployed to collect material for her novel, *The Battlers* (1941), and disguised herself, pretended to be drunk, and was arrested and sent to gaol when researching her novel, *Joyful Condemned* (1953).

Tennant wrote nine novels, two books of short stories, a travel book, three books of Australian history and three children's books. Her novels, which are mainly about the poor and struggling during the Depression, have won many awards, and in 1980 she was made an Officer of the Order of Australia.

AUCTION SALE IN STANLEY STREET

The auction was being held in the yard behind the auction rooms. The only patch of shade, cast by a big pepper tree, was jammed with people. A group of stout old women had established themselves there in armchairs and on a sofa, where they sat stolidly fanning. There were orange trees by the empty broken-down fowl run and against the tank, but their shade was an illusion. The beds and dressing tables had been placed where it should have fallen, but they were so hot in the blaze of the sun that the varnish had almost a quiver of heat haze over it. Chairs baked until the leather seats were too hot to touch; and the wardrobes, palm-stands, pot-racks, all the poor litter of wood cheaply nailed together, looked as though they would crack and snap apart at any moment.

Dogs circled about yelping when they were trodden on; bicycles leant against the entry-gate; a row of shining cars was drawn up along the footpath outside the auction rooms; a horse tethered to the fence beat its front hoof impatiently. The babies in their perambulators, the small children wandering about grizzling, the auctioneer with a knotted handkerchief over his head — all felt the heat.

Along a row of tables laden with the dead woman's china and glass, with pepper castors and teapots and sugar-bowls, spoons, forks and kitchenware, the women bobbed their black umbrellas, pushing, murmuring, nudging each other with shopping baskets and hand bags. They stood chatting in groups, linen dresses, floral dresses and stripes making a pattern of pink and green, of mauve and grey and yellow. Mostly they wore white hats and shoes because it was such hot weather. Older women, wrinkled and shapeless, in black that shone white with the heat, crawled about like cockroaches upset by the disturbance. The few men lounging about were creatures of a different species from the coloured throng of women. 'I never seen such a big crowd at an auction since I been living here,' one old lady with whiskers like a tom-cat remarked to another stout old lady who was sitting on a box to rest her swollen feet.

'Well I don't suppose now it would make any difference to a wardrobe . . . what happened to her.'

The noise and the heat, the shifts and changes of the crowd, beat down the shouting of the auctioneer. 'Ten, ten-a-half! Over there Joe. Gone at ten-a-half. Mrs Armstrong. No, not you, Mrs Clancy. Pass them over there. Now next lot. Two . . .'

The noise rose up round him, making an undercurrent to his rapid babble, as the pebbles in a stream have each a separate ripple under the roar. They were selling off the woman's iron roasting dishes.

'I remember the time mother cooked a sucking pig in the big one,' her daughter Julie said. 'You remember, Maisie, when mother cooked that sucking pig and two roast fowls?' They stood together in the shade of the auction-room doorway.

'I can't see for them black umbrellas bobbing up and down,' Maisie said fretfully. 'You look a sight, Jule. You got a big smear of dirt by your nose.'

'Well I had to unpack all them things, didn't I? Doing all the dirty work. I hadn't time to clean up.'

'Oh look at that chap with the horse! It nearly stepped on that little child. They got no right to bring horses in a crowd.'

'Did you see all the cars outside?'

'It was a good thing she lived next-door and we could just lift all the furniture over the fence.'

They were stout women with glasses, with pearl necklaces, with big bosoms and tight corsets and grey bobbed hair. Their aprons and bare arms cut them off from the crowd.

The auctioneer was holding up a handful of knives. 'Come on.' He cast a glance round the crowd. 'Why don't you bid? They haven't ever been used.'

There was a deadly silence and then smothered laughter that was half-shocked.

'It was with the bread-knife he did it,' someone murmured.

The bidding began again rapidly. 'Three. Three-a-half. Four. Four . . . Gorn to Mrs Sorby. Pass 'em across, Joe, over there . . .'

The sisters exchanged glances. 'He hadn't ought to have said that,' Julie said. She looked with a vague hostility at the milling black umbrellas, the green and flowery frocks, the white hats and shoes in the shade of the pepper tree.

'They all come to get things cheap because they knew she kept the linen and towels from the time we had the hotel in Stanton.'

They could think of their mother as she had been, stout and jolly and coarse. It wouldn't do to think of what had happened to her since she bought the business in Stanley Street. Just a small shop with a residential attached. They had talked it over a hundred times, but they still couldn't realise that their mother had been murdered. It had been in all the papers, 'Woman found Murdered in Residential'. Just another sordid crime, a drunken man who had been on good terms with mother. It didn't do to think of it. Now there was nothing of her except the chairs cracking with the heat; the rugs tossed down in a heap in the dust; the wardrobes and dressing tables and beds. There would be no bids for one of those beds. You could see by the way the people huddled away from those iron bedsteads that they knew. They joked and laughed more than usual at sales. It was as though in the strong sunlight they had to keep their courage up.

The old men and women gossiped as they sat in the shade on the dead woman's chairs and sofas; old wrinkled men leaning on their sticks; stout matrons who had come from curiosity just to stare; they sat and fanned themselves and did not think. Sometimes one woman would say to another in the crowd with a half-joking, half-nervous laugh, 'Why, Millie, what are you doing here?'

'I come to see if I could get some glasses, May. You know Alf's always bringing home fellows and I'm real ashamed of those old chipped cups.' But there was an edge of defence on her voice.

Only the auctioneer's eyes moved in his face, a yellow face cracked and seamed. His mouth was just another crack bellowing.

His eyes were screwed up against the glare. 'Nine, nine-a-half.'
The two women stood immobile in the doorway.

'It's the dinner service I'm worried about. If they put it up in
separate lots, it'll never fetch what it's worth. They don't know
what she paid for it. It's real good china.'

They had been two little girls when mother bought that dinner
service. It had cost twenty pounds. A dozen of everything.
Nothing had ever been broken. It had been treasured, scarcely
ever brought out.

Run down and tell George to put it up in one lot. Don't let them
have it' — Maisie's voice was fierce — 'just in half-dozens.'

Her sister nodded and waddled off very fast to look for her
husband somewhere down in the throng. 'I'd sooner we kept it
for the children,' Maisie confided to one of the stout old women
who sat on a box. 'We could divide it among us.' There was a
greed in her eyes. 'It's too good to sell, but Julie *would* have it
put up. That's just like her.'

The auctioneer had bent down and was talking earnestly to the
dead woman's elder daughter. 'All right, all right,' he said rapidly.
'Just as you like.'

Presently the stout woman came back panting, her arms full
of plates, her husband following behind with the rest of the dinner
service. 'I wasn't going to let them have it,' she said grimly, 'not
for that price.'

The old woman who had been sitting on a box, began fingering
the linen which overflowed from another box beside her. 'A pity
it's stained,' she grunted. 'It'll go cheap.'

'It's only water-stain,' the daughter said quickly. 'It 'ull bleach
out.' The terrible, terrible stain, it had run through the sheets,
it was all over the floor. In the strong sunlight, with the stout
women crowding to finger the things mother had touched, it did
not do to remember. 'It's only water-stain,' she said again
anxiously.

The auctioneer, standing on his box, was holding high above
the black umbrellas and white hats a china ornament. At first they
thought it was a jug, a shiny black china jug. Then as he turned

it around, it was a cat, hideous, elongated grotesque. He waved the black china cat carelessly above his head.

'Here you are.' His carven face jutted expressionless over the moving and shuffling, fidgeting mob. 'Here you are. A black cat! A black cat for luck! Who wants a black cat? A lucky black cat?'

There was silence and then suddenly the crowd burst into a roar of laughter. They laughed and laughed, under the green shade of the pepper tree, in the baking sunlight. The stir and rush of their laughter went through the thin orange tree boughs where the green oranges hung tarnished with scale. The horse tied to the fence turned its head and twitched its ears, then dropped its head again. They were laughing out in the strong sunlight, roaring the defence of life against the terrible shadow that was there among the kitchen pots, the linen, and the smell of sweat, laughing high and nervously to banish the thought that the murdered woman had touched that cat, that she had thought black cats lucky.

'Two, two-a-half, three,' the auctioneer chanted. He waved the cat with a triumphant leer at his own success. 'Four, five, seven, eight, -a-half. Here you are, Mrs Garetty.'

The elder sister had returned from bestowing the treasured dinner service.

'How they going?' she asked.

The other nodded, satisfied. 'Seem to be getting good prices.'

NANCY PHELAN
(1913–)

Phelan was born and educated in Sydney. She has travelled throughout Europe, the Middle East, Asia and the Pacific, and has written six travel books, three novels, a book of childhood reminiscences, and various short stories.

THE NURSE

As the new patient was lifted from the ambulance the frosted glass doors swung open and the smells of floor polish, antiseptic and mutton floated out into the pure crisp air. The patients craned their necks as the trolley was wheeled into the over-heated ward, and nervous speculation began.

'High pillows for heart and chest cases,' they whispered. 'Flat pillows for haemorrhages, strokes and meningitis cases.'

The old woman lay flat on her back, heaped over with grey blankets. An uneasy shudder passed down the ward as she was lifted to her bed, as the screens were pulled round her, as the trolley was wheeled away and the house physician began the low-voiced catechism. Melancholy and despair came furtively into the ward and circled round each bed; panic lurked in the darkest corners, and a wild longing to escape in time came beating its wings through the autumn dusk. Night was coming, but there was still time to get away; to get out once more into the outer air; away from the heating, the smell, the Dettol, the bed-pans, the boiled mutton, the white trolleys. To look up and see stars and hear trees rustling; to feel the wind and the earth and silence again, if only once more.

Those were dreams. Reality was the ceiling, the light, the locker, the helpless body in the hard bed, the fears and neuroses of the medical ward, the visitation of death behind brown screens. There was no getting away, no escape, neither was there any running to meet it bravely. Only the waiting, the tied hands and the hideous fears.

Here came the nurse. In her striped dress with starched apron and cap she was like a Dutch painting. Her hair shone, her eyes were wide and her skin was cool. Her body was young and her face was pretty but her hands were thin, hard, capable, frightening, merciless. She came down the ward smiling her wide smile, while her claw-like hands tucked themselves coyly under her apron.

When the relations of the old woman had gone greyly, soddenly, nervously out into the fog, night settled down on the ward. The heating waned, temperatures soared, beds grew harder, mouths grew parched, women snored, struggled, moaned and muttered in their sleep. From time to time the night nurse crept silently down the ward, a ghost-like face above a moving beam of light.

Towards morning the old woman began to talk. At first she muttered softly, then louder and louder.

'Bill! Bill! What have you done with the cups and saucers? Bill . . . Bill!'

In the darkness of the ward the women stirred. A frightened voice quavered out.

'Nurse!'

The night nurse came silently down the aisle.

'The new patient's talking, nurse. I don't like it.'

The nurse shone her torch on the bed.

'She's all right,' she said. 'Just rambling. She can't hurt you. There's nothing to be frightened of.'

'But . . .'

'You go to sleep. She can't hurt you. She can't get out of bed.'

The beam of light travelled across the floor and the ghostly face hung for a moment over the old woman.

'Well, Gran, what is it?'

'I'd better go downstairs,' said Gran loudly, staring ahead with blank brilliant eyes. 'I'm always much better when I go downstairs.'

'That's right,' said the nurse, pulling the covers straight. 'You go downstairs, Gran. And now, how about a little sleep?'

'Downstairs,' said Gran. ' They're burning something. Can't you smell it?'

'Yes,' said the nurse. 'They're burning rubbish . . . that's all.'

Another ghostly face appeared by the bed.

'All right?'

The night nurse tucked in the sheet and shrugged.

305

'Rambling,' she said.

The sister bent over the old woman.

'Comfy, Gran?' she asked.

Gran stared at her blankly.

'What did you do with them onions?' she demanded.

There was a frightened titter from the women in the ward.

'They're all right,' the sister said cheerfully. 'You ate them. Don't you remember?'

Gran mumbled.

The sister shrugged and turned her lips down significantly.

The two beams of light moved together towards the door.

'Nurse!'

The beams of light turned towards the nervous voice.

'Nurse . . . sister . . . How — how is she?'

The sister moved forward.

'She's fine.'

'But . . .'

'A bit light-headed, that's all.'

'Is she . . . is she going to . . .'

'She's fine,' said the sister. 'As right as rain.'

'Is she . . . will she . . . get better?'

'Of *course* she will. Now, go to sleep or I'll be cross.'

'She's not . . . she's not going to . . . die?'

'What a funny thing to say,' said the sister. 'Of course she isn't.'

The beams of light moved towards the door.

'If it happens tonight I hope it will be before midnight,' whispered the night nurse. 'There'll be no porters on duty after twelve and I can't carry her to the mortuary. And we don't want her here all night.'

'I doubt if it'll be tonight,' the sister murmured. 'It might be days. Or it might be tomorrow.'

'The day staff will be furious if she does it just as they come on duty,' said the night nurse. 'There's nothing so maddening in the middle of all the washings and bedmaking.'

The glass doors swung behind them.

In the morning the day staff found the ward in a bad state.

The women were hysterical, irritable, frightened, overwrought. They cried for no reason and bickered savagely among themselves.

'I wish to God this new patient would pack up quickly,' said the harassed staff nurse to the day sister. 'The women have had no sleep all night and they're all in a state of hysteria.'

'It's ridiculous,' said the day sister. 'They'll have to get used to it. She won't last much longer.'

'Can we move her down to the corner?' said the staff nurse. 'She's out of the way there.'

The sister picked up her pen.

'Very well,' she said.

The old woman was still muttering and shouting when the nurses came to wheel her bed into the far corner. As the procession moved down the aisle the more knowledgeable patients began to whisper urgently among themselves.

'They're moving her to the back door. That means she's going to die. They always put you in the back corner when you're going to die. It's easier to get you out.'

There was a sudden burst of sobbing from the bed of a new patient. A probationer hurried to her.

'I won't have her next to me!' the woman sobbed. 'I'll get up. I'll run away. I won't have her next to me!'

'There, there,' said the probationer. 'She won't hurt you.'

'She's going to die,' wailed the woman. 'I won't be next to her if she's going to die.'

The probationer turned her periwinkle blue eyes upon the hysterical woman.

'How can you be so cruel?' she said. 'That poor old woman can't hurt you. She's paralysed and she can't move.'

'But . . . they say she's going to die!' sobbed the patient, a little ashamed. 'And I'm frightened. I've never been near anyone dying before. I don't want her next to me. I don't *want* her!'

The probationer stroked her hair.

'You only say that because you're sick,' she said. 'If you were well you could never be so unkind.'

'Nurse!' called the staff nurse acidly from the corner where the old woman lay. 'Come and help me change this bed. She's soaked it again!'

Towards midday the relations appeared, poor and shabby and frightened. They filed out of the raw bitter mist and sat nervously on the edge of the waiting-room chairs, oppressed by the hospital smells and sounds, aching with love and anxiety for the old woman, timid and awkward in their ugly clothes, abashed before the starched lightness and daintiness of the nurses.

In their creaking shoes they walked clumsily down the ward, afraid to look at the patients in the beds, afraid to see anything in this unfamiliar place of white terror. Screens were brought and put round the old woman's bed and they sat themselves down on the hard stiff chairs, an awkward, pitiable semicircle.

All day they sat watching the bed so silently that the women in the ward forgot their presence and talked loudly of the night before, discussing their fears and horrors until the probationer shut them up angrily.

The old woman lay on her back, speechless, her eyes shut and sunken, her face grey and the skin drawn tightly over the bones. Her face was now beginning to resemble a skull. It was no longer her own; it had become a universal death mask. Her whole being was concentrated on breathing. In her coma she frowned fiercely with the effort of each noisy breath.

Her daughters sobbed quietly into their handkerchiefs; her husband, as grey-faced as she, sat staring at her, helpless and bewildered.

Night came again, the curtains were drawn, the heating increased, women moaned and snored and the night nurses flitted about the ward. The light over the old woman's bed was covered by a green bag that threw a ghastly greenish light upon her. The relations crept away and disappeared into the bitter night. The old woman concentrated on her breathing, snoring loudly and angrily, as though defying death. Death waited patiently, stealing through the ward, filling the women with terror, circling round the bed in the corner.

From time to time the night nurse glanced round the screen,

shrugged her shoulders and went away again. The new patient, ashamed of her morning outburst, now sobbed quietly into her pillow, sobbed with pity for herself and for the old woman, struggling alone in her corner.

About midnight the breathing changed. It became quieter, lighter, quicker and more irregular. The new patient began to hold her own breath the better to hear if it still continued. There were long pauses of silence in which it seemed the breathing must have stopped for ever; then it began again, quick and flustered. Sometimes there was a soft moan.

In the morning the patients at the far end of the ward began to recover their spirits. They began to talk brashly about the night when the old woman had been rambling and one of them gave an impersonation, calling out, 'Bill! Bill! What have you done with them cups and saucers?'

The pretty nurse with the claw-like hands came on duty, with the blue-eyed probationer and a VAD. The doctor's rounds came and beds were tidied and bedclothes twitched into place. In her corner the old woman proceeded with her dying. Indifferent to the importance of Matron's round, she haemorrhaged all over the bed.

Peeping round the screen to see if she was tidy enough for Matron, the pretty nurse was speechless with rage. She called the probationer.

'Just as Matron is coming into the ward!' she stormed. 'The whole bed will have to be changed. Every stitch. Hurry!'

The probationer was a Catholic and had a tender heart. She was shocked.

'How can you?' she whispered, with tears of pity in her eyes. 'She's dying.'

'My God, you don't need to tell me that!' said the nurse. 'I'll have to hold up Matron till you're ready. Get those sheets out to the sluice and for Christ's sake step on it.'

When the blood had been washed from the old woman's face, when all was restored to order, when Matron had looked round the screen, nodded wisely and perked down the ward, the daughters came in. Fatigue and misery and a hopeless resignation came with them. Outside the ward the sun suddenly shone and a cold fresh wind blew dead leaves about the garden. The morning was at once cheerful, high-spirited and hopeful. So quietly that no one noticed, the old woman stopped breathing.

'Come back,' said the probationer gently. 'Come back in an hour or so. Then you can take her things away with you.'

The daughters nodded, choked with their sobs.

'Dad wasn't here,' said one. 'Too late . . .'

'He can see her and say goodbye when you come back,' said the probationer. 'You can all come back and say goodbye in an hour's time.'

Love casts out fear, but not loving the old woman the patients were now afraid. They were white-faced and lay in a strained silence, trying to see nothing; trying harder to hear nothing. Again the wild longing to escape came beating its wings down the room. Panic crept up to each bed and threatened to choke each inmate.

The pretty nurse came briskly down the ward in her starched cap and apron.

'Morris,' she said to the VAD, 'you had better come and help me get her ready.'

The VAD started, flushed, turned pale. She began to feel sick and shaky.

'Yes, nurse,' she said.

The probationer stepped forward.

'Nurse,' she said, 'Morris has never done one before.'

The pretty nurse shrugged.

'Well,' she said, 'she must start some time or other. Go and get the tray ready, Morris, and the water.'

The VAD backed into the sluice-room, followed by the probationer. The women in the ward heard scraps of sound floating out — voices murmuring, muffled sobs. The nurse shrugged and sighed with exasperation.

'What is it?' she demanded, going to the sluice-room door. 'What's all this about?'

'Morris is upset,' said the probationer.

The nurse controlled her temper.

'Listen, Morris,' she said, 'are you frightened or something?'

There was a shamed sniff from the VAD.

'I suppose I am,' she said hoarsely.

The nurse spoke with professional kindness.

'There's nothing to be afraid of,' she said. 'She can't hurt you.'

The VAD sniffed again.

'It's not that,' she said. 'I've never seen a dead person before. And I feel sick.'

'But, my dear,' said the nurse, with less kindness, 'if you are going to do nursing you must get used to those things. You can't nurse without doing so.'

There was a pause during which the VAD sniffed obstinately.

'All right,' said the nurse impatiently. 'All right. O'Hara, you come then.' She paused. 'Have you ever laid anyone out before?' she asked.

'No,' said O'Hara.

'Christ!' said the nurse. 'Isn't there anyone of any use at all? The doctor will be coming and the relatives will be back and there's no one to help me.'

'I'll help you,' said the probationer. 'I'm all right. I'm not frightened.'

'Thank God for that,' said the nurse. 'Well, come on then, for Christ's sake.'

The patients who had radios now began clapping earphones upon their heads. Those who had none fidgeted nervously, talking in loud strained voices to each other, pretended to sleep, pulling the covers over their heads. They turned away as the nurses rustled up and down the ward with enamel basins, with white, covered, sinister trays, with rolls of cotton wool, with sheets, with a fold of cold blue-white material.

'The shroud,' whispered one old woman to another. 'The shroud.'

Behind the screen there was activity.

'Get all the bedclothes off,' said the nurse briskly. 'Quickly, O'Hara. You must be quicker than that.'

'I don't like to push her about,' said the probationer. 'She's still warm.'

'Be careful how you move her,' said the pretty nurse. 'She may vomit. Sometimes they start to heave as soon as you touch them.'

There was a soft moan all down the ward and the women turned despairingly to their pillows.

From behind the screens came the sound of water splashing.

'It sounds as though they're scrubbing a floor,' said one patient to her neighbour.

'Oh!' said the probationer. 'Don't be so rough with her.'

'She can't feel it,' said the nurse.

Slosh . . . slosh . . . slosh . . . The water splashed out upon the floor.

'But have you no pity for her?' said the probationer. 'Do you feel no pity for her at all?'

'None,' said the nurse, briskly scrubbing. 'None. I've done so many of them I don't feel anything.'

'Oh,' whispered the probationer. 'She's sighing.'

'Nothing,' said the nurse, clattering among the instruments on the tray. 'Wind.'

'Perhaps . . . is it the soul going?' the probationer whispered. 'How strange.'

'Open her mouth,' said the nurse. 'See if she had any teeth to remove. Now, give me the forceps and hold her jaw while I pack her throat.'

A shudder passed down the ward.

'I can't bear the way you handle her,' said the probationer.

'You're crying,' said the nurse irritably. 'Don't for God's sake be sentimental. She can't feel. She's no more now than a piece of meat.'

'No, no,' said the probationer. 'She's not. She's one of God's creatures. You mustn't speak of her like that. She's dear to someone even if not to you.'

'Look here,' said the nurse. 'When I was eighteen and starting my training I may have had those ideas. But now it's nothing to me at all. I've done too many of them. She's dead. Finished.'

'Don't you believe in . . .?'

'I do not,' said the nurse. 'I do not. We live; we die; that's all. Now hold that buttock while I plug her.'

At the far end of the ward a woman began to smother herself with sandalwood talcum powder. The sickly smell drifted over the beds and associated itself with what went on behind the screens.

'Horrible, horrible, horrible,' the new patient sobbed into her pillow. 'The way they talk of us—the way they handle us. Horrible to die in your bed. Better to be blown to pieces and never found.'

There was a final clatter and scuffle from behind the screen and then the sounds of a bed being made.

'Smooth the sheets,' said the nurse. 'We'll tidy her up and let the family in. Then we can tie her up properly for the mortuary. I told the porters to come at twelve-thirty. It's nearly a quarter past now. Pick up those sheets.'

'Who will bring the relatives in?' asked the probationer.

'I will,' said the pretty nurse. 'I'll just run and change my apron. I'm in such a mess. You clean up here and I'll come back in a minute.' She paused at the edge of the screens. 'She looks quite tidy,' she said with satisfaction. 'It's not bad for a rush job.' She gathered up her white tray. 'I think I can lay them out now in the absolute minimum of time,' she said. 'And, by the way, keep me that big bottle of eau-de-cologne in her locker.'

At half past twelve the relations came down the ward. They trailed in in a sad procession headed by the old man. He carried a bunch of white chrysanthemums and his face was grey, pinched and stunned. He stumbled towards the screens and was met by the pretty nurse. She was starched and fresh in her clean apron. Her wide eyes were clear and her hair shone in curls round her white cap. She was neat and pretty, reassuringly warm and alive. Outside the back door two porters waited with a canvas stretcher, smoking, yarning, leaning against the wall, warming themselves in the wintry sun.

'I'm so glad you got here,' said the nurse to the relations. 'To say goodbye to her.'

The daughters sobbed into their wet handkerchiefs. The old man stared blankly.

The nurse stood by the bed.

'Don't cry dear,' she said to a weeping girl. 'She's happier where she is.'

The girl choked.

'If she had lived . . .'

'She would have been paralysed,' said the nurse. 'It was best for her to go. She is so much better off now . . . where she is.'

The girl turned hopefully.

'Do you really think . . .?'

'Of course,' said the nurse. 'She's just sleeping now.' She gave a smile of great sweetness. 'You wouldn't wish her back from where she is, to all that suffering.'

'Oh, no,' sobbed the girl.

The nurse continued.

'I am so glad some of you were here with her when she . . . went,' she said. 'So glad for her. And for you, too.'

'Yes.' There was a sudden spasm of sobbing. The nurse glanced carefully at her watch, thinking of the two porters waiting and of the lunches due to come round the ward.

'She went so peacefully,' she said. 'And now she's at rest.'

'Thank you . . . thank you for all you have done for her,' said the eldest daughter. 'I am glad it was you who was here with her. Though I'm sure all the nurses were good to her. You couldn't help being,' she added. 'She was so lovable.'

The nurse sighed.

'Yes,' she said.

'And now,' she added, 'would you like to kiss her goodbye?'

One by one the pitiful figures bent over the bed, kissed the pale face and turned away, blinded with tears. To each one of them a gleam of comfort shone from the figure of the nurse.

At last it was the old man's turn.

'Goodbye, Mother,' he whispered, bending over the bed.

The nurse stared at the back of his head dispassionately, wondering how long he would be. Suddenly he straightened up and looked at her.

'God bless you, nurse,' he said, 'for making her look so pretty. You must of loved her.'

The nurse smiled at him sadly; then lowered her eyes.

'Yes . . .' she said gently. 'We all . . .'

His lips trembled.

'You're an angel, nurse,' he whispered. He shuffled down the ward after his daughters.

The nurse relaxed.

'O'Hara,' she called. 'Hurry! Help me tie her up. The porters are here and the lunches will be round in a minute. We must get her out as quick as we can. For Christ's sake, O'Hara, hurry!'

MARGARET TRIST
(1914–1986)

Trist was born in Dalby, Queensland, and spent her childhood there. She later moved to Sydney. She has published three novels and two collections of short stories, *In the Sun* (1943) and *What Else is There?* (1946). Trist records with insight and realism a woman's view of the world.

HALCROW STREET

In Halcrow Street the late milkmen passed and the footsteps of early workmen echoed along the pavement. Pale sunshine filtered over the brick semi-detacheds and penetrated chinks between the drawn blinds. Milk bottles stood chastely in front of resolutely closed front doors. In each narrow strip of garden hydrangea bushes swayed with the breeze that came up from the harbour.

Halcrow Street was shaped like a lop-sided crescent moon. It ran upwards from the harbour, curved outwards, curved again, then ran into a dead-end at the stone wall of an old quarry. From it could be seen a little blue bay with white yachts lying at anchor and the dirty, humpy buildings of the gasworks. To the left of it ran a maze of narrow, twisting streets crushed tightly with dingy houses; to the right of it were strong, well-preserved homes standing each in its acre of land and the expensive atrocities of the modern rich. Halcrow Street did not resent the first nor envy the second. It belonged to neither extreme and was intent, entirely, upon itself.

The sunlight, strengthening, pushed a yellow ray through the blind chinks of Mrs North's bedroom and fell across the polished wood of her dressing-table. It glinted on the assortment of cut-glass oddments and rested soberly on the bowl of stiffly arranged flowers in the centre of the table. Mrs North turned drowsily in bed, vaguely resentful in her half-sleep that day had come upon her before she was ready for it. Beside her, her husband lay like a thin curled log under the bedclothes. She settled back into sleep, only to be awakened by a sharp cry from the cot in the corner of the room. She lay still hoping it would subside, but it grew louder and more insistent every second. A clock at the back of the house struck six. Each of the six strokes seemed to enter her body like a shaft. Nerves she was unaware of having jangled, sending over her a feeling of nausea. The baby ceased his crying and began a loud, savage sucking of his fists. The sound stirred her as no cry could. Resigned, she got out of bed and went to him, lifting him clumsily out of the warm dampness that surrounded him. His hunger was greater than his discomfort. He pursed his mouth and made fat, gurgling sounds of annoyance while she changed his napkin, fumbling with the pins, sticking the sharp points into her own thumbs. Back in the bed he nestled against her and drank, first greedily, then with a steady guzzling sound, stopping at intervals to convey his satisfaction and once even taking time to smile complacently and vacantly into her face. Mrs North watched the little clock on the dressing-table and fought the drowsiness that threatened to engulf her. She brought herself to wakefulness by thinking about the breakfast and figuring out whether the butter would last till the grocer came the next day. 'Perhaps, if I fry some bread —' she thought.

The baby, satisfied, went to sleep. She put him back in his cot and tucked a blanket over him. She hurried into her clothes and sat on the edge of the dishevelled bed to push her feet into loose house-shoes. She gazed down unseeingly at her thin, white legs with their sprinkling of black hairs. In front of the mirror she ran a comb through her hair and hastily adjusted a pin. 'Must wash it one of these days,' she muttered, apologetic about its lankness.

In the bathroom she sluiced her face and brushed her teeth. In the sitting-room she turned on the radio. Its sudden blare shook the house, hurtling into consciousness the sleeping man. The baby, conditioned to the noises of the year of his birth, slept unstirring. In the kitchen she unclipped the window, allowing it to open three inches. Through the window she could see into her neighbour's kitchen and Mrs White, trim in a bright blue overall, moving briskly about. Such energy so early made Mrs North yawn. She started fumbling about her own breakfast arrangements.

'Water ready yet?' asked Mr North from the kitchen doorway. He was a thin, dishevelled man with a shock of untidy dark hair and a stub of a cigarette stuck in the corner of his mouth.

'Just on the boil,' answered his wife, and wondered if she really ought to fry the eggs again today. They had had them fried each morning for the last fortnight. But it was so easy. She hurried the fat into the pan. Mr North set up his mirror and gear on the kitchen window-sill and began to lather his face. He whistled with the radio and scraped at his thrust-out chin.

They sat down to breakfast at a quarter to eight. Mr North gulped porridge and eggs and the morning news.

'Not too good,' mumbled Mr North. 'Not too good at all.'

Mrs North swallowed her tea and squashed an uneasiness that rose inside her. It was nothing to do with her. Nothing at all. She allowed herself to be cheered by other items of news and forgot the rest.

'I don't like it,' said Mr North and rolled himself another cigarette. 'My lunch ready?'

Mrs North went with him to the front door. He kissed her. Though neither ardent nor romantic, it was sincere. In it were the memories of the past and the hopes of the future.

'I'll fix up the garden over the weekend,' he called as he went out the gate.

His wife nodded and waved and knew quite positively that the garden would not be touched that weekend nor the next nor the next —

Halcrow Street was alive now. Women shook mats or made one of a group who, having seen their menfolk off, congregated round Mrs White's gate. Mr Rowe, who was on holidays, and who lived across the road from Mrs North, mowed his lawn with an enthusiasm which was soon to fade in favour of the morning paper. Schoolchildren called farewells. A bread carter rumbled past in a red and yellow cart. A bottle-o followed him crying cheerily, 'Bottles, bottles, any empty bottles, bottles, bottles, any kind of bottles.' The dwellers in Halcrow Street looked at him. They had no bottles. Vinegar came in bottles, and when the vinegar was finished the grocer refilled the bottle. Lemonade was in bottles, and when the lemonade was finished the storekeeper gave you a penny for the empty bottle. The bottle-o winked to himself and urged his lean brown horse on with a 'Git up, can't yer, yer brumby.' Then he lifted his voice again. 'Bottles, any kind of bottles.' After he vanished at the harbour bend his voice lingered for a long while on the air.

Down in the bay the water was very blue. White boats stirred lazily on it. Mrs North stood at her door watching for a second. She would have liked to join the group round Mrs White's gate, but the wakening cry of the baby kept her back. She went inside, picked him out of his cot, patted him a moment, then laid him in his pram. She put the pram in the sunshine of the front verandah and left him there sucking his hands and frowning with deep concentration at the green of his mosquito net. She walked slowly back through the house, feeling depressed because of the unmade bed and crooked hallrunner, the damp towels in the bathroom, last night's paper spread over the sitting-room floor, the litter in the kitchen. She sat down in the kitchen and looked at the mess. But when a thing had to be done it had to be done, and there you were. She brushed her hair back with her hand and got up to fill the kettle.

There was the washing up and the tidying of the house and the baby's washing. Hanging the washing on the line she looked out over the narrow streets and dingy houses. A faint odour came up from them, a human smell mingling with escaped gas and blocked drains. She wrinkled her nose. Why did people live in such places she wondered?

The baby was crying now. She hurried inside to put on the water for his bath. He was a nice baby, blue-eyed, fair-haired and with sun-flushed skin. His hands were strong and dimpled and his body firm with a straight back. He gurgled in the water and tried to move his fat legs. He mouthed sounds, then, sure of his cleverness, grinned lopsidedly. Sometimes he went to laugh then forgot what he was about to do, and shrieked with annoyance. By the time that every crinkle and crease of him was clean he was used to the bath and objected to coming out. He hated being muffled in towels and he remembered that he was hungry. By the time he was dressed his small hands clawed fiercely at the empty air and his face screwed with impotent rage.

When he was settled to sleep once more, Mrs North felt in need of recreation. Tidying herself a little — a very little — she went and stood at the front gate.

The butcher boy rode a push-bike with a basket perched on its handlebars. The boy's hair was fair and straight, blowing back from a too-fair face. He whistled as he rode up the hill manoeuvring the bike in zig-zag fashion on the grade. He left Mrs White's meat, then came on to Mrs North. She took the newspaper-wrapped parcel and opened it. She looked at the meat then dug the forefinger of her right hand into it. 'Tough as old boots,' she said. 'I've a half mind to send it back. How much?'

'One-and-three. It's written on the outside there.'

'One-and-three! Talk about robbery.'

'Killer's strike,' said the boy briefly.

'What are they striking about?'

'I dunno. Strikes aren't anything to do with me.' He made to move off towards the Prices'.

'Mrs Price is out, I'll take her meat,' put in Mrs North quickly. 'She visits her mother on Wednesday.'

The boy, glad not to have to go any farther up the hill, handed over the meat. Mrs North opened it.

'Pork chops,' she said. 'What are the Prices doing eating pork chops these times?'

'They have 'em a couple of times a week,' the boy answered with his eyes on the downward slope.

'Hmm! It's good to be some people.' She dug her forefinger into each chop in turn.

The butcher boy went and Mrs North stood hopefully for a few minutes, but there was no one in sight. She went inside.

There was the bed to make and the bathroom needed attention. A man on the radio was talking about books. She turned it on to something interesting.

She put on the steak to braise slowly and made a pudding. She felt free with the dinner on the way and set about her own lunch. A pot of tea and a tomato sandwich sufficed. Then she rested on the lounge while a man sang a lovely song about blue birds

321

and roses and another about moonlight on a blue lagoon, between which was sandwiched a very nicely worded advertisement for sanitary paper.

At two o'clock she fed the baby, then took a rug on to the front lawn. She took off the baby's pants and let him kick unrestricted. He discovered the sky and stared up into it unblinkingly. She went and stood at the gate.

The greengrocer came slowly up the hill walking at his horse's head, his hand firmly on the head piece of the harness. He was a stockily built man with broad shoulders and a sun-tanned face. His head was bare. Over his working clothes he wore a canvas apron. Having negotiated the steepest grade he patted the horse and gave it a carrot. The horse rubbed its head against him. He halted outside Mrs North's gate—it was level there.

'Good day,' he said. 'Peas are thruppence, and apples two for thruppence, turnips thruppence a bunch, potatoes thruppence.'

'How much are the pineapples?'

'Aw, awful dear the pineapples. I wouldn't advise you to take a pineapple. Not worth the money!'

'I think I'd like a pineapple.'

'Aw, I don't think you would. Taste real terrible.'

'Oh, I'll risk it.'

The greengrocer coughed. 'Well, I'm not advising it,' he said. He looked at her awhile and then turned his attention to the baby. 'Fine kid!' He went to the fence and leaned over it whistling to the baby. It looked at him soberly, then fixed its eyes again on the all-absorbing sky. 'Kids are great,' he said.

'My pineapple?' Mrs North reminded him.

'Oh, yes,' he said heavily. He paused a second looking very sad, then went slowly to the cart. He looked among the vegetables and fruit then turned back to her. 'Well, I'm blowed!' he said. 'There's not a pineapple in the whole caboosle. Must have clean forgot them this morning. Peas are thruppence,' he ended hopefully.

Mrs North opened her gate and stepped over to the cart. Then Mrs White came, and Mrs Rowe from over the road, and Mrs Jones from the end of the street, and Mrs Smith from the middle of the street. The greengrocer served them slowly, then carried the vegetables and fruit to each verandah in turn, writing down the prices with a stump of pencil on a piece of newspaper.

As he was moving off the first batch of home-coming children rounded the corner. They broke into a run and the boys whooped, 'Peas-are-thruppence! Peas-are-thruppence! Hey, wait on old Peas-are-thruppence!' He waited, feeding his horse with a little red apple. They charged up to him and he handed out fruit ungrudgingly. Then he went on slowly with the children following. 'Never had no kids of my own,' he called back to the group of women. 'They're great things, kids!' The kids yelled their approval.

Mrs Rowe looked after him uneasily. 'I don't know if I'd like my children hanging round him,' she said. 'I don't like his giving away fruit. What's he get by it?' She went and leaned against the fence and made clucking sounds at the baby. But the baby, having made the discovery that he could transfer himself from his back to his tummy, was lost in his own proud thoughts.

Mrs Rowe was a plump woman with a soft face and a determined chin. She had brought up a family of seven and considered that she had had all the experiences necessary for a successful life. She was an authority on church work, a mild form of politics, where to shop for bargains, holiday resorts, babies, weddings, and birth-control — not that she believed in birth-control, but it was handy to know these things sometimes. Mrs White knew a lot of things, too, but she never told them, merely expressing with a wise shake of her head the things she could unfold if she so desired. Mrs Jones sniggered before she spoke, and when she had finished speaking covered her mouth with her hand and sniggered again. Mrs Smith had three children and was interested in Mrs Rowe's birth-control reminiscences. On Mrs Rowe's advice she had once taken a bottle of castor oil and it had worked very well.

'I see Mrs Price is out again today,' said Mrs Rowe. 'I wonder where she gets all the money for her gallivanting.'

'They have pork twice a week,' put in Mrs North.

'You don't say!' Mrs Rowe's eyes glinted. 'How do you know?'

'She told me herself,' answered Mrs North casually.

'Oh, just showing-off, I suppose. People don't tell anyone what they eat unless they want to show off.'

'She's a show-off, all right,' sniggered Mrs Jones.

Mrs White nodded her head.

'Living next door, I can see on to her back verandah,' said Mrs Smith, 'It's always in a frightful mess. I feel at times I'd like to go in and scrub it myself.'

'Well, she certainly can't keep her house properly when she's out all the time.' Mrs Rowe sighed heavily and squared her chin disapprovingly. 'Her poor husband!'

'They seem to get on all right,' ventured Mrs White.

'They do outwardly, but things can't be right in a house like that. No man could be comfortable with a woman of her type.' Mrs Rowe spoke with quiet conviction.

Mrs North slipped inside to look at her meat.

'Wouldn't you think she'd keep herself tidy about the house?' sniggered Mrs Jones.

'You would,' said Mrs White; 'but she keeps the baby real nice.'

The meat was doing satisfactorily. On her way to rejoin the group Mrs North picked up the baby.

'How much does he weigh now?' asked Mrs Smith.

'He's just on fifteen pounds,' answered Mrs North. 'He was seven and a half pounds at birth and he's put on six ounces every week since.'

'Babies make a lot of work,' said Mrs Rowe.

'But they're worth it!' Mrs Smith put in quickly.

Mrs Rowe looked at her, then looked away and went on speaking. 'Yes, thank goodness! My seven are out of the baby stage now. I tidy my house and it stops clean.'

'My husband is worse than the children,' complained Mrs Jones. 'I can manage them, but he leaves his things everywhere.'

'You've spoilt him,' said Mrs Rowe. 'I keep Mr Rowe out of the house except when there's visitors. My laundry is good enough and clean enough for him to read his papers and smoke his dirty old pipe in.' She nodded complacently, 'There's a lot in training, of course.'

Mrs Smith prepared to depart. 'Well my meat isn't on yet, and Joe will be home at a quarter to six. Ta-ta little oogle-oogle-dums.'

The baby blinked his eyes, stared, and wobbled his head uncertainly. The women watched Mrs Smith retreat along the street.

'She's a caution that one,' said Mrs White.

'No more miscarriages lately,' remarked Mrs Jones. 'She must be playing safe.'

'Here's Mrs Price,' put in Mrs North.

Mrs Price with two small children in tow advanced from the harbour bend. She was fat and jolly with masses of curly brown hair showing under a good brown hat. She came upon the group like a brisk good-natured breeze. Her eyes were brown and twinkling.

'I've got your meat,' said Mrs North. 'I'll pop in and get it.'

'Here, give me the baby.' Mrs Rowe took him with strong, determined arms. The baby looked at her speculatively.

Mrs North came back with the meat. 'I put it on the ice but I didn't unwrap it. I thought you mightn't like me to.'

'Oh, that would have been all right. It's only a few pork chops.'

The women looked at each other significantly.

'We were just talking about Mrs Smith,' said Mrs Rowe. 'She's a caution, isn't she?'

'Caution!' Mrs Price turned her eyes upward expressively. 'If you heard the hours of the night she was up after hot water you'd say so. I hear every sound from my place.'

They all laughed delightedly.

'I'd murder a husband like that,' declared Mrs Jones.

'Don't suppose he can help it,' shrugged Mrs Price.

'Nature, you know, nature,' murmured Mrs Rowe wickedly.

After Mrs Price had moved on conversation flagged and one by one the women drifted back to their homes.

Mr North was due home at half past six. It was nearing six now, so Mrs North sponged the baby, undressed him, fed him, and put him to bed. His look was very wise tonight and somehow very sad. Whether it was the stupendous discoveries the day had yielded, or his first contact with women *en masse*, it was very hard to say. He lay awhile in the gloom talking softly to himself.

Mrs North had the dinner dished up when Mr North's latch-key sounded in the door. She liked the sound of the latch-key. It gave her a protected feeling.

'Any news?' asked Mr North.

'No,' answered Mrs North. 'Have you any?'

'No.' Mr North kissed her.

Mr North told her at dinner what the boss had said to him and how he had explained to the boss where he (the boss) was wrong, and how the boss had admitted his mistake and shaken hands with him saying, 'You're a good man, North. I've got my eye on you,' and how some of the juniors had him snouted because of it. 'The trouble these days,' he said, 'is that no one wants to work for anything. Specially the young mob. Think they've only got to ask for something and have it handed to them. Spineless, young idiots.'

Mrs North related the conversation about Mrs Smith and the hot water, and Mr North guffawed loudly and said that Mrs Price oughtn't to repeat such things and hoped that she, as his wife, would respect herself more than to relate gossip.

'I never mention anything private,' answered Mrs North.

After the dinner washing up they read the evening paper and listened to plays on the radio. At ten Mrs North gave the baby its last feed. Then with deep thankfulness she went to bed herself to sleep unbrokenly till six o'clock next morning. Beside her, her husband slept like a thin, curled-up log.

To the right of Halcrow Street soft lights shone dimly, the lights wavering as the night breeze stirred among old trees. There was a sound of subdued laughter and music. Life was trickling on in a thin cool stream, dreaming placidly of a long-dead past. To the left of Halcrow Street there was a blaze of lights, lights yellow as old butter and bright as a million marigolds. The stars were pale beside the lights. Laughter floated on the air, voices shouted, music jangled. Life was surging strongly there. Life vibrant with a thousand emotions. Hunger, privation, love, and hate. The pangs of birth. The peace of death. Dreams were strong there too. Strange dreams of a future which held no dingy yellow houses crushed in a maze of narrow streets.

Halcrow Street was dark by half past ten. The sparse street lights made shallow pools ringed about by blackness.

NENE GARE
(1919–   )

Gare was born in Adelaide and educated at Adelaide Art School and Perth Technical School. Due to her husband's work in Native Welfare, Gare travelled extensively in the outback of Western Australia. The insight she gained into the problems of part-Aborigines is reflected in her first novel, *The Fringe Dwellers* (1961).

Gare has published two novels, a collection of short stories and two autobiographical works. One of these, *A House with Verandahs* (1980), is an account of the struggles of women's lives during the Depression.

ECLIPSED

Having a grown-up daughter means making a total reassessment of yourself and admitting that you've dropped too far behind ever to catch up again. You try, of course, but you keep failing: clearing away too quickly after dinner; using your scent to the last 'gone bad, mum' drop; totally unable to be nonchalant about her throw-outs (yesterday I found half a tin of Carnation corn pads and a tiny phial of Indian marigold ointment in the bin); tiring of sophisticated dinner parties after only two (Chris prefers roasts); being content with dull people to talk to or, rather, unable to summon the effort necessary to attract intellects; taking notice of one's husband's ideas of suitable frocking and hair-dos (why should you, mum?); and, last but not least, failing one's own idea of integrity by becoming garrulous on one's husband's faults.

What is it about a twenty-year-old daughter which loosens the tongue? Is it a desperate attempt to interest her in one's humdrum life at all costs or am I throwing the spotlight on Chris so my own imperfections can remain decently interred? Does that smooth young face with its faintly censorious gaze impel me to offer some other one for the slaughter?

I think I have become immune to Chris's frailties by now. I know I have. Left alone we are Darby and Joan, holding hands before the television, fitting snugly in our marital bed, complimenting each other on each's occasional effort to surface above the rest of suburbia, surely finding bearable the habits that formerly drove us mad. So long as Chris sits at the other end of the table I can endure the sound of mangled food and off my own bat I am teaching Chris to ignore my 'Beg your pardons' when I have heard perfectly what he has said. I am not deaf. I just take a while to process what I have heard.

I love my daughter. How I love her! But my days seem much

fuller of work and of waiting when she is at home. Odd empty intervals vanish and the hard part is that not only is there more work to do but I must do it secretly or be accused of fussing to make things hard for Helen. If I work, she feels she must also. She does not but she feels she should — doubly irritating.

In three years my daughter has lived in two flats and a house and honestly to see these immaculate young people doing their amusing bits of shopping at the supermarkets one would never believe the filthy nests from which they stroll forth. My sister Margaret, widowed and working on old terrace houses, told me it takes her daughter Julie up to two hours to put on her make-up. Whilst Margaret is dashing hither and yon, washing up after breakfast, straightening the rooms, peeling things for dinner, starting the washing machine, Julie is sitting at her dressing-table selecting face pastels. In the time it takes Margaret to strip the bed and re-make it with fresh linen Julie will have perfected the curve of the top lip and be starting on the bottom one. Margaret says she does not have time to stop and complain.

I was at Helen's flat one day when a friend called to take her out to dinner. Helen introduced us. 'My mother has just come to clean,' she explained me. And I may say that I am becoming immune to grubby kitchens with over-flowing kitchen tidies strung with tea bags, where cockroaches rustle forth at night and little mice eat bits out of unwrapped bread and where refrigerators are defrosted once a year so that it is a wonder they function. The backs of refrigerators is where the cockroaches live. Judith, a friend of mine, once lent Helen a small refrigerator she was not using. Helen returned it with enough eggs in it to contaminate a couple of houses. Judith said she kept finding baby cockroaches all over the place. No wonder people are dropping like flies with hepatitis — around the flatting district near the university they are, anyway.

I have the greatest admiration for Helen despite all this. This is her honours year and as well she is a trainee journalist, working one morning and one afternoon a week. She earns enough to buy her clothes and a few chicken legs. We pay the rent of the flat.

I wanted to be a writer once but there wasn't the time.

The dark sapphire colour which had spread halfway to the beach had been drawn back toward the horizon so that it formed the merest rim. I could see rain slanting down from the sky. Soon it would reach across the sea and over the beach and up the hill to the hut. I could smell it coming — washed clean air blowing over the wattles and banksias and greeting my nose with its sweet tang.

My daughter does not eat the same kind of food as us. Too fattening. Whilst we eat rotisseried chicken and four vegetables Helen cooks an omelet with tomato and parsley or she will eat natural yoghurt with wheatgerm and honey plus a plate of chicken jelly. I make this chicken jelly from the drippings of the rotisseried chicken plus vegetable water. I think to use it to strengthen the flavour of my soups and casseroles. Not if Helen is about, however. She has discovered it is nourishing, nice and contains no calories. Wherever I hide it she finds it. I don't really grudge it her but I too have to think of things to eat. On bad days my mind feels swept clean.

This morning a letter came from my sister for me but none from Ian for Helen. I'd have given a lot to have my letter change to one from Ian. Are one's daughters ever happy? We, Helen's parents, are never privileged to witness happiness. If it is not one thing it is another. At the moment, love. And so private the affair we are not allowed near its object. I don't know if we are to be broken to him bit by bit or vice versa. Before he went away he helped Helen babysit our grand-daughter. We were not available. Ian was not permitted to dine with us. Helen proposed to prepare his dinner after we were out of the way. 'What are we raising, a Queen Bee?' Chris asked.

My son Christopher had his dinner with us and thereafter stayed in his room unless he wanted to go to the bathroom. Helen and Ian sat down to a four-course dinner with an avocado for starters. I bought that, hoping to please, and Chris said, 'How do I get to travel first class in this outfit?'

Having had my instructions that she herself would prepare the food I kept out of it except for the pear, thinking, erroneously as it happened, that any food I might buy would be the wrong food. There had to be some hasty Saturday morning shopping when I discovered my mistake.

Ian is good-looking, tall, nicely spoken, and after we got home I managed a sentence or two before he was whisked away. We'd rather like to have a yarn with Ian. He has offered to drive Helen to Sydney at the end of the year and I feel we should know a little more about him, other than that he did not finish university but knows a good deal about Europe. One thing to be said in his favour; he can't be afraid of work. He has gone to Newman to make some money so he can stay in Sydney for a time looking for film work. Directing, I think, or he may start a restaurant. Helen says he is a good cook. Helen says his whole family cooks.

I wish often that my whole family cooked so I need not. Some days, this is one of the days, I feel a big block between me and ideas for dinner. I not only can't think, I don't want to think. The ideal thing would be to choose an illustration from a cook book and have it come to life. I wish that everyone would get whatever he feels like and wash up after. I don't think I'd mind keeping a refrigerator full of ideas so long as I didn't have to make the final decision. I could stay here reading and writing and doing a bit of water-colour and go in when I felt hungry to eat rye bread and cottage cheese and lovely cold salad. Which Chris loathes.

Almost out of the town a small boy with a dedicated face bounded forward four or five slow paces, raised his right arm from behind him in a wide arc and let fly. His hand was empty.

Yesterday, Sunday, Chris took Helen and me for a long drive into the blossom-covered hills where, as usual, I saw at least six places I would rather live than here. Helen read in the back seat. I know better than to call, 'Helen, do look at this.' She seemed content, though, if not actually happy. We stopped twice, once for coffee and buns for Chris and me — nothing for Helen — and once for lunch. Helen had brought her own — two slices of chicken and three lettuce leaves. It turned out she had seen everything a couple of times before this but I had not. There was a perfectly lovely old house at Toodyay overlooking the town and the Avon — I'd have given a lot to have moved straight in.

One good thing about living miles from one's family; my children might start buying their own records instead of pinching mine. Though they'd probably come to stay for longer and the records might go back with them just the same. Only more of them at a time. I wish I could remember about the records when I am at their places instead of always when I am at home and can do nothing about it.

Would a telephone call sound too peremptory?

Pale yellow grass sprang from the red summer roadside. Only the bunchy wattles cared nothing for the heat, and the scornful feckless sunflowers.

Helen has just been into town to shop. She was to have picked up my photographs. I ordered three of the one used at the top of her column. It is sweet. Every time I look at it I am reassured that the engaging Helen is there still behind that Helen-once-removed façade. But maybe this Helen is good for me. She keeps me alert. My son Christopher is too indulgent, minds nothing and laughs at some of my worst faults. But then he doesn't see so much of me, locked into his room with his philosophy books. Helen and I are together often and try as I might I continue to make mistakes which she zealously picks up. My biggest fault is my ingratiating manner. Expect to be found wanting and that's what you'll surely be.

I see Helen as a challenge. I WILL please her. Somehow! Not with food, though. That is a lesson thoroughly learned. Offering food means you are deliberately trying to make her fat. You know perfectly well that she's still on tomato and egg and can't eat another thing for four days more. I am always lying to her about thickening in the gravy and butter under the chop. Chris will eat watery gravy but he doesn't like it, preferring to eat less of the things he likes providing they are cooked the way he likes them — i.e., stodgy.

My point of view is lost in yours. I defend myself from the point of view of what you believe and only remember later what are my own beliefs. I betray myself.

Helen came home last week with two articles purchased from robbers at Cottesloe. A bolero of smudgy floral taffeta that was in fashion twenty years ago, for $18, and a scarf of pure silk, vintage maybe 1918, for seven. The scarf is terribly grubby, the bolero cracking in places. I am learning to convert sharp indrawn breaths into beginnings of sentences.

Like 'What!' to 'It is perfectly lovely.'

Today I have laundered them and I use the word in its most precious sense. Lux flakes and rainwater and lukewarm at that. Rolled into a towel to dry and ironed with a warm iron. The bolero came up beautifully, three shades lighter and proving to have a warm cream background, not dirty fawn. Fondly I smooth it with my fingers. This is the stuff of my youth.

The scarf, sadly, remains badly stained.

Helen is pleased.

He forces us to recognise that good and evil spring from the same source. He will not let us love his characters unless we do so knowingly, seeing them whole. If there is a single facet we do not embrace then our love is no such thing.

Helen rang at six this morning to tell us they have reached Mildura. So thankful to know this after hearing that snow and floods will hold up travellers for a couple of days. Helen says they are ahead of this and will reach Sydney in two days' time. Charges reversed—thank goodness Chris asked her to do this. Helen sounded as if her cold were worse but she said no, just the same. Thank goodness again that Ian is with her. She said it took 10 hours to drive over the rough patch just over the border. She also asked me to telephone Ian's mother, which I was happy to do until I came to do it. Who knew but what she might be thinking Helen had enticed her son from his loving home to live a life of sin in Sydney and my daughter not like that at all. But of course she has met Helen and must have recognised a well-brought-up girl. I hope I sounded respectable over the telephone. I tried to.

Ian's mother said she had been going to ring me later today to see if I had heard anything of them because she knew they wouldn't ring twice. Nor even once, I nearly told her, had it been going to cost them.

Rang my friend Judith after. She disclosed casually that she and Chris were at school with Mrs Bannister, Ian's mother. The Rookes are an old south-west farming family. That was her maiden name. I am delighted.

The first thing I noticed was the wind, though it was more like a profound disturbance of the air—a threat. The dry rustle of leaves accompanied the wind. Helen's room, which normally does not receive much sun, became a cavern. Then the whispers of the leaves stopped. The air was still, apprehensively calm. The light became dimmer inside. Outside it was like the reflection in a dark mirror. Shadows trembled and blurred at the edges. The loveliest were thrown by the leaves—light and feathery, dark only at their centres. The black moon glided over the rim of the sun.

Then it was bright again. The stillness left the air and life began again. The eclipse had passed.

OLGA MASTERS
(1919–1986)

Masters was born in Pambula, New South Wales. She spent many years working as a journalist, but did not begin writing fiction until she was in her late fifties. She wrote two collections of short stories, three novels and two plays.

THE SNAKE AND BAD TOM

Mother and the five children were around the table for midday dinner one Saturday in the spring of 1930.

Mother had passed out the plates of potato and pumpkin and corned beef except Father's, and the children anxious to start kept looking at the kitchen door.

'Now everyone behave when Father comes,' Mother said, her dull blue eyes skimming over them all without resting on anyone, even Tom.

But the children's eyes, from twelve-year-old Fred to Rosie the baby swung towards Tom next in age to Fred. Tom lifted a shoulder and rubbed it around his ear.

'Tom's doing it, Mother,' said Letty.

Mother was about to tell Tom not to, because the habit irritated Father, and Lord knows what it might lead to when the door opened and Father was there.

'There you are, Lou,' said Mother bustling to the old black stove and taking his dinner from the top of a saucepan she set it in his place.

Father hooked his old tweed cap on the back of his chair and fixed his eyes on Rosie, who was in her highchair with her head tipped back and her blue eyes glittering with the brilliance of her smile for him that showed every one of her pearly teeth.

'That cheeky one will get a hiding before the day is out,' said Father sitting down.

Fred, Letty and Grace laughed because it was wise to laugh when Father joked and the idea of Father's favourite, beautiful innocent four-year-old Rosie being belted with the leather strap was quite laughable.

Mother sent a small smile Father's way thanking him for his good humour. Tom was opposite Father and Father fixed his brown eyes suddenly gone hard on him, because Tom, lifting a shoulder again and rubbing it around his ear, hadn't laughed.

Tom had stolen a look at the strap hanging behind the kitchen door. It surprised him the way things were always being lost in and around the house but the strap, long and broad and shining and curled a little at one end, never strayed from its nail except when it was flaying the air and marking the children's legs, nearly always Tom's, with pink and purple stripes.

Tom felt his legs prickle at the sight of it. The old clock on the dresser with a stain in its face where Mother had poured separator oil into the works to get it going showed one o'clock. Tom dropped his knife and fork and counted on his fingers under the table. Two, three, four and up to eight o'clock when everyone was sent to bed.

Could he stay out of trouble that long? There were once ten Saturdays in a row when Tom got a hiding. As soon as Saturday dawned the topic was whether Tom would get a hiding before the day was out. Tom ashamed and fearful would lift his shoulder to his ear and wish for time to race away as fast as old Henry the cattle dog fled for the safety of the corn paddock from Father's blucher boot.

Tom was wishing that now, counting carefully with both hands from one to eight. He was slow at school, in the same class with Letty two years younger, so it took him a long time. Father saw, Tom's lips moving and not with pumpkin and potato behind them. Rancour rose inside Father churning at his innards and making him stand his knife and fork upright beside his plate with a noise like bullets from a double barrelled gun. The young whelp! The dingo! Neglecting food slaved for under the hot sun and orders barked out by old Jack Reilly on whose farm Father did labouring work because his own place couldn't keep the seven of them. Seven! My god, he should be free to go to Yulong races this afternoon with money in his pocket and an oyster-coloured felt hat, a white shirt and a red tie. He clenched his jaws on the tough meat and snapped his head back, eyes with the whites showing fixed on Tom.

'You!' he yelled and everyone jumped. 'You! Eat up! Eat up

or I'll skin the hide off you! I'll beat you raw as a skinned wallaby!
S-s-s-s-s-s — ' When angry Father made a hissing noise under his
tongue that was more ominous than a volume of words. Knives
and forks now clattered vigorously on the plates.

'Eat up, everyone,' said Mother hoping to pull Father's eyes
away from Tom.

'Everyone is eating up except Tom,' Grace said looking at Father
for approval.

Father held Tom's mesmerised eyes. 'Up straight in your chair!'

Tom took up his knife and fork and glanced down at the
wooden bench he shared with Fred and Grace.

'It's not a chair,' he said. 'It's a stool.'

Even to his own ears the words sounded not his own. They were
his thoughts and they had rushed from him like air from a blown
balloon pricked with a pin. Perhaps he only thought he said them.
He looked around the table and saw by the shocked faces that
he had. Then he saw Father, who was long and lean and sinewy,
grow longer as he reared up above the table. Tom scarcely ever
thought of more than one thing at once. Now he only thought
how much Father reminded him of a brown snake.

Father dropped his knife and fork with a terrible clatter and
seized Tom by his old cambric shirt. There was the noise of
tearing.

'Oh, Lou!' Mother cried with a little moan. 'Don't Lou!'

'Don't Lou!' said Father mocking her. 'Won't Lou! I'll kill him!'

Father had risen from his chair and it fell backwards onto the
floor.

'I'll pick up Father's chair,' said Letty looking at everyone and
anticipating their envy because she thought of it first.

'I'll get the strap,' said Grace feeling she had gone one better.

Father let go Tom's shirt but held onto him with his eyes, his
body hooped over the enamel milk jug and the tin plate of bread.

Tom saw Father's red neck running down inside his unbuttoned
grey flannel.

He's like a red-bellied snake, Tom thought and the corner of
his mouth twitched.

'Oooh, aah,' cried Letty aghast. 'Tom's grinning!'

She was on one side of Father having put the chair upright. Grace was on the other side holding out the strap. The only sound was the busy ticking of the clock.

Rosie spoke first. 'I love Tom!' she cried.

Eyes swung to Rosie and breaths were let out in shocked gasps.

The words had rushed from the small, sweet, red mouth the way Tom's words had. Rosie too seemed shocked at herself and looked around the table, pressing the spoon to her mouth as if to hold back more.

Eyes flew to Father. What would happen now? But Father still held Tom by the eyes, one hand groping in the air for the strap.

'Here it is, Father,' said Grace and Letty moved Father's chair to make it easier for him to make his way around the table.

'Finish up your dinner first Lou, while it's hot!' Mother urged.

Father began to lower himself slowly towards his chair.

He's going back into his hole, Tom thought and his mouth twitched again.

Eyes were on Tom so no one could shriek a warning when Father lowered himself past his chair and hit the floor with a thud.

'Oh, Lou!' Mother cried out. 'Lou, are you hurt?'

'Poor Father!' cried Letty, anxious to shift any blame from herself. 'It's all Tom's fault!'

Mother helped Father up, pressing him into his chair deliberately cutting off his vision of Tom. If Mother's back could have spoken it would have said Run Tom, run. Go for your life. If he hits you now he might kill you. Run, run. Please run.

'Finish up your dinner first Lou,' Mother said.

Father sat with the strap across his lap.

Suddenly Rosie cried out, 'Don't hit Tom!'

Oh my goodness, said the breaths jerking from Mother, Grace, Letty and Fred. Father would hear this time!

Father did. His head snapped back as he reared up. He swung the strap around the table like a stockwhip, flicking Rosie's cheek and missing Fred who was skilful at ducking. The strap wrapped itself with stinging force around Tom's neck. Without a sound he leaped from the stool, sailed across the corner of the table and out through the kitchen door leaving it swinging behind him. Even before Rosie started to scream they heard the rustling of the corn as Tom fled through it.

'Oooh, aah,' cried Letty and Grace scuttling back to their places on either side of the shrieking Rosie.

Rosie had flung her head over the back of her chair.

Her eyes were screwed tight and tears ran down her face over the three cornered white mark rapidly cutting into the pink of her cheek.

'Fred should go after Tom, shouldn't he Father?' Letty shouted above the noise.

'Father only meant to hit Tom, didn't you Father?' shouted Grace.

Father took up his knife and fork again. This uncaring gesture caused Rosie to shriek louder.

Father cut savagely into his meat. Rosie leaned towards Grace for comfort but Grace frightened at Father's profile jerked away from her. The pitch of Rosie's scream increased. Mother got up and filled the teapot at the stove.

'Your tea's coming Lou,' she shouted.

The cruelly unloved Rosie stretched both arms across the tray of her highchair. Father dropped his knife and fork, seized the strap and slapped it hard across her arms.

She bellowed now like a young calf and flung the wounded arms towards Fred. But Fred pulled himself away from her and made chewing motions without swallowing, keeping his eyes on his plate.

'Take her outside,' said Mother to Letty and Grace.

Grace lifted a stiffened Rosie from her chair and bore her out with Letty trotting alongside. Rosie's arms now marked identically to her cheek, stretched piteously over Grace's shoulder towards Mother.

'Go after that animal,' said Father to Fred. 'And bring him back for me to belt the daylights out of him.'

'Yes, Father,' said Fred and left the table. He began to run before he reached the kitchen door.

Father's eyes bored into Mother's plate with so little of her food eaten. She began at once sawing into her meat.

'I baked a batch of brownies this morning, Lou,' she said. 'I'll get you one while they're all away.'

But Letty and Grace were in the doorway, Rosie in Grace's arms. Rosie's hair was damp with sweat, her face scarlet. Hiccuping she looked pathetically towards Father. Grace set her down on the floor.

'Rosie has something to tell Father,' Grace said.

'Go on Rosie,' Letty said, giving her a little push.

Rosie stuck half a hand in her mouth and stared at the floor. After a moment she removed the hand and cried out 'I hate Tom!'

Father stopped chewing and snapped his head back staring ahead. Then without turning his face he put an arm out in Rosie's direction. She raced for him, climbing onto his knee and laying her head against his flannel she began to sob again.

'See! Father loves you, Rosie,' Grace cried.

'Stop crying now Rosie!' said Letty.

Mother fixed her dull eyes on Grace and Letty. 'You two finish your dinner,' she said.

'What about Fred's dinner?' Letty asked, sitting down.

'Pass it up and I'll put it on the saucepan,' Mother said.

'We'll put Tom's in the pig bucket,' Grace said importantly.

'Tom might get bitten by a snake if he's hiding in the corn,' said Letty.

Rosie lifted her face from Father's chest.

'Yes, a big black snake might bite bad Tom,' she said.

Mother reached for Fred's dinner. She saw Father in a sideways glance. He stretched and snapped his head back at the sound of Tom's name. His swallow moved his red throat running down inside his flannel and turning brown at his chest.

His jaws snapped shut and his hard brown eyes darted at Tom's place.

He made a hissing noise under his tongue.

Mother had a vision of Tom flying through the green corn. She blinked the dullness from her eyes.

One corner of her mouth twitched.

OODGEROO NOONUCCAL
(FORMERLY KATH WALKER)
(1920–   )

Oodgeroo Noonuccal grew up on Stradbroke Island in Moreton Bay, Queensland. She left school at thirteen to work as a domestic, and later joined the army.

Her first book of poetry, *We Are Going* (1964), was the first book ever to be published by an Aborigine. It was an immediate success running into many editions. She published further collections of poetry and also collections of Aboriginal legends, stories of her childhood and some essays and speeches. In her work she speaks for Aborigines with courage and eloquence, and emphasises the innate value of the Aboriginal people and their way of life.

THE TURTLE

Robert knew little of the ways of the Aborigines, because his parents lived now like the white people. He knew his parents were not very happy. He often heard his mother and father talk about the old ways of their people, and about their childhood friends. But they spoke of things that happened a long time ago. Before the white people separated and scattered their tribe. Before they were forced to live in a white society. They often talked of their homes in the bush, made of tree branches. In summer, they longed for the gunyas of their people. Now, their homes were made of wooden planks, built high on stilts to catch every breeze in the hot, sub-tropical climate. For this was how the white man built his home.

Robert had a lot of white playmates, but he often thought he would like to have black friends of his own race to play with. Sometimes he would think and dream about the way of the Aborigines, and he would say to himself: 'If I was with my own people I would have an Aboriginal name like Tuddawalli, or Namatjira. That would be better than my white man's name of Robert.'

His white friends called him Bob. After all, perhaps it was better. They would have found it difficult to pronounce the Aboriginal names.

One afternoon when school was out, Robert went to meet his friends down at the creek. He ran barefoot down the street and across the wide paddock where the grass grew abundantly and the tall blue-gum swayed in the wind above a patch of bright yellow wattles.

'Hi, Bob,' Bruce called. 'We found a plover's nest. Be careful — the mother plover will peck your eyes if you go too near.'

Robert moved closer to see where Bruce was pointing. The nest was well hidden, but mother plover hadn't hidden it well enough for those inquisitive boys. They did not intend to destroy the nest, but the plover did not know that. She declared war on the intruders by flying up high and then swooping down on them. Her anguished cries told them to go away.

'Oh, come on,' Bob said. 'Let her alone in peace.'

The boys moved off along the creek bed and the plover stopped her swooping and screeching.

Bob, Allan and Bruce were feeling fed up and bored. They often felt this way. They told each other that their school teacher worked them almost to death. Every time they went to the creek they compared notes on the ways of teachers, parents and adults in general. They promised each other that they would remove themselves from adults as often as they could, because it was clear that grown-ups just did not understand boys, and boys could not understand grown-ups. Soon, however, their conversation would dry up, and they would realise that they felt hungry. Their thoughts would transfer to what their mothers might be cooking for tea — and they would go their separate ways home. Today, after walking some way along the creek, the familiar pangs of hunger cut short their talk and they retraced their tracks towards home.

Bob waved goodbye to his friends. Hands in pockets, he made his way back across the paddock. Barefoot, he kicked at anything that caught his attention. His gaze was fixed on the ground. Suddenly, he saw something lying quite still beside a tree-stump. He bent down to get a closer look. There, fast asleep, was a turtle which had come out of the creek to bask in the sun.

Bob gave the turtle a poke with his big toe. The turtle stayed quite still. Maybe he was dead? Bob rolled him over and peered under the shell. A slow movement reassured him that the turtle was alive. He picked him up and carried him home.

'Hey, Mum,' he called from the garden gate, 'look what I've found. A turtle!'

His mother came to the house door, wiping her hands on a towel. 'Oh, what a lovely little creature,' she exclaimed. 'He's a beauty.'

345

'May I keep him?' Bob asked.

His mother looked thoughtful. She gazed sadly at her son. She knew all the things that troubled him.

'What will you do with him?' she asked.

'Keep him in the backyard.'

'He won't like that; it's not natural,' she warned.

'I'll look after him and feed him and love him—truly I will, Mum,' Bob pleaded.

'That turtle wasn't meant to live shut up in a backyard. He was meant to be free, to swim in the creek and sunbake on the bank. Don't take him away from his own way of life, son.'

'Do I have to take him back to the creek, then?' Bob asked.

'You have to do what you think best,' his mother answered.

The boy's chin quivered. He knew his mother and her ways well. Sometimes he hated having to make the decision, but his mother often trapped him into having to do just that. He thought, Why can't grown-ups be reasonable? Why couldn't his mother say either he must take the turtle back or keep it, instead of leaving it to him to decide?

Bob thought, and made up his mind. 'I'll keep him and I'll make him happy,' he said. 'I'll prove to him I mean him no harm. I'll feed him, and he'll understand, and then he will grow to love me.'

His mother did not answer. She turned her back and went inside the kitchen.

Bob carried the turtle into the backyard, put him carefully on the grass, and set to work to build him an enclosure of his own. He found an old tub under the house and dug a hole so that he could set it in the ground. Then he filled it with water from the tap. He sat down to see what his friend Turtle would think of his new home. The turtle's head slowly emerged. He looked carefully around him at this strange place, and set out to explore. He ignored the sunken tub and walked slowly round and round until he realised there was no way of escaping from the small backyard. It seemed as though he was bewildered. The water in the tub did not smell at all like the creek water, so he kept away from it. Bob sat and watched.

The boy's mother, looking out of the kitchen window, watched her son's hard-working efforts and wondered about the ways of a twelve-year-old. In his desire to make the turtle comfortable and prove his friendship, he had completely forgotten about his tea.

Five days passed. Bob invited all his friends in to see his new playmate. He found himself having to prevent them poking Turtle with a stick or wanting to pick him up — and he also found that when he would not let them play with Turtle the way they wanted, they abandoned him for other interests.

On the sixth day, Bob took stock of the situation and came to another decision. In spite of his loving care, in spite of his protection, Turtle seemed content just to walk round and round the fence, looking through it to the world beyond the small backyard.

Bob picked up his friend and carried him into the house. His mother was busy washing up the breakfast dishes.

'I'm taking Turtle down to the creek, Mum,' he announced.

His mother looked straight ahead at the kitchen wall. 'Don't be late for lunch,' she said.

Bob moved towards the gate. He looked back, but his mother had stayed in the kitchen. He headed for the creek.

He returned home in time for lunch, without the turtle.

'I've got your favourite lunch ready for you, son,' his mother greeted him.

'Don't feel hungry,' Bob replied. He went to his room and closed the door.

His mother looked at the closed door with loving eyes. 'Growing up to be a man is a hard business, son, but you'll make it,' she thought.

Bob stayed in his room until late afternoon. When he emerged he called to his mother: 'I'm going down to the creek to play with Allan and Bruce. Want to read what I wrote this afternoon?' He thrust a piece of paper at his mother, then ran from the house.

His mother hurried to the door to wave him goodbye, fluttering the paper he'd given her. When he had gone out of sight, she began to read what he had written on the paper. When she had finished there was a happy, contented smile on her face and her wise eyes were shining.

This is what Bob had written:

THE TURTLE

I went down to the creek and found him,
An old turtle with a crinkled hide.
Dozing he was near a tree-stump
With his eyes half-closed and head on one side.

I turned the old fellow over
And he quickly pulled in his head,
So I carried him off through the paddock —
At first I had thought he was dead.

But the old man proved he was much alive
And took off at a leisurely pace,
And the look on his face made me wonder
If he was challenging me to a race.

But I grew tired of his slow-motion action
So I carried him back to the bank,
And he swam with ease to the middle of the stream
And in the deep water he sank.

To Mum from your loving son, Robert.

GWEN KELLY
(1922–   )

Kelly was born in Sydney and educated at the University of Sydney. She has taught at both secondary and tertiary levels. She has published four novels, many short stories and, with A.J. Bennett, a volume of poems. Kelly has won four Henry Lawson prose awards, as well as the first Hilarie Lindsay Award in 1981 for achievement by a woman writer. Her novel, *Always Afternoon* (1981) was made into a film in 1987.

THE SHADOW

Today I ceased to exist. I looked in my mirror and I could see two pools of deep shadow floating in a bony cage. The cage was delicate, bones spun like fine thread out of the substance of a human being, and I knew that no one saw them. I drifted from the bedroom to the lounge room but no one noticed me. Threads of shadow across the sunlight-streaked carpet, shadow already crystallising into pinpoints of dust.

All the A's were there: big mother Arbuthnot swathed in a voluminous caftan, black and orange striped reality; and Alan whom I had married, fleshed in the assurance of liberated masculinity. His sisters leant eager-eyed above the table, Amy, Agnes and Amelia, tongues tripping in chorus over the shibboleths of emancipated womanhood. On the other side were Alison and Andrew, the A's whom I had created, filtering them through the bone-locker of my body into the solidity of the world.

They were all seated on solid chairs at a solid table planning the future, including my future, for they did not notice that I had ceased to exist. My shadow fell across Alan but he merely picked up his cardigan as if a cloud had passed across the sun. I put my arms around Amelia, cuddliest of all the A's, but she shuddered and Agnes laughed and said, 'Someone walked over your grave, Amelia,' and Amelia said, 'No, not that. It felt like a ghost'; and Mrs A bridling in reproof said, 'Don't be silly. There are no ghosts.' But she was wrong.

She turned back to her plans spread out in foolscap on top of the table. 'So that is that,' she said. 'Everything is organised, I'm pleased to say, Alan. The rally in the Domain should be a great success. You can now leave for New Zealand without a qualm. By the way, I don't think we should include Meg, do you? Too unreliable.' I floated to the ceiling. There is something so inconspicuous about a ceiling.

350

Alan nodded. 'I don't think Meg is well enough,' he said. 'Such a pity,' said Agnes. 'What are you going to do with her in New Zealand? You'll be so busy in your new post.'

Alan smiled, a head-of-the-house smile, free from all prejudice. 'There is no need to worry about Meg,' he said. 'I have arranged for her to take up her studies again. As you know, she never finished her degree. It will help her through the trauma of middle age.'

Middle age. I felt a tremor in my bones which I thought was a laugh. Shadows are never middle-aged. Age cannot wither a shadow. Only the public-spirited wither. My bones rattled together as I gathered my joints into a chuckle. To think of all that Grade A Arbuthnot flesh diminished like the grass of the field. Cast into the oven. I floated down from the ceiling because I could not stand the plaster dripping on my bones and dropped onto the carpet. The Arbuthnots pushed back the oak chairs on firm oak legs and they walked over my shadow, padding the soles of their shoes into my bones and after they passed I could see only a patch of dust on the carpet.

Alan glanced back as he shepherded his womenfolk out of the room. 'There is dust under the table,' he said. 'I didn't notice it before.'

Mrs Arbuthnot folded her huge arms across her bosom. 'You must ring the cleaning service, Alan. Meg simply cannot manage. And I am far too busy; anyway, housework is against our principles.'

Principles, principles, principles! Basic to my destruction. 'Your turn to wash up, Alan.' 'Help your sisters with the shopping, Alan.' Clackety, clack, clackety-clack. Dish after dish in the world of equal opportunity that demanded even so that he allow them to enter a room first, carry their heaviest parcels, escort them to teenage dances.

When I first knew Alan I was flesh and blood. I adored Alan; handsome, co-operative Alan. Alan was a feminist. His mother was a feminist. His sisters were feminists. His father was dead. In the wake of mother and her feminine counterparts he bobbed like

351

flotsam and jetsam. Yet illogically she loved him above all his sisters so that he harboured within his subconscious the knowledge of his ultimate importance. Alan, Amelia, Agnes and Amy. All A's. Leaders of principle heading the alphabetic queue. A. A.

I came in with my dainty frocks, curled hair, my glossed lips and my feminine, feminine coat and I looked at the brooding bulk of the combined feminists and they looked at me with gorgon eyes and kissed me with huanaco lips and said, 'Meg Watkins, well, well. It will be nice to be Arbuthnot, won't it. Such a change after W. Perhaps girls *should* change their names when they marry.' I was young enough to laugh. I believed I was invulnerable. 'It's a nice name,' I said, 'I shall be quite happy to change from Watkins.'

Alan kissed my heartshaped face and we floated in the bosom of our own first home. Flesh and blood, blood and flesh. Co-operative being. I dusted while Alan cooked; I cooked, while Alan dusted. We flew hand in hand down the street to catch our bus. We put out the milk bottles. I put out the cream and Alan put out the milk. 'Fly through the day on milk,' we chanted with the radio, and we tumbled flesh to flesh, on the new fawn rug on our fawn wood floor.

'My boneless darling,' he said, smoothing his fingers over my nubile flesh, 'My little boneless darling.'

Off and on the bevy of A's swept through on a tour of inspection. 'Good old Alan,' said Agnes. 'Good old Alan,' boomed Amy. 'Good old Alan,' squeaked Amelia. 'That's the girl, Meg, make sure he pulls his weight,' said the swirling mass of psychedelic colour that was Mrs A. Their eyes passed through my flesh and dismissed me as they rumpled Alan's hair, and clung to his arms and legs with touches that were not touches and fired his body with tiny silver darts and bound his limbs with tiny silver threads. I raised a plump little hand to protest and I found, instead of my little finger, a tiny frangible bone and a thin, tiny shadow of flesh. So I hid it behind my back and said nothing while they propelled Alan around the room, rearranging my lampshades and removing their frills, exchanging old-fashioned lounge chairs for hard little boxes spattered with cushions. 'You mustn't be middle class, Meg dear. And not gladioli, darling. Not these days.'

'I'm pregnant,' I said desperately, 'I'm pregnant.'

Their eyes turned on me simultaneously. 'You are still in the middle of your degree,' they said.

'Alan has not finished his doctorate.'

'Surely you took your pill.'

The other A, Abortion, loomed in the air, spread its wings over me; but I still had flesh. It was sticking to my face, sticking to my body, curled in my womb, protected by my blood. And I said again, 'I'm pregnant and I don't believe in abortion.'

There was silence, dead silence, as if the devil had risen in church. Then Mrs Arbuthnot and Amy and Agnes kissed me and said, 'Well, it can't be helped. I suppose we all have a subconscious urge to reproduce ourselves.'

'No,' I said, 'no,' but the waves of their assertion broke over my negation.

Amelia settled her leather skirt and straightened her leather boots. 'It's disgusting,' she said. 'Think of all those millions in Asia; all that pollution.'

'I am not Asian,' I muttered.

'Anyway,' said Mrs Arbuthnot, giving me a beaky peck, 'the important thing is not to get broody. You're lucky to have Alan.'

'No,' I said again, 'no, no, no,' although I was not sure what I was denying. It did not matter. No one appeared to hear me.

That night as we lay in bed I drew Alan into my arms. I felt the prickles of the silver pins in my flesh and the silver cords burrowed into my throat. I raised my hand to break them but my hand broke instead and in the moonlight on the quilt, I could see only a shadow. The silence of the house reverberated like thunder and I struggled to fight my way through the sound. Dimly I could hear Alan's voice and it was saying, 'Of course I'll help, darling, but I did think we were partners. You shouldn't have left off your pill without telling me. You could have told me.' I said nothing. There was nothing to say. After a while he said, 'We'll call him Andrew.'

353

'John,' I said, 'John.'

But one of the silver pins pierced my breast and I cried and cried. In my sleep I felt the baby move and he said, 'Andrew. Andrew. It is my birthright. I am an Arbuthnot.'

I struggled awake at daylight and there was Alan with the lemon drinks, the medically approved breakfast. I vomited. I could see quite clearly the shadow of my rib bone across the sheet. Hastily I pulled my bed jacket around me.

By the time Andrew arrived my arm had completely disappeared. Alan was so busy running the house, pursuing his studies, organising marches for Mother that he did not notice. I bought a number of long-sleeved frocks; and I always put my left arm around Alan in bed; and of course my shape made fun on the rug quite inappropriate. So he never knew.

Alone I worried. I shut myself in the bathroom and looked at tne bony outline and the shadow of my arm stretched across the tiled floor.

When I came home from hospital I cocooned the helpless infant in his shawl and slung it across my left shoulder blade. I did not want anyone to see that the baby's mother was partly shadow. But I could not deceive myself. Even as I chatted and chatted to Alan, I was conscious of the shadow encircling the tiny body like a scrap of cobweb. I was surprised that he did not notice it, but he was after all so busy arranging my schedule that he had no time to look at me.

'A fine little chap,' said Mother Arbuthnot. She was now wearing a turban like an old-fashioned rajah. It increased her air of authority. 'You'll be back at work in no time, Meg dear. We'll get that BA finished yet.'

'I'm not going back to work,' I said, but my voice was faint.

'Alan can help with the bottles,' said Agnes. 'You'll soon adapt to the routine.'

'Alan has no milk,' I said.

The horror of my obscenity hung in the air.

'You don't mean . . .' said Amy.

'It's too disgusting,' said Amelia.

They swept on me like a flock of birds and scooped the baby out of my arms. I clutched frantically, but shadows and bones are ineffective against flesh. Alan took Andrew in his firm muscled hands, held him in his well-covered embrace. And I knew I had lost him.

'You'll feel better when you've had a rest,' said Mrs Arbuthnot. 'Birth is traumatic.'

I sought in despair for outside help. Perhaps a doctor. When I returned for my post-natal visit I showed him the arm. Above the arm I could see the shadow of my shoulder clinging to the shadow of my ribs.

The doctor smiled benignly and tapped my abdomen. 'Good and healthy,' he said. 'We'll have you back to your old shape in no time.'

'But my arms . . .'

He flexed my legs, tapped my knees, sounded my chest, took my blood pressure. 'Excellent reflexes, excellent bones. Motherhood suits you. Now let us take a look at the little man.'

The shadow of my body fell across the child while the doctor listened and tapped. 'You have a fine son, Mrs Arbuthnot. We'll be starting his injections in a couple of months. Keep him on his present formula for the moment.' He began the ritual of ushering the patient to the door.

'But my arms . . .'

'You must not worry. Anxiety is a natural post-natal condition.'

'But, but . . .'

He patted my shoulder, the solid one, to conceal his impatience. I read in his eyes the line of patients glued to the chairs in the waiting room all expecting their due modicum of time.

'I'll write a prescription for a tranquilliser,' he said. 'A mild one. Women become addicted to drugs.'

'I don't wonder,' I said. He did not hear. I already owned three unfilled scripts for tranquillisers. I noted as I went through the door that my feet had become shadows. I floated through the waiting room where the patients prowled around the magazines like animals at feeding time.

Six months later I was pregnant with Alison. Alan barely spoke to me. I had forgotten to mention that I had lost my prescription for the pill. I had taken a tranquilliser instead. As I said, he barely spoke to me, but he remained helpful. He insisted on bathing Andrew before he left in the morning. As I grew bigger he even peeled the vegetables for the evening meal. Mrs Arbuthnot cleaned the house in grim-mouthed silence while the girls propped my legs on stools, fed me drinks and took me for long walks. No one spoke to me.

'We must all pull our weight,' said Mrs Arbuthnot to her daughters. 'Otherwise Alan will never finish his doctorate.'

I sat with my knitting wool twined uselessly in the bones of my fingers. I had nothing to do. I saw my baby swimming in the cage of bones. I looked curiously at the undulating infant. Boy or girl? But it swam cunningly with its sex concealed from me. I pulled my coat around me. I did not want to share my baby with the Arbuthnots. But it was no use. Nothing is private to the communal. I lost Alison just as I lost Andrew.

By my third pregnancy we were all living together. 'The extended family is the only solution,' said Alan. 'It is sense,' said Mrs A. She wore the keys of the house woven into a necklace, hippy fashion, around her neck. The necklace bounced on the solid bosom of the caftan like the belt of a mediaeval gaoler on his leather jerkin.

They wrapped my bones in a cloak and drove me to the abortionist. He was kind, efficient, and clinical. They said they put me to sleep but shadows don't sleep. I watched through bony sockets the last piece of flesh wrested from my body and I saw for the first time that the bones of my hand were crumbling into dust. I floated above the operating table where no one could touch me and I began to laugh. Ashes to ashes, dust to dust.

Tomorrow Alan and Andrew and Alison leave for New Zealand. Tomorrow Mother Arbuthnot leads the daughters of liberation through the Domain. I lie, a pool of dust under the table. This afternoon the cleaning service is coming.

ELIZABETH JOLLEY
(1923–   )

Elizabeth Jolley was born in the industrial Midlands of England. She was educated at home until she was eleven and then she attended a Quaker boarding school. In 1959 she moved to Western Australia. She has worked as a nurse, a door-to-door salesperson, a real estate agent and a teacher.

Jolley has written short stories, radio plays, poetry and seven novels — one of which, *The Well*, won the Miles Franklin Award in 1987. Jolley writes with sensitivity and humour about women. Her short stories, while complete in themselves, often contain the same characters whose situations develop from story to story.

WEDNESDAYS AND FRIDAYS

Wednesday 4 June

Dear Mr Morgan,

You will be surprised to have a letter from me since we are living in the same house but I should like to remind you that you have not paid me board for last week.

Yours sincerely,
Mabel Doris Morgan
(landlady)

Wednesday 11 June

Dear Mr Morgan,

This is to remind you that you are now owing two weeks' board and I should like to take the opportunity to ask you to remove the outboard motor from your room. There is an oil stain on the rug already and I'm afraid for my curtains and bedspread.

Yours sincerely,
Mabel Doris Morgan
(landlady)

Friday 13 June

Dear Mr Morgan,

I know there isn't anything in the 'Rules of the House' to say outboard motors cannot be kept in bedrooms. I didn't think anyone would want to. Since you mention the rules I would like to draw your attention first to rule number nine which refers to empty beer cans, female visitors and cigarette ends, and to point out that rule eleven states quite clearly the hour for breakfast. It is simply not possible, I am sorry, to serve breakfasts after twelve noon.

Yours sincerely,
Mabel D. Morgan
(landlady)

Wednesday 18 June
Dear Mr Morgan,

I am writing to remind you that you now owe three weeks' board and the price of one single bed sheet which is ruined. Please note that bed linen is not to be used for other purposes. Thank you for moving the outboard motor.

Yours sincerely,
Mabel D. Morgan
(landlady)

Friday 20 June
Dear Mr Morgan,

No. Black oil and grease will not wash out of a sheet furthermore it's torn badly in places. I can't think how it's possible to damage a sheet as much as this one has been damaged.

I am afraid I shall have to ask you to move the outboard motor again as it is impossible for anyone to sit in the lounge room to watch TV the way you have the propeller balanced between the two easy chairs.

Yours sincerely,
Mabel D. Morgan
(landlady)

Wednesday 25 June
Dear Mr Morgan,

Thank you for the two dollars. I should like to remind you that you now owe four weeks' board less two dollars.

Yours sincerely,
Mabel D. Morgan
(landlady)

Friday 27 June

Dear Mr Morgan,

Leaving a note on the mantelpiece does not excuse anyone for taking two dollars which does not belong to them even if you are only borrowing it back as you say till next week. Board is at four weeks now. I'm sorry to have to tell you that the hall is too narrow for the storage of an outboard motor. And, would you please replace your bedspread and put up your curtains again as I am afraid they will spoil and they do not in any way help to prevent people from falling over the outboard as they go in and out of this house.

> Yours sincerely,
> Mabel D. Morgan
> (landlady)

Wednesday 2 July

Dear Mr Morgan,

Board is up to five weeks. With respect, Mr Morgan, I'd like to suggest you try to get a job. I'd like to suggest the way to do this is to get up early and get the paper and read the *Situations Vacant, Men and Boys*, and go after something. I'd like to say this has to be done early and quick. Mr Morgan, five weeks' board is five weeks' board. And, Mr Morgan, what's been going on in the bathroom. I think I am entitled to an explanation.

> Yours sincerely,
> Mabel Doris Morgan
> (landlady)

Friday 4 July

Dear Mr Morgan,

Thank you for your very kind thought. The chocolates really look very nice though, as you know, I don't eat sweet things as I have to watch my weight but as I said it's the thought that counts. Do you think it's possible you might be smoking a bit too much. Perhaps you could cut it down to say sixty a day for a start.

> Yours sincerely,
> Mabel Doris Morgan
> (landlady)

Wednesday 9 July
Dear Mr Morgan,

I'm still waiting for an explanation about the bathroom. I must remind you that you now owe me six weeks' board and the cost of one single bed sheet ruined plus the cost of one bottle carpet cleaning detergent plus the price of the four pounds of gift-wrapped confectionery charged to my account at the Highway General Store. Early payment would be appreciated.

Yours sincerely,
Mabel Doris Morgan
(landlady)

Friday 11 July
Mr Morgan,

Get a Job. And clean your room. I never saw such a mess of chocolate papers under anyone's bed, ever. In my whole life I never saw such a mess. Never. I must point out too that I do not intend to spend hours in the kitchen over the hot roast and two veg. for someone who is too full up with rubbish to eat what's good for them. I'd like to remind you how to get a job. You get up early to get a job. I see in the paper concrete hands are wanted, this should suit you, so GET UP EARLY as it's a question of being first on site.

Yours sincerely,
Mabel Doris Morgan
(landlady)

And Mr Morgan, Bathroom? Explanation? And Mr Morgan. Smoking!

Wednesday 16 July
Dear Mr Morgan,

I appreciate you have troubles. We all have our troubles and I do see you have yours and it was kind of you to think of sending me flowers when you have so much on your mind. Thank you for the thought.

Miss, I forget, if you said, what you said her name was, had no business to miss her last bus. In future no guests are to stay in this house without me. See that this does not happen again. You seem to have forgotten the outboard motor. There simply is not room for it in the hall and it's all wet. Please see that it is removed immediately. And please Mr Morgan, Board seven weeks.

Yours sincerely,
Mabel D. Morgan
(landlady)

Friday 18 July
Dear Mr Morgan,

First I must ask for an immediate explanation about the bathroom please. And secondly, I must ask you to ask Miss whatever her name is to leave. I suggest you ask her what her name is if you didn't get it the first time.

I hope you won't feel offended about this but there really is not room for you to sleep in the hall, you know it has always been too narrow. There simply is not room there for you and the outboard motor. One of you will have to go. And see that young Miss leaves at once. And, Donald, always make sure you know what a girl's name is beforehand. You not knowing her name makes me feel I haven't brought you up right.

Yours sincerely,
Mabel Doris Morgan
(landlady)

Wednesday 23 July
Dear Mr Morgan,

I have to remind you Board eight weeks and Board one week for Extra Person. Perhaps you could persuade Pearl to go back to her lovely boarding school? Could you? I'm sure she's a nice girl but I really can't do with the two of you lazing round the house all day using up all my electricity and hot water. And I don't need to tell you that there really isn't enough space in the hall for your bed, her bicycle and her extra cases and the outboard motor.

Donald it's silly blocking up the hall with your bed. The neighbours will talk in any case. They'll think immorality is going on and what about young Mary? What ideas is she going to get? Donald I'm warning you I'm putting my foot down furthermore the outboard motor is not to be used in the bath. Where can it get you? AND what about a Job?

Yours sincerely,
Mabel Doris Morgan
(landlady)

Friday 25 July
Donald, No more roses please. I haven't got vases. Besides how am I going to pay for them? You know me, I'd just as soon see a flower growing in someone's garden. Thank you all the same for your lovely thought.

Your loving landlady,
Mabel Doris Morgan

Wednesday 30 July
Mr Morgan, This is to remind you Board nine weeks and Board two weeks for one Extra Person. I must say young Pearl has a healthy appetite. I wish you would eat properly.

As I was saying. Board as above, also cost of one single bed sheet, one bottle carpet cleaning detergent plus the price of the four-pound box of assorted confectionery and four dozen red roses, two deliveries, long stalks extra, and to dry cleaning and dyeing one chenille bedspread (purple) and two pairs curtains (electric green). With dry cleaning the price it is it would have been better to consult me first and about the extraordinary choice of colours, especially as I don't think the oil and grease stains will be hidden at all.

Donald, I do seriously think a Job is a good thing. Get a Job. Do try to get a Job.

Yours sincerely,
Mabel Doris Morgan
(landlady)

Friday 1 August
Donald, No more presents please. You know I never use lipsticks and certainly never a phosphorescent one. You must be off your brain. Though I suppose there is always a first time.

Your loving landlady,
Mabel Doris Morgan

Wednesday 6 August
Dear Donald,

I'm pushing this note under your door since you won't come out. I'm leaving a tray on the table outside. Do try to eat something. I'm sorry I said what I said. I am sorry too about the outboard motor. I suppose it wasn't fixed on to the boat properly. You say it's about thirty-five feet down? I didn't know the river was so deep there. Of course I'll lend you twenty dollars to hire a boat and a grappling iron. We'll simply add it onto your Board which is at ten weeks now and three weeks for one Extra Person, plus the cost of one single bed sheet, one bottle carpet cleaning detergent, one four-pound box assorted confectionery gift wrapped, and four dozen red roses, two deliveries (long stalks extra) and to the dry cleaning of one chenille bedspread and two pairs of curtains and the dyeing of the above, purple and electric green, respectively, plus the cost of one Midnight Ecstasy lipstick (phosphorescent frosted ice). I do hope we can find the outboard motor. I'm really looking forward to going on the river in a row boat, it's years since I was in a boat. We'll take Pearl and Mary with us and our lunch.

Your loving mother,
Mabel Doris Morgan
(landlady)

RUTH PARK
(1923–)

Park was born in Auckland, New Zealand. She worked as a journalist and in 1942 moved to Australia. She lived in Surry Hills during the Depression and gained a knowledge and sympathy for the lower classes, which she demonstrates in much of her work.

Park has written eight novels; of these *The Harp in the South* won the 1948 *Sydney Morning Herald* novel competition and *Swords and Crowns and Rings* won the 1977 Miles Franklin Award. She has also written a guide to Sydney, plays for radio and television, and many children's books.

THE HOUSE TO THEMSELVES

The two little girls watched the cottage-loaf back of Mrs Pearson vanish between the moss-bearded quince trees at the bottom of the hill. Instantly a new and enchanting air stole through the house; their elongated reflections leaped gnome-like in the brass platter over the mantel; the red curtains blew inwards as though there was an urgency in the wind; and the smell of new bread was like a charm.

'I like it best of all when Mum's gone out,' said Margaret. 'I like it when we're by ourselves.'

Her friend Dossie, who had come over to spend the afternoon, was a pale pudding of a child with a depressed squiff of hair and a solemn, elocutionary manner.

'Let's go and see how the baby is,' she suggested.

Margaret said: 'Wait a moment,' then she stuck her head through the window and shouted grimly towards the back of the house: 'You lie down and be a good dog, Tich, or I'll wallop you,' though there was no sound save the somnolent clinking of a chain.

She slid along the floor, pausing by the range to spit sizzingly on its polished surface. Dossie considered an instant, then spat too, watching the droplets round themselves and dance on the shining black.

The baby was asleep, his fuzzy head sticking out of a blue cocoon of rug. They looked for a while at his pouchy cheeks, and the shadows where his eyebrows were going to be. Then Margaret, with a calm, proprietary air, hit him a smart slap on the head.

'My, you'll get it,' said Dossie, breathlessly. The baby wrinkled up a red face and showed a toothless half-moon.

'You shut up, gummy,' said Margaret boldly, peering interestedly into the baby's throat as it yelled.

'Can I bash him, too?' asked Dossie.

'Sure,' said Margaret open-handedly. 'He's my brother, isn't he? I've often wanted to clunk him one.'

Dossie raised her hand with a half-thrilled, half-frightened feeling, and then, far away as a seagull on a sand bar, there sounded a voice, broken and attenuated by the wind.

'Crumbs!' said Margaret. 'It's Cheap Billy!'

She raced out into the kitchen, and Dossie started after her. Then she came back and gave the baby a kiss on its forehead, tucked it strangulatingly under the blue rug, and went out with the firm decisive tread of Mrs Pearson.

Margaret was already on the verandah. Up the track was coming a small bowed figure in a pudding-basin hat. He was driving an old weary mare with a small yellow cart behind her. Every now and then Cheap Billy lifted his head and gave a long soprano howl, in which words reared their heads for an instant and then sank back indistinguishable from the coloratura notes.

'He's saying "Bones, rags, bottles and bags",' translated Margaret proudly. 'But he buys anything. Once he gave Mum sixpence for two jars of her chutney, and another time he bought an old rug that had fleas in it, so we couldn't keep it.'

'But he can't come here when your mummy's out,' breathed Dossie. 'What would she say?'

'Pooh, I know,' boasted Margaret, her chestnut eyes scornful. 'I'll say Mother's out and we've nothing to sell, thank you.'

Dossie said quickly: 'But then he'll know we're all by ourselves and he might come in and do things.'

Margaret turned her head and stared at her friend, half-bewildered comprehension in her eyes. Things! Might steal the baby perhaps, or the silver teapot in the sitting-room cabinet. Might take all the chooks in the henhouse. Or perhaps might choke Dossie and herself to death in the course of all those vague and unnameable 'things' that happened to little girls who spoke to strange men.

'Pooh! He's only old Cheap Billy,' she said uncertainly. But it was too late, anyway. The old mare plodded to a stop in front of the verandah, and Cheap Billy, with a great cobbled hessian bag over his shoulder came and stood at the front of the steps. They stared down at him; his skin like chamois leather, the way his hair grew in little spikes over his frayed collar, his eyes as red and hard as garnets; the curious humps and wrinkles in his boots, his pockets bagged out like panniers with the host of mysterious objects within them; and his little, smooth, dirty-nailed hands, curled around the rail of the steps.

Margaret said hoarsely: 'Mum says we haven't got anything to sell today, Mr Cheap Billy.'

'Ach!' he said in disappointment. 'And your mumma promised me some picture frames last time I was here. Maybe she forgets, eh? You go and ask her, like a good liddle girl.'

The two little girls stood there, their hands frozen in their pockets, their faces feeling tight and swollen with embarrassment. Dossie wanted to go to the door and call out: 'You said you didn't want those frames to be sold, didn't you, Mrs Pearson? All right, I'll tell him.' But her feet, huge, immobile, and nailed to the verandah, would not move.

The man saw at once that the children were alone. He heard the jingling of the chain in the backyard and knew that the dog was tied up. He rubbed a knuckle under his red nose, wondering about his chances.

'You got any old clocks, any old clothes your papa do not want, maybe?' he said insinuatingly. His wrinkled boot rose to the next step, and his hand slid up the rail. Margaret's freckled nose twitched, and Dossie squeaked:

'We haven't got anything, Mr Cheap Billy. Honestly we haven't.'

'Maybe if I just go inside for a liddle while, and have a look round, I see something, yes?' he suggested. He came up another step, and the children smelt a dry musty smell rising from his clothes, as though he often slept under houses and in woodsheds.

He looked consideringly at Margaret, her long coltish legs and pink rosette of a mouth. Margaret felt a strange prickling feeling run over her, as though her blood had turned in its course and was flowing back the way it had come. All at once the simple sounds of the countryside, the little creaking of a cricket under

368

the verandah, the chuckle of the water under the weir, the distant yelp of a magpie, took on a mysterious significance, as though she were never to hear them again. She said in a sudden basso croak:

'I'll tell my father on you.'

He spread out his hands. 'Now, why? Your father and I are very good friends, ain't it? I just don't like to go away and not buy something. You understand. You are a smart liddle girl?'

Dossie stared at Margaret standing there, her mouth vacant of the words that should be said, her bronzy eyes stupid. Dossie knew that at any moment the little man with his dirty hands and his smooth foreigner's voice would come up the rest of the steps. And then . . . There slid through her mind the picture of Margaret and herself with their throats cut like the sheep she had once accidentally seen on a drought-stricken farm.

'Wait,' she said squeakingly. 'I'll find something for you. You wait here.' Ignoring Margaret's anguished little snort at being left alone, she darted into the laundry which opened off the verandah and looked frantically about. There was a big basket of clothes there, with the hem of a torn cushion-cover hanging over the side. Dossie gulped with relief. These old things wouldn't matter. Mrs Pearson wouldn't mind. She staggered out with the basket. Cheap Billy was on the top step. He seemed a little disappointed when he saw the basket, but as Dossie set it down, he ran his fingers quickly through what it contained.

'Not much good,' he grunted. 'One shilling. One shilling!'

He scrabbled in his pocket, hitching up his coat so that a strange medley of waistcoats and cardigans showed. He thrust a shilling in Dossie's trembling hand, and hoisted the basket to his shoulder. With hurry in his heels he clumped down the steps, his little garnet eyes scuttling from side to side like beetles, with something of frustration or regret in them. The old mare raised her greying muzzle and grunted as the whip flicked around her wealed shoulders. But Cheap Billy, hastening down the hill, did not look back.

'Oh! Oh-oh!' sobbed Dossie, loudly. Margaret turned on her and hit her hard on the ear.

'You've sold Mum's washing for a measly bob, that's what you've done,' she shrieked, her eyes blazing with fury and relief. 'You-you-you big lump of dough!'

'Let's set Tich on him,' hiccupped Dossie, her face a mask of misery. Margaret's eyes, their fire rekindled, flashed.

'Yes, yes, we'll do that!'

With delirous hope they rushed to the back of the house and hauled the drowsy black pup out of the kennel. He opened one eye and looked filmily at them, grinning lazily at their shrieks and pleas. Then he turned on his back and showed them his bended pink paws. They looked at each other and sat down in the scattered straw of his bed, weeping loudly.

THEA ASTLEY
(1925–   )

Astley was born in Brisbane. She has taught at primary, secondary and tertiary levels. In 1980 she left her teaching position at Macquarie University to write full time.

Astley has published nine novels. She has won the Miles Franklin Award three times for *The Well Dressed Explorer* (1962), *The Slow Natives* (1965), and *The Acolyte* (1972). Her collection of short stories won the 1980 James Cook Foundation of Literature Studies Award, and *A Kindness Cup* (1975) won the *Age* Book of the Year Award. Astley often writes from the point of view of the sensitive outsider who is observing the shallow, vain people on the inside. Her fiction is critical of exploitation and pretension.

A NORTHERN BELLE

The night Willy Fourcorners sat with me, awkward in his Christian clothing, he told me, between the clubbing blocks of rain, what it was like sometimes to be black in these parts. He's sat with me other nights as well and what he told me of this one or that, this place or that, was like taking a view from the wrong side of the fence. Wrong's not the word. Photographing in shadow, the object that is? No. I'm still hunting the wild simile. It was . . . it was like inspecting the negative, framing and hanging its reversals, standing back to admire, then crying in despair, 'But it's all different!'

People I knew, he knew, but he knew them some otherhow— as if he saw Lawyer Galipo and Father Rassini from the lee side of the banks of heaven. I asked him once why he'd ever left his little house on the outskirts of Tobaccotown, and he was silent a long time. I coddled his silence and at last he told me. I put his story onto their stories and still I get one story.

This is Willy's story, my words.

She was born in one of those exhausted, fleetingly timbered places that sprang up round the tin mines of the north. Not in the poverty of a digger's shack, let it be understood, but in the more impressive verandah'd sprawl of one of those cedar houses that loiter in heavy country gardens. How to capture the flavour of those years? Horse-rumps, sweat, hard liquor, crippled shanties, all forgotten in the spacious hours after lunch and before tea when baking fragrance settled as gently as the shadows across and into the passion-vined trellis.

A porky child with a fine cap of almost white dead-straight hair, her body gave no indication of the handsome bones that were to emerge in late adolescence. Skip some years. Now we have her at fourteen bounding confidently across the town hard-court, shimmering with sweat, her hair longer now, darkening now, still fine and unmanageable; but it's still no pointer to the strong-minded Clarice of nineteen who, despite a profile of pleasing symmetry, still boyishly racquet-scooped balls, served low and hard, and later dispensed lemon squash in the tin side-line shed where other acceptables of the town gathered each Saturday afternoon.

She had early the confidence of her class. Her father was a mine manager and owner. 'AG' they called him, and he knew to a nicety what line of familiarity to draw with the blacks who still hung about the perimeters of town, even instigating a curfew for them, but was less certain when it came to men of his own colour. Which was either bright red or mottled white. In snapshots from the period he, heavily moustached and mutton-chopped beside his wife, dominated rows of sawney after-picnic guests. She always appeared formidably silked and hatted and her bust was frightening. 'Breasts' is somehow too pretty, too delicate a word to describe that shelf of righteousness on which many a local upstart had foundered. Along with the bust was a condescending familiarity with the town's priest, two ministers of other religions, and four members of parliament whom she had seen come and helped go. Clarice was an only child, not as much of a son as the father had hoped for and something less of a daughter; but with the years her looks fined and softened; and if she was not in fact a beauty privilege made her just as desirable in a country where a fine bank account is as good for launching a thousand ships as a face: it's even better.

Her mother was determined Clarice would marry well, but no one was ever quite well enough.

Motor-cars and Clarice's teens created small tensions. There were various young men; but the town had little to offer beyond bank- and railway-clerks, or the sons of Italian tobacco farmers whose morals the mother suspected to be doubtful. Should too long a time elapse between drawing-up of a young man's car and Clarice's flushed entry to the house, her mother would tighten her mouth, draw up that juridical bust, and struggle to find words that were at once proper and admonitory. She was rarely able to draw that nice balance and one afternoon, as she worked with her daughter in the kitchen crumbing butter and flour for scones, she said without preamble and quite formally:

'I was once attacked by a sexually maddened blackfellow.'

Clarice was startled.

'That is why.' Her mother shut her lips tightly and a little line was ruled.

'Why what?'

'Why you must keep men — all men — at a distance.'

'All men?' inquired Clarice. 'Or just sexually maddened blackfellows?'

'You are too young, Clarice,' her mother said sharply, 'to use such words. Girls of sixteen should not even know such words.'

'But I don't understand,' Clarice persisted. 'Were you — ?' she hesitated. 'Harmed' seemed not an exact enough word. 'Were you carnally known?'

Her mother fainted.

'I do not know where,' she later gabbled to Clarice's father, 'where this — this child — could pick up such . . . I have done all . . . appalling knowledge . . . how the good nuns . . . wherever . . . she must be protected from . . .'

She spoke at length to her daughter on the necessity of virtue, the rigours of beauty, of chastity, the clean mind, and the need to expunge lust. She went so far as to summon Father Rassini to give spiritual advice. She read her daughter an improving poem. Clarice listened to all this with an expression on her face as if she were trying to remember a knitting pattern. Young men were discouraged from calling. Her current bank-clerk went away in the army and Clarice, after dreadful scenes in which she finally proved herself her father's daughter, took the little branch train to the coast, caught the main line south, and burrowed into essential war industry.

The city was only partly strange to her, for she had been educated at a southern convent where her only achievements had been to stagger the nuns by the ferocity with which she played badminton and Mendelssohn's *Rondo Capriccioso*. She revealed no other talents. They taught her a little refined typing and book-keeping, insufficient to addle or misdirect any feminine drives; enough French to cope with a wine list in the better restaurants; and some basic techniques in water-colours. She had a full and vigorous voice that dominated, off-key, the contralto section of the school choir for three years, but even this mellowed into suitable nuances before the onslaught of the mistress in charge of boarders.

'My dear Clarice,' she would reprove icily, 'you are not a man.'

'Non, ma mère,' Clarice would reply dutifully, giving the little curtsey this particular order required.

'And further, you seem to forget that men do not . . . oh, never mind!' Mother Sulpice rolled her fine brown eyes upwards, a kind of ecstatic St Teresa, and swished off with her beads rattling.

The boarders pondered Mother Sulpice.

'You can see she was quite beautiful,' Clarice's best friend, a thumping girl, commented doubtfully. 'Quite Renaissance.'

'Do you think she was jilted in love?' The students spent much time in these speculations.

'Oh, I heard. I heard.'

'What? What did you hear?'

'I shouldn't say.'

'Oh, come on! What?'

'My mother told me something.'

'Told you what?'

'I shouldn't really say.'

'Oh, yes you should,' Clarice insisted. She kicked quite savagely at the iron railing of the terrace that looked out over Brisbane hills. 'By not telling me you are creating an occasion of sin.'

Thumper went pink. 'I'm not. How could I be?'

'Who knows what I shall think,' Clarice said cunningly. 'I could think almost anything. In fact, I do think almost anything.'

She looked slyly at her friend and observed the moral contortion with interest.

'You've got to promise,' Thumper said, 'that you won't tell.'

'Well?'

'Do you promise?'

'Of course.'

'Well,' Thumper said with a pretty play of hesitancy, 'well, she was engaged. Before she entered.'

'And what then?'

'He died. He was killed in France. It wasn't,' she said, lowering her voice in horror, 'a true vocation.'

'Oh, stuff that,' Clarice said. 'How did it happen?'

'Mummy said it was quite tragic.' Clarice saw her friend's eyes grow moist and noticed she was getting a new pimple. 'He was running to regain the trenches and he ran the wrong way. He was dreadfully short-sighted.'

Clarice wanted to laugh. Instead, she looked at her friend hard and asked, 'Do you think they'd had sexual intercourse?'

'Now you *will* have to go to confession!' her friend said.

'Poor Mother Sulpice!' Clarice sighed.

But it was for her, perhaps for the wrong reasons, transfiguration.

She studied the nun's graceful walk, imitated the Isadora-like arabesques of her hands, modulated her voice, and began training her hair into expressive curves across her ears.

'How Clarice has changed!' the nuns observed with relief. 'She's growing up at last.'

In class, her mind closed to the finer points of the redundant *ne*, she sought for and thought she discovered the delicate prints of tragedy on Mother Sulpice's completely calm face.

'That will be the way I will bear it,' she said to herself.

After she left home the first job she obtained was as an office assistant in a factory supplying camouflage tents to the troops. She left the day the senior accountant, who was married, suggested they take in dinner and a show. When she leapt offendedly onto a tram, an American serviceman asked could he help her with her bag. She had no bag but was so confused by the nature of his offer that before she had gone three blocks she found herself in conversation with him. He told her many lies, but those she most vividly remembered were about a cotton plantation in Georgia, an interrupted semester at Yale, and no engagement of the heart, legal or otherwise. As she dressed in her YWCA cubicle for her third outing with him, she kept telling herself it was Mother Sulpice all over again, and she dropped her firm tanned neck, glanced back into the speckly mirror, and lowered her eyes in unconscious but perfect parody.

On the sixth outing seven days after they had met, he attempted to take her to bed, but she resisted with much charm. On the seventh he told her he had been drafted to the Pacific and they then exchanged deeply emotional letters that she read again and again, all the time thanking God for the good training which had prevented 'that' from happening. 'That' was happening all about her. Thumper was pregnant to a marine who had crossed the horizon without leaving any other memento of his visit. Men were all like that, Thumper assured Clarice between her sobs. Clarice thought it a pity her nose got so red when she cried.

Clarice managed to repress her feelings of righteousness and exultation that she was the one spared, and after she had seen her friend take a sad train back to her stunned parents up country she slid into Thumper's job in an army canteen. She was totally unprepared for a letter some months later from Roy telling her he had married a nurse in Guam because he had to. 'Honey,' he wrote, 'you will always be very special to me. You will always be my one true love, the purest I have ever known.' He was lying again, but she was spared the knowledge of this.

She was not built for pathos. The troubles of others found in her a grotesque response of incomprehension. She kept meeting more and more men, but they all failed to please, were not rich enough or wise enough or poor enough if wise, or were too worldy or unworldly. And through all of this, growing steadily older and handsomer, she bore her singleness like an outrageous pledge of success.

At parties when other girls more nervous than she spilt claret cup or trifle on the hostess's carpet at those endless bring-a-plate kitchen teas she seemed always to be attending, she would say offhandedly, 'Don't worry. It's not *her* trifle,' and go on flirting tangentially and unconsummatedly with this or that. She was moving up the ranks and knew a lot of colonels now.

When the war was over she settled more or less permanently into a cashier's desk at a large hotel where for half a dozen years she was still courted by desperate interstate commercial travellers who, seeing her framed between the stiff geometry of gladioli, found a *quattrocento* (it was the hairstyle) mystique which they did not recognise as such but longed to explore. She accepted their pre-dinner sherries with every symptom of well-bred pleasure, went to films, dog-races, and car-trials with them, but always bade them firm goodnights outside her own apartment.

Then her hair began to show its first grey.

Her father died suddenly shouting at a foreman; and after Clarice had gone home to help out, her mother held onto her for quite a while, determined to see her daughter settled. Rallying from grief, she arranged picnics, dances, barbecues, musical evenings, card suppers; yet even she gave up when Clarice returned home far too early from a picnic race-meeting with a *fin de siècle* languor about the eyes.

'Where's that nice Dick Shepworth?' her mother demanded from a verandah spy-post.

'At the races, I suppose.'

'You left him there?'

'Yes. He is suffering from encroaching youth.'

'But, my God!' cried her mother. 'He's the manager of two cane mills with an interest in a third.'

'He holds his knife badly,' Clarice said, picking up a malformed piece of knitting.

'You must be mad,' her mother said.

'And he chews with his mouth open.'

'Oh, my God!'

She was dead by the end of the party season. Clarice got Father Rassini to bury her alongside AG, sub-divided the property, sold at a profit and, having invested with comfortable wisdom in an

American mining corporation, retired into her parents' house and spent her days in steady gardening. It became a show place. It was as if all her restrained fertility poured out into the welter of trees and shrubs; and if the rare and heady perfumes of some of them made occasional sensual onslaughts she refused to acknowledge them.

The day she turned forty she bought herself a dog.

He was a fine labrador who established his rights at once, learnt smartly to keep away from the seedling beds and to share her baked dinner. They ate together on the long verandah which stared down at the mined-out hills beyond the garden, and the tender antithesis of this transferred the deepest of green shadows into her mind, so that she found herself more and more frequently talking to Bixer as if he had just made some comment that deserved her reply. Her dependence on him became engrafted in her days: he killed several snakes for her, barked at the right people, and slept, twitching sympathetically with her insomnia, by the side of her bed. She only had to reach down to pat Roy, a colonel, a traveller, or even Dick Shepworth, and they would respond with a wag of the tail.

Although so many years had passed since her parents' deaths, Clarice still believed she had a position in the town and consequently gave a couple of duty dinner parties each year — but not willingly — to which she invited old school friends, townsfolk who still remembered her father, and occasionally Father Rassini. He dreaded the summons, for she was a bad cook; but attended, always hopeful of some generous donation. Aware of this, she would keep him sweating on her Christmas contribution till it was almost Easter; and when she finally handed him the envelope they both remembered her stoniness as he had talked to her, thirty years ago now, about the sins of the flesh. He'd been young, too; and whenever he sat down to an especially lavish meal at some wealthy parishioner's home he recalled her cool look as she had asked, 'Are you ever tempted, Father?'

As her muscles shrank the garden acre flexed its own, strengthened and grew more robust than a lover. There were

379

rheumatic twinges that worried her. One day when she went to rise from where she had been weeding a splendid planting of dwarf poinsettia, the pain in her back was so violent she lay on the grass panting. Bixer nosed around, worried and whimpering, and she told him it was nothing at all; but she thought it was time she got a little help.

She was fifty when she took in Willy Fourcorners as gardener. He was an elderly Aborigine, very quiet, very gentle, who had been for a long time a lay preacher with one of the churches. Clarice didn't know which one, but she felt this made him respectable. Willy wore a dark suit on Sundays, even in summer, and a tie. He would trudge back from the station sometimes, lugging a battered suitcase and, passing Clarice's house and seeing her wrenching at an overgrowth of acalypha, would raise his stained grey hat and smile. The gesture convinced Clarice that though he was a lesser species he was worthy, and she would permit herself to smile back, but briefly.

'Willy,' she said one day, emerging from the croton hedge, 'Willy, I wonder could I ask your help?'

Willy set down his bag in the dust and rubbed his yellow-palmed hands together.

'Yeah, Miss Geary. What's the trouble then?'

She came straight to the point.

'I need help with the garden, Willy.' She was still used to command and the words came out as less of a request than she intended. She was devastated by the ochreous quality of his skin so close to hers and a kindliness in the old eyes she refused to admit, for she could not believe in a Christian blackskin, preacher or not. 'It's all getting too much for me.'

Willy's face remained polite, concerned but doubtful. He was getting on himself and still worked as a handyman at the hardware store. On weekends he preached.

'Only got Saturdays,' he said.

'Well, what's wrong with Saturday?'

'I like to keep it for m'self.'

Clarice struggled with outrage.

380

'But wouldn't you like a little extra money, Willy?'

'Not that little, Miss Geary,' Willy said.

Clarice's irritation riveted at once upon the simple smiling face, and unexpectedly, contrarily, she was delighted with his show of strength.

'I'm a fair woman,' she said. 'You'd get regular wages. What I'd give anyone.'

Willy nodded. He still smiled through the sweat that was running down his face, down his old brown neck and into the elderly serge of his only suit.

'Please,' Clarice heard herself pleading. 'Just occasionally. It would be such a help, Willy. You see, I can't handle the mowing these days.' And she produced for him what she had managed to conceal from almost everyone, a right hand swollen and knobbed with arthritis, the fingers craned painfully away from the thumb into the beginnings of a claw.

Willy looked at her hand steadily and then put out one finger very gently as if he were going to touch it. She tried not to wince.

'That hurts bad, eh?' he said. 'Real bad. I'll pray for you, Miss Geary.'

'Don't pray for me, Willy,' Clarice said impatiently. 'Just mow.'

He grinned at that and looked past her at the thick mat of grass that was starting a choking drive about the base of the trees.

'Saturday,' he said. 'Okay.'

He came every few weeks after that and she paid him well; and after a year, as her right hand became worse and the left developed symptoms, he began to take over other jobs — pruning, weeding, planting out, slapping a coat of paint, fixing a rotted verandah board. She grew to look forward to the clear Saturday mornings when with Bixer, ancient, dilapidated, sniffing behind her, she directed him down side paths as he trimmed and lopped the flashy outbursts of the shrubs. Although at first she tended to treat him and pay him off as she would imagine AG to have done, gradually she became, through her own solitariness, aware of him as a human; so that after a time, instead of returning to the verandah for her cup of tea after taking him his, she got into the habit of joining him at the small table in the side garden.

'Where is it you get to, Willy,' she asked one Saturday morning as they drank their tea, 'when you take the train down to the coast?'

'Don't go to the coast, Miss Geary.'

'Where do you go then?'

'Jus' down as far as Mango.'

'Mango?' Clarice exclaimed. 'Why would you want to go to Mango?'

'Visit m'folks there,' he said. 'Got a sister there. Visit her kids. She got seven.'

'Seven,' Clarice murmured. 'Seven.' She thought of Thumper. 'That's a large number, I must say.'

'They're good kids,' Willy said. 'My sister, see, she'd like me to go an' live down there now they're gettin' on a bit.'

'She's younger than you, then, Willy?'

'Yeah. Fair bit younger.'

'And have you any, Willy? Any children, I mean?' She knew he lived alone, had done since she had come back to live.

'Two,' he said. 'Two boys. Wife died of the second one. But they been gone a long time now. Real long time.'

'Where to?'

'South,' he said. 'Down south.'

'And what do they do? Do they write?'

'Yeah. Come home sometimes an' stay with m'sister. One's a driver for some big factory place. Drives a truck, see? Other feller, he's in the church. He's trainin' to go teachin' one of them mission places.'

'Well, he's certainly done well,' Clarice said. 'You must be very proud of him.'

'Pretty proud,' old Willy said. 'Teachin' up the mission when he's through. Up Bamaga way he'll be. Might get to see him then, eh?'

'Do you get lonely, Willy?' she asked. But he didn't answer.

Bixer developed a growth. When Clarice noticed the swelling in his belly she summoned the vet from Finecut who took one look and said, 'I'll give him a shot if you like.'

'Get out!' Clarice said.

She cared for him as far as she was able, but he could only shamble from bedroom to verandah where he'd lie listless most of the day in the hot northern sun, not even bothering to snap at the flies. He lost control of his bladder and whimpered the first time he disgraced himself on the bedroom floor. Clarice whimpered herself as she mopped up.

Willy found her crying over the dog one Saturday morning. Bixer could hardly move now, but his eyes looked their recognition as Willy bent over him.

'Best you get him put away, Miss Geary,' Willy advised, touching the dog with his gentle fingers. 'Pretty old feller now.'

'Help me, Willy,' she said. 'I can't do that.'

He brought along an old tin of ointment he'd used for eczema on a dog of his own, and though he knew it wouldn't help he rubbed it in carefully, if only to help her.

'There y'are, Miss Geary,' he said looking up from where he knelt by the panting dog. 'That might do the trick.'

She was still tearful but she managed a smile at him.

'Thank you, Willy. You're a good man.'

It didn't do the trick; and when finally on one of the endless bland mornings of that week she found he had dragged away to die under the back garden bushes she could hardly bear it. She sat for a little on the verandah, which became populous with the ghosts of the endless summer parties of her youth. The smack of tennis balls came from a hard-court. The blurred voices of bank-clerks and railway-clerks and service men and travellers, and even the sound of Dick Shepworth eating, hummed and babbled along the empty spaces where her mother still sat in her righteous silks.

She put on her sun-hat and walked down town to the hardware store, where she found Willy sweeping out the yard.

'You've got to come, Willy,' she said. 'He's dead.'

'Strewth, Miss Geary. I'm real sorry. Real sorry.'

'You'll have to help me bury him, Willy. I can't dig the hole.'

'Strewth, Miss Geary,' Willy said. 'Don' know whether I kin leave.'

He propped himself on his broom handle and regarded her awkwardly. She was trying hard not to cry. He felt all his age, too, leaning there in the hot sun thinking about death.

'I'll fix that,' she said. She was still AG's daughter.

After it was over she made some tea and took it out to the garden. Willy looked hopelessly at her with his older wisdom.

'Don't you worry none, Miss Geary,' he kept saying. 'I'll get you a new little pup. A new one. Me sister, she got plenty. Jus' don' worry, eh?'

But she was sobbing aloud now, frightful gulping sounds coming from her as she laid her head on her arms along the table.

'Please, Miss Geary,' Willy said. 'Please.'

He touched her hand with his worn one, just a flicker, but she did not notice, did not look up, and he rubbed his hand helplessly across his forehead.

'Look,' he said, 'I got to be goin' soon. But true, me sister she's got these two dogs an' they jus' had pups. I'll get you one of theirs, eh? You'd like that. There's this little brown feller, see, with a white patch. He's a great little dog. You'd like that, eh?'

Slowly she lifted her head, her face ruined with weeping, and saw the old black man and the concern scribbled all over his face.

'Oh, Willy,' she said, 'that's so kind of you. It really is. But it won't make any difference.'

'But it will,' Willy argued, human to human. 'Nex' time I come to mow I'll bring him back. You see. You'll love him.'

He pushed his chair back, came round the table and stood beside her, wanting to cry himself a bit, she looked that old an' lost. She looked up at him, messy with grief, and Willy put his old arm round her shoulders and gave her a consoling pat.

'There,' he said. 'Don' you mind none.'

He'd never seen a face distort so.

She began to scream and scream.

ELIZABETH HARROWER
(1928–   )

Harrower was born in Sydney, but lived for her first eleven years in Newcastle, New South Wales. She finished her education in Sydney and worked as a clerk. Later she went to England to study psychology, but instead decided to write a novel, *Down in the City* (1957). After eight years in London, she returned to Australia and worked for a short time for the ABC and as a reviewer.

Harrower's other novels are *The Long Prospect* (1958), *The Catherine Wheel* (1960), and *The Watch Tower* (1966). She has also written short stories. Her work is often concerned with women's effort to achieve self-realisation and emotional liberation in a man's world.

THE BEAUTIFUL CLIMATE

The Shaws went down to the cottage on Scotland Island every weekend for two years. Hector Shaw bought the place from some hotel-keeper he knew, never having so much as hinted at his intention till the contract was signed. Then he announced to his wife and daughter the name of a certain house, his ownership of it, its location, and the fact that they would all go down every Friday night to put it in order.

It was about an hour's drive from Sydney. At the Church Point wharf they would park the car, lock it up, and wait for the ferry to take them across to the island.

Five or six families made a living locally, tinkering with boats and fishing, but most of the houses round about were weekenders, like the Shaws' place. Usually these cottages were sold complete with a strip of waterfront and a jetty. In the Shaws' case the jetty was a long spindly affair of grey wooden palings on rickety stilts, with a perpendicular ladder that had to be climbed getting in and out of the boat. Some of the others were handsome constructions equipped with special flags and lights to summon the ferry-man when it was time to return to civilisation.

As Mr Shaw had foretold, they were constantly occupied putting the house in order, but now and then he would buy some green prawns, collect the lines from the spare-bedroom cupboard, and take his family into the middle of the bay to fish. While he made it obligatory to assume that this was a treat, he performed every action with his customary air of silent, smouldering violence, as if to punish misdemeanours, alarming his wife and daughter greatly.

Mrs Shaw put on her big straw sun-hat, tied it solemnly under her chin, and went behind him down the seventy rough rock steps from the house. She said nothing. The glare from the water gave

386

her migraine. Since a day years before when she was a schoolgirl learning to swim, and had almost drowned, she had had a horror of deep water. Her husband knew it. He was a difficult man, for what reason no one had been able to discover, least of all Hector Shaw himself.

Del followed her mother down the steep bushy track, not speaking, her nerves raw, her soundless protests battering the air about her. She did not *want* to go, nor, of course, could she want to stay when her absence would be used against her mother.

They were not free. Either the hostage, or the one over whom a hostage was held, they seemed destined to play for ever if they meant to preserve the peace. And peace had to be preserved. Everything had always been subordinated to this task. As a child, Del had been taught that happiness was nothing but the absence of unpleasantness. For all she knew, it was true. Unpleasantness, she knew, could be extremely disagreeable. She knew that what was irrational had to be borne, and she knew she and her mother longed for peace and quiet — since she had been told so so often. But still she did not want to go.

Yet that they should not accompany her father was unthinkable. That they should all three be clamped together was, in a way, the whole purpose of the thing. Though Del and her mother were aware that he might one day sink the boat deliberately. It wasn't *likely*, because he was terrified of death, whereas his wife would welcome oblivion, and his daughter had a stony capacity for endurance (so regarding death, at least, they had the upper hand): but it was *possible*. Just as he might crash the car some day on purpose if all three were secure together in it.

'Why do we *do* it?' Del asked her mother relentlessly. 'You'd think we were mental defectives the way we troop behind him and do what we're told just to save any trouble. And it never does. Nothing we do makes sure of anything. When I go out to work every day it's as if I'm out on parole. You'd think we were hypnotised.'

Her mother sighed and failed to look up, and continued to butter the scones.

'*You're* his wife, so maybe you think you have to do it, but I don't. I'm eighteen.'

However, till quite recently she had been a good deal younger, and most accustomed to being used in the cause of peace. Now her acquiescence gnawed at her and baffled her, but though she made isolated stands, in essence she always did submit. Her few rebellions were carefully gauged to remain within the permitted limits, the complaints of a prisoner-of-war to the camp-commandant.

This constant nagging from the girl exhausted Mrs Shaw. Exasperation penetrated even her alarming headaches. She asked desperately, 'What would you do if you *didn't* come? You're too nervous to stay in town by yourself. And if you did, what would you do?'

'*Here*. I have to come *here*, but why do we have to go in the boat?' On a lower note, Del muttered, 'I wish I worked at the kindergarten seven days a week, I dread the night and weekends.'

She could *think* a thing like that, but never say it without a deep feeling of shame. Something about her situation made her feel not only, passively, abused, but actively, surprisingly, guilty.

All her analysis notwithstanding, the fishing expeditions took place whenever the man of the family signified his desire for some sport. Stationed in the dead centre of the glittering bay, within sight of their empty house, they sat in the open boat, grasping cork rollers, feeling minute and interesting tugs on their lines from time to time, losing bait and catching three-inch fish.

Low hills densely covered with thin gums and scrub sloped down on all sides to the rocky shore. They formed silent walls of a dark subdued green, without shine. Occasional painted roofs showed through. Small boats puttered past and disappeared.

As the inevitable pain began to saturate Mrs Shaw's head, she turned gradually paler. She leaned against the side of the boat with her eyes closed, her hands obediently clasping the fishing-line she had been told to hold.

The dazzle of the heavy summer sun sucked up colour till the scene looked black. Her light skin began to burn. The straw sun-hat was like a neat little oven in which her hair, her head and all its contents, were being cooked.

Without expression, head lowered, Del looked at her hands, fingernails, legs, at the composition of the cork round which her line was rolled. She glanced sometimes at her mother, and sometimes, by accident, she caught sight of her father's bare feet or his arm flinging out a newly-baited line, or angling some small silver fish off the hook and throwing it back, and her eyes sheered away.

The wooden interior of the boat was dry and burning. The three fishers were seared, beaten down by the sun. The bait smelled. The water lapped and twinkled blackly but could not be approached: sharks abounded in the bay.

The cottage was fairly dilapidated. The walls needed painting inside and out, and parts of the verandah at the front and both sides had to be re-floored. In the bedrooms, sitting-room and kitchen, most of the furniture was old and crudely-made. They burned the worst of it, replacing it with new stuff, and what was worth salvaging Mrs Shaw and Del gradually scrubbed, sanded and painted.

Mr Shaw did carpentering jobs, and cleared the ground nearby of some of the thick growth of ecualyptus gums that had made the rooms dark. He installed a generating plant, too, so that they could have electric light instead of relying on kerosene lamps at night.

Now and then his mood changed inexplicably, for reasons so unconnected with events that no study and perpetuation of these external circumstances could ensure a similar result again. Nevertheless, knowing it could not last, believing it might, Mrs Shaw and Del responded shyly, then enthusiastically, but always with respect and circumspection, as if a friendly lion had come to tea.

These hours or days of amazing good humour were passed, as it were, a few feet off the ground, in an atmosphere of slightly hysterical gaiety. They sang, pumping water to the tanks; they joked at either end of the saw, cutting logs for winter fires; they ran, jumped, slithered, and laughed till they had to lean against the trees for support. They reminded each other of all the incidents of other days like these, at other times when his nature was in eclipse.

'We'll fix up a nice shark-proof pool for ourselves,' he said. 'We own the water-frontage. It's crazy not to be able to cool off when we come down. If you can't have a dip here, surrounded by water, what's the sense? We'd be better to stay home and go to the beach, this weather.'

'Three cheers!' Del said. 'When do we start?'

The seasons changed. When the nights grew colder, Mr Shaw built huge log-fires in the sitting-room. If his mood permitted, these fires were the cause of his being teased, and he liked very much to be teased.

Charmed by his own idiosyncrasy, he would pile the wood higher and higher, so that the walls and ceiling shone and flickered with the flames, and the whole room crackled like a furnace on the point of explosion. Faces scorching, they would rush to throw open the windows, then they'd fling open the doors, dying for air. Soon the chairs nearest the fire would begin to smoke and then everyone would leap outside to the dark verandah, crimson and choking. Mr Shaw laughed and coughed till he was hoarse, wiping his eyes.

For the first few months, visitors were non-existent, but one night on the ferry the Shaws struck up a friendship with some people called Rivers, who had just bought a cottage next door. They came round one Saturday night to play poker and have supper, and in no time weekly visits to each other's house were established as routine. Grace and Jack Rivers were relaxed and entertaining company. Their easy good-nature fascinated the Shaws, who looked forward to these meetings seriously, as if the Rivers were a sort of rest-cure ordered by a specialist, from which they might pick up some health.

'It was too good to last,' Mrs Shaw said later. 'People are so funny.'

The Rivers' son, Martin, completed his army training and went down to stay on the island for a month before returning to his marine-engineering course at a technical college in town. He and Del met sometimes and talked, but she had not gone sailing with him when he asked her, nor was she tempted to walk across the island to visit his friends who had a pool.

'Why not?' he asked.

'Oh, well . . .' She looked down at the dusty garden from the verandah where they stood. 'I have to paint those chairs this afternoon.'

'*Have* to?' Martin had a young, open, slightly-freckled face.

Del looked at him, feeling old, not knowing how to explain how complicated it would be to extricate herself from the house, and her mother and father. He would never understand the drama, the astonishment, that would accompany her statement to them. Even if, eventually, they said, 'Go, go!' recovering from their shock, her own joylessness and fatigue were so clear to her in anticipation that she had no desire even to test her strength in the matter.

But one Saturday night over a game of cards, Martin asked her parents if he might take her the next night to a party across the bay. A friend of his, Noel Stacey, had a birthday to celebrate.

Del looked at him with mild surprise. He had asked her. She had refused.

Her father laughed a lot at this request as though it were very funny, or silly, or misguided, or simply impossible. It turned out that it *was* impossible. They had to get back to Sydney early on Sunday night.

If they *did* have to, it was unprecedented, and news to Del. But she looked at her father with no surprise at all.

Martin, said, 'Well, it'll be a good party,' and gave her a quizzical grin. But his mother turned quite pink, and his father cleared his throat gruffly several times. The game broke up a little earlier than usual, and, as it happened, was the last one they ever had together.

Not knowing that it was to be so, however, Mrs Shaw was pleased that the matter had been dealt with so kindly and firmly.'What a funny boy!' she said later, a little coyly, to Del.

'Is he?' she said indifferently.

'One of the new generation,' said Mr Shaw, shaking his head, and eyeing her with caution.

'Oh?' she said, and went to bed.

'She didn't really want to go to that party at all,' her mother said.

'No, but we won't have him over again, do you think? He's got his own friends. Let him stick to them. There's no need for this. These fellows who've been in army camps — I know what they're like.'

'She hardly looked at him. She didn't care.' Mrs Shaw collected the six pale-blue cups, saucers and plates on the wooden tray, together with the remnants of supper.

With his back to the fire, hands clasped behind him, Mr Shaw brooded. 'He had a nerve though, when you come to think of it. I mean — he's a complete stranger.'

Mrs Shaw sighed anxiously, and her eyes went from one side of the room to the other. 'I'm sure she didn't like him. She doesn't take much interest in boys. You're the only one.'

Mr Shaw laughed reluctantly, looking down at his shoes.

As more and more of the property was duly painted and repaired, the Shaws tended to stop work earlier in the day, perhaps with the unspoken intention of making the remaining tasks last longer. Anyway, the pressure was off, and Mrs Shaw knitted sweaters, and her husband played patience, while Del was invariably glued to some book or other.

No one in the district could remember the original owner-builder of their cottage, or what he was like. But whether it was this first man, or a later owner, *someone* had left a surprisingly good library behind. It seemed likely that the builder had lived and died there, and that his collection had simply been passed on with the property from buyer to buyer, over the years.

Books seemed peculiarly irrelevant on this remote hillside smelling of damp earth and wood-smoke and gums. The island had an ancient, prehistoric, undiscovered air. The alphabet had yet to be invented.

However, the books *had* been transported here by someone, and Del was pleased to find them, particularly the many leather-bound volumes of verse. Normally, in an effort to find out why people were so peculiar, she read nothing but psychology. Even after she knew psychologists did not know, she kept reading it from force of habit, in the hope that she might come across a formula for survival directed specifically at her: *Del Shaw, follow these instructions to the letter!* . . . Poetry was a change.

She lay in a deck-chair on the deserted side-verandah and read in the mellow three o'clock, four o'clock, sunshine. There was, eternally, the smell of grass and burning bush, and the homely noise of dishes floating up from someone's kitchen along the path of yellow earth, hidden by trees. And she hated the chair, the mould-spotted book, the sun, the smells, the sounds, her supine self.

And they came on a land where it was always afternoon.

'It's like us, exactly like us and this place,' she said to her mother, fiercely brushing her long brown hair in front of the dressing-table's wavy mirror. 'Always afternoon. Everyone lolling about. Nobody *doing* anything.'

'My goodness!' Her mother stripped the sheets off the bed to take home to the laundry. 'I thought we'd all been active enough this weekend to please anyone. And I don't see much afternoon about Monday morning.'

'Active! That isn't what I mean. Anyway, I don't mean here or this weekend. I mean everyone, everywhere, all the time. Ambling round till they die.' Oh, but that wasn't what she meant, either.

Mrs Shaw's headache look appeared. 'It's off to the doctor with you tonight, Miss!'

Del set her teeth together. When her mother had left the room with her arms full of linen, still darting sharp glances at her daughter, Del closed her eyes and raised her face to the ceiling.

Let me *die*.

The words seemed to be ground from her voiceless body, to be ground, powdered stone, from her heart.

She breathed very slowly; she slowly righted her head, carefully balancing its weight on her neck. Then she pulled on her suede jacket, lifted her bag, and clattered down the uneven stone steps to the jetty. It always swayed when anyone set foot on it.

When the cottage had been so patched and cleaned that, short of a great expenditure of capital, no further improvement was possible, Hector Shaw ceased to find any purpose in his visits to it. True, there was still the pool to be tackled, but the summer had gone by without any very active persuasion, any pleading, any teasing, from his wife and daughter. And if *they* were indifferent, far be it from him . . .

Then there was another thing. Not that it had any connexion with the place, with being on Scotland Island, but it had the side-effect of making the island seem less — safe, salubrious, desirable. Jack Rivers died from a heart-attack one Sunday morning. Only fifty-five he was, and a healthier-looking fellow, you couldn't have wished to meet.

Since the night young Martin Rivers had ruined their poker parties, they had seen very little of Jack and Grace. Sometimes on the ferry they had bumped into each other, and when they had the Shaws, at least, were sorry that it had all worked out so badly. Jack and Grace were good company. It was hard not to feel bitter about the boy having spoiled their nice neighbourly friendship so soon before his father died. Perhaps if Jack had spent more time playing poker and less doing whatever he did do after the Saturdays stopped . . .

On a mild mid-winter night, a few weeks after Jack Rivers' funeral, the Shaw family sat by the fire. Del was gazing along her corduroy slacks into the flames, away from her book. Her parents were silent over a game of cards.

Mr Shaw took a handful of cashew nuts from a glass dish at his side and started to chew. Then leaning back in his chair, his eyes still fixed on his cards, he said, 'By the way, the place's up for sale.'

His wife stared at him. 'What place?'

'*This* place.' He gave her his sour, patient look. 'It's been on Dalgety's books for three weeks.'

'What for?' Del asked, conveying by the gentleness of her tone, her total absence of criticism. It was dangerous to question him, but then it was dangerous not to, too.

'Well, there isn't much to do round here now. And old Jack's popped off—' (He hadn't meant to say that!) Crunching the cashew nuts, he slid down in his chair expansively, every supra-casual movement premeditated as though he were playing *Hamlet* at Stratford.

The women breathed deeply, not with regret, merely accepting this new fact in their lives. Mrs Shaw said, 'Oh! . . .' and Del nodded her comprehension. Changing their positions imperceptibly, they prepared to take up their occupations again in the most natural and least offensive ways they could conceive. There was enormous potential danger in any radical change of this sort.

'Ye—es,' said Mr Shaw, drawing the small word out to an extraordinary length. 'Dalgety's telling them all to come any Saturday or Sunday afternoon.' Still he gazed at his handful of cards, then he laid them face down on the table, and with a thumb, thoughtfully rubbed the salt from the cashews into the palm of his other hand. It crumbled onto his knees, and he dusted it down to the rug, seeming agreeably occupied in its distribution.

'Ye—es,' he said again, while his wife and daughter gazed at him painfully. 'When and if anyone takes the place, I think we'd better use the cash to go for a trip overseas. What do you say? See the Old Country . . . Even the boat trip's pretty good, they tell me. You go right round the coast here (that takes about a week), then up to Colombo, Bombay, Aden, through the Suez, then up through the Mediterranean, through the Straits of Messina past some volcano, and past Gibraltar to Marseilles, then London.'

There was silence.

Mr Shaw turned away from the table and his game, and looked straight into his wife's grey eyes—a thing he rarely did. Strangers were all right, he could look at them, but with relations, old acquaintances, his spirit, unconscious, was ashamed and uneasy.

'Go away?' his wife repeated, turning a dreadful colour.

He said, 'Life's short. I've earned a holiday. Most of my typists 've been abroad. We'll have a year. We'll need a year. *If* someone turns up on the ferry one day and *wants* the place, that is. There's a bit of a slump in real estate just now, but I guess we'll be okay.'

And they looked at each other, the three of them, with unfamiliar awe. They were about to leave this dull pretty city where they were all so hard to live with, and go to places they had read about, where the world was, where things happened, where the photographs of famous people came from, where history was, and snow in cities, and works of art, and splendour . . .

Poetry and patience were discarded from that night, while everyone did extra jobs about the cottage to add to its attractiveness and value. Mrs Shaw and Del planted tea-trees and hibiscus bushes covered with flowers of palest apricot, and pink streaked with red. Mr Shaw cemented the open space under the house (it was propped up on columns on its steep hillside) and the area underneath was like a large extra room, shady and cool. They put some long bamboo chairs down there, fitted with cushions.

Most weekend afternoons, jobs notwithstanding, Del went to the side-verandah to lean over the railing out of sight and watch the ferry go from jetty to jetty and return to Church Point. She watched and willed, but no one ever came to see the house.

It was summer again, and the heatwave broke records. Soon it was six months since the night they had talked about the trip.

Always the island was the same. It was scented, self-sufficient; the earth was warm underfoot, and the air warm to breathe. The hillside sat there, quietly, rustling quietly, a smug curving hillside that had existed for a long time. The water was blue and sparkled with meaningless beauty. Smoke stood in the sunny sky above the bush here and there across the bay, where other week-end visitors were cooking chops, or making coffee on fuel stoves.

Del watched the ferries and bargained with fate, denying herself small pleasures, which was very easy for her do to. She waited. Ferries came and went round the point, but never called at their place.

They lost heart. In the end it would have been impossible even to mention the trip. But they all grieved with a secret enduring grief as if at the death of the one person they had loved. Indeed, they grieved for their own deaths. Each so unknown and un-understood, who else could feel the right regret? From being eaten by the hillside, from eating one another, there had been the chance of a reprieve. Now it was evidently cancelled, and in the meantime irretrievable admissions had been made . . .

At the kindergarten one Tuesday afternoon Miss Lewis, who was in charge, called Del to the telephone. She sat down, leaning her forehead on her hand before lifting the receiver.

'Hullo?'

'Del, your father's sold the cottage to a pilot. Somebody Barnes. He's bought the tickets. We've just been in to get our cabins. We're leaving in two months.'

'What? . . . A pilot?'

'Yes. We're going on the *Arcadia* on the 28th of November. The cabins are lovely. Ours has got a porthole. We'll have to go shopping, and get injections and passports . . .'

'We're *going*?'

'Of course we are, you funny girl! We'll tell you all about it when you get home tonight. I've started making lists.'

They were going. She was going away. Out in the world she would escape from them. There would be room to run, outside this prison.

'So we're off,' her mother said.

Del leaned sideways against the wall, looking out at the eternal afternoon, shining with all its homey peace and glory. 'Oh, that's good,' she said. 'That's good.'

MENA KASMIRI ABDULLAH
(1930–   )

Abdullah was born in northern New South Wales to migrant
Indian parents, and grew up on the family sheep property. She
contributed short stories to several *Coast to Coast* collections and
other anthologies, and collaborated with Ray Mathew on *The
Time of the Peacock* (1956), a sensitive portrayal of people living
exiled from their own culture.

GRANDFATHER TIGER

Grandfather Tiger was a secret and he lived at the bottom of the garden. He was Joti's tiger and no one else in the world dreamt of him.

She found him there by the river after grandfather died. Wonderful grandfather that you could talk to had died and left Joti with no one to tell how she missed him – only the Tiger. She had found *him* when she was crying by the river. She had looked up and there he was, terrible and beautiful, like the gold silk tiger on the cushion in the room that used to be grandfather's.

The Tiger's voice was growly and kind, the voice of grandfather. And Joti told him everything. So this day she ran down the yard that, until this day, had been almost her only world. She ran as fast as she could, her bare feet hardly touching the ground, to tell Grandfather Tiger her great news. He was there, the way he always was now, behind the clump of lantana, on a grassy bank at the river's edge.

She made the Hindu sign of greeting, joining her hands gently before her face. 'Salaam, Tiger Sahib,' she said. 'I am going to school.'

'Salaam,' said the Tiger. 'You have everything to learn.'

'And I will wear a dress, like the other girls. I will be the same.'

The Tiger swished his tail and smiled, very tired. 'A dress cannot make you the same,' he said. 'It will only be pretending.'

Joti looked at him, scared. Grandfather had once said something like that. 'Will school not be good?' she asked in a little voice.

'Perhaps,' said the Tiger. 'Perhaps there will be friends there.'

'Friends!' said Joti. 'Friends!' She smiled, danced two steps, salaamed and hurried back to the house where her mother was calling her to dinner.

Their home was in the suburbs. Joti's father, Raj, went every day into the city to his work, like any father in the suburbs. Her mother stayed at home with the children, and sometimes took Joti with her up to the shops, like any mother in the suburbs. And their house was like all the homes in their bushy suburb.

The house was the same but the home was different because Joti's parents kept the customs of their people. They took off their shoes before entering the house. They decorated the garden path for the Hindu festivals. They cooked curry and rice and chupatties. The friends who came there for dinner sat on the floor and felt at home.

Dinner was always a formal affair and the children never sat down to it with the grown-ups. Joti, who was the eldest, stood near the table and passed whatever was required. She had to be quick enough to do this before she was asked, and polite enough never to seem in the way. But this night she made mistakes. She could think of nothing but school.

'The little one is going to school tomorrow,' said Raj, her father, to excuse her. 'She can think of nothing else.'

Old Ram-Sukal, the guest of the evening, smiled at Joti. 'You are going to become a clever lady, like your mother,' he said.

Everyone laughed but grandmother. 'Oh, it is not right for her to go,' she said. 'It is not right! She will learn the white people's ways and think we are ignorant. She will call me stupid.'

'No, Mother, no,' said Raj. 'My children must learn to live here. They cannot stay in the house always. They must learn all they can. Then they can go to India and teach what they know.'

'They have never known India,' said Ram-Sukal. 'They may not wish to go.'

'But now that India is free,' said Raj, 'there is so much to be done. Schools to be built, hospitals and people to run them. India will be great again.'

'I thought,' said Ram-Sukal, 'that you were an Australian.'

'I am. I was born here,' said Raj. 'But my people —'

'Your people,' said Ram-Sukal. 'I have been back and I have seen your people. There is a line through your father's village.

Who are your people? Are you Indian or Pakistani? They will kill you if you do not know.'

'Old friend,' said Raj, shamefaced, 'old friend, you are always right and always wise. But what are we to do? I belong here. I am Australian, but who will believe me? My skin, my face, my thinking contradicts me, and who will accept me—or my children?' He looked at Joti.

'Accept you!' said grandmother. 'You talk like a child. It is you that must accept. Can't you understand?' She looked around at them all. Do not let us part, she thought. Do not let us part.

Next morning was first-day-at-school morning, and Joti put on her white-girl's dress. She fixed it in front of the mirror and hurried downstairs to show it and to get grandmother to plait her hair.

The family looked at her doubtfully.

Her arms and legs are so thin, thought her mother.

She looks ridiculous, thought grandmother.

'I look beautiful,' said Joti. And she smiled.

She went to school alone because she insisted, and Miss Adams, the teacher, was there on the verandah looking out for her.

'Hullo, Josie,' she said. She had thought about this new girl, off and on, ever since she had interviewed her mother. She was a difficult case and her enrolment card was going to be a worry. The cards had a space to tick for Australian and another space to tick for New Australian. What was to be done with a dark-faced Indian child who was a second-generation Australian?

'Come in, dear,' said Miss Adams. 'You had better sit there.' She pointed to an empty desk.

Joti sat in it. On the side nearest the window. Suddenly she felt a sharp poke in the back.

'That's where Dorothy sits,' said a red-headed girl from the desk behind her. 'You have to sit on the other side.'

Joti wriggled across. 'I'm sorry, I *am* sorry,' she said.

But the two girls behind didn't hear her. They went on whispering between themselves. And all day, whenever Miss Adams spoke to Joti, she called her Josie.

401

At playtime no one spoke to Joti, though they kept looking at her and giggling. At lunch-time they were bolder. One of them spoke to Joti and the others laughed.

'You're awfully skinny,' she said.

Joti smiled at her. She didn't know what to say. She didn't think it right to tell the girl that *she* was awfully fat.

They all watched her as she unwrapped her lunch. They all stared as she began to eat.

'What are you eating?' said one of them.

'Only kababs,' said Joti.

'*Kababs*!' The girls sniggered.

'That's only what black people eat,' said the red-headed girl. 'And I know what they're made of.' She whispered something and the girls that heard her opened wide their eyes.

'Eating *those*!' said one girl.

They all gazed at Joti.

She sat there as long as she could; then she gathered up her lunch and walked to the far end of the playground. She sat there, with her back to them so that they could not see her crying.

She started home from school very slowly, thinking of the endless number of days that school would be. Then she began to run, run as if bears were chasing her. She did not stop running until she had reached her home, raced through the front gate and was standing in the yard.

Everything was the same. The babies were playing on the lawn. There was the smell of curry cooking. It was her own home, safe and the same. She took off her shoes at the door and went quietly in.

As soon as she was in her room, Joti took off her new dress and put on her old *sulwa*. Then she went down the yard to talk to the Tiger. He was lying in his favourite spot by the river, and he stretched contentedly as Joti greeted him.

'It was horrible, horrible!' said Joti. 'There are no friends there. They think I am black-people. They laugh at me, and I hate them.'

'Ha!' said the Tiger. 'I thought that might happen.'

'Then what am I do to?' said Joti. 'What am I to do?'

'Accept,' said the Tiger. 'And they will accept you. If you run you will fail. If you fight you will fall. You must only accept.'

'I *cannot* go back!'

'You *have* to go back,' said the Tiger. 'You are the eldest. You are not the only one; there's your brother and sister. And your mother and father had the same trouble and pain, but your mother was patient and your father was brave — the bravest in the school. It is for you to be patient like your mother and brave like your father, little one.'

Joti looked at the ground and said nothing.

'It is hard,' said the Tiger. 'But when they accept you they will accept you for always.'

Joti stared at her feet and noticed for the first time how dark they were.

'The lessons are good,' said the Tiger. 'Your teacher is good.'

'Oh yes,' said Joti, 'I like the lessons. The teacher is nice, but she calls me Josie.'

The Tiger banged his paw on the ground so that Joti jumped. 'That is a different matter,' he said. 'You'll have to stop that or it will last you all your life. Your mother's name is Premilla and they call her Milly. Your Aunt Halima was called Alma. And your Uncle Shamshir' — the Tiger shuddered — 'they called him Sam!'

Joti giggled and the Tiger glanced at her sourly. 'You may think it funny now,' he said. 'And another thing, I would not wear that dress again. Wear your own name and your own clothes and they will understand you better.'

Joti came down to breakfast the next morning in her white sulwa. 'Look,' she said, 'I am *me* again!'

Her mother looked relieved and grandmother clucked approvingly as she plaited her hair. Her father said he would drive her to school.

During the drive, Raj tried to think of something encouraging to say to his daughter. He knew what schools were like, but he did not know what to say to a seven-year-old who had dressed herself in a sulwa to be herself again.

'Tonight, Joti,' he said at last, as he stopped the car, 'I will bring home some lollies.'

But already Joti was out of earshot. They were late and she could see that the class had gone in. She hurried to her seat with hardly time to look at the girl who was sitting beside her on the side near the window.

Miss Adams smiled at her and began to call the roll. 'Dorothy Johnson.'

'Present,' said the girl beside Joti.

'Josie Kausheed.'

Joti stood up, her legs shaking. 'Please, miss,' she said, 'my name is Joti.'

'I must have you down as someone else,' said Miss Adams. 'And Joti is too pretty a name to waste.'

Joti breathed again and sat down. The Tiger was always right.

At playtime Miss Adams showed them all a new game and helped them play it. Joti was shy about joining in, but soon she was laughing and leaping with the rest of them. At lunch-time she sat with them defiantly and, ignoring their glances, began to eat her lunch.

'What are you wearing?' asked one of the girls.

'Sulwa,' said Joti.

They thought about this.

'Why are you wearing it?' asked the red-headed girl. 'Why don't you wear a dress?'

'Because the Tiger said so,' said Joti.

'What Tiger?'

'My Tiger,' said Joti. 'He lives in our garden.'

'Oh, you are a fibber!' said the red-headed girl. 'Tigers can't talk. And you couldn't have one living in a garden. He'd eat you up . . . And serves you right: you're a terrible fibber.'

The others did not need to think about this. They had found a word. 'Fibber!' they called. 'Fibber! Fibber!'

Joti walked away, leaving the voices behind her. She sat at the end of the yard, and this time her tears were tears of anger. How dare they doubt her Tiger!

'White pigs,' she muttered. 'White pigs.'

'What's your Tiger's name?' came a timid voice near her. It was Dorothy, the girl who sat beside her in school, who had been away the day before.

'He has no name,' said Joti. 'I call him Grandfather-Tiger-Sahib. He lives at the end of our garden. He is always lying on the bank near the river.'

'I suppose,' said Dorothy, sitting down beside her, 'that's because he likes to swim. I would like a Tiger. I've got no one to talk to, except Auntie.'

'Where are your mother and father?'

'Mummy died,' said Dorothy. 'And Daddy works on a big ship and is always away.'

'No mother!' said Joti, horrified. 'No mother at home!' And she offered the girl some of her lunch.

'Thank you,' said Dorothy. 'This tastes nice. Would you like one of my biscuits?'

'Thank you,' said Joti. They sat side by side and ate. But Joti was remembering something. Was it something Tiger Sahib had said! No, it was grandfather who said it. He had been talking about the trouble in India and Joti had listened.

'All men should be brothers,' grandfather had said. 'And they become brothers by sharing. They share what they have — small things, big things — then they are brothers.'

Joti grabbed Dorothy's arm. 'We have shared our food!' she shouted. 'We are sisters, sisters!'

Joti ran home from school again, flew as though she had wings. She burst into the kitchen, forgot to take off her shoes, and danced and shouted. 'Grandmother! Mother! You have to make more kababs tomorrow. I have to share them with my friends.'

'Yes,' said her mother. 'Yes, lots more.' And she and grandmother listened, and smiled at one another while Joti chattered about her friends and her lessons and school.

She had so much to say that she forgot about the Tiger. It was almost tea-time when she remembered him. She ran down through the garden to talk to him. But he was not there.

She called to him, but he did not come. She pushed aside the bushes with her hands, but she could not find him. And it was growing dark.

Suddenly she knew that he would never come again. He had gone away because she did not need him; she was a schoolgirl now.

LEONE SPERLING
(1937-   )

Sperling was born in Sydney and studied at the University of Sydney where she won a playwriting competition. She spent thirteen years establishing her family and returned to writing in 1975. She has written a novel, two novellas, plays, and various short stories. She is currently a teacher at North Sydney Technical College.

THE BOOK OF LIFE

It is Kol Nidre night. Tomorrow is the Jewish Day of Atonement, the day on which God decides whose name will be written in the Book of Life for the following year.

He is eighty-three years old and he wants to live for another year. Not only does he want to live; he must live. It is his sacred duty to stay alive to look after his wife. His wife is eight years younger than he is and physically fitter but she needs looking after, nonetheless. They have been married now for fifty years. There was a time when he thought he might not make it to his golden wedding anniversary, but he did make it and now he needs to go on living for at least another year.

His wife has lost hold of her memory. It has flittered out of her grasp. She has entered a twilight timelessness where minutes and hours, days and dates, months and years are meaningless. He must be her constant clock. He is her timekeeper, guardian, father and friend. He unravels her confusion and imposes pattern and order onto her chaos. Without him she could not function in the real world.

He has lost his faith. He has lived his life in goodness, guided by the sure knowledge that God the Father looked down upon him and blessed him. But his wife's deterioration has changed all that. If there is a God, how can He have allowed such a thing to happen? Such a clever woman! Incomprehensible. He has lost his mate, his friend, his fifty-year companion. She has retreated, contracted. He cannot crawl for comfort into her inner world.

He has gone through all these married years in peace and harmony. No fights in this marriage; no disagreements; no harsh words. But lately he's been getting impatient, irritated, losing his temper. She must ask him the same questions over and over again in her enormous effort to engrave the answers on her sliding mind.

Sometimes he cannot control himself. The irritation builds and mounts and, before he knows it, he explodes in anger. And then she cries and he feels guilty. He keeps reminding himself that she can't help it. It's not her fault. He manages to stay calm most of the time. The thing that upsets him most is the enormous effort she makes to please him. She warms his pyjamas on the electric blanket every night.

He has lost his faith but it is Kol Nidre night and the habit of ritual is strong and, after all, how can anyone be so certain? Maybe God exists. Better to be safe than sorry. Better to go to the synagogue tonight and again tomorrow. Better to fast, better to pray, better to ask for another year of life—just in case.

She is waiting for him in the lounge-room. She is wearing her fur coat. She is always cold. She even wears her coat when she sits outside, eating fruit in the sunshine. He does not know how to keep her warm.

If only that fire hadn't burned his business down. He'd planned to keep working for another six months but thieves had broken into his shop and, finding no money, they'd expressed their frustration by setting fire to the whole place. Too old to start again. Too late to rebuild.

Retirement. Strolling with her each day around the safe, known streets; letting her tell him, over and over again, the names of all the flowers and plants; walking slowly up the hill to the Scoop grocery store to buy a few cartons of yoghurt, a litre of milk. Going to the bridge club twice a week. The only thing that keeps him sane. But how much longer can he go there? She's an embarrassment. She can't remember even the last five minutes' play. The other players won't tolerate her too much longer. What will happen to him then? They've had to give up playing bridge at home. The anxiety caused by having to provide people with sandwiches and cups of tea is too great for her to bear. They buy all their meals from the gourmet food shop.

He remembers her as she used to be. Chief pharmacist of a large hospital. How proud of her he had been! He wouldn't let her work, not for a long time. Not his wife. His wife didn't need to work. After all, he earned enough money, didn't he? Enough to support her and the children — all quite comfortably. But she wouldn't give up. She pestered and begged and finally he'd let her go back to work. What a difference it had made to her! She could whip through her day with lightning precision; dash home with swift steps, feet flying; cook dinner, wash dishes, iron clothes, help the children with their homework. Phenomenal! Her momentum propelled her through the days, the months, the years. No one could keep pace with her.

And the Friday nights, the family dinners, children and grandchildren spilling around the swimming pool. How can it have come to this? Now, now when he needs her companionship, her friendship, her understanding; now when they should be enjoying the rewards of his hard-working life. He thinks of his children. All successful, thank goodness. All well-educated. Not like him. Not reliant on the business world. And yet, he'd done well, hadn't he? Comfortably off. Not rich, but comfortable. 'The whitest man in the rag trade.' That's what they'd called him. Too honest to be rich. And too much given away to charity, so some people would say. But isn't that the most important part of being a Jew? Doing mitzvahs — giving to those less fortunate than yourself. They could have gone on a world cruise if only she'd managed to keep hold of her mind.

He looks at her, sitting in the lounge chair, waiting for him. Frail now. So thin. Her upper lip trembles. Her gloved hands grasp her handbag very tightly. He tells her it won't be long. Soon the taxi will arrive to take them into the city.

They are walking down Elizabeth Street towards the Great Synagogue. It is 5.45 p.m. He knows that the service begins at 6 p.m. but he has to get there early. He is a man of extreme punctuality. If he is not fifteen minutes early, then he considers himself to be late.

It is difficult for him to walk quickly because the arteries in his legs no longer function properly and he suffers from angina. Her pace slows down to match his. The wind claws into her. If she did not have her fur coat on, she would surely die.

410

They reach the synagogue and find that the gates are closed. Not only are the gates closed, but heavy, locked chains hold the gates together.

'We must be very early,' he says to her. 'I must have mistaken the time. Perhaps the service doesn't start until 6.30 p.m.'

'It's so cold, dear,' she complains. 'I can't just stand still. I'll have to keep walking.'

'Come on, then, Mummy dear, we'll walk round to the Castlereagh Street entrance. It's bound to be open.'

By the time they walk around the block to the back entrance of the synagogue, it is 6 p.m. The tall, brown doors are closed and locked. The street is empty.

'Let's walk back to the front, dear,' he says. 'By the time we do that, they must be open.' He walks swiftly now and her pace quickens to keep up with him. He should slow down, he should be calm. He knows that if he gets upset his angina will get worse but his agitation is beyond control.

The front of the synagogue is still locked. He moves away from her and stares at the gates in disbelief. She pulls the collar of her coat up around her chin. 'There must be some reason, dear, why the synagogue is closed,' she says. 'I don't know what that reason could be, but there must be a reason.'

He does not hear her. Where are all his fellow Jews? Don't they know, as he does, that they must begin their fasting and their atonement on this night? Why are they so late opening the synagogue? He goes to the gates and rattles them. He pulls at the chains. His mind is mathematical, decisive and precise. He never makes mistakes about dates and times. The synagogue must be open. It must! No other possibility is tenable. He grabs the heavy iron gates and shakes, shakes, shakes them. 'Open the gates!' he cries. 'Open the gates and let me in! God, let me in! Put my name, my name . . . down—my name, write my name in the Book of Life!'

She stands apart from him, waiting, whipped by the wind. She folds her hands into the sleeves of her coat.

He stops, lets the gates go. His hands drop, head sags. He stares

411

at her in blank confusion and a tear spills out of the corner of his eye. He takes her arm and they lean against each other, tightening themselves against the wind, shuffling through the darkness, along deserted Elizabeth Street.

BARBARA HANRAHAN
(1939–   )

Hanrahan was born in Adelaide. She pursued a career as an artist, and has become a painter and printmaker with an international reputation. She later turned to writing with a memoir of her childhood, *The Scent of Eucalyptus* (1973), and has published eight novels and a collection of short stories, *Dream People* (1987).

Hanrahan has a simple, straightforward style which explores the contradictions and contrasts of respectable society.

ANNIE M.

I like chicken legs, I don't like the top part of a chicken — I just don't, I like the legs. Sometimes I make a custard or a jelly. I sit down at the table — I sit down to do everything, even to have my wash. I've got no strength to grip things. I hold the spoon with my best hand and sort of steady it with the other hand while I stir the jelly crystals. Sometimes I do it with the left hand, sometimes I do it with the right, it all depends which hand is sorest. I can't straighten my fingers. My right thumb gets the wobbles and I hold him up straight so he doesn't wobble, my knuckles have come up like eggs. I dropped some wool pieces from my crochet and I had to scoop them up with the fly-swatter.

I have bread and margarine and honey, or bread and margarine and jam for breakfast. I have a hot meal for lunch — I manage somehow with my hands. I get the carrot and saw the ends off, then I stand up and scrape it, and do the same with the potato, and then I put them in the saucepan with the chicken leg. I have bread and margarine and honey, or bread and margarine and jam for tea, or when I feel like bananas I have a banana sandwich.

But they said at the hospital I passed out in the supermarket because I didn't eat enough. The cashier went and got a bag of beans for a pillow. It was quite comfortable. The ambulance man was an Aborigine and he talked so nice, but the nurses were a rough lot, they hurt me every time they touched me. They brought a bedpan and shoved it right against my tailbone — oh boy, did it hurt. When I told the male nurse he got rid of them and fixed me up. He had a way with him and though I'm deaf (but not stone deaf) I could hear what he said. I told him I was cold and every hour he took the quilt out of the hot room and wrapped it round me and put another quilt on top to keep the warmth in. He said, 'You can't be worried about modesty,' and washed me all over.

He washed everything and it didn't worry me (I thought it would but it didn't—once you don't feel well you don't seem to care any more). With my bone trouble I couldn't lift myself up, so he put his arms round me and I put my arms round his neck—just to be out of the road—and he lifted me straight up and I never felt a thing. I told him to call me Annie because I don't like to be called by my surname, it's a Scots name and people don't pronounce it right.

They tried to make me go into a nursing home but I wouldn't, so they sent me back to Pearl Street with a walking-frame and a seat-raiser for the lavatory. I was high up in the ambulance and could see out. They made me have Meals on Wheels and the first two dinners were all right, but then the two old girls spilt the soup. I didn't want soup and I'm not fond of lettuce (I never eat any green stuff) and you have to pay, you don't get them for nothing, so I told them I didn't want Meals on Wheels.

Elly, the small Greek woman, lives up the top end of the street next to Ritsa, the big Greek woman who's all swollen up with something under the skin. They were friends, but Ritsa's creeper keeps going over into Elly's yard so now they don't speak. I can't walk to the supermarket any more so Ritsa gets my chicken legs, Elly gets my bread and margarine, and I've got to work it so they don't meet when they come to see me. I leave the front door open for Elly and she comes in the morning; I leave the back door open for Ritsa and she comes in the afternoon.

Elly can't read and once when I asked her to get extra things she got different things, so now I don't ask her to get anything fancy. Ritsa will get anything I want but I don't like too much fruit and that's the trouble with Ritsa. If I ask her to get me two small bananas or one big one she comes back with half a dozen. I don't want bananas, bananas, bananas—I'm not that fond of them and they go funny in the fridge. But I owe Ritsa a lot. She cashes my pension cheque and pays my bills and puts the rubbish out and washes my sheets and cuts my toe-nails—she sits on the bed with my foot on her lap and trims them down, both feet. I gave her the money to buy the wheelchair in the front room and she'll take me for a walk when I'm ready. I've put a neck rest at the back so when I sit in it I can support my neck. She'll take me round to the supermarket — I've never been further than the front gate with my walking-frame for fifteen months. When you see the food there you start fancying a bit of this or a bit of that. Perhaps a little bit of ham or a little bit of fish, and I'd like a few new magazines and some lollies.

But you don't get much fish now, not nice fish. The fish at the supermarket's not what I want. I want some fish from Port Noarlunga. I waded in the water. We went there for a holiday, and my girlfriend wouldn't go in. I waded in the water and caught a fish with my hands. We took it back to the house where we were staying and the landlady let us use her kitchen and I cut the fish in half — it was a big one and we couldn't eat it all. I gave her the bit with the head on and Gwen and I had the tail.

It's rheumatoid arthritis, not just arthritis. No one knows what it's like except those that've got it, but I suppose it's better it's me than somebody that can't put up with it. I can't think of any part of my body I haven't got the pains in except my eyes. And my private parts, they don't ache (I'm still a virgin, I never had it — poor old pussy). My tailbone is the worst because I lie on it in bed, but I've got a soft pillow I put up under my bottom so it sort of hangs over and then it doesn't hurt. Bed is the best place. I don't get bored. Long as I'm comfortable I'm all right. If I feel lonely I have the wireless going and I do some crochet-work. Ritsa's got six doilies I made, she reckons she can't get enough of them; she'd put a doily under anything. I can crochet for five minutes, and then it takes me an hour before I can pick it up again. The magazines are light and I can hold them to read but they're always about the Prince, the Duchess and Princess Diana. I had a book once — it wasn't a new book but it was heavy and I couldn't read it, my hands just dropped, so I sawed it up in pieces at each chapter with the bread-knife. Then I read it and threw it out.

I'm thinking things in my head all the time. Sometimes I write down words. Anything that'll rhyme with the other words: *masquerade marmalade lemonade promenade parade esplanade persuade* (they just come into my head, I'm smart) *barricade balustrade serenade renegade cascade cavalcade* (you'd never dream there'd be so many) *colonnade accolade cannonade crusade* and: *edge wedge ledge sledge hedge bridge ridge fridge forge fudge smudge nudge trudge budge badge cadge dredge pledge.*

Sometimes I write down songs. I sing some of the old songs I used to know: 'Moonlight on the Silv'ry Rio Grande', 'Beautiful Isle of Somewhere', 'By the Watermelon Vine, Lindy Lou'.

I have my tea at six o'clock so I can get back into bed for the seven o'clock News. I never listened to the wireless once, but since I've been in bed I don't want to miss anything. Times are bad now, very bad, things are not right. People killing one another and doing awful things. One woman, they stabbed her in the stomach a couple of times and cut all her fingers off; she's in hospital and doing all right but she's lost her fingers. It was here, in Adelaide, I think, but it might have been Melbourne. There are more murders over in the other states, mostly up in Queensland — they have a lot of murders up there, they don't seem to be able to look after themselves and yet it's hot there, you wouldn't think they'd be worrying about being violent. But it was terrible here at the Zoo. Boys got in and killed the baby animals they were keeping for the children to see. They put those boys away and they're still away and there was some talk of doing away with them.

I have 5DN, turned up loud, and KG comes on at four o'clock and has his say about the football and when he doesn't know he says so, but he knows just about everything. He's not rude, not if you get the real KG. Now and then you don't get the real one — somebody else takes over while he's gone home to have a sleep. He's got a car but he goes home on his motorbike, it's quicker, he can slip in and out of the traffic.

At nine o'clock the one comes on who has the phone-ins. I've listened so long I know his tricks. Any of them that are abusive (they never say hello, they just start jawing), he shuts them up pretty quick. Some people cry and I said, 'Oh, shut up, you big boob,' to the man crying about his wife. Father Bob, the Catholic priest, comes on round midnight. But I go to sleep when he's

417

talking because I know my religion and they don't use the Bible I use — they've got a different Bible, and they talk their own talk. And I don't believe in this Our Lady business because Jesus' mother, she was his mother, and that was all.

I've got my wireless on the cupboard by the bed, and my emery board and my glasses and my scissors. In the drawer are my handkerchiefs, my purse, my pencil and pad, the peroxide I dab on if I scratch myself, the Vaseline I rub on my neck and face, my barley sugar lollies (I don't suck them, I leave them at the side of my mouth and let them melt). I never shut the drawer. If I leave it just open it's no pressure on my hands to pull it out, but if I shut it right tight — wow!

You've got to have everything handy. I have the walking-frame next to the bed and my wool for crocheting goes in the box in the middle and on one handle is a plastic bag for lolly papers, on the other a bag for dirty handkerchiefs. I don't ask other people to wash my hankies or any soiled garments, I put them in to soak in a dish of water with a spoonful of Morning Fresh. I tried paper hankies in the hospital but I didn't like them. There was a big bag to put the dirty sheets in and I threw the used paper hankies right in and the male nurse looked and said, 'You're a good shot.' I said, 'I always have been.' I have, too. I've got a straight eye. Dad would come in and say, 'Will you give me a straight eye?' There was a tennis-court across the road, before the offices were built, and Mr Williams asked me to play. I said I didn't belong to the tennis club but he said, 'I'm asking you, it's my tennis club and I'll have who I like there.' So I went, but I won every game because of my straight eye and I knew the other girls were jealous.

Mum's photo is up on the mantelpiece. I put it over to the side first but the light wasn't right, I couldn't see her face, so I shifted it over to the centre. She had brown eyes but Dad had blue eyes and I've got hazel eyes. My brother, Tom, had brown eyes and my sister, Dorrie, had green eyes. I call her my sister but really she wasn't, but Mum brought her up and she was like our family in every way and she had Dad's dark hair and those green eyes —

418

everybody remarked about them. They were always wide-awake eyes, as if they were going to miss something.

Even before I went to school I had a good memory. I'd go up the street to Mrs Fry's place and get all the news and come back and tell Mum. I went on the first electric tram down North Terrace with the nurse, but I don't remember, I was only a few weeks old (perhaps I was the first baby to ride on the first tram). I'm not bragging, but I think I was cleverer than the other children at school, though I talk-talk-talked and Miss Vaux stood me behind the door. When it was the First World War, Sammy Lunn was dancing on the steps of the Grand picture theatre with his walking-stick but the mothers and wives never threw him a penny, and it was their sons and husbands that got any money Sammy collected. So I took the end of his stick and watched his feet and did the same steps as he did and sang the songs he sang, and when I did that they started throwing the money.

A lot of people don't think I'm the age I am. I'm seventy-seven, but even with my bone trouble I still feel young. The skin of my face is very smooth — smile lines don't count because everybody wrinkles up their eyes a bit, same with your forehead. I've got wrinkles elsewhere, though; my bust is a bag of wrinkles. I don't know why I've got so thin, unless it's lying in bed. My whole body is thin. My chest is all knobs, there are knobs all over the place, they even try to poke out of my skull. But I've never had a cold since I was a child. I had the influenza then, when everybody else was dying with it. But I lived through it and I've never had a cold since. I must have an angel looking after me, or a good constitution.

My bust went, it just flopped. I don't wear a bra, I haven't got anything to put in it. Once I wore size 34 and I wore it over my singlet to keep me warm in the wintertime. Now I wear a jumper and my pyjama pants to keep warm. Even in the hot weather I still wear jumpers and I don't go out to sit in the sun — I couldn't sit on the seat with my bones, and even when it's a heatwave it doesn't make any difference, I still feel cold. The cold goes right down to my knees, but when I get back into bed it disappears.

And I wear a black nylon turban to keep my head warm and a pillow round my neck done up with a safety-pin to keep my neck warm. I made my jumpers before I got bad hands; they're fairly big in the neck and I can get them off over my head, even with it done up in a turban. When I take them off I work each sleeve down till the elbow pokes out at the armhole, then it pulls off as easy as anything. I don't like hair hanging round my face and often wear a few rollers. But it's awkward for my hands, putting in rollers. It takes me nearly two hours to do five. I do one and then I have to have a rest. My hair has grown down to my shoulders and I'd like to get to Feres Trabilsie's in town to have it cut. I thought I might go in a taxi with Ritsa one day. I'd pay for it and take my walking-frame (they could unscrew it and fold it up and put it in the back). I'd let Ritsa go to the shops and buy something while I went into the hairdresser's.

I haven't got a bath and I'm glad; I couldn't lift my legs to get in (even if I could and had one, I might slip and fall and break my ribs). When I wash myself, I get things ready in the kitchen the night before, my towel and my wash-cloth and everything. The kettle's full and after breakfast I put it on. I can't lift the kettle, it's too heavy, so I fill it up with a small saucepan. When the water's hot enough, I put the saucepan on the stove and tip the kettle on its side — it can't slip off because of the things poking up round the gas jet — and the hot water pours in and I add a drop of cold, then pour it over my hair and rub in the shampoo. Then I rinse it and roll a towel round my head to soak up the water and sit down and wash my body with another dish of water, and the last thing I do is my feet. I put them in the water and let them wash themselves and then I take them out and stand them on a towel to dry and then I put my feet in my slippers.

Once I went out dancing. I danced all night and I was fussy, I never danced with anybody that couldn't dance. I liked waltzing and if they put their cheek on mine I left it there, it didn't worry me, because that was as far as they got. Though some kissed me when they took me home and I didn't mind that, but I never kissed back. Some girls were larrikins, they went out with anything, they

weren't my type. I went out with Edmund and Skeeter and Eric
and did the Moonlight Waltz, the Hyacinth Waltz and my dance
dresses were every colour you could think of: red, blue, lavender,
pink. I had three pinks because I was a pink bridesmaid three
times — a pink lace, a pink French crepe, a pink taffeta.

I was a sewer. I had sewing on the brain. When I was fourteen
I started at the Perfection Shirt Factory, then I went to the sewing-
room at Moore's, the big department store in Victoria Square.
Then I started sewing at home and I made Mum's clothes and
my sister's clothes and my clothes and Mum always dressed very
smart, she preferred navy and black, she didn't go in for colours.
I made her a black chiffon and a navy crêpe satin and I made
her dresses for knocking round, she didn't like getting round any
old how. And I made anybody's clothes that came along and
wanted clothes. I sewed silk shirts and alpaca coats, bridal dresses
and evening dresses. But the girls with too short a neck always
wanted high necks to their dresses when they should have had
more open necks — not necessarily low necks, but not high.

As well as my dressmaking, I looked after the garden and there
was never a weed out of place. A rose tree grew in a diamond-
shaped bed; it had bright pink buds and then as they came open
I didn't care for them (I only like roses when they're half open).
There was a rockery, a fern house and a coprosma hedge I
trimmed — it kept me busy, that garden. I had a fig tree but it
wasn't a long fig or red; inside, it was a very pale pink. I loved
those figs and I had a lemon tree, an apple tree, a Satsuma plum.
A grapevine trellis went down the side: muscatels, lady's-fingers,
sweet-waters, and then there was a little tiny one like currants.

Now it's terrible, that yard. I've never had a yard like that in
my life. There are so many weeds, and the blue flowers have gone
wild. They're not hard to pull up, you can pull them up easy, but
I've got no pull or I'd have a try.

I don't want the Domiciliary Care from the Council, but I could
get a pop-in maid. They advertise in the newspaper and she'd only
have to do that room and this room and the kitchen. She'd charge
according to what she did, and could come once a fortnight. But

I do my best, I try to keep things tidy. I sit on the bed and sweep any wool pieces down into one place, and then I dab them with the broom and they stick to it and I turn the broom up and take them off, and then I put them in the rubbish bag on my walking-frame.

I only have four cups of tea a day but some nights I have to get up every two hours. But of late I've been going every four hours, so it's been very good, it saves this business of getting up. It must be the weather. In the cold weather you make more water, but now it's getting warmer. It's painful to get out and it's painful to get in. Sometimes I think I'll wet the bed and I make an effort and get out, but it takes me so long and I'm wishing and praying I can hold it. I get inside the walking-frame and sometimes I think I might drop my water on the way. I no sooner sit down on the lavatory seat-raiser than away she flies.

The old girl next door, she's no lady, she wets the bed and sleeps in it. She stinks. She sleeps in it and wets it and sleeps in it and wets it. You can smell the stink coming from her window — I've got a good smeller. I don't want her here. I only talked to her once, I couldn't understand her. She had her teeth in but they don't fit, they wobble round and she has to hold them in with her finger. She talked about a husband but she has hallucinations, I don't think she ever had one. She's not right in her head. She should be put away.

I never wanted to get married, I never wanted it, that's just me. When Audrey's husband came round wanting it I didn't feel upset. It doesn't matter what they think they're going to get, they don't get it from me, my mind's made up. Scots people are more that way and I took after Dad. We weren't a sexy family, not a bit. I don't know how Mum had my brother and me, but she did. After that, Dad didn't want it any more. But he loved Mum — he'd put his arms round her and kiss her, but that's as far as it went. There are a lot of people like that.

You hear of girls now, they're not married but they live with their man, they're happy, that's enough. After all, saying a few words doesn't make you any different. But I never wanted to get

into bed with a man and I wouldn't like to marry an old man—
he'd be too used to it, he'd wear you out. Though I liked talking
to men and dancing with them and having a bit of fun, and I liked
Hazel's brother, Eric: we danced the snake dance. After he lost
his leg in his accident he never worried about women. I might
have married him if things had been that way. But he might have
got tired of me—and yet again, I don't know, he might have been
something like myself. Could have been.

My girlfriend, Mabel, was like that for a while, but then she
got married and had children. If Harold wanted something from
Mabel at night he'd go on so silly. Sometimes when I was there
to tea, I couldn't hear what he said, but the way he was going
on, I could have clouted him. It made me shudder to think of
getting into bed with Harold and Mabel wasn't very sexy and I
suppose he didn't think he was getting enough because he started
bringing home flagons of wine. She tried to look as if she hadn't
been drinking, but I could always tell. Her words didn't slur and
she didn't walk crooked, but it was the effort she put into trying
to look as if she wasn't and I knew she was. Then one day when
Mabel was under the influence, she got abusive with me and I
said if that was all she had to say, I was going. I grabbed my bag
and walked out and I never went back. When I finish, I finish.

When it was the Second World War, I worked at Holdens and
had full authority over a hundred and twenty girls and five blind
men and five deaf and dumb women. Then I worked in the butter
room at the Co-op. Then I did sewing and looked after the
children for Mrs de Dear. The de Dears were millionaires and
after five girls they had Alasdair, and after that Mrs de Dear
didn't want any more kids so a nurse came the next time she was
pregnant and put it down the toilet—I don't blame her. The
de Dears had a party in their ballroom with oyster patties,
crabmeat puffs and stuffed eggs and when the children were put
to bed I mingled with the ladies. But not one of them was really
smartly dressed. I supposed they thought they'd just wear ordinary
and have a few drinks and one thing and another, like they did,
those types. I'd put on my party dress of black taffeta and silk

velvet (real soft silk velvet, you can't buy it now). Mrs de Dear looked and then realised she was staring. I was too well-dressed to be with them, so I disappeared into my sewing-room and took the dress off and folded it away in my case. Then I put on a pair of slacks and a jumper and a jacket because it was cold weather and went home on my scooter.

Mum died and then Dad died and then my brother died and then my sister died. I'd had such a good time when I was young that when I lost all my people I just went flop. Mrs Warne up the street took me to see a spiritualist, though I said I didn't believe in them. The woman was meant to go into a trance and I thought, You're not going to get any information today, I'm going to control you. I did, too. I broke her concentration. She was getting everybody under her control, but she couldn't get me.

Once I took pills for the arthritis, but they didn't do me any good, I don't believe in pills. I had a laboratory test and they charged me eighteen dollars to check a sample of my water. I won't have injections: over the wireless they said that anybody that's taking any injections must stop immediately — there's something wrong with the injections. The doctor came to see me once; I kept my hands under the sheets so he couldn't see the knobs. I knew he couldn't do anything, so we had a good yap and I'm silly as a wheel at times and he went out the front door still laughing.

I read in a magazine that eating Fairy margarine would help you in a lot of ways with your troubles. I'd been eating it for a while when I suddenly felt my toes move. I thought I must have dreamt it so I swung the bedclothes back and had a look and sure enough my toes were opening out, and then my fingers started to straighten out, too. I'm still eating Fairy margarine and I keep a supply in the fridge. I eat two tubs a week and might get better and live to be over a hundred.

When I go to sleep I have food dreams, but every time I dream I'm going to have a nice dinner I wake up before I get a chance to eat it.

I used to have fowls. I had a big black Orpington rooster, a Rhode Island Red, white fowls and two burnt-orangey bantams called Darby and Joan. After the old black Orpington did the dirty, Joan sat on four eggs; but she was too small to sit on them properly, so Darby helped her and they brought out four chickens: a black, a buff, a cream, a speckly. And I had pigeons and ducks, and Mickey was my last cat. I brought him home from the Co-op as a kitten and he sucked his milk off my little finger (my fingers weren't like they are now) till he lapped from the saucer. He was grey with white paws and a biscuit-coloured front. In the end he went thin and rubbed himself on my legs and, months after, I found him in the bottle-oh's paddock. He was trodden flat, but it was poor old Mick.

All the things I had. I used to love having them. I think about them sometimes. I think, Oh well, they're gone now, but still . . . I still think about them.

GLENDA ADAMS
(1940–   )

Adams was born in Sydney. She taught Indonesian at the University of Sydney. In 1964 she moved to New York in order to write and study. She has published two collections of short stories and two novels –one of which, *Dancing on Coral*, won the Miles Franklin Award in 1988.

MY SECRET LIFE

I got excited watching the Watergate hearings. All those mediocre people leading secret lives, getting found out, going on national television, making three-line heads every morning.

Since I've always been just a mediocre gal, I wanted a secret life, too. My friends were supportive. 'You can do it,' they said. 'You've got what it takes.'

I decided to plummet to fame.

First, I changed apartments and told no one my new address. I got an unlisted phone and blacked out the number on the dial. I peeled the address labels off my *New York* magazine as soon as it arrived, since I didn't want my name, address, and expiration date falling into the wrong hands. I then began to practise the secret arts of equivocation, dissimulation, subterfuge, and outright lying.

At parties I no longer mentioned people or places by name, referring only to 'a friend in retail' or 'a predominantly English-speaking island northeast of the Canaries'. When people asked, 'Where are you from?' I replied, 'Somewhere else.' The answer to 'Where did you go to school?' became 'A certain urban, Ivy League institution.'

My new secret life began to demand an unfailing will and supreme sacrifices as well. Once, at an elegant dinner, I forgot myself for a moment and talked intimately with an incredibly attractive man. When he asked where I lived and if he could take me home, I knew what I had to do. Choking back tears and smiling bravely, I said, 'I live in a racially mixed area south of the Bronx combining academics, workers, ethnics, and the elderly.' Then, recalling a ruse I had read about once, I pointed out the window and cried, 'Look, there's a little dog chewing that bicycle tyre!' and rushed out of the room.

About that time I stopped seeing people and also changed jobs.

427

I chose a location in the West Village so that I could go to work in the garb of an Episcopalian nun without causing a stir. Soon I found the shame-guilt-ecstasy habit exhausting, and decided it was time for a vacation. I left false clues about where I was going, to foil the exterminator, the Con Ed man, and the occasional friend who had tracked me down and sometimes stopped by with chicken broth and the *Sunday Times* to see if I was all right. I left *The Last of the Midwest* and an Amtrak ticket to Chicago on the coffee table.

I cleaned my sneakers, had my tennis racket restrung, and placed them next to a Qantas airline bag in the hall closet.

At the last moment I changed my reservation on a group flight to Sydney, no stopovers, to a round-trip first-class flight to Malta. I bought snorkelling equipment, which I carried home during rush hour in the subway, holding my newspaper open at the shipping page, where I had circled the temperature in Rio de Janeiro.

When the time came to leave, I dyed my hair black, put on green, four-inch platform shoes, and, in a rented car, I drove upstate and spent two weeks in a secluded cottage using the name Babs McTavish.

In the fall, I switched to a Hare Krishna outfit and carried an empty one pound Maxwell House coffee can. Sometimes I made a couple of dollars on the way to work, especially if I sang 'Swing Low, Sweet Chariot'.

Right now I'm concentrating on the apartment, getting rid of all telltale signs that might reveal something about me. I've replaced the Delvaux and Magritte prints and a painting I did myself with a snowscape, a port scene, and a pencil drawing by a Dutch master. All my books are stacked in a closet. (I daren't throw them out in case someone goes through my garbage.) But I've left out a few titles for decoration, like the *Zip Code Directory* and *Webster's Seventh New Collegiate Dictionary*. Sometimes, I casually leave the dictionary open at a page that has no significance. A favourite is page 263, which begins with 'ectomere' and ends with 'effacer'.

The challenge now, as I see it, is making my way undetected down Broadway to the twenty-four-hour Greek grocery, which I do every third Tuesday at 2 a.m.

BEVERLEY FARMER
(1941–   )

Farmer was born in Melbourne and educated at the University of Melbourne. She has worked as a teacher, a dishwasher and a waitress. She spent three years living in a Greek village, which provided her with the background for many of her short stories. She has written one novel and two collections of short stories. One of these collections, *Milk*, won the 1984 New South Wales Premier's Literary Award for fiction.

A WOMAN WITH BLACK HAIR

Her front door locks, but not her back door. Like the doors on many houses in her suburb, they are panelled and stained old pine ones, doors solid enough for a fortress: but the back one opens with a push straight into her wooden kitchen. Moonlight coats in icy shapes and shadows the floor and walls which I know to be golden pine, knotted and scuffed, having seen them in sunlight and cloudlight as often as I have needed to; having seen them lamplit too, cut into small gold pictures by the wooden frames of the window, thirty small panes, while I stood unseen on the back verandah. (The lampshades are lacy baskets and sway in draughts, rocking the room as if it were a ship's cabin and the light off waves at sunset or sunrise washed lacily inside it. Trails like smoke wavering their shadows over the ceiling are not smoke, but cobwebs blowing loose.) These autumn nights she has a log fire burning, and another in her front room just beyond. With the lights all off, the embers shine like glass. They fill the house all night with a warm breath of fire.

An old clock over the kitchen fire chimes the hours. One. Two.

Off the passage from her front room is a wooden staircase. Her two small daughters sleep upstairs, soundly all night. Beyond the staircase a thick door is left half-open: this is her room. In its white walls the three thin windows are slits of green light by day, their curtains of red velvet drawn apart like lips. There is a fireplace, never used; hardly any furniture. A worn rug, one cane armchair, a desk with a lamp stooped over books and papers (children's essays and poems drawn over in coloured pencil, marked in red ink); old books on dark shelves; a bed with a puffed red quilt where she sleeps. Alone, her hair lying in black ripples on the pillow.

For me a woman has to have black hair.

This one's hair is long and she is richly fleshed, the colour of warm milk with honey. Her eyes are thick-lidded: I have never been sure what colour they are. (She is mostly reading when I can watch her.) They seem now pale, now dark, as if they changed like water. On fine mornings she lies and reads the paper on the cane sofa under her shaggy green grapevine. She is out a lot during the day. She and the children eat dinner by the kitchen fire — her glass of wine glitters and throws red reflections — and then watch television for an hour or two in the front room. After the children go up to bed, she sits on and reads until long past midnight, the lamplight shifting over her. Some evenings visitors come — couples, the children's father — but no one stays the night. And she has a dog: an aged blond labrador, half-blind, that grins and dribbles when it hears me coming and nuzzles for the steak I bring. It has lolloped after me in and around the house, its tail sweeping and its nails clicking on the boards. It spends the night on the back verandah, snoring and farting in its sleep.

The little girls — I think the smaller is five or six, the other not more than two years older — have blonde hair tied high in a sheaf, like pampas grass. (The father is also blond.)

Tonight, though the moon is nearly full, it is misted over. I may not even really need the black silk balaclava, stitched in red, that I bought for these visits, though I am wearing it anyway, since it has become part of the ritual. I am stripped to a slit black tracksuit — slit, because it had no fly — from which I unpicked all the labels. I have the knife safe in its sheath, and my regular tracksuit folded in my haversack ready for my morning job when I leave the house.

Tonight when the clock chimed one she turned all the lights out. When it chimed two I came in, sat by the breathing fire, and waited. There is no hurry. I nibble one by one the small brown grapes I picked, throwing the skins and the wet pips into its flames of glass, making them hiss. Nothing moves in the house.

When the clock chimes three I creep into her room — one curtain is half-open, as it always has been — to stand watching the puddle of dimness that is her pillow; the dark hair over it.

431

I saw her once out in the sun untangling her wet hair with her fingers. It flowed over her face and over her naked shoulders like heavy dark water over sandstone. The grass around her was all shafts of green light, each leaf of clover held light. There were clambering bees.

There is a creek a couple of streets down the hill from here. I wish I could take her there. It reminds me of a creek I used to fish in when I was a boy. There were round speckled rocks swathed with green-yellow silky weed, like so many wet blond heads combed by the fingers of the water. (My hair was — is still — blond.) I used to wish I could live a water life and leave my human one: I would live in the creek and be speckled, weedy-haired, never coming out except in rain. I lay on the bank in spools and flutters of water light. A maternal ant dragged a seed over my foot; a dragon-fly hung in the blurred air; a small dusty lizard propped, tilted its head to take me in, and hid in the grass under my shadow.

Over the weeks since I found this woman I have given her hints, clues, signs that she has been chosen. First I took her white nightgown — old ivory satin, not white, but paler than her skin — and pulled it on and lay in her bed one day. It smelled of hair and roses. I left it torn at the seams on the sofa under the grapevine that shades her back verandah. I suppose she found it that night and was puzzled, perhaps alarmed, but thought the dog had done it; anyone might think so. Another day I left an ivory rose, edged with red, in a bowl on her kitchen table. She picked it up, surprised, and put it in a glass of water. She accused her daughters of picking it, I could tell from where I was standing by the kitchen window (though of course what she was saying was inaudible), and they shook their heads. Their denials made her angry; the older girl burst into loud sobs. Another frilled rose was waiting on the pillow in the room with the three red-lipped windows. I wonder what she made of that. They looked as if they were crumpled up then dipped in blood.

I drop a hint now: I sit down in the cane armchair, which creaks, and utter a soft sigh. Her breathing stops. She is transfixed. When it starts again, it is almost as slow as it was when she was asleep, but deeper: in spite of her efforts, harsher. Her heart shudders. For long minutes I take care not to let my breathing overlap hers; I keep to her rhythm. She does not dare to stop breathing for a moment to listen, warning whoever is there, if anyone is, that she is awake. And at last — the kitchen clock chimes four — she starts to fall asleep again, having made herself believe what she must believe. There is no one there, the noise was outside, it was a dream, she is only being silly.

I make the chair creak again.

She breathes sharply, softly now, and with a moan as if in her sleep — this is how she hopes to deceive whoever is there, because someone is, someone *is* — she turns slowly over to lie and face the chair. Her eyes are all shadow. Certainly she opens them now, staring until they water, those eyes the colours of water. But I am too deep in the dark for her to see me: too far from the grey glow at the only tall window with its curtains left apart.

This time it takes longer for her to convince herself that there is nothing here to be afraid of. I wait until I hear her breathing slow down. Then, as lightly as the drizzle that is just starting to hiss in the tree by her window, I let her hear me breathing faster.

'Who is it?' she whispers. They all whisper.

'Quiet.' I kneel by her head with the grey knife out.

'Please.'

'Quiet.'

The clock chimes. We both jump like rabbits. One. Two. Three. Four. Five. I hold the knife to her throat and watch her eyes sink and her mouth gape open. Terror makes her face a skull. 'Going to keep quiet?' I whisper, and she makes a clicking in her throat and nods a little, as much as she dares to move. 'Yes or no?'

She clicks.

'It's sharp. Watch this.' I slice off a lock of her black hair and stuff it in my pocket. 'Well?'

Click.

'Well?'

'Yesss.'

When I hold her head clear of the quilt by her hair and stroke the knife down the side of her throat, black drops swell along the line it makes, like buds on a twig.

'Good. We wouldn't want to wake the girls up, would we?' I say. I let that sink in, let her imagine those two little girls running in moonlit gowns to snap on the light in the doorway. Then I say their names. That really makes her pulse thump in her throat. 'They *won't* wake up, will they?'

'No,' she whispers.

'Good.'

I press my lips on hers. My mouth tastes of the grapes I ate by her still fire, both our mouths slither and taste of the brown sweet grapes. I keep my tight grip of my knife and her hair. She has to stay humble. I am still the master.

'I love you,' I say. Her tongue touches mine. 'I want you.' Terror stiffens and swells in her at that. 'Say it,' I say.

'I — love you,' she whispers. I wait. 'I — want you.'

Now there is not another minute to wait. I throw the quilt off and lift her nightgown. She moves her heavy thighs and the slit nest above them of curled black hair. There is a hot smell of roses and summer grasses. I lie on top of her. 'Put it in,' I say, and she slips me in as a child's mouth takes the nipple. 'Move,' I say. She makes a jerky thrust. 'No, no. Make it nice.' Her eyes twitch; panting, she rocks and sways under me.

I have to close her labouring mouth with my hand now; in case the knife at her throat slips, I put it by her head on the pillow (its steel not cold, as hot as we are), and it makes a smear where the frilled rose was. Her nightgown tears over her breasts, black strands of her hair scrawl in red over the smooth mounds of them, warm wet breasts that I drink. Is this the nightgown? Yes. Yes. Then we are throbbing and convulsing and our blood beats like waves crashing on waves.

None of these women ever says to me, How is your little grub enjoying itself? Is it in yet? Are you sure? Can it feel anything? Oh, well, that's all right. Mind if I go back to sleep now? No, move, I say, and they move. Move nicely. Now keep still. And they do.

'Now keep still,' I say, picking up the knife again. She lies rigid. The clatter of the first train tells me it is time. Day is breaking. Already the grey light in the window is too strong to be still moonlight, and the dark tree has started to shrink, though not yet to be green and brown. 'I have to go. I'll come again,' I say as I get up. She nods. 'You want me to. Don't you.' She nods, her eyes on the hand with the knife.

I never will. I never do. Once is all I want. At night she will lie awake thinking I will come to her again. Just as she thinks I might cut her throat and not just slit the skin; and so I might. But their death is not part of the ritual. The knife is like a lion-tamer's whip: the threat is enough. Of course if the threat fails, I will have to kill her. She, for that matter, would turn the knife on me if she could. Chance would then make her a killer. Chance, which has made me the man I am, might yet make me a killer: I squat stroking the knife.

'Well, say it,' I say.

'Yes.'

'You won't call the police.' She shakes her head. 'Or will you? Of course you will.' My smile cracks a glaze of blood and spittle around my mouth. In the grey mass on the pillow I watch her eyes roll, bloodshot, bruised, still colourless. 'I want you to wait, though. I know: wait till the bird hits the window.' A bird flies at her window every morning. I see her realise that I even know that; I see her thinking, Oh God, what doesn't he know? 'That's if you love your little girls.' Her eyes writhe. 'You do, don't you. Anyone would.' Girls with hair like pampas grass. 'So you will wait, won't you.' She nods. 'Well?'

'Yes.'

Her coils of dark hair are ropy with her sweat and her red slobber, and so is her torn gown, the torn ivory gown that I put on once, that she never even bothered to mend. A puddle of yellow haloes her on the sheet. She is nothing but a cringing sack of stained skin, this black-haired woman who for weeks has been an idol that I worshipped, my life's centre. The knowledge that I have got of her just sickens me now. Let them get a good look

435

at what their mother really is — what women all are — today when they come running down to breakfast, her little girls in their sunlit gowns. 'You slut,' I say, and rip her rags off her. 'You foul slut.' Just having to gag her, turn her and tie her wrists behind her and then tie her ankles together makes me want to retch aloud. Having to touch her. But I stop myself. Turning her over to face the wall, I pull the quilt up over the nakedness and the stink of her. I wipe my face and hands, drop the knife and the balaclava into my haversack, and get dressed quickly.

The dark rooms smell of ash. Light glows in their panes, red glass in their fireplaces. The heavy door closes with a jolt. I break off a bunch of brown grapes with the gloss of the rain still on them. The dog snuffles. Blinking one eye, it bats its sleepy tail once or twice on the verandah.

I have made a study of how to lose myself in these hushed suburban mornings. (The drizzle stopped long ago. Now a loose mist is rising in tufts, and the rolled clouds are bright-rimmed.) I am as much at home in her suburb as I am in her house, or in my own for that matter, though I will never go near the house or the suburb, or the woman, again. (I will find other women in other houses and suburbs when the time comes. Move, I will say, and they will move. Move nicely. They will. Keep still. Then they will keep still.) And when the sirens whoop out, as of course they will soon, I will be out of the way. I will wash myself clean.

I am a solitary jogger over yellow leaves on the echoing footpaths. No one sees me. I cram the grapes in my haversack for later.

I know that soon after sunrise every morning a small brown bird dashes itself like brown bunched grapes, like clodded earth, at the bare window of her room, the one with its red curtains agape. Again and again it launches itself from a twig that is still shaking when the bird has fallen into the long dry grass and is panting there unseen, gathering its strength for another dash. (The garden slopes away under her room: no one can stand and look in at her window.) It thuds in a brown flurry on to its own image shaken in the glass. It startled me, in the garden the first morning.

I think of her half-waking, those other mornings, thinking, It's the bird, as the brown mass thudded and fell and fluttered up to clutch at the twig again: thinking, Only the bird, and turning over slowly into her safe sleep.

But she is awake this morning. She is awake thinking, Oh God, the bird, when will the bird? Twisting to free her hands and turn over. Please, the bird. Her shoulders and her breasts and throat are all ravelled with red lace. Her hair falling over them is like dark water.

HELEN GARNER
(1942–   )

Garner was born in Geelong, Victoria, and was educated at the University of Melbourne. She worked as a secondary school teacher but was dismissed for answering students' questions about sexual matters. She has worked as a journalist and freelance writer. Her novel, *Monkey Grip* (1977), won the National Book Council award and was made into a film. She has published one other novel, two novellas and a collection of short stories.

ALL THOSE BLOODY YOUNG CATHOLICS

Watto! Me old darling. Where have you been. Haven't seen you since . . . Let me buy you a drink. Who's your mate? Jan. Goodday Jan. What'll it be, girls? Gin and tonic, yeah. Lemon squash. Fuckin' — well, if that's what you — Hey mate. Mate. Reluctant barmen round here. Mate. Over here. A gin and bloody nonsense, a scotch and water for myself, and a — Jesus Mary and Joseph — *lemon squash*. I know. I asked her but that's what she wanted. Well and how's the world been treating you Watto me old mate. No, not a blue. I was down the Yarra last week in the heat, dived in and hit a snag. Gerry? Still in Perth. I saw him not so long ago, still a young pup, still a young man, a young Apollo, a mere slip of a lad. I went over to Perth. I always wanted to go over. I've been everywhere of course in Australia, hate to hear those young shits telling me about overseas, what's wrong with here? anyway what? yeah well I've got this mate who's the secretary of the bloody Waterside Workers, right? I says to him, think I'll slip over to Perth. He says, Why don't you go on a boat? I says, What? How much? Don't shit me, he says. For you — nuthin'. Was I seasick? On the Bight? No fear. Can't be seasick when you're as drunk as. Can't be the two at the same time. All those seamen drunk, playin' cards, tellin' lies — great trip, I tell you, great trip. Course when I got off at the other end had a bit of trouble, once you're back on dry land the booze makes itself felt, but anyway there I was. Yeah yeah, I'm gettin' to Gerry. Blokes on the boat asked me where I was goin', I says, Don't worry, I've got this mate, he works at the university — I didn't tell 'em he was a bloody senior — what is it? senior lecturer? Reader. Anyway first bloke I run into was this other mate, Jimmy Clancy, you'd remember him I suppose, wouldn't like him, bi-i-ig strong bloke, black beard, the lot, always after the women, well he hasn't

439

changed, still running after 'em, I told him off, I lectured him
for an hour. Anyway it was great to see him again. He used to
hang round with Laurie Driscoll, Barney O'Brien, Vincent Carroll,
Paddy Sheehan, *you* know. Paddy Sheehan? Pad hasn't had a
drink in — ooh, must be eight years. He was hittin' it before,
though. Tell you about Pad. I was in Sydney not so long ago,
went up for the fight, well, on the way home I went through
Canberra and I tell you it was shockin'. Yeah I said *shockin'*.
Ended up in a sort of home for derelicts — the Home for Homeless
Men! Well, I come to out there, I had plenty of money see, it
was the fight, the time Fammo beat Whatsisname up Sydney, I
had tons of money, tons of it, I says to this Christian bloke out
there — he wasn't one of those rotten Christians, he was one of
the ones with heart — I says to him, Listen mate, I don't want to
stay here, I've got plenty of money, just get me out of here — I've
got this mate Paddy Sheehan who's a government secretary or
something, so the bloke comes out to pick me up in a bloody
chauffeur-driven car, bloke in front with a peaked cap and that,
Paddy with his little white freckly face sitting up in the back in
his glory — he really laid it on for me. So I says goodbye to the
Christian bloke, I says Here, have some of this and I give him
some money. How much? Oh I dunno, I had handfuls of it, it
was stickin' out of me pockets, I just passed him a handful of
notes and away I went in the big black car. All right all right,
I'm gettin' to Gerry. Perth wasn't I. Yeah well we sat and we talked
of the times that are gone, with all the good people of Perth
looking on. Ha ha! Course we did. He's still a boy, full of charm,
like a son to me. He was a young tough buck then, love, all
handsome and soft, wet behind the ears, and Watto
here done the dirty on him, didn't you Watto! Yes you did, you
broke his heart, and he was only a boy, yes sweetheart — what was
your name again? Watto here she hates me to tell this story, yes
she does! He was only a child, straight out of a priestery — no,
must have been a monkery because he said he had to wear
sandals — course he'd never fucked in his life! Didn't know what
to do with his prick! And Watto here goes through him like a

packet of salts! Makes mincemeat out of him! Poor bloke never knew what hit him. Drove us all crazy with his bloody guitar playing. She told him didn't you Watto that she didn't want no bloody husband but he wouldn't listen, he was besotted, drawin' her pictures, readin' her the poems of W.B. Yeats, playin' his flamin' guitar—they used to fuck all day and all night, I swear to you love—no shutup Watto! it's true isn't it! I dunno what the other young Catholics in the house thought was goin' on in there—but one day I gets this lettuce and I opens their door a crack and I shoves the lettuce through and I yells out, If you fuck like rabbits you better eat like 'em too! He he! Look at her blush! Ah Watto weren't they great times. Drinkin' and singin' and fightin' over politics. I remember a party at Mary Maloney's place when Laurie Driscoll spewed in the back yard and passed out— next morning at home he wakes up without his false teeth—he had to call poor Mary and beg her to go out in the garden and poke around and see if he hadn't left his teeth behind as well as the contents of his guts. Oh, all those bloody young Catholics— 'cept for Gerry, who was corrupted by Watto here—don't get me wrong Wats! you done him a favour—they were all as pure as the driven snow—dyin' of lust but hangin' on like grim death for marriage, ha ha! They thought they were a fire-eatin' mob in those days but they're all good family men now. Course, *I* was never allowed to bring no women home, bloody Barney he tells me, Don't you dare bring those hooers of yours back here, you old dero—I had to sneak them round the lane and into me loft out the back. And finally Watto here gives young Gerald the khyber, he moons tragically for weeks till we're all half crazy—and then he met Christine. *Byoodiful.* Wasn't she Watto. *Byoodiful . . .* ah . . . she's still me best mate. Gerry was that keen to impress her the first time he got her to come back to our place, he says to me, Now you stay away, I don't want no foul language, she's a lovely girl. So I stays away and that night I come back real late from the Waiters' Club with this sheila and we're up in the loft and in the morning I didn't know how I was goin' to get her out of there! They were all down in the yard doin' their bloody exercises, Barney and Dell and Derum — so in despair I pushes her out the door of the loft and she misses the ladder and falls down into the yard and breaks both her flamin' legs. Lucky Barney was a final year medical student. Oh Christine was beautiful though — I'll never forget the night you and her brought Gerry back here, Watto, he was that drunk, he'd been found wallowing with his guitar in the flowerbeds outside that girls' dormitory joint you two lived in — youse were draggin' him along between you and he was singin' and laughin' and bein' sick — and then you went off, Watto, and left the poor young girl stranded with this disgusting drunk on her hands! Laugh! Aaahhhhh. Course much later she goes off with Chappo. I remember the night she disappeared. And years after *that* she took off with that show pony McWatsisname, McLaughlin. Didn't you know that? Yeah, she went off with him — course, she's livin' with someone else now. Oh, a beautiful girl. Gorgeous. They fought over her, you know. They fought in the pub, and bloody McLaughlin had a fuckin' aristotle behind his back while poor Chappo had his fists up honourable like this — I got the bottle off McLaughlin. At least if you blue you should do it proper. Cut it out, I says, look you don't have to fight over cunt! If I was to fight over every sheila I'd ever fucked there'd be fights from here to bloody Darwin! Why do they have to fight over them! Those bloody young Catholics. Gerry. All right all right. And fighting over women! You don't have to *fight* for it! Look if I can't get a fuck there's a thousand bloody massage parlours between here and Sydney, I can go into any one of them and get myself a fuck, without having to *fight* for it. I never put the hard word on you, did I Watto, in all those years? Well, Gerry. Yeah, he was in great form, lovely boy, always felt like a father to him, I taught him everything he knew, I brought him up you might say. Oh, he's been over London and all over the place but he's back over the west now, just the same as ever. Aaaah Watto I've been in love with you for twenty years. Go on. It must be that long. Look at her — turns away and giggles. Well, fifteen then. You're looking in great shape. Gerry. Yeah, yeah . . . he was a lovely boy. Don't I remember some story about you and him in Perth once? Something about a phone box in the middle of the night? Oh. Right. I'll stop there. Not a word more. You're lookin' in great shape Watto. Your tits are still little though aren't they. How's the baby, my girlfriend? How old is she now? *Nine*, Jeesus Christ. She still goin' to marry me? I seen her come in here lookin' for your old man one time, he was drinkin' in here with some of the old crowd, she comes in the door there and looks round and spots him. Comes straight up to him and says, Come home! And bugger me if he doesn't down his drink and get up and follow her out the door as meek as a lamb. *Pleeez* sell no more drink to my father/It makes him so strange an' so wild . . . da da dummm . . ./Oh pity the poor drunkard's child. A real little queen. Imagine the kid you and I would have had together eh Watto— one minute swingin' its little fists smashin' everything, next minute mai poetry, mai music, mai drawing! Schizo. Aaah Jesus. Have another drink. You're not going? Ah stay! I only ever see you once every five years. Give us a kiss then. I always did love ya. Ha ha! Don't thank me. Happy New Year and all the best. Ta ta.

GABRIELLE LORD
(1946–   )

Lord was educated in Sydney and Armidale, New South Wales. She worked as an employment officer for the CES until a New Writer's Fellowship enabled her to take a year off to write her first novel, *Fortress* (1980), which was later made into a film. She now writes full time.

Lord has written three novels as well as short stories and newspaper articles. Her work demonstrates a great anger and indignation at the powerlessness of women and children and suggests that it is possible to fight back.

MATI

Kieran walked into the wine bar. It was crowded with bodies and the lights were mellow and soft.

'Baby, I cry for you
Baby, I'd die for you . . . '

the juke box played as he fronted the bar. He stood there, pulling at the crotch of his jeans. They were too tight, he knew, but they accentuated the small bulge between his legs, and made the most of his matador's backside. He looked around. There were a lot of chicks tonight. Most had partners and Kieran's practised eye paused but briefly on them. What he was looking for was a single one; perhaps two chicks together. He enjoyed that. He liked to play with both of them, never letting them guess which one was to be favoured with his final interest until the last, when one chick's face would fall with disappointment and resentment. Sometimes, he would play up to the prettier and leave with the plain one. The pretty chicks couldn't get over that one; they were so used to leaving their less attractive girlfriend with a shrug of phoney regret. He ordered a drink and continued to look around slowly. Tonight, he didn't feel the usual excitement of the chase. Was it that lately it had all been so predictable? Maybe it was time, as some of his married mates had suggested, to get a good chick and marry her. He shied away from the idea. Once chicks got married, they changed. He'd seen it happen before. Where once your slightest wish had been their command, they started fencing you off. They didn't like football anymore, although before, they'd go to every game with you. He took a long pull at his cider and straightened up. He showed to advantage in the lit area of the bar and he wanted whatever lucky chick it was to get a good eyeful. He knew he had a beautiful body. Hadn't he been told over and over again until it was almost a bore? And he knew he was a great lover, he'd been told that plenty of times, too. He couldn't understand why there was all that stuff written about technique. It was easy, screwing. A few kisses to get you in the mood, a hand under the dress, push her back, and wow! Kieran prided himself on not hanging back.

His attention was taken by a chick sitting alone with a wine glass in her hand. She looked all right. From his position, he could see the top half of her body; lovely silky hair hanging simply from the crown of her head, nice boobs covered in a flowing dress, and best of all, a sweet open face without paint all over it. Kieran didn't like paint. He didn't like a chick to rub off on him; he hated to find that the skin and eyes he had admired the night before had rubbed off on his pillow and that a very plain, blotchy lady was snoring beside him. He ordered two drinks and carried them over to her. Yes, she was alright, all right. She'd do. Perhaps their thoughts coincided because she looked full at him as he advanced and he liked that. No looking around the room pretending she hadn't seen him coming. He put the drinks down.

'Mind if I join you?'

'No, not at all. In fact, I've been wondering when you would.'

He liked that too. A bit of aggression is good in a chick, as long as it doesn't go too far. He sat down and had a closer look. Her voice had been soft and low, with a slight accent. Good. Some of these foreign chicks were really something. Her eyes were regarding him steadily. They were large and frank, glowing with an inner light. He wasn't sure of the colour; green perhaps, or that in-between shade.

'My name's Kieran.'

'Mine is Mati.'

'That's unusual. Where are you from?'

'Oh, a little place. A tiny village in Finland.'

'Finland. I've never met anyone from Finland before.'

She laughed, and they chatted a while. Kieran found it easy talking with her. She had none of the coyness he'd met in other chicks. Her soft voice with its odd intonations charmed him.

Sometimes, she would reach for the right word and he would laughingly supply it. She looked him straight in the eye when she addressed him, just like another bloke would, he thought. There were no sliding glances from behind sticky lashes; her eyes were rimmed with feathery gold, the same soft colour as her brows and hair.

'Hey, I like that dress.'

'Do you?' she asked without surprise. It was of cotton, he supposed, and covered with rich embroidery of flowers and grasses, wheat and leaves.

'It is a special dress that I made myself for the garden. I love to garden. I have a small farm and I grow all my own vegetables. I will be planting soon.'

Kieran was further intrigued. He'd never met a gardening chick before, in fact, he'd never met a chick before who was interested in more than clothes, make-up, shopping and Rod Stewart.

'I will be planting vines and herbs, grain crops and vegetables,' her beautiful voice had a sing-song quality, 'but first I must fertilise it.'

'Like with manure and stuff?'

'That too.'

The night wore on.

Kieran was finding her more and more attractive but somehow his usual confidence had dissipated. You couldn't just say to a chick like this 'your place or mine'. He had the feeling she'd just fix him with those frank eyes, and maybe laugh. But then, she had said that she'd been waiting for him. He ordered two more drinks and placed his hand over hers. She made no attempt to remove it and her skin was warm and faintly damp.

He was aroused by her, but it was more, much more than the usual physical response. He was aroused by her — What was it? That elusive quality she had? A simplicity and softness, a total lack of artifice. This might be the sort of good chick a guy could marry. He day-dreamed a little, imagining himself helping her in the garden, watching the moonrise, making love on the warm earth . . .

447

Her lips were very close to his ear, her words gently moving the soft hair that fell near his own. They stood up, Kieran awkwardly trying to find the right words. Then to his joy, he saw he needn't worry, she had taken his hand in hers and was moving outside with him.

'Come with me,' she was saying. 'Come with me to my farm. We will make love on the earth, the beautiful, warm earth.'

She had seen into his soul. He kissed her gently and they were driving through the city, through the spring night, across the river, into the mountainous country where her farm lay. By the full moon, he could see her tiny house but she drew him away.

'Not there,' she murmured. 'Tonight is special.'

And it was. Kieran was used, more than most, to the variety of women, their secrets, their intimacies. But tonight was special. He had never been so aroused, so close to another. For the first time, his partner was a real part of his own experience and the excitement that this generated was almost more than he could bear.

'Mati, Mati,' he whispered to her as they lay on the earth that still contained the warmth of the great sun. 'Mati, oh Mati.' Earth, oh Earth. The very ground they lay on was like a warm, moist woman, ready to love. He could contain himself no longer, and he exploded in her arms like a sun-burst. She leaned over him, very tenderly, murmuring to him and the stars swung above them. She plunged the three tynes of the fork straight through his new velvet shirt, severing soft skin and ribs, searching out his heart with steel claws. She held him close while his body arched in a last, desperate ecstasy. 'Did you not know, my love,' she murmured reverently, as the blood welled blackly and soaked into the radiant earth, 'did you not know, that the king must die?'

INEZ BARANAY
(1950–   )

Baranay was born in Italy. She has been a schoolteacher, an activist, an actress, a traveller and a television researcher. Her short stories have been published in many modern anthologies.

THE SEX PART

How could she do it? What if she didn't like him?

The unknown man. He puts his papers in a neat pile. He puts them in his briefcase. He has a shower and puts on a bathrobe. He has a shower and gets dressed again. He waits to have a shower with her. He doesn't think about a shower until she arrives. He thinks about a shower but does he want her to know he just came out of the shower? He has a shower and smears on the deodorant. He hopes she's a girl who appreciates personal freshness. He hopes she's as good as the last one. He hopes she's better than the last one. He doesn't think about it. He catches up on some phone calls while there's time. He has a drink. He orders champagne. He doesn't order yet, not until he has a look at her. He remembers why he called. He hopes it'll be worth it. He doesn't care.

She knocks at the door. She's immediately at home, sitting at ease, kicking her shoes off, hoping he hasn't waited too long, it was hard to get a cab. She lets him notice her relief and pleasure that it's someone more attractive, young, distinguished or something more than she had dared to hope. She'd love a drink. Better get you-know-what out of the way, enjoy ourselves. Is it cash? He wants to know how much, how long, how good. He doesn't ask a thing. It's ready. It's in an envelope. He has to find his wallet. Is there any hurry?

He can see he has her attention. He has her interest. Interesting. Where does he live? Oh yes, so he said. Never been there, is it nice, interesting. He's looking at her. She's got nice tits. She's got tits. She's got nice legs. Those awful pantyhose or real stockings? Suspenders, lace, black, red, flesh, silk, nylon? He wonders. He hopes. He doesn't care about these things. She's wearing pants. Casual, kinky. She's got personality. He likes the smile, a mind of her own. Smart. Professional. But not too blasé. Oops. He likes her passive, feminine, dumb, admiring. That's better. Has she been doing this long? Of course, it's relative. But he can tell it wouldn't be long — she's not hard. Don't get hard. That's right, he laughs — nervously, heartily, not at all — ladies shouldn't be hard. Men should be hard. A hard man is good to find. (A good man is harder.)

Another drink? Maybe later. After. Get comfortable now. Take off the tie for a start. How do you feel? It'll be good. He watches her undress. She loves it. Show-off. Nympho. Sex maniac. Bullshitter.

Her hands on her own breasts, her own thighs, the hips moving against the cold sheets, the cold sheets making her giggle. Come here, make me warm. Put your hands here. She replaces her hands with his own over the cunningly hardened nipples. He lowers his face to hers. The big moment: does she kiss? She moves her head swiftly at the last second, bites his shoulder, leaving him thrusting his tongue at the air stupidly like a fish. She's got a boyfriend, you can tell that if she doesn't kiss him. He doesn't think of kissing her. Kissing has no part in this. He doesn't want to kiss. He begs for a kiss. He won't ask again. He'd better not. She pushes his head to her breast. There, nice, like that, don't bite, careful, gently please, no teeth. He kisses the nipples. He sucks gently. He sucks hard. He's not into tits at all.

He hasn't got this far. He's sitting on the end of the bed. He has to tell her. He sometimes has a bit of trouble. It's all right, and she looks him in the eye, steady, confident, you won't have any trouble with me. She undoes the top button of his shirt. She pulls the shirt apart and presses her mouth to the bare triangle of flesh. Next button, her wet mouth sliding down. Next button. Down to the belt. Her tongue flicking over his nipples. One side. The other side. Down to the belt. He takes it off, she can't. Good. Pushes him back, says don't do a thing. Her wet sliding mouth on his bare stomach. Lifts the underpants, eases them over, aside. He's growing. He's hard and eager. He isn't yet. He soon is. Her hands underneath him, cupping, holding, stroking. Her hair on his bare stomach. Her tongue flicking, slurping, sliding. No

451

trouble with me. He's ready. A bit more. That'll do. She tugs at the pants. He takes them off. She rolls over on the bed. He's busy pulling his pants off his ankles. She quickly spits the gathered saliva onto her fingers and applies it. She is posed, classical, her hands pushing on her thighs. She's wide open. She glistens, she beckons, she flows. Come on, come on.

Oh god he's the nouvelle cuisine type. He had minted eggplant puree for dinner topped with pickled prawns in a marmalade glaze. He knows these days it's ladies first. Gentlemen come later. It's his turn for her turn. All right then. Good, don't bite, gently please, no teeth, no, there, like that. She's tensely ready to jerk his head off by the ears. She's never been so relaxed, sinking, flowing. She can't stand it anymore. It's time for the killing to start. They should never have been told about the clitoris. Her most hated question, did you come? Oh god he's a talker. Tell me what you want. What do you want? Where will I put it? What am I doing? Tell me. Say it. Do you like it? Where is it? What is, what's in your cunt? Baby. Baby.

It wasn't like that. He had a plain steak for dinner. He grabbed her arse, got on top, said nothing, grunted once, it was over.

It wasn't like that. He's a stayer, an athlete. He turns her over, he's read magazines, he wants her on top, he turns her over and over again. He knows tricks, he can make her move, he can make her moan. Don't stop, she moans to him, don't stop. He has stopped. He's finished, she said the wrong thing. She listens. He moans, she sighs. He yells, she cries out. He doesn't make a sound, she's dead, coming slowly alive. She places her hands to check his heart. He's already quietly finished. He's just starting, building up speed, ready to pound furiously, announce his arrival, a fanfare. He takes her with him. He fills her. She's throbbing, streaming, clutching.

Are you wet? Are you hard? Can you feel it? Do you like it? What am I doing? Do you believe me? Do you want more?

Suppose there's more. He's well read, he knows things. He goes for the works. The endless falling into darkness, falling into his iron manly flesh, the hot kisses gulped like wine adding heat to her body drinking deeply, the sucking mouth melting into mouth seeking the leaping tongues, the eyes alight, the febrile waves trembling there, the pools of madness, the exquisite torment, her hair damp as seaweed, her taste like a seashell like a camellia like a rose, the velvet the silky salty flesh; tigerlike he's tearing open the fur, the frenzy, the steaming tides, the hot springs, the wound of ecstasy which rents her body like lightning, the beatitudes, the tightness like a sheath closed over him softly caressing, gripping, the sweet insistent stabbing, her back arching to meet his thrusting, the flicking darts of fire, the molten languor spreading through her body.

It wasn't like that. He rolls over silently and turns his back to her. He rolls over and lights a cigarette. He holds her as if it should never end. He asks about her boyfriend, children, interests. He pays for another hour. He says she can go. He wonders why he does this. He feels gratified. He doesn't think. She has a shower, careful not to get her hair wet, drying herself hurriedly (or slowly) she looks at his after-shave, his pills, his toothbrush. It's a night to remember. They never think of each other again.

There's something about it that's rather like the real thing.

KATE GRENVILLE
(1950–   )

Grenville was born in Sydney and educated at the University of Sydney. She has worked as a film editor and as an assistant director. She has published a collection of short stories, and three novels, including *Joan Makes History* (1988), which was written with the support of a grant from the Australian Bicentennial Authority.

THE SPACE BETWEEN

The banana-shaped tourists lie in chairs by the swimming pool and stocky Tamil waiters on bare feet bring them drinks. The daring ones have ice. The manager himself has assured us that yes, the water for the ice is boiled. Boiled and then frozen. Oh yes yes. Boiled, of course boiled.

For myself I avoid the ice. It's not exactly that I don't believe him. But I prefer to smile and shake my head. No ice, thank you.

Outside the cool marble corridors of this palace-turned-hotel, beyond the graceful arches framing the sky, the streets of Madras are hot. Out there the sun is a solid weight on the top of the head, a heavy hand across the back of the neck, but beside the blue water of the swimming pool the sun has been domesticated by umbrellas and palm-leaf screens. Where the guests sit turning brown or scarlet, Madras is as far away as a travel book.

Here by the pool, under a blue umbrella, Mr and Mrs Partridge involve me in kindly conversation.

—Travelling alone are you? You don't find it a bit . . . ?

Mrs Partridge's crepey old face puckers as if encountering a bad smell.

—A bit, you know, unpleasant?

Mr Partridge tries to clarify his wife's query. He rubs a hand over his bald head, red from the sun, and says:

—You don't find that these chaps. Ah. They don't let their own women out on their own. Of course.

They're kindly folk who do their best to conjure up the girl in white frills who must be underneath my baggy shirts. They even have a go at a little matchmaking. Mrs Partridge leans in and murmurs while Mr Partridge stares off across the pool.

—Sandra dear, we were talking last night to the young man who's here with the tour. A very nice type of young man.

455

Her husband brings his stare back from the middle distance and speaks energetically.

— Nice group of people here. The McFarlands. The Burnetts. The Pruitt chap. Good company helps, doesn't it? In this heat?

Mrs Partridge nods and shows me the pink plastic of her gums.

— That's him. Ted Pruitt.

I've seen Ted here by the pool carefully browning himself like a chop on both sides. I've seen the way the water pools around his body on the cement and the way the hairs on his legs stay flattened to the skin even after they've dried. I've enjoyed watching the hairs on his legs, and the shell-pink soles of his feet, that the sun makes translucent. In the small of his back is a dark mole, pleasingly symmetrical, the kind that can turn into a cancer. I have avoided looking at his face, filled with too many teeth, too much flesh, eyes of too knowing a blue.

On cue, Ted appears at the edge of the pool. His muscular arms glint with ginger hairs as he hauls himself out. The water streams down his head and makes it as flat as a dog's. He flicks his head sideways and glittering drops land on the concrete. As I watch they evaporate into the dense sunshine.

— Ted, we were just talking about you, says Mrs Partridge. Come and meet Sandra.

He stands over me, blocking out the sun. I squint up at him, at his face invisible against the glaring sky.

— Hi. What was it again, Sandra?

— Sandy, actually.

He stands above me, legs apart, water running down his body and spreading in pools around his feet.

— Sandy? Used to know a bloke once called Sandy.

He runs a hand over his shoulders, where skeins of muscle lie side by side under the skin.

— I mean, no offence of course.

He gestures and grins and watches me under cover of rubbing his head with his towel. I see him looking at my baggy pants and shirt, and my face half-hidden under the hat. When he stands up to dry himself, the muscles of his chest flex as he rubs his back, and twinkling water is caught in the hairs of his curved thighs. He bulges heavily, thickly, unabashed, into the taut weight of stretched red nylon between his legs.

Mrs Partridge looks away as he rubs the water off his legs. Mr Partridge breaks the silence.

—I was just saying to Sandra . . . Sandy?

—Sandy.

—Ah. Just saying what a good bunch of people we've got here. Lucky, really.

Ted shakes water out of his ear.

—Too right.

He sits down, leaning back on his hands. I see his chest gleam in the sun but have to look away from the red bulge offered towards me.

—You been going around on your own all this time?

—Yes. It's been a lot of fun.

My voice sounds prissy in my own ears.

—Yeah?

He doesn't quite close his mouth after the word, so I can see blood-pink inner lip.

—Why'd a good-looking chick like you want to get around on your own?

He stares at me, waiting for an answer, but although I wet my lips with my tongue, I can't find one.

—You must have a bit of, you know, from the fellas.

He glances again at the shapeless pants and I wonder if he's thinking, on the other hand maybe she doesn't.

—Anyhow, any time you want to come around with us, just say the word. We'll look after you. No worries.

He smiles. It's the wide blank smile of a man who's looking down his own strong legs, safe in muscles and red nylon.

When the waiter comes over to pick up our glasses, I recognise him by the moustache, such a thin line on his upper lip that it might have been drawn with a ballpoint. Each morning this waiter brings my breakfast, knocking inaudibly before coming in immediately with his tray of pawpaw and the dazzling smile that

457

makes his moustache go crooked. I put a hand over my half-finished drink and he bows. He wonders too, when he sees me each morning lying in splendour in the canopied bed, why I'm alone. His black eyes dart from Ted to me and he bows again before padding off. He shouts in Tamil across the pool to another waiter and their laughter echoes between the arches.

The Partridges excuse themselves. They walk off arm-in-arm, slowly, like an advertisement for retirement. Ted and I sit in silence, and watch the waiter remove a toothpick from behind his ear and clean his fingernails with it. When he has finished, Ted sighs and says:

—Well, where you going next?

His voice seems very loud.

—I thought I might go to Bombay.

—Yeah? Look, we're all going there too, for the silver. Why don't you come with us? No good being on your own. For a girl especially.

He's watching me and I'm conscious of the size of his very white front teeth. His hair is starting to dry, fluffing out around his temples like down. I squint into the glare of light off the pool and picture myself diving in, trying to drown. Ted would rescue me, using the approved hair, chin or clothing carry to pull me to the side of the pool before administering artificial respiration. It would take determination to drown beside Ted.

—Well, thanks. But I don't think so.

Ted has not heard properly, shaking a last drop of water from his ear.

—Eh? That's settled then? We'll have a ball.

I have to raise my voice to say again:

—No. No, I don't think so. No.

Ted is in the middle of winking at me, thinking of the ball we'll have, when he understands that I have refused. The wink goes wrong and all the features of his face fight each other for a second. When they have resolved themselves into a coherent expression, it is one of suspicion and dislike.

—Okay. Suit yourself.

He gets up, flings his towel over the chair with a flourish, and dives in. He is a powerful swimmer, reaching the end of the pool in a few strokes and showing those pink soles in a flurry of water as he turns. He would hardly be able to imagine drowning.

— You've lost your young man!

Mr Partridge beams down at me. He and his wife are no longer arm-in-arm, but Mrs Partridge tweaks a thread off her husband's shoulder as he speaks. Behind the kindly uncle, winking at me from under white eyebrows, a sharp voice can almost be heard. Some people just don't want to be helped.

— We were counting on you to look after him!

Mrs Partridge's eyes disappear into a web of kindly wrinkles as she smiles teasingly. Behind the smile, embedded in the lines that pucker her mouth, is doubt. They both watch me, but I have nothing to tell them, and my smile is exhausting me.

Not far from the hotel, there is a cluster of shacks that squat in the dust, lining a path of beaten earth. Hens scatter under my feet and skeletal dogs run along nosing the ground. Pieces of cardboard cover the walls of the huts. DETER UPER WASH. They *are* the walls, I see when I look more closely. Women sit in the shade, picking over vegetables, while beside them their other sari hangs drying in the sun — tattered, dust-coloured with age, but washed. Is there another one in the dark interior of the hut? Is there, somewhere, the wedding sari, best quality cotton or maybe even silk, with the lucky elephant-border or the brocade border that reads GOOD LUCK GOOD LUCK GOOD LUCK all the way around the hem? As I pass, the women look up and stare, their lips drawn back to reveal stained teeth. They are not smiling, but only staring, and they look away when I smile.

Out of doorways a few small children appear, staring shyly, their huge dark eyes full of astonishment as they look at me. They curl one foot behind the other in embarrassment when I look at them and twist their bodies away as if fleeing, but their eyes never leave my face.

As I pass the huts the children drift out after me and at each hut more emerge. I can hear their feet padding in the dust behind me. When I turn around to smile they all stop in mid-stride. They all stare, motionless except for a hand somewhere scratching a melon-belly, a foot rubbing the back of a leg, a finger busy up a nostril.

On the fringes of the silent group the girls stand, curious but listless, holding babies on their hips. They stare blankly, shifting the baby from one hip to the other, automatically brushing away a fly.

At last one of the boys lets out a nervous giggle and the tension breaks. Suddenly they're all shrieking, dancing around me, bravely reaching out to dab my arm and springing back, squealing and giggling.

They seem to know a bit of English. They yell:

—Good morning! Good afternoon! Good night!

When I speak to them they explode and cover their mouths with their hands to keep so much laughing hidden. They don't point, but they nudge each other and gesture around themselves, miming my clothes. One boy, bigger than the rest, wearing only a tattered pair of shorts that hangs precariously under his round belly, sweeps his hands around and stands before us. He stares up at me and says:

—You boy or girl?

His voice does not prejudice the question one way or the other.

—Girl. I'm a girl.

He stares, not believing. After a moment he grins enormously and laughs in a theatrical way to show how well he understands the joke. Then doubt clouds his face. He ducks his head as if overwhelmed by his question, but pulls at my sleeve:

—You boy or girl?

He stares up at me waiting for the answer. His round head, under its short fur of hair, seems too large for his frail neck. He cranes up at me for the answer.

—Boy. I'm a boy. Like you.

He considers that, but after a moment of looking at the front of my shirt he bends over with laughter again. Now he's embarrassed and won't look at me. He says something to the other kids and they all stare at me. They're waiting for a proper answer. It's very quiet in this back lane. The horns of the taxis on the main road seem puny and very far away. It seems the kids could wait forever for an answer.

I start to walk back to the main road, but the kids follow, straggling after me along with the dogs and a hen or two. When I walk faster, some break into a run to keep up, even the girls, with the babies on their hips bouncing and crying. One by one they dart around in front of me and run backwards for a few yards to watch my face as they try again.

—You boy or girl? Boy or girl?

They're all doing it together so that the words have become a chant. Bah yo gel bah yo gel bah yo gel.

At the edge of the shack village they stop as if on a line drawn on the road. I walk on until finally I can wave goodbye before turning a corner that takes me out of sight. But they are still calling out even after I've disappeared. Bahyogel bahyogel. Their voices carry a long way down the quiet street.

SALLY MORGAN
(1951–   )

Morgan was born in Perth, studied arts at the University of Western Australia, and completed a post-graduate diploma in Counselling Psychology and Computing and Library Studies. She has also established a reputation as an artist.

As a young adult, Morgan began to research her Aboriginal background and she wrote about this rewarding search in her first book, *My Place* (1987), which has been widely acclaimed. She is writing a second book with the support of a grant from the Australian Bicentennial Authority.

THE LETTER

The bus swayed back and forth making my tired old head hurt even more.

Really, I wanted to cry, but no-one cried on a bus. I glanced down sadly at the old biscuit tin sitting on my lap. Scotch Shortbreads, they weren't even her favourites, but she'd like the colour of the tin so I'd given them to her.

I sighed and wiped away the tear that was beginning to creep down my cheek. She was gone, and I felt old and lonely and very disappointed.

My fingers traced around the lid of the tin and slowly loosened it.

Inside was all she'd had to leave. A thin silvery necklace, some baby photos, her citizenship Certificate, and the letter. I smiled when I remembered how it had taken her so long to write. She'd gone over and over every word. It was so important to her. We'd even joked about the day I would have to take it to Elaine. That day had come sooner than we both expected.

I've failed, I told myself as I lifted out the necklace. It'd been bought for Elaine's tenth birthday, but we hadn't known where to send it. Now we knew where Elaine lived but she didn't want the tin or anything in it.

I placed it back gently on top of the photos.

Elaine had said the baby in the photos wasn't her. She'd said it was all a silly mistake and she wished I'd stop pestering her.

It was the third time I'd been to see her and it looked like it would be the last. I picked up the letter. It was faded and worn. I opened it out carefully and read it again.

To my daughter Elaine,
I am writing in the hope that one day you will read this and

understand. I suppose you don't want to know me because you think I deserted you. It wasn't like that. I want to tell you what it was like.

I was only seventeen when you were born at the Settlement. They all wanted to know who your father was, but I wouldn't tell. Of course he was a white man, you were so fair, but there was no love in his heart for you or me. I promised myself I would protect you. I wanted you to have a better life than me.

They took you away when I was twenty. Mr Neville from the Aborigines Protection Board said it was the best thing. He said that black mothers like me weren't allowed to keep babies like you. He didn't want you brought up as one of our people. I didn't want to let you go but I didn't have any choice. That was the law.

I started looking for you when I was thirty. No-one would tell me where you'd gone. It was all a big secret. I heard they'd changed your last name, but I didn't know what your new name was. I went and saw Mr Neville and told him I wanted to visit you. That was when I found out that you'd been adopted by a white family. You thought you were white. Mr Neville said I'd only hurt you by trying to find you.

For a long time I tried to forget you, but how could I forget my own daughter? Sometimes I'd take out your baby photo and look at it and kiss your little face. I prayed that somehow you'd know you had a mother who loved you.

By the time I found you, you were grown up with a family of your own. I started sending you letters trying to reach you. I wanted to see you and my grandchildren, but you know all about that because you've sent all my letters back. I don't blame you and I don't hold any grudges, I understand. When you get this letter I will be gone, but you will have the special things in my tin. I hope that one day you will wonder who you really are and that you will make friends with our people because that's where you belong. Please be kind to the lady who gives you my tin, she's your own aunty.

From your loving Mother.

My hands were shaking as I folded the letter and placed it back in the tin. It was no use, I'd tried, but it was no use. Nellie had always been the strong one in our family, she'd never given up on anything. She'd always believed that one day Elaine would come home.

I pressed the lid down firmly and looked out the window at the passing road. It was good Nellie wasn't here now. I was glad she didn't know how things had turned out. Suddenly her voice seemed to whisper crossly in my ear. 'You always give up too easy!'

'Do not,' I said quietly. I didn't know what to do then. Nellie was right, that girl was our own flesh and blood, I couldn't let her go so easily. I looked down at the tin again and felt strangely better, almost happy. I'll make one last try, I thought to myself, I'll get a new envelope and mail it to her. She might just read it!

I was out in the yard when I heard the phone ring. I felt sure that by the time I got inside it would stop. It takes me a long while to get up the back steps these days.

'Hello,' I panted as I lifted the receiver.

'Aunty Bessie?'

'Who's this?' I asked in surprise.

'It's Elaine.'

Elaine? I couldn't believe it! It'd been two months since I'd mailed the letter.

'Is it really you Elaine?' I asked.

'Yes, it's me. I want to talk to you. Can I come and see you?'

'Ooh yes, anytime.'

'I'll be there tomorrow and Aunty . . . take care of yourself.'

My hands shook as I placed the phone back on the hook.

Had I heard right? Had she really said, take care of yourself Aunty? I sat down quickly in the nearest chair and wiped my eyes.

'Well, why shouldn't I cry?' I said out loud to the empty room, 'I'm not on the bus now!' Nellie felt very close to me just then. 'Aah sister,' I sighed, 'did you hear all that? Elaine will be here tomorrow.

'Did you hear that sister? Elaine's coming home.'

ANIA WALWICZ
(1951–   )

Walwicz was born in Poland and came to Australia in 1963. She attended Art School in Melbourne, where she now writes and paints. She has published one collection of her writing, and her short stories have appeared in many magazines and anthologies.

HOSPITAL

I go to hospital. I go to the hospital again. I went there very early in the morning. I go there today again. In the hospital there are very clean and shiny. Linoleum floors. And everybody saying kind things to me. And I get lost and they find me. And everything makes sense. And what is the name and address. And please. And talking slowly. And I really exist. Here. And everything you do has a point to it. They tell me to follow the line. A red one. I know what to do. And I had to have a tooth taken out. And they did. I didn't sleep all night. The dentist asks me. How old I am. I'm only twelve everywhere. In here. I'm always twelve. Or even less. And they had these kind girls. Nurses. From the country. With rosy red cheeks. And a nice smell. And they tell me. Don't worry. Don't worry. Don't you worry baby. Gave me a cup of coffee. Tell me. To wait. Try to make me comfortable. Are you easy now. Gave me my card. And is somebody looking after you. Nobody is. So I can always go to hospital. I go to hospital. They have these big buildings. Meant to save my life. They let me go on. This hospital. Had pink curtains. Around the beds. And green ones. And yellow ones. Pastel and the colour. Glows. So sharp. This hospital. Has blue cards to fill in. And red ones. And white ones. But I don't like the white ones. At all. No I don't. And I sat on the red rubber couch. On grey linoleum. And the disinfectant smell that was like the school. First grade. And the shiny walls they painted. So you can wash them. And I was waiting. And there were these trolleys. And elegant thin aluminium. And instruments. And they sat me on a kidney bowl. And I wasn't embarrassed. At all. And they told me to press my bare chest against the machine. And it was cold. And I didn't mind. And the nurse was very nice to me. And the lady doctor had a starched white coat. I'm always going to the hospital. And

467

they put me on a special chair. And turned these lights on. And the dentist was very young. And it was his first time. And he pulled my tooth out. And I heard him drop it in a little dish. And he was so scared. That I was so scared. And a drop of sweat fell like a tear on my cheek. And they told me to lie down. And there were such nice clean sheets. And the air was warm. And I was slower here. And peaceful. And they put a needle in my arm. And I didn't have to pay anything for this. And there were these very kind ward attendants. That would do anything to make you smile. And they saw everybody the same. And they liked me. And when she came to the hospital. I could tell how she was. Just about to jump out of herself. Through the top of her head. And I go to hospital. And when everything was very bad. I'd take a taxi. I took taxi. When I can hardly walk. And I would call him on the phone. And he'd say do come down. And they would go where. And in my father's clinic there was this operating table for horses with big rings where to tie down. And I used to think that I was a gelding. And born horse. And my father did it to me. And I don't want to go to hospital. And I do go to hospital. And I was nearly crying and so weak. And I stood in Royal Parade with a wad of cotton in my mouth. They take care of me here. And the trolleys glisten. And the pincers took the cotton in my mouth so sure of every movement. And everything anybody did. Made such sense to me. And nothing to spare. Or laugh at. And everyone so serious. And kind. And I fell on the street. And my knee ran through my stocking. And they clean me here. And comfort me. Yesterday. The liqueur bottles shone at me all evil red. And I was feverish. And hot in the head. And today I'm well. And at ease with me. And these red skaters moved in my television set much too quickly. And now I'm just so peaceful. I get love here. I get loved.

MARGARET COOMBS

Coombs was born in Mudgee, New South Wales, and was educated at the University of Sydney. In 1980 she held a general writing grant from the Literary Arts Board of the Australia Council. A collection of her short stories is soon to be published.

NOTHING HAPPENED

It is seventeen years ago. I am waiting at the bus stop just up the road from our house. Our house is the big one on the corner of Beresford Road, the one with the funny-looking staircase out the front and the ornamental arch between the chimneys. I am waiting for the bus.

Today I am going to the beach with Anne. I am meeting Anne at Double Bay and from there we will catch the 365 to Bondi Beach. We'll make our way to the end of the beach right away from the baths and the life-saving club, and find a spot under the Lost Children sign where everyone meets. All the Scots and Cranbrook boys and all the Ascham and Kambala girls who belong to a sort of a *set* come here to sit, all the ones who learn dancing at Miss Cay's and go skiing in the May holidays and hang around the VJ yacht club all summer and in winter watch the GPS football, or play it, and who always have the right clothes to wear and all that. I guess the vital thing they all have in common is that they all have the right kinds of *bodies* as well as the right kinds of clothes. I don't. If I were by myself, I'd go out of my way to avoid this part of the beach. One of the girls who comes here is a model for the *Teenagers' Weekly*, and another has actually been in a film on TV! The film star girl is thirteen like me. Her name is Janey Wynne-Williams. She goes to Ascham. She is also a friend of Anne's.

Anne is neither a model nor a film star but I'm sure she could be if she liked. She's fourteen. She and I go to Kambala. She's the nicest girl in our class. She's not the cleverest, not the richest, not even the most fashionable; but she's kind-hearted and happy, and everybody likes her, even I do. She can afford to be my friend even though I am neither nice nor happy. I am not rich or fashionable either, and if I am clever (I think I am) it does not always show in my marks.

I am neither a model nor a film star and I know I never could be. I have no boyfriends, not even friends of the family or cousins. My family has no 'family friends' and I have no cousins of a suitable age, or none that I've met. What if I did? My nickname is Pud. What boy would be caught dead with a girlfriend called Pud?

I have read the collected works of Havelock Ellis, all seven volumes. But so what? I am not a social asset.

I am not fat, I am just *called* Pud from when I was new and got teased. I used to tell myself it didn't matter, it gave me distinction, it proved I was tough, things like that. *A rose by any other name would smell as sweet*, I used to chant to myself. A lie, that is! I hate everybody calling me Pud. Everybody does, even the fat ones, the ones much fatter than me. I know they can't help feeling they must be better than me because I let them call me Pud. I don't know why I do. I can't help it. I can't protest, not with my voice.

Anyway, the fact is that though I am not fat, I am not as slim as Anne. And if Anne were fat, she would just look voluptuous. So would Janey Wynne-Williams. If I were fat, I would just look fat.

I think of what it must be like to be Anne . . . a girl so certain she is loved that she can go with me, Pud, to Bondi Beach to sit under the Lost Children sign and chatter to people like Janey Wynne-Williams and not even try to pretend she's not with me — with the body in which I am. She's not like me! When I'm at the beach, I try to pretend this body has nothing to do with me, I would like to be able to disown it completely. I lie leadenly there on my stomach, sweaty and dazed, my sunglasses on, pretending to read while Anne darts about like a little bird and chatters and dashes off into the surf and swims. I never go in. I hate to expose myself, hate the crowd, the stares, the freezing water, the waves that threaten to knock me down. Surfing is sport and I am no good at sport, I don't like it. Only the pretty, popular girls go in. I stay with my face hidden in a book. I am waiting. I am hoping for something to happen to me.

471

What is it that I'm always hoping will happen? I try to think: what, exactly, am I waiting for?

I am waiting for the bus.

The bus sure is taking a long time to come! I gaze vacantly at the oncoming cars.

A taxi pulls up at the kerb just in front of me. It startles me. I look round to see who has hailed it. There is no one there.

'Where are you going, pet?' the driver asks.

I realise he is speaking to me. He is old, with grey hair. He looks older than my father. He looks kind. I take all this in at a glance.

'To Double Bay,' I reply automatically. 'But I'm just waiting for the bus. I haven't got enough money for a cab.'

I wish I did! I wish I could just open the door and step into the cab and say, 'Double Bay, thank you driver,' and pretend I'd intended to catch the cab all along, pretend I'd hailed it. I didn't hail the cab, I didn't even blink. Did I? But he'll say I did. He'll accuse me of having waved him down, tell me by rights I should pay him the flag fall, drive off angry at me, thinking I'm a bloody nuisance and a liar. It's not fair! How can I make him believe he's made a mistake, stop him from hating me?

'Hop in. I'm going that way. I'll give you a lift,' he says.

I look blank. Then I look puzzled. I keep thinking: *I haven't got enough money for a cab*. I turn around to make sure again that nobody else is there.

'Come on, pet, I'll give you a lift,' he repeats. 'I'm going that way.'

By now he has opened the front door of the cab. He gestures for me to get in. He smiles. He has a lovely smile, friendly and kind. I like his smile.

'But I haven't got any money,' I say. 'Not enough for a cab.'

'That doesn't matter,' he answers. 'I'm going that way anyway. I'll give you a lift. Hop in.'

I hesitate.

'For nothing,' he emphasises. He grins at me.

I should run away. I should run home. Mummy says I must

472

never accept lifts from strangers, she's told me this again and again. I should say firmly to this man, 'No thank you, my mother doesn't allow me to accept lifts from strangers,' and then I should run straight home. I rehearse all this in my head.

But if I don't go with him, the driver will be insulted, I know he will. He'll think to himself that he was only trying to do me a *favour* for goodness sake, and be disgusted that this is how I repay him. And anyway Mike, my brother, *he* accepts lifts. He's over twenty-one so no one can stop him, he hitch-hikes everywhere, it nearly drives Mum berserk. *He* says Mum's bloody paranoid, says the main reason she thinks it's wrong to accept lifts from strangers is that 'It Isn't The Done Thing'. He pipes 'It Isn't The Done Thing' in a funny voice, mocking my mother. She becomes furious, calls him a smart aleck and a lout, seethes with hatred for him. She says you just *cannot* trust everybody. He says that *her* trouble is she's never trusted a soul in her life. He always walks out at that point. Slams the door. My mother always turns on *me*, tells *me* if I ever accept a lift from a stranger she'll kill me, *kill* me.

But taxi drivers aren't strangers. Are bus drivers strangers? I know taxi drivers aren't strangers because once when I was a little girl, eight, I got lost at Kings Cross and it was a taxi driver who found me and brought me home safe. That was when we'd just arrived in Sydney from the country and were living in a flat at Elizabeth Bay. One day I went for a walk by myself and got lost and couldn't find a policeman so I asked a taxi driver the way and he gave me a lift home. For nothing. He didn't even wait to be thanked. Mum and Dad kept saying what a decent chap he must have been and what a pity they didn't know who he was and wishing there was some way of rewarding him. I remember all this without even thinking of it.

'Are you coming?' the taxi driver asks.

Well, why not? I *can't* go home. Anne is waiting for me at Double Bay. We are going to the beach. My mother doesn't like me going to the beach, she doesn't understand that everybody goes to the beach, everybody who isn't a droob. She'll make a dreadful fuss if I run home. She'll grill me endlessly about what has happened. *Nothing* has happened. An old man has offered me a lift, that's all. She will suspect . . . I don't know exactly what she'll suspect, but she'll suspect me of *some* unmentionable crime. She'll blame Anne. She'll blame going to the beach. I'll never be allowed to go to the beach again.

I am going to the beach with Anne.

I climb in.

The driver leans across and locks the door. He looks respectable. I don't dare look at him, but the blurred impression he makes on my brain tells me he looks respectable—what my mother would call respectable: neat and clean and suitably dressed. There is nothing odd about him, nothing unusual. *Of course* there isn't! I am limp with relief.

Now I am quite proud of myself for having climbed in, for not having been such a child as to refuse this lift, be afraid, go running blindly home to Mumsy-Wumsy. I think of Mike. I am on his side against Mum, glad that I've used my common sense and realised it was quite all right to accept this particular lift, behaved like an adult. *I'm* not afraid to trust people or do what's 'Not The Done Thing'. *I'm* not like my mother. Stupid old bitch.

The taxi is turning.

My eyes confirm the fact that the taxi is turning.

The taxi is doing a U-turn across New South Head Road. My brain reels. Something collapses inside me. I am dizzy. I am sick with dizziness. Is the cab turning or am I just dizzy?

The cab is turning. I watch the world outside the window turn back to front. Everything seems upside down. I feel sick with terror, my heart contracts with terror. I feel as if all the blood has gone out of my head. All the blood has fallen down out of my head.

'Isn't Double Bay the other way?' my voice asks meekly. I *know* Double Bay is the other way. I know the only *possible* way to Double Bay is the other way.'The bus goes the other way,' I explain, not wanting him to think it presumptuous of me to question *him*.

'Oh yes,' says the driver. He seems perfectly calm. 'I just thought we'd park over here for a little while and look at the view. You'd like to do that, wouldn't you?'

I can't think how to say no.

'Okay,' I say.

So he parks in the parking bay just down from the pier. He switches the engine off. Something inside me switches off. My heart sinks. Suddenly it seems very quiet. My heart is thumping inside me in a way that is making it difficult for me to breathe.

'Pretty, isn't it?' he says, gesturing towards the water.

I agree. 'Yes.' Well, it's true. It is! I smile to show I am not afraid. I think of Mike. It's silly of me to be so frightened. All the same, I am stiff as a doll and fuddled with fear. I stare at the view seeing nothing. I concentrate on hiding my feelings. The taxi driver must not know how I feel, must not guess what I'm thinking. He must not guess that I'm the slightest bit afraid.

'Do you live near here?' he asks casually.

'Yes.'

'Where?'

I am terrified. This man must not find out where I live. My mother will murder me if she ever finds out about this old man. If this man ever finds out where I live, my mother will find out about this man, and then she will murder me. I am almost panting with fear. I control my breathing carefully. As long as this man beside me does not find out where I live, I will be all right, I'll survive whatever it is that is happening to me now, it will never happen again. But if he does find out, I'm done for, finished.

And yet I can't lie. 'Over there,' I say.

'Where?' he asks again.

Perhaps he already knows where I live. Perhaps he's just testing me to make sure I trust him. He'll know if I tell a lie, and he'll despise me for it.

'Over there,' I say. I nod vaguely towards the other side of the road. For the first time I notice we're parked right opposite my house. That shocks me. If my mother comes out on the balcony with the binoculars, she will . . . What will she do? Kill me? Save me?

The driver looks.

'Which house?' he asks. He sounds as if he's just curious, just wondering.

I feel it must be *obvious* which house. I'd hardly live in a shack on a building site and you can see the other place is a private hotel.

'Oh, over that way,' I say with a shrug. I pretend I'm simply not very interested in where I live. I turn back to peer intently at the view: boats, pier, sea.

'What, in a flat or a house?' he asks.

He might still be just curious. Mike would say he was just curious.

'In a house,' I find myself saying. I feel cornered, helpless.

'Do you? Which one?' he casually insists.

What does he mean *which one*? There *is* only one!

Unless he thinks I mean up Beresford Road somewhere.

'Oh, just over there,' I shrug again, doing my best to sound bored. I pretend to yawn. I stare hard at the sea. I am terrified this man will find out how frightened I am of him. What right have I to be frightened? What has he done to me? Nothing. *Nothing*! It's not fair of me to be frightened like this.

There is a silence. Somebody toots in the distance. The traffic hums by.

'What's your name, pet?' he asks.

I freeze.

'Just your first name,' he says. 'I don't want to know your second name. Just your first name.'

That makes it worse. But I tell him. 'Helen.' I don't tell him everyone calls me Pud.

'Helen? That's a lovely name,' he says warmly. 'Helen. Lovely.'

He *makes* it sound lovely, pronounces it carefully — like in a poem or something. I like the way he says 'Helen' but I am terrified almost out of my wits. I am finding it almost impossible to think. His eyes are studying me. I can feel them. He is really noticing me, really paying attention to me. I look down and stare into my lap. My fingers are busy unravelling the fringe of my beach towel. My beach towel is bright pink and has a black fringe. I sewed it on myself.

'A lovely name for a lovely young lady,' he adds.

That's a bit corny. But, 'Thank you,' I mumble.

I notice there is ink on one of my fingers.

'And how old are you, Helen?' he asks.

'Almost fourteen.' I am thirteen years and ten months.

'Do you like being fourteen?' he asks. 'Do you like being a woman?'

I should run away.

'Yes,' I say.

Silence again.

I pull a thread out of the towel and knead it into a little ball.

'Your parents must be pretty mean—not giving you much money,' he says. 'Don't they give you much pocket money?'

Oh Christ! Does he want me to pay him after all?

'Not much,' I say.

'Your parents are mean to you, are they?'

His voice is full of the promise of sympathy. I am petrified. My mother would murder me if she knew I was here.

'Oh no, they're okay really,' I manage to lie, brushing non-existent hair out of my eyes.

I'm sure he doesn't believe me. He *knows* what my parents are like.

'How much do they give you a week?' he asks.

'Ten shillings,' I say. I know that's what Anne gets. I don't get pocket money as such. I'm not supposed to be interested in money.

'Gosh, that's not much! I'd give you much more than that if you were *my* daughter,' he says. 'I'd give you twice that if you were *my* daughter!'

I don't comment. I flick the pellet of thread onto the floor.

'I haven't got any daughters, you know, Helen,' he says—and adds wistfully, 'I'd love to have a daughter. I've always wanted a daughter.'

Silence. I pick at the fringe.

'Helen . . .?' he says. His voice is soft, intimate. My breathing ceases. I am stiff with apprehension. I say nothing.

'Helen . . .?'

He takes my hand. My heart lurches. The blood rushing up to my heart turns to ice. 'I like you, Helen,' he says. *My mother will murder me*. I should scream, run away.

I don't move a muscle. I stay riveted to the seat.

Gently he puts my hand palm-down on the bulge between his legs, cups it over the bulge between his legs. He cups his own hand down over mine. My hand is like ice. His hand on mine is heavy and warm.

'You don't mind if I do that, do you, Helen?' he asks me languidly.

My mind is a blur.

'No,' I murmur, polite as ever. I glance sideways to where the end of my arm disappears under his hand. Does that arm belong to me? I look away.

'What did you say? Mmm?' he asks, leaning forward attentively.

'No,' I say, 'I don't mind.'

Yes, those *are* the words I speak.

Something in my head explains to me that I'm not supposed to know enough to mind, I'm not supposed to have the faintest idea what this man is doing. All I should know is: NEVER ACCEPT LIFTS FROM STRANGERS. I am a well-brought-up thirteen-year-old girl and I oughtn't really to understand the gist of what this man is doing. I'm not supposed to have read Havelock Ellis *et cetera*, I'm not supposed to know about men and all that. My mother would murder me if she ever found out how curious I am about all that, if she found out a fraction of the things I know. As far as I'm supposed to know, there's nothing wrong, nothing wrong at all: an old man with grey hair and neat clothes and a young girl in green bermuda shorts are sitting on the front seat of a taxi parked on the esplanade at Rose Bay admiring the view, and the old man just happens to be holding the young girl's hand cupped over the bulge between his legs. It *is* a funny place for him to put her hand and it's fair enough for the girl to be puzzled, but she should explain to herself that he's put it there absent-mindedly, it just *happens* to be there, the old man would be disgusted, utterly scornful, very indignant if the young girl let

478

on he was frightening her. He wouldn't think of hurting her, she must be mad if she thinks he'd do her any harm — he's only trying to be kind to her, trying to help her. Hasn't he offered to drive her to Double Bay? For nothing?

I don't want to seem rude and ungrateful to a man who has offered to drive me to Double Bay. For nothing.

I don't want anyone to think *I'm* obsessed by sex, that *I'm* mad.

I smile. I try to look innocent and calm. I try to look indifferent.

He presses my hand down harder on the bulge. He begins to stroke my wrist with his thumb. I am close to delirious. I cannot think.

'I'm so glad you don't mind,' he says softly. 'You're not embarrassed, are you, Helen?' His question sounds concerned, not bullying. I have only to say, and he'll take my hand away. He's not forcing me to keep my hand there.

'No,' I mumble.

'I'm glad you're not,' I hear him telling me. I'm so frightened that I hardly know what is happening any more, hardly know what I'm doing. I am drunk with fear. I go on pretending to be rapt in the view.

He squeezes my hand on the bulge between his legs.

'Don't you think it's wonderful how God's made men different from women,' he says.

Oh Christ! I don't know what to say. Is it *disappointment* I suddenly feel? I'm an atheist. I don't believe in God, despise droobs who believe in God. The man's a droob!

'You know how God has made men different from women, don't you, Helen?' he asks. 'Don't you think it's wonderful?'

Is he trying to talk down to me? I'm not a child! I glance sideways at him again. He is looking solemnly down at his hand on my hand on the bulge between his legs. Silly old fool! I realise he actually means what he says, that he's being quite serious. It scares me more to think that he must be some kind of crackpot, some kind of nut. How can I explain to him that I'm an atheist? Hasn't he ever heard of Darwin and Freud?

I'm too frightened of him to explain. I am too polite. 'Yes,'

I gush, 'yes it *is* wonderful.' My voice is peculiar, though. It sounds guilty and false as well as childlike and terrified. I can tell just from my voice that I'm trying to humour him.

He can't. Or won't. Or doesn't care. He goes on talking about God. All the time he is speaking, he is gently pressing down on the bulge beneath his trousers with my hand. I try to seem not to notice. I try to seem totally absorbed in what he has to say and in the view, but it's like trying to pay no attention if my hand were being held down on a lump of burning coal. A voice is rambling on in the distance about God and our bodies and love and forgiveness and sin. He is murmuring on and on about there being more joy in heaven over one sinner who repenteth than over ninety and nine just persons or something, but all I am really thinking of is that bulge. There must be a ridge of cloth where the zipper is, and I can't feel anything definite, just a lump: it doesn't feel much like the thing in the diagrams in books. My mother would murder me if she knew I were here, she would never forgive me for this. The old man keeps pressing my trapped hand down on the firm lumpy bulge and talking of God.

He lifts my hand slightly. He sort of adjusts the lump thing sideways a bit. He closes my fingers around the firm lump thing through the cloth. My heart stops.

'Does that feel nice?' he asks me softly.

I stare at the dashboard.

'Does that feel nice, Helen?' he asks again.

I mumble yes. I am dizzy, scared rigid. The inside of my body is in turmoil, the outside as stiff as a china doll's. I am like a china doll whose hollow body is filled with a tumult of feelings. I stare straight ahead of me at the meter, my eyes like a doll's eyes — painted on. I concentrate on the words FLAG FALL on the dial. FLAG FALL. I *am* those words.

'You feel it, Helen,' he offers, he pleads, squeezing the firm lump with my stiff hand. My brain reels again. I can hardly breathe. He tells me how wonderful it is that God has made this part of a man to fit inside a woman to give her babies, that it's all part of His Design. I hear. This is not real. This is not really part of my life. He asks me gently if I'd mind if he undid the zipper of his trousers and got me to put my hand inside so I could feel this part of him properly, hold it in my hand, feel for myself what a man is really like. He doesn't want to hurt me, he says. He just wants to show me how different from a woman God has made a man, he just wants to show me the work of God. There's nothing wrong with looking upon the work of God, he says. There's nothing to be ashamed of about the way we've been made by God. 'Will you do that for me, Helen?' he asks. 'Will you do that for *me*?'

I'm so frightened I think I will die. *My mother will murder me.* I am shocked. I am dazed with shock, panic and shock. How will I stop myself saying yes? How will I stop myself?

'Oh, well, I haven't time really,' is what I say.

I can sense how crestfallen he is.

'I think I should really be going now,' I add.

'Do you?' he asks.

'Yes, I think I'd really better go.'

'Why?' There's resentment in his voice. Oh God, let him not be angry with me! He'll say I led him on. Oh God!

'Oh, well, you see, I've got to meet my friend at Double Bay. She'll be waiting for me, you see. She's expecting me. I really do think I ought to go.'

'Who's your friend?'

'Oh she's my friend from school. I really should be going.'

'Are you sure?'

'Yes, I really do think I should.'

There is silence. My heart pounds. I listen to my own breathing.

'Well if you really have to . . .?' he says petulantly.

'Yes I do, I really do, my friend'll be waiting for me.'

'What time do you have to meet her?' he asks.

I tell him the truth. 'Eleven o'clock.'

He looks at his watch. I can't see what it says. I don't dare look at mine.

Silence. Cars toot. Seagulls screech. Traffic hums.

'All right then, pet,' he says at last.

But still he doesn't release my hand.

I don't dare try to drag it away. I sit there helplessly. He says nothing. He is gazing out at the bay.

I decide to try again.

'I don't mind getting out and catching a bus if you're not going that way right now after all,' I offer, desperate to appease. 'Buses come pretty frequently along here, it would be no trouble.'

He snaps out of his trance. 'No, no, I'll drive you, I said I'd drive you, pet,' he says, affronted. He puts my hand back in my lap. Just like that. It is just a thing, of no further interest to him. He discards it the way my father discards a book he's been leafing through but has found doesn't tell him what he wants to know after all; in the way you discard what has now become an encumbrance.

He leans forward to switch on the ignition.

'To Double Bay then, eh?' he says, entirely matter-of-fact.

'Yes thanks,' I say.

He does a U-turn back across New South Head Road and begins to drive towards Double Bay.

He doesn't say anything else at all. Nor do I. I watch the scenery go by.

I glance sideways at him as we go down the hill past Cranbrook. He is concentrating on driving. I realise that he has completely lost interest in me, he has forgotten me. I am just a young girl in green bermuda shorts with a pink beach towel on her lap whom he is driving to Double Bay. That's all I am.

When I turn round to look at him again, he is craning to see beyond the car in front of him, intent on passing. He is a respectable-looking elderly taxi driver carefully driving a young girl in green bermuda shorts to Double Bay. There is nothing odd about him. He has grey hair. He is just a man.

I am just a girl, thirteen, taking a taxi to Double Bay to meet her friend, Anne.

I think of telling Anne about what is happening to me. How will I tell her? I think of crying on Anne's shoulder, pouring the whole story out to her: her big blue eyes will be wide with amazement, alarm. She will make a fuss of me, comfort me, *admire* me, almost, for having such a strange thing happen to me. Something exciting and dreadful has happened to me! I think of how interested she'll be, how kind, how concerned. I can't wait to tell her about it. It will be our secret. I can't wait to tell Anne.

All the time I am thinking this, I'm aware of the taxi driver beside me, driving. I shouldn't be sitting in the front, I realise. Mummy says never to sit in the front of taxis. Never mind. We're almost there, almost at Double Bay.

I see Anne see me coming in the cab. Her face lights up. She darts forward smiling as I get out. The taxi driver shouts goodbye, good-naturedly, just as if nothing had happened. I thank him, smiling. My face is twitching, but I am smiling.

Anne doesn't notice that I don't pay my fare. She doesn't seem to notice that I am trembling, that my face is ashen. Am I flushed or ashen? It doesn't seem to surprise her at all that I've arrived late in a cab, she takes lateness and cabs for granted. She doesn't notice how close I am to tears. I can't wait to tell her what has happened to me, can't wait for her to pity me.

The taxi is held up at the lights. I'm afraid to stop smiling until it has driven away. As soon as it's out of sight I will break down and cry, will tell Anne all that has happened to me. But there are dozens of people around. I wish there weren't so many people around. They'll stare when I begin to cry.

The lights change. I'm aware that the taxi drives off. Anne is still talking about the beaut bikini she has seen in the window of The Squire Shop while she's been waiting. I can't think of how to butt in, how to begin what I have to say.

I can't think what I have to say. What is there to say?

I realise: Anne will not understand. Nice Anne. She won't understand what happened to me. Did anything happen? It would make a better story if he *had* made me look at his penis or tried to rape me or something like that. Now I wish he had! I feel obscurely cheated. It is terrible to have felt so much terror and yet not be able to explain what caused it. I *couldn't* have been more frightened no matter what he'd done, but Anne can't be

483

expected to understand that. Anne can't be expected to believe
I felt in such dreadful danger, so afraid, when really almost
nothing happened to me: what happened to me was all my own
fault or all in my head. It's not fair, this! I want to cry, I long
for someone to understand how I feel and to pity me. How can
I explain to Anne what was in my head? She'll ask why on earth
I didn't take my hand away, why I didn't just jump out of the
cab and run away. 'The taxi was *stopped*, wasn't it?' she'll say,
baffled. It will be beyond her comprehension why I didn't run
away, why I didn't run home and tell my mother, why I let this
man do what he did with me. Did he *force* me to do anything
against my will? No, nothing at all. I acquiesced to everything.
Anne will be horrified, she'll think I'm quite depraved. Why didn't
I scream, she will say. She won't understand at all why I didn't
scream. She won't understand why I don't ring my parents now,
straight away, and tell them every detail of what happened. How
can I explain?

How can I explain to Anne what I don't myself understand?
There is nothing to say. Nothing happened.

When Anne stops talking, all I tell her is that the bikini sounds
really terrific. I go on smiling. Together we walk across the road
and catch the 365 almost straight away. She chatters brightly to
me all the way to Bondi Beach. All the way to Bondi Beach I
chatter back. We talk about the kids at school. I feel myself grow
calm.

I forget what has happened to me. Nothing happened.

We make our way to the end of the beach right away from the
baths and the life-saving club. All the Scots and Cranbrook boys
and all the Ascham and Kambala girls who have come to the beach
to meet each other are here, clustered beneath the Lost Children sign,
rubbing oil on each other's backs, laughing and talking, flirting.

Anne sits with me under the Lost Children sign and chatters
to people like Janey Wynne-Williams and introduces me as her
friend and is surprised, really *surprised*, when we haven't actually
met before, when it turns out that I've only *heard* of them. The
people like Janey Wynne-Williams aren't surprised. I can see they

can see I'm a waste of their time.

I lie there leadenly on my stomach on the hot sand, sweaty and dazed, my sunglasses on, pretending to read while Anne darts about like a little bird and chatters and dashes off into the surf and swims. I don't go in. I stay with my face hidden in a book. I am waiting.

I am waiting for something to happen to me.